SYNTHETIC BI PRODUCTS

SPARROW L. PATTERSON

Akashic Books
New York, NY

Published by Akashic Books
©2001 Sparrow L. Patterson

Cover design by Alexis Fleisig
Design and layout by Will Croxton
Author photo by John Rakow

ISBN: 1-888451-18-1
Library of Congress Catalog Card Number: 2001087221
All rights reserved
First printing
Printed in Canada

Akashic Books
PO Box 1456
New York, NY 10009
Akashic7@aol.com
www.akashicbooks.com

Lovingly dedicated to Mark and Willow

And to my best friend and muse Matthew

Acknowledgments

My sincerest thanks go out to Johnny Temple at Akashic Books for his patience and belief in my work; to Gabrielle Danchick for her unbelievable dedication, support, and editorial skills; and to the whole Akashic staff.

I would also like to thank those who stood by me, holding my hand and drying my tears: my Mother, JLPIII, Matthew, Patrick, Nita, Auds, and Wolff; and a special thanks to Andrew for all his hard work.

PART I

Heather

I Kissed a Girl

CHAPTER 1

With the exception of the shopping mall, there wasn't a whole fuck of a lot to do in Geneva, Illinois. Unfortunately for the "young adults," the town left much to be desired. We had a movie theater, a Denny's to eat at when shopping at the mall, and the field that separated the high school from all the distractions mentioned. I was just thankful for the company of Heather; if it weren't for her I would have surely died of boredom.

It all started during summer school, after classes on our long walks through the tall wispy grasses of the field, on the way to our beloved hangouts. That was when Heather became the best friend I ever had, and when feelings beyond friendship began brewing inside me.

"What do you think will happen when we die?" Heather asked as we walked.

"Do you mean us in particular, or people in general?" I replied.

"Either way, it doesn't matter," she said, her droopy brown eyes becoming alert and focused, settling on my face.

"I believe there's no heaven or hell. I don't believe in the Bible or that Jesus crap that my mother goes crazy for. See, I think the Bible was a horrible joke that the disciples or maybe just some guys tripping on acid put together to freak us out—a story about some superior being that takes care of all the pathetic people in this world. How crazy is that?" I was curious to see if she had her own opinion or if she would just go along with me as usual.

"Well, what do you believe in then?" she asked.

"Reincarnation, I guess." I looked down at the ground, wondering what it was I really believed in, or if I believed in anything at all. "See, I know I'll eventually be diagnosed with lung cancer because I smoke like a fiend, and I never intend to quit. So, as soon as they tell me I have cancer I figure they'll be able to give me an estimated time of departure. When that time draws near, I'll go to the ocean, cut myself all over with a razor blade, and feed myself to the sharks. You see, I believe that if you are eaten by something, you'll be reincarnated as what ate you," I said, realizing that my side of the conversation had turned slightly grim.

"So according to you, it's not 'you are what you eat' but 'you are what eats you.' Okay, then what will I be reincarnated as?" She looked directly into my eyes, biting her lower lip. Then she gazed at the horizon over my head. She looked beautifully perplexed.

"You will be a butterfly, so damn beautiful but always flitting from one thing to another."

"Then I'm going to be eaten by a butterfly?" She thought about it. "What do you mean, flitting?"

"Of course you aren't going to be eaten by a butterfly, silly. I just meant that you're not focused," I sputtered, immediately wishing I'd kept my mouth shut.

"Not focused, huh?"

"You're just so carefree," I said, suddenly becoming conscious of how stupid the word *carefree* sounded.

Heather closed her eyes and dropped with a sigh into the tall grasses of the field. I felt so close to her, and even if she thought I was crazy, at least I had told her something substantial. She looked strained under the purple sky, her eyes shut tight and her lips pressed together so hard it looked painful. I thought I would like to kiss her, but then I thought that it might freak her out. I tried to imagine what Alyssia might do in this situation. Hell, I knew what Alyssia would do, but instead I just gazed at Heather's face, her long brown hair spread out across the grass, her flat stomach, her beautiful round breasts, the nipples pert under the cotton fabric of her tank top. I wondered if she ever thought about me in this way. I wondered if Alyssia had had these same doubts initially with me. I knew Heather was boy crazy, but then so was I. In a hopeful moment of anticipation, I decided to ask her what she was thinking.

"Just trying to focus my pea brain on something, you know, trying not to flit around too much," she said, her eyes shut.

"Cute, really cute. No, really, what were you thinking?"

"Nothing, just about how good a friend you are and how happy I am that we lucked out and had the same class together—even if you do think I'm flighty." She opened her eyes and smiled a little smile at me.

I lay next to her and lit two cigarettes. I placed one between her lips, wishing I could just do something, like reach out for her hand or kiss her, just touch her in a different way than we normally touched. I wanted to; I tried but my courage left me when she rolled onto her side, smiled, and thanked me for the smoke. I knew for some reason that my opportunity was gone, and I doubted we would ever be that physically close again, doubted that the same butterfly feeling would return to my stomach with such force and desire. But I hoped that it would.

On the frequent journeys Heather and I made to the mall, Heather met a boy, and when I say boy, I really mean *boy*. His name was Baker. He was thin and straggly, and when he wasn't in his mom's apartment across the parking lot from the mall, he was at the mall. He took an instant liking to Heather, which I, of course, understood. I never felt threatened by Heather; in fact, I knew I was better looking, but that made no difference. We never competed. Baker was a child in my eyes—he was even younger than Heather who was a year and a half younger than my recently achieved eighteen years. I guess Baker had some cute, childlike appeal that affected Heather in a way I couldn't comprehend.

Summer school was nearly over, and I started to notice that Heather and I had not been spending as much time together. She'd been hanging out with Baker at the mall the majority of her free time, and I had recently given in and taken a job at a video arcade. I was sick of stealing shit with Heather at the various stores we frequented. We were really good at it. We could get anything we wanted, and we never got busted, but it was getting tiring. Besides, Baker was moving in on our hot thieving spots, stealing anything Heather said she wanted, and I felt that too much stealing was going to catch up with one of us sooner or later. I didn't want it to be me, so I took the job at the arcade in the mall to make some money.

Heather, Baker, and I sat outside the mall smoking cigarettes. I was killing time until I had to work at five, so I suggested we go over to Baker's house and drink some beers. This was never difficult because Baker's mom was an alcoholic and she was never at home. Baker said that she worked at the K-Mart in the mall, one of our favorite places to steal from, but I never saw her there, so that information was inconclusive. Baker told us she was always in the back smoking cigarettes; I think she actually spent most of her time at the little pub across the street from their apartment complex.

Heather and I sat on the couch at Baker's place while he got us each a Miller Lite out of the refrigerator, then he went to the bathroom.

"So why are you hanging out with Baker," I asked Heather, immediately tired of watching TV.

Heather was holding the remote, flipping absently through the channels. "Well, it's not like it's serious or anything. We hang out together, that's all. But who knows, maybe we'll end up getting married someday."

I sat quietly, but on the inside I was laughing. I knew I was a completely fucked-up person, but even so I had a better concept of marriage. In fact, I thought the whole concept was bogus. How could you just be with one person your entire life? Heather and Baker would never make it. Eventually one of them would get it on with someone else and the marriage thing would be over.

The beer tasted good and Baker put some music on, which loosened things up. Heather and I went into Baker's room to chill out and listen to tunes. We sat on Baker's bed, and he sat on the floor. A Neil Young CD was playing, and Baker realized he wanted us to hear a specific song, so he fast-forwarded to "Old Man." Instantly, it became Heather's and my song. The part about "twenty-four and there's so much more" reminded me of how boring and uneventful my life really was, and I was only eighteen. We listened to it probably twenty times before our little party broke up. I had to go to work at the arcade, and it was time for Heather to get home. One thing she had to deal with on a daily basis was her completely psychotic mother—it just never seemed to stop. She mingled in Heather's business and never allowed her to do anything at night.

Especially now that summer school would be over in three days, her mother seemed to think she should be studying. Apparently she didn't realize that summer school classes were designed to be passable. We both knew we were going to pass. You just had to show up.

Heather leaned over and gave Baker a long, semi-passionate kiss that made my stomach hurt. Afterwards, Heather and I exited quietly, and Baker informed me that he would be heading over to the arcade shortly.

As we walked toward the mall, Heather looked sullen. "What's up?" I asked, then tripped over a crack in the sidewalk, stumbling a bit until I regained my footing.

Heather giggled at my clumsiness. "I just wonder what it must be like to have a *real* boyfriend. You know, someone you can have safe sex with, someone you can always have sex with. Know what I mean?"

As if *I* had all the answers to the game called Love. "Yeah, I had one of those once. It's comforting but seriously overrated. It puts a damper on the freedom thing. Plus, I think I'm too freaky to get serious," I said, trying to dissuade her from running into the arms of another loser guy.

Heather looked at me as if I were crazy. "What do you mean, too freaky? You're too smart. That's about the only thing freaky about you. You know people almost instantly, and you know too much about them."

"I don't feel that way. I wish I knew more about certain people."

"Like who?"

"Like you," I said.

She was silent. We trudged through the parking lot, past the cars of mall patrons who were spending their afternoons partaking in the great American pastime otherwise known as shopping. Then we walked through the glass doors that separated us from that great buying extravaganza and from my job. I felt nervous. I was so close to saying something to Heather or asking her something I knew I would later regret. I wanted to tell her that I had feelings for her, different than normal feelings. I was desperate to ask her if she ever had such feelings herself. I wanted to allude to the fact that I thought about her in certain ways, that I wanted to touch her in a way that was more than friendly.

"Well, there's always time to get to know each other better," she said. "See you later. Oh, and call me if you get bored at work."

I felt slightly relieved that our conversation was over, but I was also slightly disappointed that I didn't get a chance to explain my feelings more clearly.

I walked into the arcade, heading toward the back room, thinking of how close I'd come to screwing up a really good friendship. Really, how could I tell her these things and expect her to just deal? I couldn't.

The day before my final I was on my way to a Grateful Dead concert at the World Music Theater, dreading that I was going to be up all night and certain that some illegal substance would somehow find its way into my system. But I wasn't really worried about the test. I knew I could pass it even if I were dead, just as long as my body and my number-two pencils were present. So I had begged the idiots I was going with to make sure I made it to school by eight the next morning. This was the only way I would pass, and I needed to graduate or my mother would kill me.

It was weird how I ended up getting to go to the Dead show in the first place. There was this girl Lisa who I don't think anyone really liked in my high school. She was that slutty kind of trailer-trash girl, and somehow I got roped into being her friend. At the beginning of the last semester of high school, before I decided I wasn't going back to school for the remaining four months (which was the reason I had to complete one class in summer school), we had to do this bowling thing in gym class for about four weeks, which really sucked, but at least I had a friend in the class to be partners with. Unfortunately, the trailer-trash girl couldn't find anyone who wanted to be partners with her, so my friend and I got stuck with her. During the four weeks of bowling we got to know Lisa more than we wanted to. She was annoying, crude, rude, and basically impossible to like. But now she had invited me to see the Dead because she had some extra tickets. This was a totally cool gesture, and after Lisa threw in an additional ticket to sweeten the deal, Heather and I decided we had to go.

So here we were in this guy Jerry's truck on our way to see the Dead. Even though Jerry was a friend of Lisa's, I was instantly attracted to him, having given up on my ridiculous thoughts of Heather. The feeling seemed to be mutual—he had asked me to ride in front with him, which I did. He was gorgeous. He had long, dark brown hair and rosy lips. He was built, really built, and older, about twenty-one, and I had a thing for older guys. If anything, he had sex appeal, but that was probably all there was to him.

The ride to the show was long, and we got stuck in major traffic. I looked out the truck window and watched the line of VW buses, bugs, and various other autos meander down the highway. Right in front of us was a bus completely covered with Dead stickers. Drum circles and Hacky Sac games had started on the side of the road. Guys were shirtless, girls dressed in long skirts, their hair loose. It was another world at these Dead shows, a world that reminded me of what I envisioned the sixties might have been like. A drug-induced vacation from reality. Jerry watched me watching these people and occasionally talked about loving the Dead. Other than his mindless babble about what was obvious to me, he had nothing of substance to offer. I turned and looked out the back window, thinking about poor Heather stuck in the bed of the truck with Lisa and her whacked out friends. The unfortunate thing was that Lisa never had anything relevant to discuss other than drugs or her sexual conquests. Her topics of conversation always revolved around greasy guys with no lives and no jobs, but who somehow could afford cheesy cars that impressed trailer-trash women. So my heart went out to Heather, who I knew was enduring stories about these Jiffy Lube guys who greased Lisa's tubes. I watched Heather nod her head, then stare off toward the horizon. Thankfully the ride wasn't killing me. I inched over toward Jerry to change the radio station, and he placed his hand on my thigh. This was fine by me. I looked down at his hand and watched the fingers slide slowly up and down the inside of my leg, then I looked out the window and realized we were approaching the entrance of the World Music Theater. It was a massive eye-sore that could be seen from miles away.

For some reason, the Dead were becoming popular again. It was 1989 and everyone I knew suddenly seemed drawn to a kind of hippie lifestyle. But unlike the generations of the sixties and seventies who fought for social reform and justice, my generation preferred slacking off, begging for change, watching MTV. They liked the grungy clothes, the revival of sixties music, and the drugs, but they didn't seem to have it in them to fight for anything. Our parents had already been there and done that.

Once cars pulled into the entrance of the World, there was usually another half hour wait until you could actually park. Jerry's truck lurched along, barely making any progress. I had never seen so many people in line for a concert this early. We had left three hours before the show was to begin in order to avoid traffic, but it appeared everyone else had done the same. After a while I got antsy and suggested that Heather and I meet Jerry in the parking lot.

"I'll catch up with you there," he said. "Are you taking everyone with you?" He looked back toward the bed of the truck.

"I was going to leave the three freaks with you, if you don't mind," I said, following his gaze.

"Hey, don't knock them, they're the ones with the weed." He gave me a huge smile. Go figure! I thought, here's this hot guy who I really wouldn't mind doing, but he's all involved in this drug shit. I guess it didn't matter because I honestly wasn't looking for something long-term, more like a good fuck once or twice a week.

Heather and I took off in a hustle to get to the parking lot, and once we'd covered enough distance from the truck, Heather said, "Thanks a lot for making me ride in the back."

"What, you didn't love schmoozing with the grease monkeys?" I faked surprise.

"Honestly, I can't imagine being that ignorant. It's all about guys with jacked-up cars, and loose, easy women who rock their worlds."

"Hence the reason we don't hang out with them unless there's some form of bribery involved," I said, and Heather gave me a knowing smile. For a moment I thought about grabbing hold of her hand and intertwining my fingers with hers, but I was too shy. Instead, we jetted along to the scrubs vending in the lot. These were people of an entirely different caliber than the grease monkeys. They were high school dropouts with a sort of lower-class artistic talent. They were able to tie-dye shirts, bead jewelry, collect freaky, little tokens they could sell—and we mustn't forget their remarkable ability to make friendship bracelets. I was glad that I would graduate from high school, then at the least do something more than vend in parking lots.

A Head with long, bone-dry dreads and gua pants was coming towards us. As he approached, we were almost knocked over by his characteristic Deadhead patchouli scent.

"Can I interest you two princesses of Mother Earth in some tie-dyes?" he asked, and I couldn't help thinking how Deadheads were always such poetic geniuses.

"How much?" Heather asked.

"Two for twenty, for you two beauties," he said, and offered a stunning brown-toothed, gaping smile.

Heather and I looked at each other and simultaneously blurted out, "What the hell."

After purchasing two fly T-shirts that we thankfully didn't have to make ourselves, we moved on to the "oh so talented" bongo drummers, mesmerized by the thump of their drums. We silently grooved to the music. Suddenly, I was grabbed from behind, and I turned and saw Jerry smiling idiotically with a joint hanging from his bottom lip. Unfortunately, the rest of the creep crew was with him. Anne, the quiet one, was obviously stoned out of her gourd. Her head drooped toward the pavement, her long greasy hair clumped together at the roots. Anne's boyfriend, Chuck, seemed equally stoned. He was short and thick in the middle—probably too much beer. He stood next to Anne playing air guitar, singing the chorus of "Jack Straw." And let's not forget Lisa, leading the pack, her gaze darting through the crowd, a possessed glint in her eye.

"Hi, Jerry." I rolled my eyes in the direction of his entourage.

He took my hand, and we marched caravan-style toward the entrance where the ticket takers diligently frisked us. Finding no obvious illegal substances, they allowed our entrance into the already overcrowded theater. Lisa was being her usual obnoxiously loud self, and immediately after gaining entrance she began freaking out. She was so obviously out of place in the peaceful circle of the Dead show. She started cackling, literally, then bellowing at the top of her lungs, "DOSE ME!"

I'm sure the acid was flowing freely around the pavilion, but nobody wanted to deal with the screaming five-ten, one-hundred-and-ninety-pound-blonde-with-black-roots freak. It was clear that this was the wrong place for her. I could see her more in her own element at, say, a Guns N' Roses concert.

Jerry, Heather, and I slowly separated from the acid-deprived maniac and her friends. We trudged up the hill to the already gloriously muddy mess of a lawn where all those who couldn't afford seats temporarily resided. The Dead were beginning to jam on the stage, and Jerry was standing behind me with his arms encircling my waist. I liked the way he felt, breathing on my neck, all hot and moist.

"I have a surprise for you two," Jerry said as he dropped his hand from my waist. Digging into his pocket, he pulled out a piece of cellophane that contained tiny perforated pieces of paper. He pulled off three squares of paper—for Heather, himself, and me—which he ceremoniously placed on our wagging tongues.

From that point on all I remember is the beat of the music, the calm, soothing sounds; the deep sway of Jerry's hips as they pressed rhythmically against my backside; Heather dancing next to us; the colors flashing on the video screens; and the mystical feeling of my passive soul, that for this instant in time had ceased raging loudly and painfully from within.

I was back in the front seat of the pickup, and Jerry was being awfully attentive.

"Do you want to stop for water or something?" he asked, his pupils dilated so much from the acid that I could no longer detect the color of his eyes.

"I guess I could use something to drink; I feel really funny still."

"You will for about six more hours—it's good acid." His smile shifted from evil to good within seconds.

"Six hours—that's crazy. This shit's really potent," I said, then I slipped into a somewhat unconscious state. The road moved from side to side, and I felt like Speed Racer as we drifted in and out of traffic. I was completely transfixed by the pitch-black road with its bumblebee-yellow stripes. The lines spread out, then became slim with the sway of the truck. Sometimes they were no longer lines at all but splashes of yellow flung onto an empty black canvas. It seemed like hours of this until we pulled into a gas station for drinks. Jerry got out to buy me some coffee; he was acting worried about me being all right for class in the morning. How goddamned thoughtful of him, I thought. Ten minutes later he returned to the truck accompanied by Heather. They were involved in some deep conversation about the color patterns in the sky. I looked up. Until now I had not found anything remotely interesting about the sky, but it completely grabbed my attention. The stars glowed a bright phosphorescent green against the midnight-blue backdrop streaked with deep purple clouds. I was in complete awe of the beauty before me. I wanted to reach up and touch it, dip my fingers into the large pool of blue. Jerry interrupted my thoughts.

"Orleigh, do you mind sitting in back for a while? I'm gonna let Heather ride in front for a bit; she's cold."

"Sure, that's cool," I said, realizing Heather had complained to Jerry and convinced him to allow her to usurp my seat. I wasn't going to say anything, so I got into the slimy beer-soaked bed of the truck.

"Did you see Heather and Jerry lip-locked in the gas station?" Lisa asked immediately as I sat down, and I chalked another one up for her subtleties.

"No, I didn't." I looked away from her, hoping she would shut up.

"Well, isn't it interesting that you're stuck back here with us now?" she asked in a snide tone.

I looked over at Anne in the corner of the bed. She was inhaling a large drag from a joint. "It's cool," I said. In reality it sucked, of course. I couldn't stand being with these three losers, and I wasn't about to get involved in Chuck's current speech on the quality of rolling papers. Actually, they had no idea that I was tripping, so I figured I would just groove with the ride, and they would think I was being bitchy as usual. I certainly didn't want to reveal any emotion over this Jerry and Heather thing. I didn't want to let anyone know I had feelings, well, for either of them. I would've preferred to be hung by my toenails before I'd let these trailer-trash idiots see me agitated. But I was pissed. What did Heather think she was doing anyway? It should have been obvious to her that he was mine. I guess neither of them really cared, and he really wasn't mine anyway. But it hurt like hell. I didn't want them to get together, though it wasn't because I wanted Jerry. It was an ego blow, and I still longed for Heather, which the crew in the back of the truck would never have guessed. They thought I was bummed because of Jerry.

"So why did you let her move up there with him?" Lisa asked, trying to keep up the conversation that I wanted her to let die.

"Because she's cold, and I really don't care."

"But you've been with him all night," Anne said, coming out of her marijuana haze just long enough to comment.

I turned toward Anne, watching her fiddle with her yucky long brown hair, her eyes red and puffy. Chuck said nothing; he just sucked down a warm Miller Lite and watched Anne play with her hair. I'm sure he didn't care about this kind of shit.

"Not really, we were just hanging out. He can do whatever he wants. I'm not really that concerned about a guy like Jerry," I said. What was I supposed to do, cry about it? That would get me nowhere but mocked by the ever-trashy Lisa and her stony cohorts. Instead I kept to myself and watched the road move behind the truck and the flickering head-lights of the cars behind us. I resigned myself to this calm sedateness, until I saw the flashing blue and red lights. I realized we were in Lisa's neighborhood, and it appeared that we were about ten feet from her driveway. I felt the truck jerk into park, and I watched the officers get out of the squad car. I was completely paranoid that we were all going to jail. The bed of the truck reeked of beer, and Jerry was both tripping and drunk. I sat there, absorbed by thoughts of having to tell my mother I was in jail, while the lights spun round and round, making little flecks of color on the dew-moistened pavement. When I looked up from the ground, I saw Jerry getting out of the truck and the officers asking him how much he had drunk. I was starting to freak out again, so I distracted myself with the lights and occasionally glanced at Jerry as the cops made him walk on the yellow line.

My trance was broken when an officer asked if anyone knew how to drive stick, and a whole round of no's erupted from the bed of the truck. A cop leaned his head into the passenger window and spoke to Heather. She got out and walked around to the driver's seat. Jerry was allowed to get back into the truck, and I fell back into a daze. Then Heather was pulling into Lisa's driveway, and Lisa and her friends were stumbling drunkenly out of the bed.

"Goodbye," Lisa shouted, evidently unaware that it was early in the morning and she was probably waking up the entire neighborhood.

"Bye. And thanks for the wonderful experience," I said sarcastically.

Anne fell down on Lisa's driveway and Chuck hurried to help her up. "Nice to meet you," she called to me, and I could have sworn I saw chunks of vomit hanging from the ends of her straggly brown hair.

Chuck winked at me. "Good luck with Jerry," he said, struggling to hold onto Anne as she stumbled toward Lisa's door.

I watched them go into the house, and the truck pulled out of the driveway. Quietly I chanted, "I don't need any fucking luck with anything, Chuck."

The truck pulled to a stop, and I realized we were at Heather's. Heather jumped out, walked around the front, and leaned in the driver's side window to give Jerry a dispassionate kiss on the cheek. She told me she would see me in class, but I simply shrugged my shoulders and stared at the driveway, and she walked off.

"Hey, why don't you climb back up here with me?" Jerry shouted through the window at me.

I scuttled out of the bed, then climbed into the passenger seat.

"Do you want to go home?" he asked, as if there were some other option I hadn't considered.

I watched Heather go inside her house. I was sorry we'd parted so coldly. "Where else would I go?"

"You could come over to my house," he said, placing his hand on my knee.

"Well, you see, I have class in the morning, and I can't miss it."

"I can get up and drive you to class," he told me as the hand began to slide up and down the side of my thigh once again.

What an asshole, I thought. "Actually, this is really important, and I think I should probably go home," I said. "It's my last class, and I really need to be there to take the final. So I think I should just sleep at home." I wasn't stupid; I realized he wanted to get laid. He couldn't get Heather, so now he was hitting on me. Wasn't that how all the guys operated?

"I'll just take you home then," he said. I could tell by his tone that he was annoyed. "Maybe we could get together tomorrow after you're done with your final?"

"Maybe," I lied.

We pulled into my driveway, and the sun was already beginning to rise. I only had about three hours to sleep before I had to take the fucking test. I jumped out of the truck with a brief good-bye, no kiss, and an I-don't-give-a-damn attitude.

CHAPTER 2

My wake-up call was only slightly rude; it involved my mother coming into my room with a mouthful of gleeful greetings, pulling the covers off my bed. "Long night last night, Orleigh?" she asked with a snicker.

"I guess," I said, not really in the mood for her sarcasm.

"You have a test in half an hour, and I already let you sleep in. Get up!" she insisted, while I relished in the joys of our mother-daughter relationship.

I didn't want to get up, and personally, at this point, I did not really care about the test or graduating. It all seemed like too grueling an experience, and I really just wanted to get some rest. I actually wasn't so convinced now that I was going to pass the stupid test. I was hung over, hazy, and tired. My mother was busying herself getting my clothes together as I tried to shake off my sleepiness. I stood there feeling like I was five years old. My mother was laying my clothes out while I stretched. It was ridiculous, but it was the way she was and always would be. She had to take care of me, no matter how old I was. I constantly reminded her that I was old enough to get my clothes together, old enough to make my own decisions, and old enough to wake myself up in the morning. But regardless, she was my mom and deep down inside I loved her. After all, she had raised me on her own. Coming to terms with my pathetic situation, I got dressed and ran downstairs to the car, which my mother had already pulled into the driveway.

Heather sat on the school steps, smoking a cigarette. She looked up at me and said, "You're late."

"I know. I had to deal with my mother. Plus, I'm still feeling like shit from last night."

"Yeah, that was a lot of fun."

"It was fun until you started hitting on Jerry." I could taste the contempt in my mouth.

"Well, I just wanted to test him to see if he really dug you or not." She smirked.

"Next time, why don't you let me do my own legwork," I replied, pissed.

We snuffed out our butts and climbed the six stairs covered with other varieties of butts and crusty gum. I dreaded having to take a test. The sick feeling I had all morning was burrowing through my stomach. As we walked into the classroom of losers, I felt like I was going to puke. I ran to the lovely black-walled bathroom (the janitor continually painted it to cover the graffiti), which made me feel even sicker. I leaned over the toilet. The hideous bathroom disinfectant smell made me more nauseous. Soon, the bile started to move slowly up my esophagus until I was drooling, then I let it all go. Of course, almost immediately after, I felt fine again. I rinsed out my mouth, then headed back to the white walls of the classroom where all the others were diligently filling in circles with their number-two pencils. The teacher gave me my little packet of materials, and I began to do my own filling in.

Heather finished before me. She watched the teacher grade her test, then left. I was worried that she would take off for a better place without me. I scrambled to finish my own test, which the teacher graded while I waited to be released. I tapped my foot impatiently as he made two red check marks on the answer sheet, then I received my passing score of ninety-eight, and I busted out of the room to search for Heather. Luckily, I found her in the smoking section behind the school that was designated for us, by us.

"So how'd it go with you?" she asked me, as she ashed her cigarette against the wall.

"Ninety-eight," I answered, not really caring.

"Seventy-two."

"Who really cares?" I said, hoping this would not set the tone for the day.

"Not me. Let's go get some ice cream." She stood and crushed her cigarette into the ground under her Birks.

"Sure, sounds good," I said, pleased that her grade had not put her in a foul mood.

We ended up at Denny's, scooping spoonfuls of super-chocolate ice cream into our mouths. It was nice to be done with the stress of school. It was a relief to graduate, even though dropping out proved to be a really good time. At the very least, I now knew if I ever wanted a future I could go to college, stressing the *if* in that one.

"So what do you want to do today?" Heather asked, lifting another spoonful into her mouth.

"Well, I guess we could go hang out at the mall or Baker's house," I said.

"Yeah, do you have to work today?"

"No, they finally let me off so I can enjoy myself a bit." I gave her one of my crazy mischievous smiles.

"Isn't that what we did last night?"

"No, actually I think I was kind of pissed off about the Jerry thing." I looked down into the bowl of ice cream to avoid her glance.

"Look, he was just a game for the night, nothing worthwhile, right?"

"I guess, but he was really hot," I said, my eyes still penetrating my last chocolate glob.

"I don't think he was that hot, but I would've done him. I've been extremely horny lately." She looked down at the table, and I began to sense maybe she was not really doing all right. I was still angry with her though. Why was she such a game player? And why with the guy that I liked?

"What, are you not getting any from Baker?"

"Baker and I just sort of hang out; it's not like we have this big *love* affair or anything. He's so young. I want to meet someone who's, like, twenty-five or so."

I knew she was telling me the truth, but I didn't know why she felt this way. "Twenty-five, why?"

"Because they're so much more experienced than the little boys we hang out with."

I immediately resented being tossed in the same group in which she classified herself. "Don't you mean *you* hang out with?"

"Whatever. You're always with us."

"Maybe, but I'm not having the same problem you are."

"What problem?" she asked, suddenly getting nasty.

"Frustration," I replied, matching her tone.

She gave me that annoyed look, the one that I really loved to see because it always turned me on, and she stood up to leave. "Come on, let's find Baker."

We paid for our stomachache-inducing ice cream and scrambled out the door, leaving no tip. We decided to take the shortcut through the field, and halfway there, Heather fell to the ground and pulled out another smoke. "Let's sit for a while," she said.

"Certainly, whatever you want." I didn't really care what we did as long as we did it together.

"Why are you that way with me?"

"What way?" I asked, not knowing what the hell she was talking about.

"You either act like a parent or like a boyfriend."

"What are you saying, I'm manly?"

"No, quite the contrary, but you talk to me differently than other girls do."

I thought this was obviously because I was smarter than those other girls, not because I was manly. "What do you mean?" I asked, hoping she would go into more detail.

"You know, like you honestly care about my feelings." She looked rather shocked by her own words.

"Because I do," I said a little nonchalantly.

"Why?"

"I don't know, I guess it's because I love you," I said, and immediately wished I could retract my words.

"You love me? What does that mean?" She stared down at the ground, reinforcing my belief that I had said too much.

"It means that in every person's life, at any single moment, they can probably count on one hand the true friends they have. So on my hand I count you, and I guess that means I love you."

"I thought you were talking about some kind of lesbo thing," she said, and giggled a little.

"No. Why do you have a problem with that?" I swallowed my words.

"Lesbians kind of freak me out," she said, and looked directly into my eyes.

"Why?"

"I don't know. Why do you care?" she asked, brushing my question off.

"I guess I can understand why a woman would be a lesbian, that's all."

"Why do you think anyone would want to be a lesbian?"

I could tell that I had struck a cord; I knew she really wanted my answer to this question. "Think about the great artists of the past. What did they paint? Nude women. Why did they paint that? Because the female body's much more beautiful than the male body. We have these beautiful curves, shapely breasts, and soft spots. I think our bodies are wonderful, much better than men's," I said, sermonizing a little but also feeling relief that I was finally getting somewhere.

"So, are you saying you're a lesbian?"

I smiled at her for her lack of tact. "No, I'm saying I think women have better bodies than men."

"So, you could fall in love with a woman and do things with one?"

"What do you mean *things?*" I suddenly felt that this conversation was hitting too close to home, and I was getting nervous that I would do or say something that would frighten her. I had already pushed it too far, already told her way more than I had intended.

"You know—like kiss or even touch?"

"I guess I could picture that . . . I don't know."

"You could?" she asked, and I could see her turning this around inside her head, behind those sleepy brown eyes of hers.

"Yeah, I guess so," I told her, thinking that of course I could imagine it; I had already done it. Vivid memories of Alyssia flashed before my eyes. I quickly pushed them away; I didn't want to think about her. I was still quietly pining for her.

"That's kind of weird, you know. I mean, why would you want to? Are you gay? Because you're always after some guy."

I felt strange, like I didn't want this door being opened. I wanted to shut it and never open it again. "First of all, I'm not always after some guy. I like guys. Secondly, I'm not gay, I just think women are beautiful. That's all."

"What do you think about me—do you think *I'm* beautiful?"

This was a weighted question. God, I didn't even know why I ever started talking about this. I could feel myself slipping further and further away from her. I felt like she would never talk to me again, no matter what I answered. But I had to come up with an answer; she was giving me that tight-lipped look, and all I could think about was kissing her. I wanted to lean over and touch my lips to hers. She gave me that "Well?" look, and in a panic, not having enough time to formulate the correct answer, the perfect nonevasive answer, I blurted, "I think you are gorgeous, extremely beautiful!" What did I do? What had I done? For god's sake, I knew I had just blown it. Somehow I blew it. I decided that I would keep my eyes focused on the grass, not daring to look into her eyes to witness her disgust.

"You're beautiful too, Orleigh. I think you're really pretty. Maybe you're bisexual. Have you ever thought about that?"

I was stunned, first to find out that she thought I was beautiful, and second because she brought up bisexuality as if it were everyday conversation. She appeared so calm and collected.

"Maybe I am; I don't really know. My experiences are limited in that department," I lied.

"Would you want to have an experience?" she asked, dead serious.

"What do you mean, with you?"

"No, I mean if you met the right person," she said, and I instantly felt crushed.

I hadn't fessed up to my time with Alyssia. I couldn't tell her that I had once thought I'd found the right person, but despite her effect on me, our differences were overwhelming. Alyssia's idea of a way of life was far too different from mine. "Yeah, I guess I would, given the opportunity. I've thought about it before," I told her, trying to play it cool.

"Have you thought about it with me?"

What the fuck did she want me to tell her? That I thought about her all the time? I thought I was in love with her or something? That I thought about my mouth on her breasts, my tongue in her mouth, and my tongue in *other places?* Was I supposed to tell her that? She saw what I was thinking—I knew when I looked at her at that moment. She read my mind, and she knew everything I'd been thinking. I didn't know how to answer. I had already taken too long. I was getting really hot, nervous. I could feel my armpits sweating, my forehead, everything.

"Well . . ." she said, letting the word trail off like a path in the dark.

I looked up at her with the coyest smile I could muster. My smile intact, I replied, "Yes, I think about you all the time."

I figured what the hell. She could read it in my face, in my hesitance, in my every move. Why should I care? And if she hated me for it, so be it.

"That's cool. I mean, it really doesn't bother me. I just want to know what you think about. I mean, what you think about me when you think that way," she said, looking at me with softer eyes now that her inquisition was over.

I was not telling her any more of the sordid details of my fantasies. Too much information can be a bad thing, and I had already told her too much. "I don't really feel like talking about it."

"Then why don't you just do it?"

I did a double take and tried to sort out her words. "Do what?"

"Do something you think about doing with me. Kiss me."

I didn't know what to do. I was pulling the grass around me out of the ground, sweating even more than before. I averted my eyes from hers and concentrated on the grass; I wondered what the fuck she wanted me to do. "Why, do you want me to do something to you? Don't you think this is kind of stupid?" Fear surged through my veins.

"No, I think it's really interesting. Just because I never thought about it before doesn't mean I'm averse to the idea. Anyway, if you don't want to, it really doesn't bother me. I just thought . . ."

"What did you just think?" I snapped, growing tired of this little game.

"I just thought it might be nice."

All I could think about was how long I'd waited for a chance to do something with her. Here, sitting before me, was a girl I had fallen in love with against my will. The whole idea of touching her sent shivers down my spine. I wanted to kiss her, touch her, anything, but probably for the first time in my life I was afraid. I couldn't look at her; I just kept pulling at the grass. Then I felt her hand on mine, and she lifted my fingers off the blades of grass. I looked at her, and she was smiling, tight-lipped, with those slanty I-want-you eyes. I really didn't know what to do. I thought I had to be dreaming or something, maybe still hallucinating from the night before. This was nothing like Alyssia—Alyssia pursued me and her feelings were clear. Heather was lifting my hand up to her mouth and kissing my fingers lightly, then she placed my hand on her breast.

I lost it; I leaned over and began kissing her neck, her hair, her face, her lips. I leaned into her slowly, easing her down into the grass. My hand was still resting on her breast, only now it came alive with the realization of what was happening. She was hot too. I could feel her quiver underneath me, and then she slid her tongue into my mouth. Her mouth seemed even hungrier than mine; she licked my teeth, my lips, everything. I lifted her shirt and started caressing her gently but getting slightly more forceful as I felt her hips rise and fall.

My hands found the place on her stomach where it caved in, and I gently passed my fingers back and forth over the top of her shorts. I wanted to inch my fingers down inside them. I was scared that would be too much for her to handle, that it would be crossing the line. I felt her hand slide under my shirt and felt her fingers softly rise up the small of my back. It felt so good, and I didn't want to push things too far; hell, I really didn't know what to do. I relinquished my control, her hand finding my small breast. I was terribly hot, in every sense of the word. She hadn't even touched me between my legs and already it was like a volcano had erupted in my underwear. I wondered if she felt the same way.

Her forehead was all sweaty, and I rubbed the back of my hand across it to remove some of the perspiration. The whole situation was really going to my head. I was seriously overheated. My hand found the button on her shorts. I was desperately trying to undo them, trying to get the courage to unzip them. I was weak all over, and she was frantically groping me. I unzipped her shorts and grazed my fingers slightly inside her underwear. Her eyes opened wide and looked right at me. I realized immediately I had crossed a line; I had gone too far.

She smiled at me as she rolled over onto her side, her shorts still open. "I'm just not really sure if I'm ready for anything else right now."

"That's totally all right; actually I'm really sorry. I just lost control."

"So did I, but it wasn't bad."

"No, I really didn't mean to freak you out."

"You didn't."

"I feel like I did."

"Seriously, you didn't."

I was pissed off. Just when I felt like things were going to really groove, I'd frightened her. I had to go and push it too far. I wanted to know what it felt like between her legs; I wondered if she was like Alyssia. I was so stupid; I mean, I was already pushing the boundaries of a friendship that I really enjoyed, that I wanted to keep. I felt like I had built a wall, a large thorn-covered brick wall that could never be crossed again. Yet I loved her, and I wanted her.

"You didn't freak me out. Why don't we just go to Baker's house and relax for a while. Is that cool?" she asked.

"Yeah, it's cool."

We got up and straightened our clothing. Both of us were covered with grass. I brushed off my shirt and shorts, then Heather came up behind me and brushed my back off.

"Would you do me?" she asked flirtatiously as she turned her back to me.

"Sure I will," I said, and brushed the grass from her back and softly brushed over her butt, all the time thinking how great an ass she had.

"Thanks."

"No, thank *you.*" I was so worried that things would never be the same for us.

She pulled two smokes out of her pack, lit them both, placed one in my lips, then smiled.

"Don't worry, I understand now everything you feel about women. It makes total sense to me now, total sense."

Great, I thought, I've heightened her awareness. Still, I had no idea what she thought about me and felt I had gone too far.

"Are you okay?" she asked me, obviously concerned.

We were nearing Baker's house, and I really didn't feel like getting too philosophical about my feelings for her right then. I decided I would put on one of my many happy facades and act as if I didn't give a shit.

"I'm all right; let's just go drink some beers. We deserve them after all—we passed our fucking class."

"Yeah, I forgot, we *are* supposed to be celebrating."

What did she think I was doing back in the grass? I was celebrating hard-core with her.

When we walked into Baker's house after knocking the "secret" knock, we found him crashed out in his bed, doing this really cute babylike breathing thing.

"Wake up, sweets," Heather said, ruffling his disheveled hair.

"Huh, what, Mom?" Baker rolled over, turning away from Heather.

"Not Mom. Me!" She bent down and kissed him gently on the lips. I was jealous, so fucking jealous.

"Hi, Heather," he said to her with a sexy, scratchy too-many-cigarettes-the-night-before voice.

"Hi, Baker, how are you doing?"

"Good. Did you pass?"

"I passed."

"How 'bout you, Orleigh, did you pass?"

"Yeah, Baker, I passed," I said, surprised that he even noticed I was there.

"Let's go have a drink then," he said.

We all moseyed into the den, turned on the TV, and popped open some Bud Lights. It just so happened that Baker's mom had consumed all the other beer I had put in the fridge the day before. We were watching MTV when the secret knock was pounded on the door again. This time it was Aaron, who entered out of breath.

"What's going on, Aaron?" Baker asked, laughing under his breath.

Aaron didn't answer but went straight for the kitchen where he grabbed some paper towels. His mouth had a silver ring around it where the paint from the inside of a plastic bag had left an imprint. He looked so pathetic. He wet the towels in the sink. After he studied the dripping towels in his hand for a while, he looked at Baker. "Nothing, man, just got followed over here by the cops. I was in the bushes huffing a bag when a cop crawled in and started chasing me. Like, what does it matter if I want to huff a bag? It's not illegal or anything. Any old fool can buy spray paint."

I couldn't really understand why people would want to suck up spray-paint fumes; it didn't make any sense to me at all. Here was this totally good-looking guy who wasted his time on an old orange couch in the bushes, inhaling paint fumes.

"Aaron, they get pissed about that kind of shit because it's so fucking unhealthy," Baker said. He seemed genuinely concerned for him; we all were.

"Well, now I'm feeling like shit—total buzz-kill trying to run from the damn cops. If someone knocks on the door, I'm not here; I'll crawl out the window or something."

Baker shook his head, looking down at the floor. "Don't worry, man, they won't find you here," he said, and pointed to a spot on the couch for Aaron to sit down and chill.

The three of us silently watched MTV, while Aaron busied himself with his paint-cleaning situation. Heather and Baker sat on the love seat holding hands. I realized how pathetic and boring we all were; how this was really all we had to do in life. I looked deep into my beer bottle and wondered if this was really where I wanted to be.

Moments later, out of the blue, Heather spoke: "I'm not going home tonight."

"Neither am I," Aaron said. He was still scrubbing off the spray-paint ring. The paper towels were crumbling apart, falling onto the shaggy brown carpet at his feet.

I didn't really have a clue about what Aaron's home life was like. All I knew was I wouldn't go home covered in spray paint, trying to explain how it happened every day. If I were his mother, I suppose eventually I would figure out something was just not right about my son's spray-painted face.

"I guess I won't go home either," I said, knowing I was the only person who really didn't have to worry about going home. My mother had no control over my comings and goings, no matter how hard she tried. I guess I was the fortunate one.

"Where should we stay?" Heather asked. She didn't want to go home, yet she had no idea where to go.

"I don't know," I said.

"You guys can't stay here; my mother wouldn't like that," Baker said.

Nobody had mentioned staying at Baker's house; I don't think anyone had even considered that an option. What a dork, I thought.

"I know where we can sleep," Aaron piped up. He'd finally given up on the spray-paint ring; it looked rather permanent. "Whenever I don't feel like going home, I sneak into the empty old barn over on the other side of the mall, and I sleep inside." He walked back into the kitchen and threw the paper towels into the trash can.

I couldn't believe Aaron actually suggested sleeping in a barn. What a screwup. That would be so goofy—me, Aaron, and Heather crashing in a fucking barn. But Heather's eyes lit up. "God, that would be so cool! I've never been in there before. Is it nice?"

Aaron smiled. "Really, it's pretty cool—filled with hay, you know."

"Sounds like fun. What do you think, Orleigh?"

"I guess we could sleep there; what do I care?" I said somewhat aloofly. Actually, the idea suddenly seemed rather stimulating. Anything could happen if I spent the whole night with Heather. She might even get past earlier events and allow the shorts to come off. Anything was possible, and my head filled with wonderful visions of the two of us basically alone, with no parents hovering over us. I saw us intertwined on a blanket in the hay. It was classic; if ever there was a perfect opportunity, this was it.

So there we were, several hours later, Heather, Aaron, and I, with our stolen food from Dominick's, mostly candy and crap like that, and a flashlight, trying to find our way around in the dark barn. Aaron kept putting his arm around me, telling me how pretty I was. In all honesty, he made me nauseous. I tried to brush him off, but when we finally found our way to all his sleeping gear, that he obviously kept there permanently, he sat down right next to me. Heather was looking rather uncomfortable, and she pulled a blanket far away from us, announcing she was going to go to sleep. I didn't want her to fall asleep and leave me with this idiot.

"Hey, why don't we just hang out for a while?" I asked, hoping to get Heather to come back over by me.

"I'm really tired, and now I'm kind of worried about what my mom's gonna say tomorrow," Heather said, making the brightness of the evening go dim.

"Don't worry about it, she's psycho. She'll get over it," I said.

"I don't know, Orleigh, you have no idea how bad it can get." She lay on the blanket and wrapped herself up in its excess.

"We have two blankets; we can put one on the bottom and one on top of us," Aaron said.

I didn't know what had given Aaron the idea that we were going to sleep next to each other. Really, I thought he was a complete reject. He must have read the look of utter disgust on my face, because he gave me this kind of sad look, then he started blabbing.

"Look, Orleigh, I didn't mean to offend you. I guess I'm just totally fucked up. It's this spray-paint shit. I can't even help it anymore."

"Why do you do it?" I asked, feeling a little ticked that we even had to go into this. I wanted to be with Heather, and here I was playing psychologist to spray-paint boy.

"I don't know; to escape, I guess," he said, grabbing fistfuls of hay and throwing them as far as he could.

"Escape from what—what could be that bad that spray paint is the only cure?"

"I guess ever since my dad left I've been totally down. I just can't get over the fact that he bailed on us. He met some young chick and took off. I don't even know where he is anymore." He was wearing a hurt-little-boy expression that made me feel a twinge of sympathy somewhere deep inside. I couldn't believe this. "Look, I'm really sorry about your dad," I said, trying to coax him back to the real world, "but I think you are dealing with this situation completely wrong. I mean, spray-paint fumes are not going to bring your father back." I could understand some of his feelings. My father was also a real prick, but I had always dealt with it. I wanted to be sympathetic, but I was pissed he was taking up my time, coming between me and Heather.

"I guess I've just been really lonely, that's why I wanted you to sleep next to me. Not because I was planning to do anything to you, but because I'm lonely. I'm completely harmless anyway. The fumes make me impotent—can't even jerk off if I want to."

I felt even more sorry for him and his pathetic existence. I decided to just lie down next to him and keep him company. I wasn't even tired.

"I'm sorry, Aaron. I guess I understand where you're coming from. My dad left too. You'll be all right; just try and stay off the spray paint," I said, but I knew that nothing I could say would make him stop.

All of a sudden he just leaned over and kissed me full on the mouth. I pulled back instantly. "What are you doing!" I yelled, losing any sympathy I'd felt earlier.

"I just wanted to remember what it felt like."

"I don't want to help you rekindle those lost memories. Sorry," I said bitterly.

He rolled over, obviously embarrassed, and almost immediately started to fall asleep. I looked over at Heather who appeared to be asleep too, and I realized this was going to be a long and boring night. I lay, trying to sleep, but my mind was filled with thoughts of my earlier encounter with Heather in the field.

I stirred, feeling a tap on my shoulder. I turned around, hay in my hair, my contact lenses foggy as hell. I rubbed my eyes to release some of the nasty little sleep that had collected in their corners. When I could focus again, I realized it was Heather waking me, not Aaron.

"Come sleep by me," she asked.

I lifted my head off the blanket. "Why, what's up?"

"Nothing really, I'm just cold." She rubbed her hands up and down her arms to show me just how cold she was. I couldn't help thinking how pretty she was, clumps of hay stuck in her long brown hair.

I stood and grabbed the blanket off Aaron. I took the blanket he was sleeping on and wrapped the corners around him so he wouldn't freeze. I placed the blanket on top of both of us, and I lay there with my back to hers.

"Are you mad at me, Orleigh?" she asked, placing her hand on my shoulder.

"No, not at all," I replied, keeping my back to her.

"Okay, are you tired?"

"A little, I guess."

"Then I'll let you sleep."

"Did you want something?" I asked, a little hopeful.

"Not really," she said, and took her hand off my shoulder.

"Goodnight then."

"Goodnight."

I wished she had wanted something, but of course, she only wanted a warm body to generate some heat. How lucky I was to be the chosen one. Eventually I fell asleep.

I felt cold hands sliding inside my shirt, a body spooning me, legs tucked tightly behind mine. The hands were traveling up my stomach, slowly reaching my chest. An incredibly hot breath gushed against the back of my neck. I wasn't sure how I had gotten back over to Aaron's sleeping blanket, but for this moment, half-asleep as I was, he felt really good. His hand was caressing me slowly, his fingers playing gently with my nipples. I could feel his lips press against my neck, his tongue gently licking my nape. For some reason, he was totally turning me on. I forgot about the spray paint, forgot about all his dead brain cells, and I turned to return his kisses. Except it was Heather.

I knew it was going to start all over again. I kissed her, but I knew that this time I wouldn't be able to control myself. I guess that didn't matter, because she grabbed my hand and slid it down her already unbuttoned shorts. She was ready for something more. I wasn't sure what I should or shouldn't do. She grabbed onto my wrist and slid it further into her underwear. I was completely unsure of what I was supposed to do. Alyssia was different from Heather; she was always in control. I closed my eyes as she pressed her lips to mine even harder. I knew what she wanted, and I knew I had to do it. I let my hand slide down to her soft spot. I slowly moved my fingers back and forth, and I guess I was doing something right because I heard her moan in the middle of our one long kiss.

CHAPTER 3

I woke not really sure what had happened the night before. I didn't know if it had all been a dream, or if it was, in fact, real. I was next to Heather though, and I knew that was not where I had fallen asleep. She opened her eyes when I moved to a seated position.

"Hi. Sleep well?" I asked, as I watched her rub her pretty eyes.

"Yeah, really well. You?" She ran her fingers through her straw-strewn hair.

"Except for a little runny nose from the hay, I slept fine," I responded, wiping my fingers under my nose.

"Cool."

"Can I ask you something, Heather?"

"Sounds serious. What's up?"

"Did anything happen between us last night?"

"What do you mean? We slept next to each other; that's about it." She waved her hand in the air.

"Just checking." So it had been a dream, a delicious dream. But part of me wasn't fully convinced. It had felt so real. I had been half-asleep, and this is why it had felt like a dream. Why was she lying? I couldn't figure it out, and I couldn't figure her out either.

"I was thinking maybe we should call Tyler; we haven't seen him for a while," she said with a dark little smile. I knew exactly why she was smiling. Tyler had a car, and we could get him to drive us around all day.

"Sure," I said, trying to brush off my confusion.

Tyler and I were friends since the seventh grade. He was a totally whacked-out guy who always told the most extravagant and unbelievable stories. These ranged from being attacked by a wolf to chasing an escaped criminal through a forest preserve. Other than his nasty habit of trying to sound larger than life, Tyler was a really nice guy. We had remained friends, mainly because I was able to see through his bullshit and not take him too seriously. I hadn't hung out with him for some time, but I knew he had a thing for Heather, and he would take us wherever we wanted to go.

After we sent Aaron on his way back to the orange couch and his spray paint stash, Heather and I walked over to Denny's and called Tyler. He couldn't be there for another hour or so. We scrounged all our remaining cash, ordered a platter of French toast to split and two cups of coffee, and waited for Ty.

Tyler and his friend Richie waltzed into Denny's just as I was pulling out two smokes. Tyler walked his preppy ass over to our table and sat down next to Heather, leaving Richie to sit next to me. Tyler was cute, definitely a suburban boy, always dressed in Polos and khakis. Richie was the complete opposite—tall, a little heavy, pretty goofy looking. The booths were small enough as it was, then Richie had to cramp my space even more. I was thrilled to have him practically on top of me.

"What's up, ladies?" Tyler asked, putting his arm around Heather.

"Nothing really, just hanging out and eating breakfast," I answered, feeling kind of pissed that Heather was getting all his attention.

"You two look like you haven't showered in weeks." Tyler laughed.

"Try one day. And it's because we didn't go home last night," Heather snapped.

Tyler looked down at the table. "Where did you go?"

Heather looked Tyler square in the face. "We slept in a barn."

"Barn? Did you say a barn?" Tyler asked.

"Yeah, we slept in a barn because we didn't have anywhere else to go." I admired the way Heather could make things sound so dramatic.

"Why didn't you just go home?" Richie asked, joining in.

"Because my mother's been so totally crazy lately. I can't even deal with her. She won't really let me go out at night. I don't know why. She's really freaking out on me lately."

"But a barn? Wouldn't you rather sleep in your own bedroom?" Tyler asked.

What did Tyler think? That she liked being cooped up in her bedroom like Rapunzel? Sometimes he made no sense. It was always like this with him and everybody else like him who had cool parents. I'd seen Heather's mom in action—scary! I couldn't blame Tyler for not understanding though; he was from a rich, over-privileged family that never had problems. He just didn't have a clue how the less fortunate lived. He was cool enough to always do stuff for us though. He asked us what we wanted to do, and I had some ideas, but Heather took over.

"I want to get cleaned up, but I really can't go home," she said.

"We could go to the stream at Leroy Oaks and take sort of a bath. The water is really clean," I said.

"That way you two won't smell like farm animals," Tyler said, laughing. He obviously thought he was extremely funny. I guess he caught himself being pompous, because then he said, "I'll drive you."

"Finished," Heather said, emphatically slamming her coffee cup down on the table.

We jumped into Tyler's dad's Saab and headed over to the grocery store. Heather and I went inside and picked out a biodegradable body wash that we could use in the stream. Unfortunately, we had no cash to buy it, so once again we had to thieve. After we cleverly concealed it in Heather's shirtsleeve, we headed back to Tyler's car, where the guys were jamming out to Van Halen's "Jump."

"Ready to go bathe, girls?" Tyler asked, as if he thought he were joining us or something. He turned to face Heather and me sitting in the backseat, his eyebrows raised. I shook my head at him. He got this dejected look, then turned his attention back to the road.

"Hey, did I ever tell you guys about the time I ran into a pack of coyotes in Arizona?" Tyler asked.

A round of no's erupted from the interior of the car. I couldn't believe he was going to tell us another fucking story. He carried on for the whole trip to Leroy Oaks. It ended with him explaining how coyotes attack.

Heather and I walked down the path that led to the stream. We headed toward some huge trees. Behind them the stream was conveniently hidden from passersby. I turned and saw Richie and Tyler moving in the other direction; they were lighting up a joint. I was relieved that they were being respectful of our privacy.

We arrived at the side of the creek. It was so pretty—you could see tiny multicolored pebbles on the bottom of the water. Large oak trees surrounded us. I began to wonder if something might happen out here, beneath the perfect umbrella of the trees, by the creek, in the green grass. Maybe Heather and I could get back to where we'd been before in the field.

"Hurry up and get out of your clothes, I want to get this over with," Heather yelled.

I turned. She stood nearly naked in front of me. She snapped off her bra. I was amazed. Her breasts were so much more beautiful than I had imagined them, feeling with my hands. I could tell that she was enjoying me watching her continue to undress. She seemed to linger as she pulled down her baby-blue drawers. She turned her back to me. I could see now that she really did have a perfect ass; it was heart-shaped and firm. Once again I was dying to touch her. I had barely undressed myself because I had been so absorbed by her little show. She ran into the stream, her breasts bobbing.

"Get in here, slowpoke, the water's really warm, and I need the soap." She slipped head and all under the water, then emerged.

I hurried to take off my bra, revealing the inadequacy of my own tiny breasts. I was embarrassed because she had such a round and lus-cious body; I had the body of a thirteen-year-old boy—no curves at all, five-ten-and-a-half, and a hundred pounds, skin and bones. I felt really stupid as I pulled off my underwear and headed into the water after her.

"Did you bring the soap?" she called, her fingers traveling through the water towards my hand.

"Yeah, I brought the soap. What's the point of washing without soap?" I giggled like a child, feeling extremely giddy to be naked in the water with her.

"Okay, give it to me," she said, then opened the squeezable bottle, squirting a dab of soap into her palm. She started rubbing it all over her neck, then she moved down to her breasts, where she made a huge pro-duction of sudsing them. I could tell she was trying to turn me on. She was caressing her breasts, cupping them in her palms, then running her soapy fingers to her nipples, squeezing them until they were hard. She removed one hand from her breast, then ran her soapy fingers along her stomach. I realized that I was just staring stupidly at her; I was in complete awe of her body. I decided I had better do something other than ogle, so I took the soap and squirted some into my own palm.

"Could you get my back with that, please?" she asked coyly.

She was really getting into this whole touching thing. I didn't understand. At first she had thought it was so freaky, and now she was more into it than I was. I didn't mind though. I still wanted her, and I found it amazingly sexy how she was leading me on.

She turned, and I started to soap her long smooth back. I moved my hands up and down, then concentrated on the small of her back, above her ass. I was really enjoying this whole process. I decided to wash her ass. I moved my hands all around it, then I moved one hand between her legs. I ran my fingers back and forth, gently grazing her clitoris. I put a finger inside her, then two, sliding them in and out. This went on for a while, until I felt her jerk away. I was so preoccupied with her body I hadn't seen Tyler and Richie walking towards us. I moved away from Heather and slid further into the water so the guys couldn't see me. Heather looked over to where they were standing. "We're almost done," she yelled.

"We'll meet you at the car," Tyler called back, staring longingly.

They walked away towards the parking lot, and Heather smiled at me. "We better hurry up; it looks like they're ready to go."

"Yeah, I guess we should motor." All of a sudden I felt weird. I wondered if I was just a game for Heather. One moment she seemed totally engrossed in me, then the next disinterested. I was at a loss. She dressed with a quickness she hadn't displayed during her disrobing. I was utterly disappointed that the show was over.

Tyler drove us to Baker's because that was where Heather wanted to go. We said our good-byes to Ty and Richie, and they drove off to go golfing. The leisure class! Heather was smirking. I could tell she was feeling good about having gotten these boys to drive us around all day. One thing I could always count on was Heather's ability to use people for whatever she wanted. Too bad she had involved them in our day, though, especially with what had happened at the stream. I felt so damn frustrated. My underwear was damp by the time we walked into Baker's. Neil Young's "Old Man" was blaring from the stereo, and even though it was our favorite song, I was wishing I were back in the water, alone with Heather. She'd walked over to Baker's bed and sat next to him. How sweet! I sat on his papasan chair thinking about how many other things I would rather be doing—with Heather.

"You're really not working much lately," Baker remarked, and I wondered where this sudden concern about my state of employment was coming from.

"No, I really haven't found it necessary, Baker, but I do get paid today." I shrugged my shoulders, feeling like I was ousted again now that Baker was around.

"Awesome, then we can party tonight," he said. Heather smiled and Baker slid his hand over hers.

I was instantly pissed that the idea of my paycheck brought to mind the notion of partying. Now I was the one being used, and I was getting seriously tired of Heather's games. Was it me or Baker she was interested in? I really couldn't take it anymore. I was fidgeting in my chair, wishing that something interesting would happen. Someone knocked on the door, but not the secret knock. We weren't expecting anyone. Baker looked at us hesitantly, then stood to go answer the front door. I could hear him open it, but he didn't say anything once he had.

"Is Heather Ray here?" A man bellowed from the hallway.

"No, I don't believe she is, sir," Baker responded. His voice sounded small.

"Well, young man, her mother claims she is, and her mother would like her to come home. I do believe you should let me take a look around."

"Well, I guess you can look around," Baker said weakly. What a wimp, I thought.

I couldn't understand how he could let a complete stranger intimidate him into allowing him into his home. I heard the man skulk around the apartment. I couldn't see Baker, but I could hear the man's footfalls down the hall. He shuffled toward Baker's doorway, then was silent. Heather and I had lain across Baker's bed trying to be completely still. Heather reached out and held my hand, and it was kind of weird that it was completely nonsexual. I closed my eyes and wished I were far away. I wanted to be anywhere but in this room. I wished I were in my bed at home, alone with Heather.

"Is one of you Heather Ray?" a voice boomed in the room. I opened my eyes. A cop was standing directly in front of us. I looked at Heather, and I could read her desperate urge to lie all over her face.

"Neither of us is Heather. Uh, Heather whatever-you-said," I replied in the most annoyed voice I could muster, which wasn't too difficult under the circumstances. I was ready to send this fat doughnut-eating moron on his way.

"Do you have any identification?"

I quickly found my backpack, then my wallet, and pulled out my driver's license, handing it to the officer. He looked it over thoroughly then handed it back. He looked at Heather. "And yours—where is it?"

"I don't have mine on me. Must've left it at home. Sorry." She smiled sheepishly.

The cop looked at me, then Heather, and then he turned his beady little eyes toward Baker. I hadn't even noticed that Baker was cowering in the corner, taking the whole episode in.

"Get up; you're coming with me," the cop said, glancing back at Heather. He tapped his foot on the floor, waiting for her to move.

"I'm not going anywhere with you; I'm not the person you're looking for," Heather said, but her voice came out all shaky.

The officer pulled out a picture, which he compared to Heather. He squinted at it, then at Heather. God, what a genius, I thought.

"Young lady, I'm taking you home."

Looking defeated, Heather rose, gathered her belongings, took a swig from a Miller Lite, then marched out the door with the cop. Baker and I watched through his bedroom window as she climbed into the backseat of the squad car.

CHAPTER 4

For two days now Heather's mother had been hanging up on me, Baker, or anyone we recruited to call Heather's house on our behalf. We were beginning to wonder if Heather was home at all. Every time we called we either got the answering machine, her mother, or her mother's boyfriend, who hung up too. We were afraid that if we showed up at her house, her mother would call the police. So instead, Baker and I sat by our phones all day, waiting to hear from Heather. I had quit my job and did nothing but bite my nails.

At three in the morning on the third day of Heather's disappearance, I got a phone call from Baker. I was groggy, but I managed to make out that Baker had heard from Heather. I couldn't really comprehend what he was talking about, but then I heard him say Mercy Center Hospital. Suddenly my head cleared, and I began to take note of what he was saying.

"Mercy Center, why is she there?"

"I guess the cop brought her directly there, not home," Baker said. I couldn't believe the cop had lied to us, but then I realized that's what they're paid to do—lie, cheat, steal, and blackmail.

"Can they do that?" I asked.

"That's what her mother wanted. Now she's holed up in a place where they keep bad kids. It's some runaway, wild kids' holding den. Some kind of mental institution. Her mother had her committed."

He gave me all the details. They gave Heather a pass that enabled her to go outside, on the Center's grounds. I took this in. I had to figure out a way to get her out, then bring her someplace safe. My mind was already scheming. When I got up that morning, it would be Thursday, which gave me one day to sort everything out.

"What time on Friday did you say again, Baker?" I asked.

"Two o'clock is when they let the monkeys out of their cages."

"God, Baker, you're so witty today. I'm impressed! Don't worry about it, babe, I'll figure it all out from here." I hung up and went to my room.

I lay in bed totally awake, thinking. I had never busted someone out of a mental hospital before. I began thinking about who I needed to call, who I could find tomorrow to help me with my master plan. As I contemplated all the obstacles I could think of, I fell back asleep.

I woke early in the morning in a state of panic. I was crazy even thinking I could pull this off. Jesus, I was honestly in love with Heather. I cared more about her than anyone in my life, with the exception of myself. I had to think fast, had to figure out who I could talk to about this hideous situation. First, I called Baker. I made sure he'd get in touch with Heather to let her know we'd bust her out on Friday. He said she was supposed to call him at four p.m. that day, when she had rights to one phone call. So that was all set. I decided my best bet would be to head to the mall and round up some friends who might be willing to help.

Two hours later I was at the mall wandering aimlessly about by myself. I guess I had actually been a little too eager. Most people we knew never made it out until about three in the afternoon, so I decided I would visit with my old boss at the video arcade, then get something to eat. I walked into the arcade and bumped into paint-sniffer boy playing pinball. Today the ring around his mouth was blue: the flavor du jour.

"Hey, what's up, Orleigh?"

"Nothing, Aaron. Just trying to figure out what to do about Heather."

"Oh, yeah, I heard she's locked up in some mental place."

"Don't tell everybody that, okay! Her mom put her in there for no reason."

"Yeah, I know, rotten deal. Too bad she didn't go home the other night, huh?" He slammed his hips against the Black Knight pinball machine, and it made some kind of awful noise, which made him slug his fist down on the glass. The "Tilt" light flashed. He turned his back to the machine and looked at me. "Come to think about it, I haven't been home for about a month and a half."

"Where have you been staying, Aaron?" I asked, even though I already knew the answer.

"The orange couch or in the barn."

"Lucky you," I said.

All I could think was what an absolute loser he was. I would never sleep in the bushes on a fucking smelly couch, not if you paid me. For god's sake, didn't he have any dignity?

I craned my neck looking around for Brenda, my old boss. The arcade's office door was locked. She must have been out getting lunch. Maybe she was hanging with one of her lesbian friends. I walked out of the arcade and saw Malick, a guy I briefly knew in high school, heading into Kmart.

"Hey, Malick," I called, and kind of half-waved.

"Orleigh, how's it going?" he asked, walking towards me.

"Shitty, and you?"

"Have to work all day."

"Sorry."

"What's wrong?" he asked.

"Well, I got this friend who's kind of in a bind." I ground my shoe into the cement floor. I was desperate. Here I was talking to this guy I barely knew about Heather.

"What kind of a bind?" he asked, concerned.

"It's like her mother is completely freaky, and she put her into Mercy Center Hospital because she didn't come home the other night." I could feel my face redden, which pleased me because I thought then Malick would see how frustrated I was. This would hopefully make him more empathetic to my situation, and therefore get him to help me. God, I was manipulative.

"Man, that's really shitty." I could tell he needed to get to work, but he kept his attention focused on me. He was just the kind of guy I needed. He cared about people.

"She gets some kind of grounds pass, so I can pick her up if I can get past security, and get her the fuck out of there. But I just don't know where I can take her afterwards. Her mom knows all of our hangouts. I really don't know what to do about all this," I said, looking down at the ground, lost and helpless.

"Well, you know I'm all the way out in DeKalb?"

"Yeah?" I said, almost too eagerly.

"That's pretty far from here, but if you could get her out there . . ." He looked at me kindly, and I realized he was offering me his home.

"You mean you would let her stay at your place?" I asked incredulously.

He smiled warmly. I had it in the bag. "Sure, you could stay too; we always have a full house."

"God, Malick, that would be perfect." I threw my arms around his neck, I felt so relieved and excited.

He asked when I thought we would arrive in DeKalb, and I filled him in on all the details of the plan I had thus far. I couldn't believe how sweet he was; he barely knew me. And he didn't know Heather at all. He was totally cool. I wondered why we hadn't been better friends in high school. He scribbled some directions onto a tiny piece of paper.

"Now, don't lose this because we don't have a phone," he said, handing me the piece of paper. "I'll tell my roommates we're having company so that they'll be expecting you. I won't be there when you get there, so just make yourselves at home."

I thanked him for his kindness and watched him walk into Kmart. I hoped I hadn't made him lose his job. Now all I needed was a getaway car. I decided to go outside and have a smoke.

I sat on the low cement retaining wall in the parking lot, looking out at all the cars, the tiny trees that had just been planted to beautify the mall, the bike rack filled with teenagers' Huffys. I leaned back, inhaled deeply on my cigarette, and tried to think of who I might trust to help me kidnap Heather. Most of the people I knew were mall rats. They had no lives, no real friends, no loyalties to anyone or anything. They cared mainly about sex, liquor, and cars. How unfortunate! While I was reflecting on all these high school dropouts, I saw a real winner pull up in a metallic blue Thunderbird. It was Zacker. I was seriously frightened that I actually knew what kind of a car he was driving. All I could think was how the mall-rat mentality was getting inside me like flesh eating bacteria munching away at my brain. A shiver ran up my spine at the thought of turning out like one of those trailer-trash chicks the guys here hung out with—like Lisa. I vowed solemnly to myself this would never happen. Absorbed by these thoughts, I watched Zacker with disgust as he got out of his lovely car. He was heading right towards me.

"Hey, hey, hey, Orleigh, what's shaking, babe?"

He had on some heavy metal T-shirt and the worst hair I'd ever seen. It was that permed-in-the-back, feathered-on-the-sides do that all the metal heads sported.

"Nothing, Zacker, absolutely nothing," I said, trying to brush him off, will him away with my mind power.

"Where's your partner in crime?"

"Away for a while," I said, keeping things simple.

"Away? Is she maybe locked up somewhere?" he asked, and I figured Baker, who could never keep his mouth shut, had already blabbed everything all over the Chicago area.

"Maybe she is. Where are you getting your info from anyway?"

"Bakity-bake Baker," he said with a grin, finding himself amusing. I couldn't stand even looking at him, his yellow teeth, all gums and gaps. He made me physically ill.

"That's great!"

"Yeah, he told me you two were going to bust her out of Mercy."

"Just great!" I said, looking away. I lit another cigarette and ignored him. I really just wanted him to get back in his car and circle the parking lot to look for chicks.

He moved closer toward me, his body swaying awkwardly back and forth. "So, do you need any help? I can help you out, you know."

"No, I really don't think we will be needing you, Zacker." I took a deep drag from my cigarette and glared at him.

Zacker's bony index finger extended out, pointing directly to the center of my forehead. "Maybe you don't have a choice. I want in on the action. I've never done anything that cool before," he said, his voice quavering a bit as he dropped his hand to his side.

"Zacker, I do have a choice, and my choice is for you to get the fuck out of here, leave me alone, and stop talking to me, period." I was feeling all huffy at this point. I honestly didn't want him standing near me, didn't want people to even think I knew him.

"Ah, I see. Now you decide to get all bitchy on me. I tell you what I'm going to do! I'm going to let the police know about this little break-out you've planned. I'm gonna fuck it all up for you. You know why? Do you know why?" he said in a snotty tone of voice.

I wasn't even looking at him. I was fixing the ash on the end of my smoke, twirling its edge against the cement wall to make it a perfect sphere shape. I looked up when Zacker had finished his ranting, and I noticed he had a bit of drool at the corner of his mouth. He had also begun sucking on a cigarette with this sickeningly slobbery sucking noise that was driving me crazy.

"I don't give a fuck, Zacker." I flicked my cigarette butt, which grazed the side of his thigh, then landed on the ground next to his high-tops.

Zacker looked down at the butt, then back at me. His face contorted, his eyes growing wider. His jaw locked tight. "Because you're such an absolute bitch to me, Orleigh. You think you're so fucking pretty. You think your shit don't smell? Well, you're wrong. You may have a nice face, a nice body, but real beauty comes from the inside." How intelligent, I thought. I was so proud that his two-and-a-half years of high school had finally paid off. He actually had learned how to do more than change a carburetor. He knew how to judge inner beauty. How beautiful he was, especially with the white slobber crusting around the edges of his mouth.

"Look, Orleigh, here comes a cop right now. I'm gonna go tell him your little plan. You have one minute to figure out what you're going to do," he said hastily. His head swiveled back and forth from the police car to me. He looked like a charmed snake.

I peered across the parking lot, and sure enough a cop was headed in our direction. The copper was probably looking for paint inhalers like Aaron who were hanging out in the bushes. I watched Zacker thoughtfully eye the squad car. I couldn't believe that someone who had been busted by cops so many times was willing to throw himself into their jaws for absolutely no reason. Out of the corner of my eye I saw the car circle the lot; it was turning away from us, then for no apparent reason it circled back toward us. It was getting closer with every passing second. Finally, when it was about ten feet away, Zacker gave me a look, signaling that this was my last chance. I didn't respond.

"Here I go."

"Go then," I said, kicking my heels against the cement wall.

"Okay."

I was sick to my stomach. I couldn't believe he was actually walking over to the cop car whose window was rolled down. I watched him wave, and the cop stopped. I was honestly going to puke. Zacker ducked his head into the window, and I could hear him talking to the cop, but I couldn't make out his words. He turned and looked directly at me, then he resumed talking to the officer. This was ridiculous. I could not believe he was going to sabotage Heather's only chance at freedom. I wouldn't give in to the slimy little bastard. I picked up my pack of Black Russians and walked into the mall without looking back. I was about to head over to Kmart to tell Malick what had transpired when someone tapped me on the shoulder from behind. I turned. It was the infamous Zacker smiling his yellow-toothed smile.

"What do you want?" I sneered at him.

"I just wanted to tell you to be careful," he said, as he placed his clenched fists on his skinny hips.

"What are you trying to accomplish?"

"I just wanted to be part of the action," he said with a pathetic look.

"Why?" I rubbed my fingers against my forehead. A sharp pain throbbed at my brow.

"Because I like Heather and because it would be fun."

"What exactly did you say to the cop?"

"Nothing. I was just making small talk," he said, then chuckled.

"Why did you look at me?" I asked.

"Just to see if you were still sitting there." His arms dropped from his waist, and he attempted to place his hand on my shoulder.

I stepped back, out of the range of physical contact. "I don't know what you think you can do for us."

"I can give you a ride when you break her out." He was visibly getting more excited, drumming a hand against his leg.

The last person I wanted to help us was Zacker. I kept thinking about my options, but every time I came up with someone, I realized they would probably not want to get involved. Tyler avoided trouble at all costs, even though he liked to tell stories that suggested otherwise. Baker was a child. I glanced around, looking into the entrance of Kmart and watching shoppers walk by. Shit, I didn't know any of these people.

"I can find someone who wouldn't mind doing it," I said. I was afraid my plan was going to fail.

"I've already told you that I wouldn't mind," Zacker replied, his hands dancing around his body as he grew more insistent.

"I know, but it doesn't seem like it would work. Especially after that little stunt you just pulled."

"That was nothing. But if you don't let me be a part of this I *am* going to tell the cops."

I could have killed Baker for opening his big mouth. Of all the people to talk to about something this important, Zacker would have been my last choice. But I was feeling like I had no alternatives. I had nothing on Zacker to bring him down, so it was either comply or let the crazy bastard fuck it all up.

"All right, Zacker, you can give us a ride. I don't give a shit. I'm really not in the mood for your bullshit," I said, surrendering against my better judgment.

"Good. Now tell me the plan," he said smugly.

I explained to him how things were going to go down, and we decided to meet at the mall the next day. He promised he would be there at one thirty in the afternoon, and I reluctantly told him I would too, then I walked away from his sleazy ass. I kept thinking about how I wanted to kill Baker. I was ready to put a brick through his skull.

Lying in bed that night, I couldn't sleep. I could hear the sound of my alarm clock tick-tick-ticking behind my head. I wondered if everything was going to run smoothly. I knew deep down inside that involving Zacker was about the worst thing I could have done. Everything else had gone so well. Malick was being completely cool about his house.

I missed Heather. I wished she had called me. I wished she were lying next to me; I wished I could touch her again. I tried to assuage myself by thinking about how we would be together tomorrow night. It was going to be wonderful. I started to drift as I thought about Heather lying next to me naked. It was going to be so beautiful, so fucking beautiful.

I couldn't believe I had slept so late. It was twelve in the afternoon. I quickly jumped into the shower and scrubbed down. I rushed to dry, dress, and fix my hair, which was flying all over the place. I bounded down the stairs to beg my mom for a ride to the mall.

"Don't you have anything better to do with your time than hang out at the mall with all those trashy people?" my mother asked snidely, her eyes betraying her misgivings about what I was really up to.

I stood in the doorway of the kitchen, avoiding her gaze. "Actually, today I don't. I need to get over there, Mom, I'm meeting someone."

"Who?" Again with the questioning.

"Please, just give me a ride," I said, thinking I had one nerve left, and she was perched on it.

"Fine," she said wearily, her arm extended over the kitchen sink as she wrung out the sponge she had used to wash the kitchen counters.

"I also won't be home for a few days." I realized this was probably not the best time to tell her, but I couldn't think of a better one.

"What!" she exclaimed, dropping the sponge into the water.

I was annoyed. I reached for my mountain pack, holding it in front of me so she could see it. I had packed the previous night, and I had just remembered that all my toiletries were still in the bathroom. Well, fuck it, I was going to be late. I could either steal or possibly buy some new things.

"I'm not going to be home for a little while, is what I said. I'm going to stay in DeKalb for a few days with some friends," I explained as I slung my mountain pack over my shoulder.

Her shoulders were slumped and she wasn't looking at me. "What friends?"

I looked at her, wondering when this interrogation would cease. "What does it matter?" I chuckled under my breath, but my mother obviously didn't find this amusing. She reached for the paper towel rack and yanked at the edge of the roll angrily. A good portion of towels ended up in a pile on the counter. I could see her body tense up even more.

"Will I see you again?" she asked, and for a moment I could tell she was truly concerned. Her wide blue eyes softened as she looked over her shoulder at me, then she began rolling the towels back up.

I tapped my foot impatiently on the floor. I always did this when we had a confrontation, and I could never understand why we always argued when I was in a hurry. I exhaled heavily and leaned against the doorframe. "For god's sake, you're really bugging me. What's the problem?"

"I just worry about you. You're telling me you're not going to be home for a few days," she said, turning around to face me again. She shook her head back and forth, searching my face for answers. "What am I supposed to think?" She sighed.

"Jesus Christ, Mom, I'll call you, okay? I'll call you to let you know that I'm alive," I said defensively. "I know you think I'm going to be murdered or maimed, mutilated or destroyed, but really, Mom, I'm finally having some fucking fun!" I hoped that my hostility would end further questioning.

"All right already; sorry I care! Let's go get you to your important people." She gathered her purse, keys, and wallet off the kitchen table and walked down the hallway to the garage. I stood another second, thinking about how badly I wanted to move away for good, not be dependent on my mother anymore. I figured that if this time in DeKalb worked out better than it did with Alyssia, I might stay permanently. I grabbed my pack and headed out to the garage. My mother had already pulled out into the driveway, and she clicked the remote to close the garage door as I walked into the garage. The door started to close, and I ran the rest of the way to the car so I wouldn't get trapped inside. Damn, she must be really mad, I thought as I slid into the passenger seat. I didn't want her to talk to me; I just wanted some peace. Unfortunately, it was never that way with my mother.

She thought everything mattered. And I'd never met a person who cared so much about what people thought. If the garage was open for more than two minutes, she believed the whole neighborhood was look-ing in at the mess. She thought people really cared about that kind of shit, that they judged her on how clean her garage was. I didn't give a rat's ass about what anybody thought about me, and I guess that was the differ-ence between us, the reason we had so much trouble seeing eye to eye.

She looked over at me as I fumbled with my mountain pack strap. "You know I just worry about you." Her voice sounded calm.

I suddenly felt bad about ragging on her. I just wanted to be free to do what I wanted to do. I hated always having to explain myself to her. I smiled warmly and said, "I know, but you need to stop. I'm doing fine."

"But you aren't even going to college." Her tone was uneven. I couldn't tell if it was disdain, anger, or resentment.

She pulled out of the driveway and headed in the direction of the mall. I was relieved that we were finally moving. I thoughtfully tugged at my mountain-pack strap and said defensively, "Not right now I'm not; I really need a break, but that doesn't mean forever."

"Don't placate me," she said with another sigh, this one exaggerated and labored. "You know all the other kids are going away." Her eyes darted from me to the road and back again. Finally, she turned on the radio to some terrible fifties music, and she began to drum her hand against the steering wheel.

It was the same old—always worrying about what people in town or the neighbors were going to think or say. I don't even think she cared if I went or not, or thought about whether I could even handle going to classes.

"Mom, I'm not all the other kids. Please, just have faith that things will work out in the end."

"I guess I should, but I still think of you as my little girl." I could see her getting sentimental on me. "Where you're going, is it safe?"

I glanced out the window at St. Peter's church, hoping it was the last time I'd have to drive down this road. "Yes, Mom." I tried to sound reas-suring, but I knew she would worry regardless. I kept catching glimpses of her face, seeing it contort as she concentrated on the road, deep in thought.

"Why are you going to DeKalb?"

"I need some time away. Consider it a vacation," I said, thinking to myself how remarkably honest I was being with her. Her tight grip on the steering wheel relaxed a little. Her tense lips parted. I studied her profile. It was visible how the stress of my dad and me had aged her. For the first time, I considered how difficult it must have been for her when my father left. Dad had basically deserted us. He decided he no longer loved my mom and disposed of me just as easily. She had to do everything on her own. I admired her strength, and she was still hip. She wore cool vintage seventies dresses and Birkenstock clogs. At least she was as hip as a mom could be—but she looked tired. For a moment I felt base about the way I treated her.

When we pulled into the mall parking lot, it was already twenty past one. As we sat in park, my mother looked at me for a while. "Do you need any money?" she finally asked.

"No, not really," I said, knowing that if I said yes my chances of getting cash were unlikely. If I said no, then she usually gave me some. It didn't make any sense. Plus with the yes answer also came the *you really need to get a job* lecture. I watched her pull two twenties out of her wallet.

"Here, in case you run out," she said, handing me the money. Her fingers brushed mine, resting for a moment, then she pulled them away.

I felt like I should pat her hand, give her a kiss on the cheek, something. But instead I just said, "Thanks, Mom." I grabbed my backpack, then opened my door. "Bye, now. I'll be fine and I *will* call. Don't worry! Please, don't worry. I love you."

"Love you too, Orleigh. Be good."

"I will," I said. I shut the door, looked over my shoulder at my mother as she pulled away, then headed to the front of Kmart where Zacker was already waiting for me. He was pacing back and forth as I walked up behind him. He wore all black even though it was hot. When he turned and looked at me, I noticed he had some black shit under his eyes, like football player makeup. I guess this was his idea of looking inconspicuous. I laughed under my breath at him, thinking this must be the most exciting thing he'd done in a long time: Zacker's covert mission.

"What took you so long?" he asked, simultaneously snapping his gum and running his fingers through his hair.

"We have plenty of time," I said.

All of a sudden Baker came running towards us.

"What are *you* doing here? You're supposed to be in school." I sounded like my mother.

"I know, but I wanted to come and see Heather, so I skipped." He crouched over, his breathing heavy and strained.

"Are you crazy? Your mother's in there," I said. I pointed to the window of Kmart, where coincidentally I saw his mother, wearing a red Kmart shirt, arranging cartons of Pall Malls on a shelf, which confirmed that she did in fact work there. Baker looked in the direction of my pointed finger.

He dodged behind Zacker, peering at me from the other side of Zacker's scrawny arm. "We need to get going. I don't want her to see me." He glanced at the window of Kmart, then back at me. "All I want to do is go with you when you break her out. I can't go all the way to DeKalb. Is that all right?"

"It's fine with me," Zacker answered smartly, shoving me forward. "Let's get fucking moving; we don't have all goddamned day."

Zacker escorted us to the beautiful blue baby he had waiting in the parking lot, the whole time telling us about some secret compartment that led from the inside of the car to the trunk. Baker crawled into the backseat, leaving me to ride beside Zacker. Instantly, Zacker began telling me his brilliant idea to hide Heather in the trunk. At this point, I really didn't give a damn, I just wanted to get to the crazy house to pick up my little monkey. Zacker turned on the stereo and the trashiest song, ZZ Top's "Legs," boomed from the stereo. The music was so loud that the passenger seat was vibrating my whole body. I thought I was going to die. I didn't relate to this kind of a person; guys who were uneducated morons irked me. I just wanted to get Heather, then move on to DeKalb.

I spaced out for the majority of the ride to Mercy, my eyes shut, trying to block out the annoying music—Metallica, Van Halen, White Snake. Eventually, we pulled onto the grounds of the hospital and passed the wooden shack that housed the security guard. He smiled at us and waved the car through. Quality security, I thought, as we pulled into a circular drive with a statue of Mary dead center. Her arms were spread out wide, welcoming all the sick, deranged, little children into their new home. Little flowering impatiens bloomed red, white, and purple at her feet. Beyond the statue, I saw Heather walking toward us across the green, meticulously manicured lawn. No one else was around, and I couldn't believe this could be so easy. Zacker pulled his car up next to her and popped his trunk. Baker and I sat there waiting to get busted, as I watched Zacker get out of the car and shut the trunk. Baker immediately pulled open Zacker's armrest that had the hole in it that led to the trunk. Through the armrest, I could faintly hear Heather.

"Hey, Orleigh. Hi, Baker," she said. "Thanks for getting me out of here."

I thought for sure we would never get off the grounds, but we were slowly approaching the exit, which was supervised by a guard. I held my breath as Zacker drove past him, my heart beating wildly.

"We did it, Heather. We made it," I hollered over my shoulder, watching the security guard wave good-bye.

"Cool, when can I get out of this trunk?" she asked. I could barely hear her, so I turned down the volume on the stereo. Zacker shot me a look of disapproval, but I ignored him.

"Just as soon as we drop off Baker."

"When will that be?" It was strange to hear her talking out of the armrest. I couldn't see her beautiful face.

"In about ten minutes," I said.

"Where are we going after that?"

"DeKalb, to stay with some friends."

"Awesome. Anything's better than that shit hole," she said.

Baker tried to hold Heather's hand through the hole in the armrest, and it was actually kind of cute, but I just wanted to drop him off and get Heather out of the trunk. Zacker turned the music up again, and he was shaking the whole car, bouncing up and down to his idiotic music. I felt like I was going to throw up.

"That was awesome! Can you believe I pulled that off?" Zacker yelled.

Whatever he thought was all right by me, because I knew I wasn't going to see him again, ever. "Yes, Zacker, you were amazing!" I said.

"I just can't believe you thought the whole thing through by yourself. And to think you were able to get Heather in the trunk, and so slickly, for that matter. You're a dream, a real fucking professional."

"Thanks, I know." He pulled around the corner and bellowed, "Baker, your stop, man!"

What a stud, I thought.

"Thanks for letting me come along." It was evident by the way Baker was gripping Heather's hand that he didn't want to leave her. How fucking romantic. I was so happy that Heather and I would soon be alone.

"No problem," Zacker said, then he got out of the car and opened the trunk.

Baker got out and walked to the back of the car, probably to give Heather a good-bye kiss. Poor kid, wouldn't see the love of his life for a while now. Heather slammed the trunk shut and strode around to the door. She clumsily climbed into the tiny backseat of the Thunderbird.

"Hey, baby, I missed you," she said, reaching over the back of the passenger seat to throw her arms around my neck.

As soon as she touched me, I felt warm and anxious. I had been waiting for this moment for too long. "I missed you too," I said.

Zacker ruined the moment by opening his big mouth again. "You know, you two can stay with me instead of going all the way to DeKalb." He flipped open his pack of cigarettes and took one out. I watched him flick his Zippo against his jeans to light the wick.

"No thanks. We already have a place to stay, and anyway your house is always crawling with cops looking for you or your brother."

"Not so much lately. You know, my bro and I've pretty much been staying out of trouble."

"Good for you, but the place we're staying at seems to be a little safer, if you know what I'm saying."

"Okay," he replied reluctantly. "Where is it anyway?"

I reached into my mountain pack and pulled out the piece of paper Malick had written on. We were already heading down Lincoln Highway, which was the beginning of the directions. So far, so good.

"Just continue down Lincoln until we hit DeKalb," I said, looking at Heather. God, I wanted to kiss her. But she was busying herself biting off her split ends.

"Whose house is it anyway?" he asked, getting all nosy.

"Oh, just a friend of mine, someone I've known for a while." I got Heather's attention away from her hair and mouthed the words, *"I'll tell you later."* I didn't want to reveal too much information in front of Zacker. Even though he was kind enough to drive us to DeKalb, I still didn't want him to know all the digs on our arrangements. I could see him totally fucking things up. That was just the way it was with Zacker. I looked out the window and spied the cornfields. People were always saying how much they loved the great Illinois flatlands—all cornfields, an occasional meadow with a cow or two grazing. I hated it here, hated the sameness. All I could see was corn: corn and flatness everywhere. I wanted mountains—peaks and valleys. We passed a huge red barn with a horse running around in a fenced-in area. That horse was just like me, believing in his little bit of freedom, but captive. We were getting close to DeKalb.

I turned to Heather, who was now spinning strands of brown hair around her index finger. "What's wrong?" I asked, reaching for her hand, then untangling her finger from her hair. She squeezed my fingers in an attempt to be reassuring.

"Nothing, I'm just sort of worried about what my mom's gonna do. The cops are probably already looking for me. I guess I'm a little scared." She released my hand and returned to her hair twirling.

"Don't worry, we're going somewhere safe, and anyway, why would your mom ever look for you in DeKalb? She doesn't even know that we know people there, right?"

"No, I really don't know anyone there at all; I don't think I've ever even said *DeKalb* in front of her."

"Then what are you worried about?"

"The cops found me at Baker's house, took me to a mental hospital, and I just broke out. Sorry if I'm a little paranoid. I just don't want to be locked up again."

"Come on, Heather, look, we're almost there. I'll make sure everything goes smoothly. Seriously, you have nothing to worry about." I hoped it was true. I couldn't even stop my own heart from racing out of control. I was so nervous, contemplating what could happen to Heather if she were caught again.

"How will you do that?"

"I said, *Don't Worry!*"

"Where to from here, Orleigh?" Zacker asked. We had arrived in DeKalb.

"Shit, let me figure this out." I looked down at the scrap of paper Malick had given me. According to his directions, his house was behind a place called Tom and Jerry's. Sure enough, I saw the sign coming up on our right. I made Zacker pull a quick right. Ahead, about a block away, was a sign for John Street the street Malick lived on. I read the numbers on the houses. Then I saw the house—it was huge.

"Zacker, you can let us out here," I said.

"What, here?" Zacker asked, looking around at the houses.

"Yeah."

Zacker's gaze zoomed in thoughtfully on Malick's house. "This is it?"

"Yeah."

"Can I come in with you guys?"

A string of no's immediately ran through my head. "I don't really think that's a good idea. See, I don't even know any of the people in there right now, Zacker. My friend lives here, but he's at work. So how about I just talk to you in a few days. Is that okay?"

"I guess, but I would really like to come inside."

"Like I said, I don't want to freak these people out. We need a place to stay, and I don't want to overwhelm them by dragging in extra people. Hell, Zacker, they might not even know who we are. So we'll get in touch with you, okay? Thanks for the ride." I grabbed my pack and opened the door. Heather was trying frantically to gather all the little things she was able to take out on her walk, and she stuffed them into a bag I had brought along for her. Zacker was watching from his rearview mirror, and he looked really pissed. Heather jumped out of the car after me and smiled at Zacker.

"Thanks a lot, Zacker, for helping me get out of there," she said, sucking up to him a little, which was good because I couldn't bear to be nice to him.

"Anytime you need anything, let me know. But next time try to leave your bitch at home." He grinned at Heather and then leered at me.

He was such a polite inbred loser. I pulled Heather away from the car toward the house. I had no patience left to deal with Zacker. Behind me, I heard him rev the engine of his disgusting automobile, then pull away with a couple of honks, just to let us know he was "outta" there. Thank god!

"I hate that guy," I said with a scowl, as we walked up the path to the front door of the house.

"He did give us a ride though."

"I know, but he's so creepy." I looked up at the door, then back at Heather. "Here we are."

"Do we knock?"

"I guess we should." I knocked, and we waited. No one was answering. We stood there looking like complete shit heads.

"What should we do?" she asked me.

"I don't know, do you think we should try to open the door?"

"I guess. What else are we going to do?"

I opened the latch on the screen door. The main door was open. We walked into a denlike area filled with four couches and six overstuffed chairs. Across the room on a green velvet sofa lay a long-haired guy reading a book and smoking a joint. He looked up for a split second, then went back to his book.

"Hello, we're Malick's friends," I said, feeling like an intruder.

He looked up again, took a hit off the joint, then continued reading. He didn't even look at us when we introduced ourselves. I was thinking something must be wrong with him, like maybe he was deaf.

"Sit," he finally said, and pointed to a yellow plaid couch across from a green one. He could actually speak. Heather kept looking at me as if she were wondering what was going on. Unfortunately, I couldn't give her a reassuring look, because I didn't know either.

I heard someone moving around in a room. There were three doors to the right. One of them was suddenly kicked open, and a pair of combat boots came flying into the den. A punk chick walked out after the combat boots. She wore a black mini dress and red tights that matched her bright red hair, which was obviously dyed. A variety of silver jewelry adorned her body, including three rings in her nose. She looked like a fucking circus sideshow. Not to mention the out-of-sync fifties horn-rimmed glasses—sans tape, thankfully.

"Hi, I'm Tammy, Malick's girlfriend," she said, patting her chest with a clenched fist. It looked like she was ready to punch us. She had a chain and padlock around her wrist.

"I'm Orleigh," I said, trying to sound hip.

"My name's Heather."

"Yeah, Malick told me about you two," Tammy said.

"We didn't know if anyone would be here or not," I said, hoping she thought this was a good enough excuse for us to barge in.

"I'm here." She smiled kindly.

We made small talk. I told Tammy how we had rescued Heather. Tammy searched Heather's face, as if she knew her or something, but then she said, "I think the first thing we should do is change that hair of yours so that you look a little different."

"What do you mean, change my hair?" Heather asked, a look of terror on her face. Heather had been working on growing out her hair for years. She thought it was the shit.

"I was actually thinking we could cut it, maybe shoulder-length, then we could dye it. Red or blond," Tammy said.

Heather held up the ends of her long brown hair and looked at them lovingly. She turned her attention to Tammy. "Do you really think that's necessary?"

"You don't want to look too much like yourself, especially if anyone comes looking for you," Tammy insisted. "I'm sure they *are* looking for you around your area as we speak. Eventually they may get smart and come out here. Whatever you think, though; I'm just trying to be helpful."

"I guess we could do it. I mean, why should I care? It's only hair," Heather said, looking to me for support. I smiled. "I really wonder if they will actually come looking for me out here."

"Heath," I said, "they may or may not hunt for you out here. Tammy just wants to do her best to keep things cool. She's right, you won't stand out if you don't look exactly like that picture the cops are carrying around."

"All right then, let's do it."

Tammy smiled and walked back into the room she had emerged from. I heard her fumble around, and Heather gave me this really frantic look. I tried to reassure her by smiling, but it didn't seem to help. Tammy came back, carrying a huge, black trunklike thing.

"Okay, I got all my stuff."

"What stuff?" Heather asked, anxiously eyeing the trunk.

"I'm a beautician. I do this for a living. Fortunately for you, this job will be free. Just don't tell anybody here because I don't do this for just anyone." She winked at Heather. I was starting to think that she was pretty cool.

We followed her past the guy on the green couch, through the kitchen, then up a flight of stairs to a hallway with several doors, all shut. Tammy pointed to a door that was painted red. "You two can put your things in here."

She opened the door to a bedroom that was really creepy—it looked like Sharon Tate's room after the Manson-family rampage. "Helter Skelter" and "Little Piggies" were painted on the walls in red. I could tell that Tammy could feel the apprehension just oozing from us. I was afraid if we opened the closet, we might find Sharon Tate's dead baby in there.

"Sorry, guys, I know it's a little strange, but the two guys who used to share this room kind of freaked out. Now Sam and TJ are supposedly in California."

Sam. I wondered if it was the Sam I knew. Wondered if he had lived here. It was quite possible. I started thinking about him again. I thought about his vampire problem, his bisexuality, his charming good looks. I hadn't seen him in such a long time. Thinking about Sam made me think of Alyssia. Tammy had no idea that she'd launched me into a major flash-back. I sat on the bed, totally unaware of Heather and Tammy. I leaned against the wall, lit a cigarette, and began thinking about how I could possibly have gotten involved in that strange cultish relationship with Alyssia and Sam.

CHAPTER 5

I couldn't believe how entirely different Heather looked. Her hair was platinum blond and very short, bluntly cut in a bob. She had put blood-red lipstick on her thin lips and heavy black eyeliner and mascara on her eyes. She looked amazing. It was a complete makeover. Tammy had even changed the way she dressed—she had gone from this chilled-out jeans-and-T-shirt chick to this totally punked-out babe. The transformation was incredible. They were both giddy, and I was happy that Heather wasn't sulking about how short her hair was.

"You look good," I said, smiling inside, thinking of how badly I wanted to be alone with her.

"Really?" she asked, concerned.

"Yeah, really good," I said.

"You know there's going to be a party here tonight," Heather said flirtatiously.

I got that queasy, sexy feeling in my stomach. I wanted to kiss her red lips, wanted to run my fingers through her new hairdo. I had to sit on my hands to resist temptation. "Really?"

"Yeah," Tammy piped in. "We're all going to drink ourselves into a stupor. Lots of people are coming."

"Cool," I replied, but I wasn't paying any attention to Tammy. My eyes were ravaging Heather's hourglass figure, which was now accentuated by a tight black dress.

Maybe at the party I could find an opportunity to get my hands on her. We could get drunk and pick up where we'd left off.

Tammy wanted to bring us downstairs to show Heather off. The guy on the velvet couch did not seem to have moved since we'd gone upstairs, and he had rolled another joint. His long hair covered his face

69

as he smoked, and he didn't look up when we entered the room.

"Hey, Joe, why are you being so quiet?" Tammy asked, coming over and hitting him on the shoulder to get his attention.

"Shut up, Tammy, I'm concentrating," he said.

"Okay, fine, but you could be polite to our guests." She looked over at us, smiling.

Joe finally looked up from his book. He didn't seem to notice that Heather's appearance had completely changed. He smiled a quirky little I-don't-give-a-shit-about-you grin. I kind of liked his attitude.

"Hey, Joe," Heather said, trying to return his feeble attempt at politeness.

I opted to give him a slanty look that matched his fucked-up grin, and suddenly he seemed very interested in me and less in his book.

"What are you doing here?" he asked, and this question was obviously directed at me, because his eyes had locked into mine.

"Just helping my friend."

"Cool. Are you staying here too or just the friend?"

"Both of us."

"Nice." He gave me a softer grin than the one before.

"So, what do you do, Joe?" I asked, making small talk.

"I go to school at NIU. Majoring in creative writing. I'm writing a novel about the real John Lennon." He looked intently at me for a response, as if he'd said something mind-blowing.

"I think that's already been done," I said indifferently.

"Not my way," he responded. I could tell he was a little hurt, but he didn't return to his reading.

I turned to walk away from him. I wanted to get back upstairs to see if I could steal some private time with Heather. "Well, good luck."

"What do you do?"

I pivoted back around and looked at him curiously. Why was he suddenly interested in me? "Currently, I break people out of mental hospitals, but I'm planning on starting at NIU this coming semester. Art major. Painting and drawing," I said, even though the thought hadn't ever occurred to me before.

"Sounds cool. Are you any good?"

"I won some awards in high school." I glanced around the room and noticed that Tammy and Heather had left. I couldn't blame them. I myself wanted to sneak away with Heather, but I didn't want to be rude to my new roommate.

"Can you paint a mural in my room?"

"Paint a picture?" I asked, feeling a nervous excitement well up in me. It had been so long since I'd even tried to picture something I'd like to paint.

"I don't know, something different, not too fancy," Joe said.

"I guess I could, but I'm short on materials—mainly brushes and paints." I sighed, half wanting to do the painting, half wanting to find Heather.

"That's okay because there's a guy, Mark, who lives here off and on, and he leaves his art supplies here." Joe stood up and stretched. He yawned loudly and scratched his stomach, then left the room to find the art supplies. I peered into Tammy's room, where Heather and Tammy were having some kind of fashion show. Heather had put on a different tight black dress that she was modeling for Tammy. Tammy twirled her finger in a circle, and Heather spun around. Neither one of them noticed I was standing in the doorway. I walked over to the green couch and plopped myself down, exhaling loudly. I felt exhausted from the day's events, but also excited to be in DeKalb. I couldn't tell exactly how many people lived here, but I hoped I would meet everyone at the party tonight. Just as I was spacing out hardcore again, the door opened and this hippie chick with a dog walked in. She was kind of fat and looked like she hadn't showered in a long time. Her legs were incredibly hairy. To tell the truth, she kind of sickened me.

She dug her fingernails into her dreadlocks, smiling briefly at me as she scratched. "Hey, I'm Lottie, and this is Bear," she said.

"Hi, Lottie, I'm Orleigh." I didn't feel like talking with her. She was so unkempt and gross. I watched her pick at her fingernail—she seemed to be digging out the flakes from her scalp. A shiver ran down my spine as she flicked whatever was under her nails onto the floor.

"What a beautiful name. Does it mean anything?"

I shrugged my shoulders and rested my chin in the palm of my hand. "I don't think so—my parents were hippies so their main focus was about always trying to be different."

"I see. I doubt that was your parents' philosophy," she said snootily. "But I love the name. Do you live here?"

"I guess I do now, and you?"

Her eyes darted around the room. She stooped down to rub Bear's ears, then adjusted her rainbow-colored sock. "Sure, off and on," she said, standing back up. "I've been at a Rainbow Gathering for the past three weeks, but I always come back here to regroup after traveling." Her focus came back to my face, and I faked a smile. My muscles tensed up when I thought about the lack of responsibility some people had.

Tammy came out of her bedroom and immediately ran to Lottie to give her a hug.

"How are you, baby?" she asked. I was surprised Tammy could be friends with a girl like Lottie—they seemed so totally different.

Lottie pulled back from Tammy's hug and grabbed her hand. They swung their arms, like little kids do when they hold hands. "I'm great. How are you?" Lottie asked.

"Good. How was the gathering?" Tammy let go of Lottie's hand, and she seemed to be studying her dreadlocked hair.

"Really stress relieving. It was probably about the most relaxing time I've had in months."

Heather came out of the bedroom and introduced herself to Lottie. Lottie actually seemed like a nice person despite my earlier judgments.

Joe came bounding down the stairs and ran to Lottie just as enthusiastically as Tammy had. "Hey, gorgeous, thought I heard you down here," he boomed, smiling like a smitten schoolboy. "Shit, I've missed you. Lots!"

Lottie's cheeks turned a little pink. "I've missed you too, Joey," she said in a girlish voice.

They kissed each other—a more-than-friendly kiss. I was kind of stunned. Joe was this totally good-looking cool-as-ice guy who thought he was better than everybody else, but here he was kissing and hugging Lottie. I guess she was his girlfriend, though it was hard to believe that he would be with a girl like her. She was nice and all, but not very pretty. They both were engaged in heavy Rainbow Gathering conversation, and Joe seemed to have forgotten that I was in the room. He had dropped a paint box on the couch, and now they were involved in a *passionate* conversation. I sat down on a chair and watched them. Tammy and Heather had returned to the bedroom, and I peeked inside to watch Heather slip another short black dress over her head. How fucking many black dresses did this chick own? I was amazed Heather felt comfortable enough to undress in front of Tammy. I felt jealous. I lit a smoke, which must have alerted Joe that someone else was in the room.

"Hey, Lott, I've got to go get this artist started painting. She's going to do something or other on the wall in my room. Can we finish catching up a little later at the party?"

"No problem, Joey, I've got to head back to Jeremiah's house anyway."

"You two still together?" he asked, genuinely interested.

"As always."

"That's just fucking fabulous." Joe kissed her good-bye, again with great passion it seemed. I couldn't figure out what their story was.

"Come on, Orleigh, let's go paint the town." Now that Lottie had showed up, Joe seemed like a different guy, not the smug bastard who sat on the couch with his nose in a book. He told me he wanted me to paint a cool picture of a chick. Didn't he know that the two went hand in hand?

He left me in his room, and I began to think about what I would paint, what I felt like painting. I thought about Eve. I really dug the idea of the Garden of Eden. Not so much the religious aspects of the story, but the idea of a woman who rocked the way Eve did—she was evil, naughty, and powerful. Just the fact that she did exactly what she wanted was impressive. She was a woman who wouldn't let a man take her for a ride. She rebelled and danced with the devil. I wanted to be more like her: strong and wild.

I must have stayed in Joe's room for hours. No one came in and disturbed me, so I grooved with the paint. I looked at the clock and couldn't believe I'd been painting for so long. When I decided I was through, I lay back on Joe's bed and looked at the picture. I had painted a beautiful Eve with a serpent wound tightly around her body. She had long, jet-black hair and tremendous breasts. Ever since my encounter with Heather at the stream, breasts had become a focal point for me. Eve sat cross-legged in a pile of leaves, her crotch hidden. I didn't want the picture to be pornographic. Insects and spiders crawled on her pale skin. The foliage in the background brought out her emerald-green eyes. I was surprised it had actually turned out as nicely as it had.

Decidedly done, I called Joe back into the room to view my work. He loved it, which made me happy; it had been a while since I'd painted anything that meant something to me.

I could hear people arriving for the party, and I had paint all over my face and hands, so I headed up the stairs to take a shower. I found Heather getting dressed into her party digs. She was sporting a mini mini; nauseatingly so. But the girl looked good. I watched her paint her lips a dark maroon. She turned to smile at me. I was dying to reach out and touch her. I stepped toward her cautiously.

"How was painting?" she asked, taking a few steps backward.

"Check it out when you get a chance." I continued to move toward her, trying to close the gap between us. I had been waiting so long to be alone with her, dying for us to get into bed. I wanted to see how much further we could go this time. I ached to have my tongue explore her body.

She twirled around for me, then asked, "Like my new look?"

I could hardly speak. She was definitely flirting. I sensed that she was trying to provoke me—she wanted it too. "It's different, but, yeah, I like it," I said, seductively licking my lips. "You know you always look good to me." I lunged at her and put my arm around her waist, pulling her close to me. I couldn't believe I was being so aggressive, but it felt wonderful. My lips were inches away from hers—almost touching. I pressed my mouth against hers, but she pulled back forcefully.

"Don't! You'll ruin my lipstick," she said, glancing in the mirror and rubbing her finger above her top lip. "It took hours for me to make them look this way."

I felt so rejected, I was shaking. "Sorry," I said. I sat down on the bed, watching her fix herself in the mirror.

I didn't get her attitude. She'd become completely uninterested in me, or too caught up in her looks—I couldn't tell which. At this point I didn't really give a fuck. Who really fucking cared that much about lipstick? "I need to shower and get ready for this soirée," I said quietly, focusing on her reflection. She was frantically fussing with her hair. Didn't she understand that I thought she was beautiful? That all this shit was completely unnecessary? I couldn't imagine what I'd done wrong. I really thought tonight would be perfect, but now she was being really bitchy.

Her features softened, and she put down the tube of lipstick. "What're you wearing?" she asked, suddenly being kind and gentle.

"Something swank and sexy." My eyes caught hers and wouldn't let go. I was trying to be saucy. I wanted Heather to forget about her lips and get more interested in mine.

She giggled a little. "Sounds groovy, baby." There was a hint of naughtiness in her tone.

"You know I can never look as good as you," I said. I stood up and took a step toward her, but I could tell she was still concerned about her lips, or her hair, or whatever superficial thing about her appearance was floating around in her head.

"Not unless you gained about thirty-five pounds," she replied, dryly.

"Whatever!" I was sick of her little mind fucks. I grabbed my shirt and dashed to the bathroom. Thankfully there was no line to shower.

I could already hear the party busting out downstairs. I stood looking in the mirror for a moment. I didn't look too bad. In fact, I thought I looked kind of pretty. I had naturally pink lips that didn't need lipstick. People always asked what color my lipstick was, and they were surprised when I said I didn't have any on. What was up with Heather? I couldn't take her messing with my mind. It was becoming unbearable. I stripped and scrubbed rather quickly, but when I headed back to the room I couldn't decide what to wear. Heather was gone. I tossed all my belongings onto the bed after trying them on and not settling. I didn't know why this had to be such a traumatic experience, but I knew that first impressions were everything. After about twenty minutes of stressing, I decided on my original choice—a pair of crushed-velvet bell bottoms and a black tube top—got dressed, and put on my obnoxiously dark trademark black eyeliner. Something about Bette Davis eyes.

The house was already jam-packed with punks, hippies, and freaks. I saw Malick and Tammy, with, to my horror, a pet rat. They sat over on a couch, sharing a bottle of wine. I decided I should say hi to them first.

I approached them gracefully and casually asked, "What's up?"

"Just having a bottle of 1989 Boone's and chilling with Sebastian." Malick lifted the rat Sebastian up to me, and I shook my head, indicating a big fat NO and backing away. There was no way I'd touch a rat. They were such dirty animals. Sebastian's beady little black eyes glared at me, and his little clawed hands doggie-paddled in the air until Malick set him back on his knee.

"Sounds like fun," I said. "I'm more of a dog or cat person." I continued to take another step backward.

Tammy dragged a painted black fingernail down Sebastian's spine. "Yeah, not everybody loves Sebastian like we do," she said gently, bringing her lips down to the rat's little head, giving him a tender kiss.

I was repulsed. I had to get away from them. I looked at Malick, who was definitely more interested in the bottle of wine, and asked, "Have you seen Heather anywhere?"

Malick took a swig of the wine and smiled, his eyes scanning the room. "Last time I saw her she was talking to Kurt," he slurred. He lifted his index finger, and I watched it shakily point nowhere in particular. The finger finally steadied, and I looked in its direction.

Heather stood in a corner, talking to some guy who looked Mexican. I decided to approach them and give Heather another chance. When I slid up next to her, I put my hand on her shoulder. She looked at me indifferently and stepped aside, causing my hand to fall lifelessly back to my side. Coldly, she introduced me to the guy, Kurt, but they seemed very engrossed in each other. I couldn't understand why she was being so flirty with this guy. He was short, chubby, and his front teeth were brown. I couldn't even imagine kissing a guy like him. I waited for her to say something to me. Watching her doing her stupid fake laugh anytime Kurt said something that wasn't even funny made me sick. She glanced at me, then she put her hand on Kurt's shoulder. I felt a pang of jealousy surge through me and quickly fled from them. Fuck her, I thought. She was obviously trying to hurt me, but I didn't know what I'd done wrong.

I roamed around a bit, got a lot of looks from strange-looking people, then decided to go upstairs to be alone. I walked through the crowded kitchen, where people were mixing drinks and spilling shit all over the floor, then turned the corner to head up the stairs and ran smack into some guy sitting on the steps with his head in his lap. He looked up at me, and I immediately thought, he's the most incredible looking guy I've ever seen. I was thrown completely off guard.

His hair was black, cut right above his chin. He wore a red bandana tied around it, which looked kind of feminine, but I thought it was really sexy. His eyes were almond-shaped, a deep, dark brown. But it was his lips that really rocked me—the fullest, pinkest lips.

"Uh, I'm sorry," I said.

"That's OK, it's only my foot."

I could feel a warm blush creep into my cheeks. "Really, I'm sorry. My name's Orleigh."

"I know."

"How do you know?"

"Because I've met you before."

He didn't know what he was talking about. I had never met him. I would surely have remembered. I stepped past him and headed up the stairs. Why I walked away, I don't know. He had even made an effort to keep me there.

"My name's Mark, by the way," he called up as I continued climbing the stairs. When I got to my new bedroom, I shut the door and lay on the bed. I closed my eyes and thought about Heather. I realized that was why I'd left this extremely sexy guy on the stairs: I wanted to be with her. But the girl was all over the place. She couldn't make up her mind as to what she wanted, or maybe she simply never wanted me. Whatever game she was playing was tiring me out. I was on emotional overload because of her shit. God, I was frustrated. My mind focused on Mark. I decided the only thing to do was masturbate, so I pulled down my tight velvet bells and went to town.

I pictured Mark on top of me, his hair falling over his eyes, me having to push it aside as he pushed himself inside of me. I could feel his arms wrapped around my waist, his fingers running down the notches of my spine. I wanted to taste his bubble gum–colored lips, feel the heat of his breath mingling with mine. After I brought myself to orgasm and pulled my pants up, the door opened, and Heather walked in.

"What are you doing in here?" she asked snidely.

"A little stress relief," I replied, visibly flustered.

"Yeah, what's up?"

"Nothing, I just had to get away for a minute."

"Did you see that super-hot guy on the stairs?" she asked.

"Yeah, he's something." I could still see him on top of me, his hair falling over his eyes.

She grinned devilishly. "Fuck, yeah, I want him. What do you think?"

What do I think? What does she think I think? I'd been waiting for this night forever. I'd done just about everything I could for this girl. First it was Baker, next Jerry, then this Kurt guy, and now Mark. When was she going to stop fucking with me? I'd had enough, and I didn't want her to start something with Mark. I liked him. I had just finished masturbating over how hot he was, and she was asking me what I thought? Well, here was one of those times when I just wanted to be selfish and rude. Like maybe *I don't think he's right for you,* or *he's not that good looking,* or *I've seen better looking guys here.* I wanted to ward her off of him, but of course I couldn't do that. Or could I?

"I don't know if he's all that great. I guess you can give it a try, see what he says." A mass of emotions swept through me. I didn't want her to be with him, but I think it was because I wanted him, *not* her. I was looking directly at her, but I felt void.

Her eyes became kind and she bit her lower lip. "I'm a little nervous to hit on a guy like that. I mean, he's just way too good looking for me. Would you get him to come up here?" she asked.

Fuck it, of course I would. Whatever she asked. The little bitch always had me right where she wanted me. "Is he still on the stairs?" I asked.

"He was a minute ago."

"I'll see what I can do."

I walked down the stairs, fuming, and found him still sitting in the same spot, his back to me. I walked up behind him quietly, then sat down on the same step next to him. He turned and looked at me with a confused look, and I figured that maybe this was a mistake.

"You're back." He smiled, running his index finger across his forehead, brushing some stray hairs out of his eyes.

"Yeah, I just had to get something from my room."

"You live here?" he asked.

"Uh, huh." I shrugged my shoulders.

"Since when?"

"Today."

"You like it?" he asked. I could tell he was genuinely curious.

I wondered who he was, and why he was sitting on the stairs alone. "I haven't really met any of my roommates yet, but so far it's pretty cool," I replied casually.

"Who do you know here?"

"Malick, and now his girlfriend too. I met Malick a long time ago, back in high school."

Mark looked toward the ceiling thoughtfully, then back at me. "I can't believe I'm talking to you," he said, laughing quietly.

I was surprised. Maybe he really did know me. "Why?" I asked.

He gave me that same thoughtful look he had given the ceiling, rubbing his fingers in little circles around his temples. He sighed heavily and said, "Because I understand from some people I know that you're a complete bitch."

I found it unbelievable that this guy would talk to me like this. He obviously didn't like me. I really didn't care. I was a bitch, and I was about to get bitchier. "Yeah, I guess. Who told you that?" There was a shortness to my tone that I hoped he was picking up.

"Just some people."

"Do you think I'm a bitch?" I asked hesitantly. I didn't want him to say *yes*.

He looked at me as if he were testing me, his eyebrows raised and creasing toward the center of his forehead. "Not yet," he said.

"That sounds like you might want to get to know me better."

"Maybe I do. Will you do something for me?"

"What?"

"Put makeup on me," he said shyly.

"Sure, I guess. In my room though." I grabbed his hand and brought him up the steps. Heather was chilling on the bed, and she smiled hugely when we walked in. I introduced them to each other.

"Will you do me a favor, Heather?" Mark asked.

"Sure," she cooed.

"Could you go downstairs so that she can put makeup on me? I don't want anyone to watch."

"Uh, sure, I guess. I'd like to watch though." She desperately looked to me for help. I had nothing to say. I wanted to be alone with him, and I was happy he wanted to be alone with me. I didn't say a word to her. I just gave her a sympathetic glance, but I really couldn't have cared less at that point. If she didn't want me and was going to continue to hurt my feelings, I wasn't going to go out on any limb for her.

Mark spoke gently: "That's all right, really. I like to do things alone. I hate an audience. We'll come back down to the party in a while."

Heather got up off the bed and glared at me. I shrugged my shoulders. I mean, all she asked was that I bring him up here. He was the one who asked for my help. I knew she would be totally pissed at me, but I was getting even. My mind had been fucked with for entirely too long. I had been turning over the question did she or didn't she love me for way too long. Her actions were starting to speak louder than her words. In fact, she hadn't even said anything about us since I had broken her out.

She stopped at the doorway, turned, and looked back at me. Maybe it was the dark eye makeup she was wearing, or maybe it was the ugly way she was looking at me, but her countenance seemed evil. Her eyes squeezed into razor-thin slits. Her eyebrows arched downward. Her thin lips were thinner than I'd ever seen them. We stared each other down as though we were the only two people in the room. Mark had his back toward us, and he was looking through a stack of CDs. Heather flashed a scary grin, then mouthed the words, "Fuck you!" She turned and walked out of the room. It was over.

Mark sauntered to the bed, oblivious to all that had transpired—shit, even his walk was sexy. I nervously flipped through my makeup case to find the right stuff. I tried so hard to pull everything off cool-like. I sat next to him on the bed and began to darken his eyes, but then decided I should start with face powder—chalk him up a little, go after a

Robert-Smith-from-the-Cure look. I didn't know if he'd like it or not but I knew I would. After I covered his face with powder I concentrated on the eyes again. He watched me fumble.

"Can I do something to make this easier for you?" he asked. The corners of his mouth were twitching up into a smile, and his eyes were wide with enthusiasm.

It was so nice to be with someone who was excited to have me around. I tugged at a strand of my hair thoughtfully. "I'm not sure."

"Do you want me to move?"

I kept twirling the eyeliner pencil around in my hand, trying to find a way to hold it at a proper angle. I couldn't get it to work. "No, you're fine." I sighed, feeling frustrated. "I'm just trying to find a way to do your eyes."

"Why don't you sit on my lap?" he asked, patting his thighs.

I hoped he didn't see the intense blush that I felt rush to my face as I slid onto his lap. I straddled him, letting my legs rest behind him on the bed. Our faces were so close I could feel the warmth of his breath. My crotch rested on his upper thighs, nearly touching his. The position was way sexual. This was definitely going to be the most difficult makeup application I'd ever performed. I could feel his warm palm resting on top of my thigh. I was growing dizzy. I pulled myself together and started working on those beautiful eyes of his. I colored and colored until they were steamy black, and when I was done he looked the carbon copy of Robert Smith, save for his hair. I decided some dark red lipstick would be the finishing touch. I outlined his lips with a pencil, and as I concentrated very intently, I felt the hand that had been resting on my thigh move gently between my legs. It wasn't an accidental slide, but a long rub, which I knew he meant to be sexy, especially when I looked into his dark eyes. They conveyed every thought running through his brain, screaming out how much he wanted to fuck me. I just smiled.

His fingers continued to graze the inside of my thigh. "You're really pretty, Orleigh," he said softly.

"Thank you. You look really good with makeup on," I said, the words getting stuck in my throat.

"I do?"

"Yeah." I felt awkward. I wanted to kiss him. I wanted him to kiss me.

I was enjoying the feel of his hand on my thigh. I wanted him to slide his fingers into the waistband of my pants, then send them crashing to the floor.

"Is it done?" he asked, his hips rising up a tad.

I brushed a strand of hair from his eye. "Yeah, now we only need to do your hair."

"Can you do that?"

"Sure, no problem," I said confidently. Inside my head, thoughts of kissing him, touching him, and grabbing the mass between his legs ran rampant.

I went and got my comb and some hair spray, then started teasing his hair like crazy. I knew I was pulling his hair, but every time he flinched I thought he was sexier. It was a difficult process; I had no idea how much hair he had until I had started. This was one of the most exciting evenings I'd ever had—I mean, this guy was incredibly sexy, and he was letting me put makeup all over his face? He was the most beautiful picture I'd ever painted. It was truly a Kodak moment.

I pulled the comb through the last section of hair, easing back on his lap to see what he looked like.

"Am I done?" he asked.

"Absolutely. You look wonderful." He looked fuckable. I wanted to press my lips to his and never remove them.

"How wonderful?" His tone was sexy. I wondered if he was thinking the same thing I was.

"Like Robert Smith."

He smiled almost with pride. "You a Cure fan?"

"One hundred percent."

"So am I. What's your favorite song?"

I exhaled heavily. I didn't want to be discussing music, I wanted to be making music with him on the crumpled sheets. "'Pictures of You,'" I said demurely.

"That's a great song, one of my favorites too."

"Cool. Not too many people I know love the Cure."

"They're probably my favorite band," he said.

We had way too much in common, and I wanted to cut the small talk.

82

"I think they're mine too." I smiled, but my thoughts were really on his mouth, dreaming of how soft his lips must feel.

He pulled back and I almost fell off his lap. He swung his left arm out and grabbed me around the waist. After I caught my balance, he asked, "Where's the mirror?"

"In the bathroom. Want to go check yourself out?"

"Yeah, I do."

We walked into the bathroom, and he stared at himself in the mirror for about five minutes straight. I just watched, admiring him admiring himself. I really wanted to touch him. After all, he had rubbed my thigh, which wasn't an oh-so-innocent gesture. But instead I played it cool.

He rested his palm on his now crunchy hair. "Thanks so much." He looked at me intensely.

"No problem."

"What can I do for you in return?" he asked, sexuality dripping from his lush lips.

"Don't ask," I said, with a touch of shyness.

"Why?"

I felt my knees go weak. "I can come up with lots of things I'd like you to do, but I better not say."

"Like what?"

I stared into his eyes, afraid of opening my mouth for fear I would tell him everything I was feeling, and he would think I was a nymphomaniac.

He took a step toward me. "Can I kiss you?"

"Yes." My stomach was burning hot, fluttering with nervous tension.

He began leaning into me. His minty breath tickled my face. His lips were inches away from mine, then the soft flesh of his lower lip grazed mine and he pulled away. Tammy had busted into the bathroom.

"God, you look great!" she said, stopping short when she saw Mark.

"Really?" he asked, turning away from me and glancing into the dingy bathroom mirror again. I could see his reflection and my own just a foot behind him. I must say, we looked like the perfect couple. He appeared tough and fragile at the same time, and I liked the fact that he was about two feet taller than me. I seemed genuinely happy. My cheeks glowed pink, and my eyes sparkled.

"Yeah, haven't seen you look this good before." Tammy giggled like a schoolgirl.

I think Mark winked at me, but I wasn't sure. "Really?" he asked.

"Yeah, who did this to you?"

"She did," he said, turning to me.

I focused my attention on the tired yellow, mildew-covered shower curtain. I felt embarrassed and was anxious for Tammy to leave.

"He looks just gorgeous." She was gawking at him.

"Thanks, I try."

I was really happy that she thought he looked so good, but I wished she hadn't come in when she did—I was still waiting for his kiss. She gestured for us to follow her, and we headed into one of the other bedrooms where some people were grooving out to the Cure, which was eerily coincidental. Tammy introduced me to one of my other roommates, Kerrie. The music was blaring. People danced around the room, guys and girls grinding against each other. Two girls were making out in a corner, and I had to do a double-take to make sure one of them wasn't Heather. I stood at the door and watched Mark out of the corner of my eye—he was leaning against the wall. He moved gently to the music, mouthing the words to "Pictures of You," which was now playing. I was stunned that he looked so much like Robert Smith. I stared at him even more closely, unabashedly, then I noticed he was crying.

Now, I know people talk about things like this all the time, but I'd never felt anything like it before. When I saw him crying, I fell head over heels. Love. I felt it deep down inside, like something curling up and making itself comfortable. Okay, maybe at first I wanted to get back at Heather. I was tired of the way she had been treating me. Maybe I was flaky, or fickle, but suddenly I didn't fucking care who Heather wanted to be with.

I tried to watch Mark dance, but I couldn't. I wanted him not to be able to stand there and dance like that, but to want me as badly as I wanted him. So, instead of standing there like an idiot by myself, I decided to go back to my room. I looked at him once more before I left and saw him look my way. I couldn't exactly tell who he was looking at through his tears.

In my room I started to unpack some clothes and put them away in a dresser drawer, while I drank another beer. I was feeling sleepy. Unpacking was going marvelously until two girls came barging in.

A short girl with tight dirty-blond curls approached me. "Hey, where's Mark?" she asked.

"Mark should be in Kerrie's room. Who are you?" I asked, puzzled.

"I'm Mark's sister Sarah, and this is his ex-girlfriend Theresa." She shot a sideways glance at a short, chunky girl with bobbed platinum-blond hair.

I looked over at this Theresa chick and tried to picture her being with as a wonderful specimen as Mark. It seemed impossible to fathom that he would go for her. She looked way too young, and she wasn't that pretty.

I sighed loudly. I didn't want to be a bitch to his sister, but also I had immediately disliked Theresa. "I'm Orleigh," I said, as I placed a pile of folded shirts on the bed.

"Nice to meet you," Sarah replied. Theresa glared at me.

Just then, Mark came walking in, not even seeming to notice his sister or his ex. He smiled at me. "Where did you go? I was looking everywhere for you."

I smiled back. "I had a little unpacking to do. Oh, you have company." I nodded at his sister and his ex.

Mark looked at them, then back at me.

"What are you two doing here?" he asked.

His sister smiled gleefully, then she came over to him and wrapped her arms around his neck. "You look wonderful, so sexy. We came to see you. I wanted to know if you were going to spend the night here or at home," she said sweetly. She was actually quite cute. She looked like a female version of Mark, except for her hair.

Mark looked down at his shoes for a moment. "I'd rather stay here," he said. He glanced at his sister, and then looked to me with a broad smile.

His sister nervously thumped her palm on the side of her jeans-clad leg. "What about Dad?"

Mark glared at his sister, and I thought he was mad at her. His jaw was clenched tight. "Fuck him," he spat.

"He'll just flip out on you," Sarah said cautiously.

"Who cares?"

"I do." She walked up to him and put her arm around his waist, giving him a sisterly peck on the cheek.

His facial muscles relaxed. "Thanks, Sis. What are you doing?"

"We're going to Ethan's." She dropped her arm from his waist and moved over to where Theresa was standing quietly.

"Have fun," Mark said.

"You too." Sarah looked in my direction, then gave her brother a little wink. She headed toward the door and Theresa followed her. Before she walked out, Theresa looked over her shoulder at me, giving me a look that was hard to place. I couldn't tell if she was hurt or angry. She just stared intensely with her sad smile, then turned and left.

I spun around with an armful of clothes. Mark was staring at me. "What are you looking at?" I asked, feigning hostility.

He ran his tongue across his upper lip. "You."

I could feel my insides get all warm again. "Why?" I asked.

"You are . . . you're . . . everything," he stammered nervously.

I tried to speak, but nothing came out. I stood there gaping at him. Nobody had ever said anything like that to me. I was overwhelmed with emotion. "What does that mean?" I asked, my heart pounding so hard in my chest I thought he could probably see it.

He looked down at the ground, then back at me. His face was so innocent, like a little boy who'd just been caught doing something naughty. "I can't explain it; I just feel it."

I already loved him so much it hurt. Even though I had pretended not to understand, I knew exactly what he was talking about. In fact, I think I finally understood what a friend of mine, Don, used to say. He would tell everyone how he felt this electricity thing. I could feel this force field surging all around us. I felt cheesy even having these thoughts, but then again I didn't give a fuck.

"I think I know," I said hesitantly.

Mark looked nervous and scared. "I need your help getting this makeup off," he said, flustered.

"Already? You want to clean off my masterpiece?" I had thought he was going to stick around for a while. I wanted him to spend the night. He looked at his reflection in the mirror above the dresser and ran a finger over his cheek.

His eyes looked pained when he turned to me. "Yeah, or my father will kill me," he said softly. I couldn't tell for sure, but he looked like he was going to cry again.

"Why?"

"Because he's a dick!" His whole body tensed. "Look, I'd leave it on forever if I could."

"I know," I replied quietly, trying to calm him down.

His face changed. He looked at me with surprise. "You do?"

"Yeah, I know everything about you." I smiled and walked toward him slowly.

"I think you do," he said. He cupped my chin is his hand and delicately brought my lips to his. Then he kissed me. It was the kind of kiss you only get once in a lifetime—worth more than any I'd ever had.

My body shuddered. I wanted him so badly I could barely breathe. I didn't want him to leave. It was too fast. "I wish you could stay," I said, my face buried in his shoulder.

He pulled away from me and his eyes were glistening. "Tomorrow." The corners of his lips turned upward. He was grinning mischievously.

"Promise?" I asked. I was desperate to hold onto him. I was afraid if he left, he would never come back again. I could almost hear the dramatic soundtrack of an epic movie swelling in the background.

We smiled, then he followed me into the bathroom so I could scrub off my beautiful work. It killed me to clean his face, but I loved the feeling of soap on his skin, rubbing and cleansing his face. Everything about him was soft and tender. I washed him about three times, thinking how erotic soap was, and how much I loved how it got his skin all slippery. I wished we could get into the shower, wished I could wash him all over. I knew he sensed what I wanted, and I knew he wanted it too. He dipped his head under the sink and rinsed the hair spray out of his hair. It was still wildly messy when he lifted his head out from under the stream of water. I handed him a towel of mine.

When he finished drying his face, he handed me the towel. "I've got to go," he said, his eyes growing sad.

I walked out the door of the dingy bathroom, and he followed closely behind me. "All right," I whispered.

He stood in the doorway, his skateboard resting against his thigh. "Thanks for everything." He ran his fingers through his wet hair.

"Sure."

He picked up his skateboard and headed down the stairs. I stepped out of the doorway, watching his back, then walked back into the bedroom and lay down. I didn't understand what the hell had happened. Part of me wondered if he had just gone downstairs back to the party. I decided I'd try to sleep it off. The music downstairs was still incredibly loud, but I soon drifted in and out of sleep. I was dreaming about Mark, dreaming that he was in bed with me, until Heather and Kurt came in the room and woke me.

"Hey, girl, what are you doing sleeping?" Heather asked.

I rubbed my eyes. "Oh, hi, what're you doing?" I sat up and leaned against the wall. Heather sat down on the edge of the bed, and Kurt plopped down in the faux-leather chair next to the bed.

"We're just hanging out. What happened between you and that guy?" Heather asked. Her tone was easygoing enough to someone who didn't know her, but I could see the venom dripping from her pearly white teeth.

"Not much. I just put makeup on him. You know, kind of lame." I wanted to keep it to myself. I didn't want to tell Heather, not because I was afraid it would ruin things between us, but because I wanted it to remain mine.

"But he's gorgeous," she said, licking her lips.

My body tensed. How dare she turn him into a sex object. He was so much more than that. "So what?" I replied indifferently. Sure, Heather, I thought bitterly, he could've been another victim or conquest of yours, just like me. She'd really hurt me.

Kurt decided to butt in. "I'm glad you didn't really like Mark."

"Yeah, why?" I sat up straight, crossing my legs. *Who the fuck was this guy? What did he know?*

"He's got a lot of problems," he said.

"Don't we all?" I spat back.

"Yeah, but his seem to get in the way more than they should."

"He takes life a bit too seriously?" I slid off the bed and stood up. I began to pace around the room. I was frustrated that this idiot came into *my* room (even though I'd only recently acquired it) and started counseling me on who I should or shouldn't be interested in. Fuck him! Fuck them both, I thought, as I paced in front of the mirror, shuddering at the anger I saw in my reflection.

"Maybe. Either that or he's really fucked up," he said, and chuckled.

Oh, everything's so goddamned humorous, I thought. "What do you think?" I didn't give a rat's ass about this guy's opinion. I just wanted the two of them to leave and go fuck each other or something.

"He's one of my best friends, so what can I say?"

"I don't know," I said, turning to face the wall so I didn't have to look at either one of them. But I did know. I could tell right away that Mark was emotional and sensitive. Just seeing him cry I knew there was something different about him, which was what had made me fall instantaneously in love with him. I didn't care if he was fucked up. All I cared about was seeing him again. I wondered if he had gone to find his ex-girlfriend. God, I hated ex-girlfriends; they always got in the way. Actually, I myself had gotten in the way of a few girls' attempts at starting relationships with my ex-boyfriends. It was never about me screwing up some girl's chances; it was because the ex-boyfriend and I were such good friends that these girls got jealous and bailed.

I kept standing with my back to them. I heard the faux-leather chair squeak as Kurt stood. "I'm gonna go back downstairs," he said. His voice sounded less confident than it had before. My behavior was probably making him uncomfortable, but I didn't care. I heard his feet shuffle across the floor. There was a moment of uncomfortable silence, while I concentrated on a crack in the wall.

"Why don't you come back down to the party and have another drink?" Heather whispered.

I continued to face the wall. I really just wanted to be alone. "I'm tired. I'm going to try to sleep," I said tersely. I refused to turn and look at her. I was so pissed I thought I might take a swing at her perfectly painted mouth.

"You sure?" she asked sweetly.

Her change in tone was making me nauseous. So, okay, now I had to turn and look at her. I wanted to see if her face would betray her voice. "Yeah," I said. I looked deep into her eyes. She smiled uncomfortably.

"Have fun," she said.

"I always do."

"I know," she said nastily, then started to walk out the door.

"Heather, wait," I called.

She pivoted around, placing her hands on her hips. "What?" she asked, annoyed.

"It's just that, well, I really do like Mark."

"I figured." She paused and looked at me inquisitively. Her hands dropped from her hips. "What happened with us?"

"Us? Was there ever really an *us?* Heather, you flit around. One guy to the next. You don't even notice I'm around unless it's convenient to you. I thought you were different, but you're not." I stared at her a moment and could see tears forming in her eyes, and I immediately regretted lashing out. She looked so hurt.

"All I ever wanted was a friend. Sorry if our signals got crossed. I'm glad you found someone you like," she said, then left, shutting the door behind her.

I looked back at the crack in the plaster. What the fuck was that all about? She must have some interesting ideas about friendship, I thought. If she had only wanted to be friends then why did all that other stuff happen? Why did she lead me on? I sat down on the bed and felt tears stream out of my eyes. I was so frustrated, I couldn't even think straight.

CHAPTER 6

I tossed and turned all through the night, regretting the fight I'd had with Heather. When I woke in the early morning, the house was very quiet. Heather wasn't in the room, and I wondered where the hell she had slept. I decided I would get dressed and check downstairs—I needed to find her and reconcile. I put on some sweats and headed down to an obscenely messy kitchen. A bottle of wine had spilled on the floor and still lay there. There were beer cans and empty pizza boxes everywhere. The stickiness of my bare feet on the floor made me gag.

I walked into the den. The carpet beneath my feet was also sticky and soaked. The smell of cigarette butts and beer wafted into my nostrils. This made me even more ill. Sleeping bodies lay on the couches and on the floor, some of them breathing heavily, others snoring loudly, some perhaps even dead, not moving at all. I know it was a party, but it seemed more like the aftermath of war. My eyes scanned over the bodies, trying to identify Heather's, but she wasn't there. I sat on the only chair that wasn't occupied and turned on the television. The regular Saturday morning bullshit was on—Superman, Smurfs, and Roadrunner. Bummer. I heard the door to Joe's bedroom squeak open, and Joe walked out in silk pajamas. "Hey, why is the television on?"

"Because I'm awake," I said. I yawned and stretched my arms above my head.

"Well, I'm not," he said, in a petty way.

"I'm sorry. Do you know where Heather is?"

"Try the attic." He yawned too and turned around to walk back into his room.

"Wait. Why the attic?"

He scratched his crotch. "She was there last night, with Kurt. That's where he sleeps."

"What were they doing?"

"You know . . ." He smiled a sickening smile that made my skin crawl. I was shocked. "You mean she slept with Kurt?"

"I heard you got lucky too." He snickered, scratched himself again, then for some reason pulled the elastic band on his pajama bottoms out and looked down at his dick. I wondered if he had a problem—like crabs. He let the band snap back into place and smiled.

"No, I didn't," I said. "Who told you that?" What an arrogant prick in his prissy pajamas, I thought.

"Word gets around."

"Well, I didn't. What do you care anyway?"

"I do."

"Why?" I asked, even though I didn't want to hear his answer. I wanted to find Heather and talk about what had happened last night.

"Because we kind of clicked yesterday, you know. And I love the way you paint. It rocks."

I felt a little flattered, but I was not interested in him in the slightest. In fact, there was something about him that scared me. "Thanks, but I've got to go find Heather."

"Turn off that TV please," he said, and I detected a quiver of disappointment in his voice. He walked back into his room.

I headed up the stairs, past my Manson-themed bedroom, then up the dimly lit, rickety stairs to the attic. Heather and Kurt lay in the bed there, wrapped in a blanket. Kurt's mouth hung open, revealing his stained buckteeth. There was a pool of drool at his mouth, spreading on the pillow. Rolls of stomach blubber peeked out from under the blanket, and I wondered if he was entirely naked. The sight of the two of them together was repulsive. I guess I had just thought that Heather was much better than a one-night stand with this ugly dweeb. This time it wasn't jealousy. I was beyond that, especially after our little catfight. Granted, what had happened might make her never want to speak to me again, but I still wanted to be friends. Maybe I had been a little too hard on her. Maybe I didn't really know her at all. I mean, Kurt, what was she thinking? He was so disgusting, and she was so beautiful. Maybe she was trying to get back at me for the Mark thing. But in the end she was the one who'd pay for it, because she'd be waking up next to this Kurt guy. I decided it would be best to leave her there and let her wake to the full horror of what she had done.

I returned downstairs and flicked the box back on. Fuck Joe, I thought. I sat, not really watching but thinking about Mark. God, he was hot.

Joe came bounding out of his bedroom, now wearing a long silk robe over the silk pajamas.

"You came back. Did you find her?" he asked, suavely. I guess he was trying to be sexy when I thought he would be pissed about the TV.

"Yeah. It was just like a love scene out of a movie."

"In the attic?" he asked, chuckling.

"Yeah, with Kurt."

"Pretty gross, huh?" he asked.

I yawned, ignoring his question. "I think Mark's coming over here to hang out," I said, feeling victorious.

"You'd like that, wouldn't you?"

"Yeah, why?" I asked, staring at the television remote clutched in the palm of my hand.

"Because he'll never show up," he said, contempt in his voice.

"What are you talking about?" I asked, a bit too frantically. I couldn't look at his face. My attention stayed focused on the tiny black buttons on the remote. I absently slid the battery cover open and shut.

"I just know him, and I know he won't be here."

I gave him a stern look, but he was busy running his fingers across the silk material of his robe. "He said he would," I said, defensively. I was pissed at him. I wanted him to go back into his room and leave me and the sleeping and dead bodies alone.

"Of course he did; he wants to get in your pants."

"I don't think he's like that."

"How much do you really know about him?" He looked me square in the eyes. I felt so uncomfortable.

"Enough to know that he's not that way."

"We will see, won't we?" he said. He was so full of himself.

I looked back at the television screen and flipped through a couple more channels. "You're being a real jerk," I said to the TV.

"Just telling you like it is."

"Whatever!"

Just then an extremely tall, lanky guy came into the den, walking an unidentifiable hairless animal on a leash. The guy's jet-black hair was puffy, as if he had ratted it out. He wore glasses that looked like the ones guys in high school wear in shop class. He had on extremely tight black jeans and a white T-shirt that he'd outgrown years ago. His face was gaunt and pale, and he was so skinny. I wondered if he was a junkie, or if he had AIDS. Maybe he was just anorexic.

Joe looked over at him and gave him an indifferent nod. "Hey, Brian, how goes it?"

"What happened, Joe? What the hell happened to the house?" Brian yelled. A few of the bodies lying around in the den bolted upright. A couple that had been sleeping on the couch stood and left the room.

"A party. Weren't you here?" Joe said, picking at his fingernail.

The animal was licking the carpet, then licking its paws. Brian twirled the leash around his hand so that the animal lifted off the floor by its neck. Brian kept looking sternly at Joe, then down at the animal, then around the room at the party guests as they began to gather their belongings and leave the house. He scooped the animal up into his arms. He pet it gently, then examined its paws.

"We had a good one last night," Joe resumed.

"Apparently. And who is this?" He pointed in my direction with this obnoxiously long finger, then gave me a look that could have curdled my blood.

"Oh, pardon my rudeness," Joe said snippily. "This is Orleigh. I guess you should know she lives here now."

I looked over at the sickly Brian and tried to smile as best I could.

He set the animal back on the floor and placed his free hand on his hip. His chin jetted out defiantly. "Did this go through a meeting?" he asked, tapping his black Doc Marten on the soggy carpet. "I'm the one who organizes all the house meetings, and I never heard anything about a new roommate."

"No, I don't think this was brought to the table. It was kind of an emergency situation, and Malick made an executive decision based on extenuating circumstances."

"Which are . . ." Brian huffed.

"Well, Orleigh's friend just broke out of a mental hospital that her mother locked her up in, and they needed a place to stay until the fuzz got sick of looking for them."

Brian gasped loudly. "So there's another one?"

"Yeah, she's in the attic." Joe laughed out loud. I just sat and watched, afraid to say anything.

Brian looked at me, rubbing his fingers across his chin. The gesture was so slimy, I could barely look at him. I wanted to say something, but the look on his face wasn't softening. This guy was not balanced. I waited for him to speak. Finally, after what seemed like hours, he dropped his hand from his chin and looked at Joe. "I don't like this. No, I don't like it one bit. The house is messy, there are criminals living with us now, and there was a party last night that was not approved. I don't like the whole situation."

"Then I think you need to call a house meeting to express your concerns," Joe said. I couldn't tell by Joe's tone if he was humoring Brian or being genuine.

"I think I don't have a choice," Brian snapped.

I couldn't take this guy seriously. I wondered how old he was. He acted like he was about fifty. None of my friends ever got this ruffled about parties. I glanced at Joe out of the corner of my eye, and he cracked a smile at me.

"I guess you don't." Joe laughed under his breath.

"When are you available?"

"Tonight," Joe said. Brian scratched his head, looking at the entryway to the kitchen. There was a calendar on the wall there, with pictures of kittens playing with a ball of yarn. A thick red marker hung from a black shoelace tacked up next to it.

"Tonight, well, I wonder if everyone else can make it." Brian walked to the calendar and studied the large squares. He uncapped the marker and wrote something in one of the boxes. The animal crept in between his legs and wound its leash around his ankles. I was worried Brian would trip and fall on the little thing.

"Probably, it's Saturday night. Who around here would have plans for a Saturday night?" Joe asked sarcastically.

"I don't see any parties scheduled on the calendar for this evening, but then the calendar doesn't seem very reliable these days," Brian responded, raising his eyebrows at Joe. They looked at each other for a moment, locked in quiet battle. Brian didn't flinch, he just gnawed on his lower lip, clutching his pet's leash tightly.

Joe broke the stare down to bite a fingernail off. He spit it on the floor. "I'm sure everyone could take about half an hour to discuss the issues you have, then we can go our merry ways." I could tell he was trying to pacify Brian. Joe leaned against the wall and chewed off another nail, spitting it onto the carpet. I felt terribly uncomfortable trying to hold my laughter inside. I sat quietly, digging my fingernails into my palm.

"It seems to me that this may take a little longer than half an hour." After all was said and done, Brian made a very poignant turn, picked up his hairless animal, stomped out of the den into the kitchen, then up the stairs. I looked at Joe and started giggling.

Joe was beginning to crack up. "You have now met Mister Serious."

"Really? God, is he anal," I said, through an outburst of laughter.

"Isn't he, though?"

"Does he ever lighten up?"

"No, I don't think he ever does."

"I don't think he liked me very much," I choked out. "What's up with that hairless creature?"

Joe caught his breath and stammered, "CAT! Melvin the hairless wondercat. Brian is allergic to everything."

"Okay, so why does he walk it around on a leash?"

Heather poked her head through the archway to the den. She looked at me with an expression that was more shy than angry. I smiled to reassure her that things were going to be okay between us. She inquired about Brian and Melvin, which started Joe and I back into a laughing fit. When we regained our composure, Joe looked at Heather. "Rough night?" he asked.

"No, a good night," she replied.

The air became tense. I sat on the couch glancing from Joe to Heather. Joe's face contorted—he looked at Heather, and it was obvious he was on the verge of saying something to her—his eyes piercing and evil. He ran his fingers across the silk collar of his robe and said, "Fuck it, it's just not worth it." He spun around on his heels and returned to his bedroom.

"I'm sorry," I said quietly.

"I guess I am too." She folded her arms across her chest, then sat next to me.

"So, you want to tell me what happened?" I asked, leaning back further into the couch cushions.

"What do you mean?"

"What happened last night with Kurt?"

"Nothing," she said too quickly.

"I don't believe you." I smiled coyly. I wanted her to feel like we were friends again. I couldn't stand the tension between us. It would kill me if she couldn't tell me things anymore, even if it was only the gory details of her disgusting experience with Kurt.

She rubbed her hands together nervously. Her hands were a pale white, and her fingernails had been bitten to the quick. "Maybe there's a good reason why you don't."

"Maybe. Want to talk about it?" I asked. I wanted to make peace. We'd been best friends for a while now. It didn't seem right to suddenly have this breach.

"Not really." She looked away from me, then stared vacantly at the wall.

"What did I do?" I asked cautiously.

"You knew perfectly well that I wanted that guy Mark, and you just moved in on him," she said sourly. She looked sad. I remembered how alive her eyes had been when we had bathed at the stream. I wanted to touch her, to comfort her, but it felt awkward.

"Look, something happened between us that I can't explain. I can't even put it into words. I'm truly sorry if the fact that I put makeup on him offended you, but it was one of the greatest things that ever happened to me."

"I don't really care anymore. I slept with Kurt," she said.

I knew she had, and it bothered me. I felt a little jealous and hurt, and I wondered if that had been her intention. Even though things were interesting between me and Mark, a part of me remembered why I had come to DeKalb in the first place—to get closer to Heather. "Do you like him?" I asked.

"I guess so. He's really nice and, uh, he's good . . ." she said. Her lips twisted up in a smile, which was the look she gave when I'd seen her lie to people. Suddenly I felt sorry for her.

"That's cool . . ." I looked down at the carpet. Heather nervously dragged her nails across the velour of the couch. I knew she was going to tell me what she was thinking. I could tell by how tense her fingers were.

"What else was I supposed to do?" Her tone was angry. I continued looking at the carpet. "You remember when I told you I hadn't been with a woman before?" she asked.

I looked up at her, baffled. "Yeah, I remember," I said, hesitating a little.

"I lied. You weren't the first. And I guess, well, I thought I was falling in love with you."

I was stunned and didn't know how to respond. She had played so many games with me. I'd given her so much. Now I wasn't sure what to think—I felt like she might be toying with me again. "I'm sorry, Heather. I, you, you never told me any of these things. I couldn't figure that out on my own—you were always giving me mixed signals. I'm sorry, I just couldn't take it. I loved you too. I still do, in a way, but I stopped trusting you. Why didn't you just tell me?" I didn't want an answer. I was afraid she might suck me in again. I studied the sogginess of the carpet, not able to look her in the eye. I felt devastated and stupid for not having been able to pick up on it.

"I didn't know if I was ready to be a lesbian. It kinda scared me," she said, her voice raising a few octaves.

Brian walked into the room with a bucket and a sponge. It was obvious by the expression on his face that he had heard at least the tail end of Heather's confession. "Sorry to interrupt. I think I'll start cleaning upstairs instead," he declared, then spun on his heels with a ballerina's agility, and left the room.

I looked at Heather's scarlet cheeks, and I felt terrible for her. I knew she was humiliated. "Hey, it's okay. I never knew how you felt, Heath, and now that I do, I guess I'm sorry it didn't work out between us. But we have a great friendship, and I think that's where we need to focus our energies. What do you think?"

"I think you're right. I have to get ready," she said, getting up from the couch.

That's pretty quick, I thought, and I was hurt by the way she could just move on with things as if nothing ever happened. "Ready for what?" I asked.

"Tammy and I are going shopping. Want to come?"

"I guess I could, but Mark is supposed to come over."

"We won't be gone long."

I really wanted to hang out and wait for Mark, but I also felt like I needed to do something with Heather. We had been friends for a long time, and with all this shit going on between us, I realized it would be best to try and work things out.

Before we left, I knocked on Joe's door, and he called me in. I stopped momentarily to admire my painting. It was awesome. Joe was sprawled out on his bed, reading and drinking coffee. "What's up?"

I asked if he could relay a message to Mark if he got here before I returned from shopping. At first, he acted all put out, but he eventually agreed. "That's *if* he ever shows up," he said.

Joe seemed to have some kind of personal vendetta against me and Mark. Tammy called me from the other room.

"Thanks, Joe," I said, though I didn't feel thankful.

He grinned. "Like I said, no problemo."

When we arrived at the Salvation Army, it was amazingly annoying—Heather and Tammy had to try on everything they laid their eyes on. I never had to try on clothes, and I found a couple of really fly used jeans that I bought for three dollars each. Tammy found two dresses and when Heather told her I sewed, she begged me to cut one of them off and sew it for her later, so it could be a mini dress. After she roped me into altering the dress, we were off to Bee's Wax.

I found two T-shirts I *had* to have—a black one with a giant monarch butterfly on the front and a baseball jersey with "Cowgirls" printed on the back. Unfortunately, other than these finds, the excursion was making me crazy. Heather and Tammy took forever looking at things, and they were getting along fabulously. I wasn't even getting a chance to try to smooth things out with Heather.

She came out of the dressing room wearing a short tie-dyed dress. Tammy had her walk a make-believe catwalk.

"You look absolutely delicious." Tammy giggled. She was making me sick.

Heather adjusted her hair and blew an air kiss to Tammy. "You *really* think so?"

It was like watching Heather and me together, only now I was the outsider. I was distressed about this turn of events. I wondered if Heather was trying to make me jealous and if Tammy would be her next victim. Maybe that was what it was really about with Heather— she needed to play with someone in order to feel better about herself. Alyssia could be like that, but she never excluded people. If anything, she was too inclusive.

I suddenly felt so lonely. Tammy was taking her turn on the catwalk, wearing a black miniskirt and a bright orange tank top. Heather was giggling like a little girl as Tammy sashayed down the imaginary runway. They were being so high school, and I couldn't believe how Tammy was playing into Heather. What bitches!

"I'm going to wait in the car," I said.

"Are you bored or something?" Tammy asked, as if she had just remembered I was there.

"I bought a couple of things, but I'm done." I squinted at Tammy and shifted impatiently back and forth, then headed toward the door.

Looking over my shoulder, I saw Tammy holding up a black dress against her body for Heather's advice.

"That would look so cool on you," Heather squealed, too enthusiastically.

I thought it looked ridiculous. I walked outside into a gust of warm air, leaned against the car, and had a smoke. I couldn't wait to see

Mark. I wanted to put makeup on him all over again—it was incredible how erotic and sexy that was.

I glanced up and finally saw the two new best buddies coming out of the store, with perfect lipstick-red smiles plastered on their faces. I wondered if they were doing it to piss me off. Heather was carrying two shopping bags, Tammy six. They jumped in the front seats of the car. How obnoxious, I thought, getting in the backseat.

Heather turned her head to kindly address me. "Do you think you could hem that dress as soon as we get back?" Her tone was snappish, as if I were some kind of fucking servant.

"I suppose," I said, seeing myself wince in the rearview mirror. "I'm planning on doing something with Mark, but if I have time I will."

"If he's not there yet will you start?" Tammy asked, peering at me in the rearview mirror.

"Whatever!" I said, kicking back against the seat.

I was hoping Mark was already at the house. I wanted to find him sitting on my bed as he had been last night. He was all I could think about. I didn't want to have anything to do with that damn dress.

I tried to play it off cool. Instead of running headlong toward the house, I waited for the two shopoholics to gather their purchases from the car. When we went inside, there was no one in the den.

"I'm going to put this shit in my room," I said. I was still trying to be smooth. I didn't want to look like I was desperately searching for this guy I'd barely met, but I doubt they even noticed. They were both laughing loudly about something stupid, no doubt, in Tammy's room. I walked up the stairs a tad too quickly (if they had seen me), worried that Mark hadn't come at all. I opened my door. The room was empty. Maybe he was in Kurt's room, I thought hopefully, so I returned to the frightening attic where Kurt dwelled. No one was in there either. Frustrated, I decided to ask Joe. I barreled down the stairs and knocked on his door. His raspy voice called out, "Come in."

I found him exactly the same as I'd left him.

"Hey, Orleigh," he said, picking up a bookmark from the bedspread and placing it between the pages he was reading. He snapped the book shut and smiled strangely.

"Hi, Joe. Did Mark come by?"

"Uh, that's a big no." He was still wearing a smile. I was certain he was pleased that his theory about Mark had proved correct.

"All right." I tried to hide my feelings, but I could feel my whole body slump as if I'd been punched.

"Don't be so blue, he could still show up," Joe said, upbeat.

"Yeah, well, you told me he wouldn't." My eyes were focused on the floor. I knew that I looked upset even though I was desperately choking back tears.

"I just know how he is."

"How's that?"

"Fickle, like a woman."

"Whatever." I walked out of Joe's room and ran right into Tammy, who was holding a dress in one hand and a beer in the other. "Hey, I got you a drink. Will you help me now?"

"Sure. Where's Heather?" I asked, defeated. I was amazed they'd unglued.

"She's taking a nap. Are you all right?"

"Fine. Put the dress on, so I can see how much hemming I have to do," I said dryly, hoping she would read my reluctance to help her and give up. But she seemed pretty stubborn. She put on her new dress, and I got to work pinning it up to an obnoxiously short length. After I had cut and pinned it, I busted out a needle and thread. The whole sewing by hand thing sucked, but I wanted to get her off my back. After about an hour and a half of painstakingly tiny stitches, I was through with the afternoon project, and Mark still hadn't shown up. I was starting to get really upset.

I wanted to hide and listen to the Cure's *Disintegration*. Sure, it would make me feel even more depressed, but I liked to pick a mood then wallow in it.

I went upstairs. I needed the relief of a good cry, but Heather was crashed out, and I didn't want to wake her up with my childish sobbing. It was getting pretty late, and I hadn't eaten dinner yet, so I forced myself to go out and pick up some grub at the Tom and Jerry's behind the house.

I walked to T & J's, watching the house out of the corner of my eye.

For a college town, I was surprised there wasn't a line inside. At the grease-covered register I ordered some mozzarella sticks and fries to go from a Greek man wearing a hair net. I didn't want to miss Mark if he actually came over, so I counted my money quickly and paid the Greek. I'd never been blown off by a guy before, and I didn't know how to handle it.

"Number thirty-one, please," the man at the counter said. What the fuck? It didn't seem necessary to use numbers when I was the only customer.

My greasy food awaited me on the counter. I picked it up and left. As I walked back, I had renewed hope that I'd find Mark waiting for me, but when I opened the door I found only Joe sitting in his usual evening couch spot. I guessed he was right about Mark all along.

"Where'd you go?" he asked, looking up from his book.

"Food." I held up the white paper bag. Then I sat across from him on the yellow plaid couch. I didn't feel hungry at all.

"Are you able to eat in your current smitten state?"

"I'm not smitten," I said defensively.

"Really?"

I knew my expression was betraying me, exposing my weakened state. "Maybe I would have been if he'd shown up," I replied, reluctant to tell him anymore.

"I told you what he was all about."

I felt like he was scolding me. "I thought maybe you were wrong." I took my food out of the bag and spread it out on the glass coffee table in front of me. I really didn't want to talk to Joe about this. Strange Brian came down the stairs and walked into the den with a broom in his hand.

"Hello," he said. "Glad you're done with the little confrontation you were having earlier."

I didn't want Brian to say anything about this in front of Joe. I tried to talk, but my mouth was full of fries. Brian started sweeping the carpet. I found this kind of funny. I'd never seen anyone sweep carpet before. He stopped momentarily to put a Jesus and Mary Chain video in the VCR. As he swept, he began to dance around the room, using the broom as his partner. Joe and I kept giving each other looks. Finally, Joe couldn't take it anymore, and he busted out in a fit of laughter, which immediately caused me to break into one too. We laughed so hard we fell onto the floor. Tears rolled down my cheeks, and I couldn't seem to gain my composure.

"What do you think is so funny?" Brian asked. "I don't think anything here is funny. You think I'm dancing crazy or something; I was only sweeping to the beat."

His protest only made us laugh harder. I felt like we were being so mean, but I was out of control and I couldn't stop.

"Look, stop laughing right now. I'm trying to get ready for the house meeting. This whole episode's making me very upset. Please shut up or go to your room, Joe."

It hurt terribly to laugh, but every time Brian opened his mouth it got funnier and funnier. Joe was standing above me laughing. He reached his hand down and grabbed mine to pull me off the floor. We laughed our way into his room where we fell on the bed and laughed more. After about a good five minutes of getting it out of our systems, we stopped. Joe looked over at me. "Do you remember what we were laughing about?"

"No, not what started it all."

"Neither do I. Are you still sad?"

"I feel better now."

Joe put his arms around my waist and got up right behind me. I wanted to pull away from him, but I couldn't bring myself to do it. I turned and looked into his eyes, and I could tell he was really serious. Then out of the blue he kissed me. This time I pulled away.

"What's wrong?" he asked.

"I don't think I want to be doing that," I said, inching back on the bed until my back was against the wall.

"With me?"

"It's not about you," I said, focusing my attention on the clutter on his bedside table.

"Who, then?"

"Me," I answered. I was taking in all the scribbled-on scraps of paper strewn over the little table, which was covered with cigarette ashes too.

"You mean Mark, don't you," he said.

"No, me."

"Really hung up on him, aren't you?"

"I like him." I tried to read the chicken scrawl on the pieces of paper, but I couldn't focus. I felt like I was going to cry.

"So it is about him," he said, this time his tone turning angry. He began backing away from me.

"No, he never came over."

"Why don't you tell me what the problem is then? I know we clicked. You know it too. If you hadn't had some mystical moment with Mark, you'd be all over me."

"Don't flatter yourself." I was getting annoyed. His sheets reeked of patchouli, which reminded me of the Dead show I went to with Heather.

"So, you wouldn't be?" he asked. His eyes were having trouble looking at me, and his mouth was twisted in a frown. It was obvious he was hurt.

"I don't really know," I replied gently.

"Why don't we find out?" Joe said, approaching me again. That did it. Joe had his soft hands sliding up the back of my shirt. His touch was warm and soothing. I was taken in by the sensation, lost because I was feeling hurt by Heather, then Mark. I let go and allowed Joe to do as he pleased. He took his time with me. It was slow and easy. I felt horrible about the whole thing, and couldn't exactly get into the groove. I felt like I was betraying Mark. I could have been fooling myself, but I felt Mark really liked me. When Joe finished having his way with me, I turned over and fell asleep. I was ashamed and sort of sickened by my feeble attempt to resist what I really didn't want.

I woke the next morning feeling worse than the night before. I stumbled out of Joe's room. I needed to find Heather, talk to her about everything, cry on her shoulder—well, actually, I just needed sympathy for my own hideous mistake. Maybe she'd felt the same way about Kurt. I walked into the room that Heather and I shared, but no one was there. Once again I checked Kurt's room in the attic. He was alone in his bed. Next was Tammy's room; after all, they were so fucking tight now. Maybe they were sleeping together now that I was out of the picture. Anything was possible. I slowly opened Tammy's door, only to see Tammy and Malick snuggled closely under their black sheets and comforter that matched the horrid black walls of their room. I scanned the lumps beneath the sheets for a possible third body, but alas, no threesome. They were obviously into

Celtic shit. There were dull-looking silver swords, shields, helmets, and breastplates mounted on the walls. Blood-red velvet curtains covered the only window. Tiny black shelves lined the walls with white and black votive candles resting on each. Wax drippings fell down the ledges of the shelves, leaving solid pools at various spots in the carpet. It looked more like a torture chamber than a bedroom.

Tammy looked up at me sleepily from beneath the comforter.

"Heather is gone," I said, fidgeting back and forth on the balls of my feet.

"What?"

"She's not in the house. Do you know where she is?"

"No." She rubbed some of the crustations out of her eyes.

"Did you hear anything this morning?"

"Maybe she left to get something to eat. I know she slept on the couch last night."

"Well, she's not there anymore."

"Don't worry. I don't think she ate last night so she probably went out for breakfast."

"By herself? This early?" I asked, hearing the panic in my voice. It didn't seem like Heather. I knew she was paranoid about being found by the police, and I didn't think she'd go out by herself. I believe she would have asked for company just to be safe.

"Maybe she didn't want to wake anyone up. She couldn't find you last night anyway. She thought you were with Mark."

All of Heather's belongings were still in the bedroom: her new dresses, her toiletries, her tennies. I figured Tammy was probably right—she had gone out to eat. I decided to take a shower and get dressed. When I was done, I went downstairs and found Kurt watching television.

"Good morning," he said.

"Hello," I said curtly.

"Did you have a nice time last night?" he asked.

"What's it to you?"

"I know where you slept."

"Nothing happened."

"Really?"

"Yes, really," I spat, annoyed that he knew where I'd been and that he was being so snoopy.

"Did you ever hear from Mark?"

"No."

"Funny, he was here when I got home," Kurt said, staring at the television.

"He was?"

"Yeah, he was talking to Joe."

"You're kidding me," I said, anger rising from the pit of my belly. Joe had lied. The bastard had lied to get me in bed.

"You should ask Mark," Kurt said. He exhaled a large cloud of marijuana smoke.

"I will."

"Good, because he'll be here in a little while."

I didn't want Mark to come over. I didn't want to have to face him. I felt like I was wearing the scarlet letter of adultery. Everyone knew I had slept with Joe. I sat on the couch across from the one Kurt was lounging on. I didn't want to be close to anyone here, I decided. I focused my attention on the Cheech and Chong movie on the TV. I was sick to my stomach. He'd been here and Joe had lied. What kind of a sick bastard would toy with someone like that? I wanted to first break open Joe's door, then break open his skull. I wanted to cry. More than anything, I didn't want to believe it could be true. I tried to laugh at the movie, tried to stop thinking about the horrible lie Joe had told me, but I couldn't think about anything else. Then the door opened and Mark walked in. He didn't say a word to me, and I knew he knew what had happened. He sat in an armchair across the room and quickly looked over at me. I sat, picking at the couch's frayed fabric, watching him out of the corner of my eye while pretending to focus my attention on the TV. I didn't know what to do.

"Hey, how are you, Mark?" Kurt asked.

"Had better days," Mark replied, not acknowledging me.

"Haven't we all," Kurt said knowingly. Smug bastard!

"I guess." Mark rolled his skateboard under his feet across the dirt-encrusted carpet. He wouldn't talk to me, but now he was looking at me.

I was looking at him, then back at the fabric I was picking, all the while dying for him to say something.

"Orleigh," he finally said, and it made me burst with happiness.

I let go of the couch threads I'd been twirling around my finger. I looked up, meeting his sharp gaze. "Mark," I said, and it came out in a whisper.

"Do you think you could put makeup on me again?" he asked.

"Sure," I said, quietly.

We went upstairs to my room. It was a mess. I looked around, ashamed of the grungy bras and underwear on the floor.

My heart beat out of control as Mark sat on my bed. He smiled a quirky little smile, but I couldn't read his eyes.

"Can you do it like you did the other night?" he asked.

"First, can I ask you a question?" I sighed heavily as I sat down next to him, discretely kicking a pile of dirty clothes under my bed.

He smiled sincerely. "Anything."

"Where were you yesterday?"

"Doing stuff," he said, as if my question weren't important.

"Why didn't you come over?"

He looked at me, stunned. "I did."

Part of me thought that maybe Kurt had been fucking with me. "When?" I asked.

"In the afternoon. Joe said you went shopping."

"Why didn't you come back?" I asked, alarmed and a little angry. If he had only come back, none of this would have happened.

"I was waiting for you to call me."

"I don't have your phone number."

"I gave it to Joe and told him to give it to you when you returned. He didn't?"

"No. He told me you never came."

"Why would he do that?"

"Because I think he likes me," I replied, and a sour feeling swept over me.

"Bastard. That's no reason not to give you my message. Did you honestly think I wouldn't come?"

"I didn't know what to think." My eyes fell to the floor. I felt so ashamed.

"Yes you did. You do. You know I wouldn't blow you off." His eyes looked hurt.

"I didn't think you would, but then I didn't see you."

"Is that why you slept with Joe?"

"What?"

"I was here last night, late, looking for you. They said you were in Joe's room, so I left."

"I don't know what to say."

"You don't have to say anything. I'm sorry he took advantage of you, but I'm happy you didn't lie to me."

"I can't lie to you," I said softly.

"Put some makeup on me." He smiled, and I felt relieved. Mark was by far the greatest guy I had ever met in my life. I wanted to love him forever. In silence, left to these thoughts, I did his makeup. When I was through, he looked even better than the time before. Again, I teased all his beautiful hair. I wanted him to touch me again, to kiss me, but I knew he needed time to get over what had happened.

"Almost done?" he asked.

"Why, are you in a hurry?" I asked. I sprayed the tangle I'd just created with some nasty Aqua Net hairspray.

"Got a date to get to."

I tugged a little harder on the next section of hair I pulled. "Really?" I asked.

"A beautiful babe I'm taking to the Morning After. You know, that funky coffee shop?"

I lifted the hairspray and shot a stream onto the back of his head. "What's her name?" My voice came out harsher than I meant it to.

"Orleigh," he said, turning to face me. He wore a huge smile and kind of chuckled at me.

"What an unusual name."

"Her parents must have been wigged out."

"What does she look like?" I was curious to hear how he'd describe me. I stood with my hands at my waist, waiting.

109

"Tall, blonde, thin but curvy." He smiled, then looped his arm around me.

"You mean like a fat little boy?" I asked, backing away from him.

"She has boyish good looks. Adolescent boyish good looks. She's very beautiful. Actually, she's very feminine."

"She might get mad if you're late," I said, swaying back and forth on my heels, trying to escape his reach.

"She wouldn't."

"Why?"

"Because she's good like that." He smiled.

"I see."

"So is she ready to go?"

"Who, me?"

"Yes." He grabbed my hand and I helped pull him off the bed.

We ordered lunch. I hadn't been to the Morning After since the whole Sam, Alyssia, Geoff, and Don thing. I definitely didn't want to run into them. I only wanted to be with Mark. I would go wherever he wanted me to. After he had ordered I didn't even have to ask, I knew he was a vegetarian like me. I couldn't eat anything that had a face and a heartbeat. We stared at each other as we waited for the food. Mark broke the silence.

"I'm not upset with you; in fact, I understand."

"How can you understand?" I asked. I knew that if he had done something like that to me I wouldn't understand.

"Because if I was waiting for you and you never came, I would be completely vulnerable. Just tell me if you have feelings for him."

"What can I say? I'm totally pissed off. His lies and everything. It makes me sick. I feel used and cheap and basically rotten about the whole thing."

"Let it go. Please."

"I want to but I'm really mad," I said. A picture of Joe in his silk pajamas flashed across the movie screen of my mind, and I cringed.

"We never know how much time we have," he said. "If this is the only day I get with you, I want it to be as perfect as we are together."

"I'll let it go." The image vanished. All I could see now was Mark sitting across from me, smiling.

"Eat," he said.

I hadn't noticed that the food had come. I was way too interested in how beautiful Mark was. He was so mature, so kind and understanding. He was different from any of the other people I'd fallen for in my life. He was sincere, whereas everyone else always seemed to want something from me. Mark just wanted to be with me. He didn't play games, like Heather. He wasn't on a power trip, like Alyssia. He just seemed good, pure, and real.

As soon as we were out the back door of the Morning After, Mark sat on the brick steps leading to the sidewalk and pulled a cigarette out of his pack. We sat on the stairs and smoked together. I sat between his legs, inhaling my cigarette deeply as he rubbed my shoulders. His hands were large, the fingers long and smooth, with perfectly manicured nails—strong hands that seemed to know just where to touch or put pressure. I felt so relaxed as I smoked. It was better than an after-sex cigarette. As soon as I tossed my butt in the bushes, Mark stood, ready to go.

"Where to now?" I asked.

He grabbed my hands and pulled me up from the stairs. "Somewhere pretty."

"Where?"

"On the campus, there's a place I go everyday between classes."

"What classes?"

"I'm an art major at NIU," he said with a smile, squeezing my hand.

I was planning on majoring in art the following semester, ever since it had slipped accidentally out of my mouth. Now I was actually looking forward to it. I had decided to go back to school because I was getting bored hanging out and working meaningless jobs. Now that I knew Mark was going to be there too, it seemed like an even better idea. I thought about how we could plan our schedules so that we could have classes together.

We walked down a bike path that led toward campus, holding hands. I kept thinking about how crazy it was that I had met Mark. I felt myself falling victim to all that mushy shit that usually made my stomach turn.

Maybe it still did, a little, but I kind of enjoyed it. I felt like such a girl.

We turned a corner and came upon a garden with four circular fountains, tall hedges all around it. Inside, the fountain's tiny white and blue lights reflected off the water and the pennies of all the wish-makers. Between the fountains were pairs of stone benches decorated with gargoyles. I felt like we had walked into a wonderland. No one was around.

"Come sit here." Mark sat on one of the benches, pressing his hand on the stone beside him.

We faced each other, gazing into each other's eyes.

"You are so lovely," Mark said.

"No, you are," I said.

"I'm no you."

"True, you're better," I said.

"No, I'm not."

"Yes, you are."

"Why?" he asked, looking confused.

I was tiring of the *who-is-better-than-who* game. I loved him, I cared about him, but I wasn't used to getting this kind of attention. He said things so easily. For me, it felt a little embarrassing talking like this. I decided I would just spill my guts and maybe we'd be done with it.

"Because you are the most wonderful thing I've ever met," I said, looking down at the bench, tracing my fingers over cracks.

We were silent. We looked at each other. Then out of the blue, Mark broke into song. "*I want somebody who cares for me passionately, with every breath and with every detail.*" It was "Somebody" by Depeche Mode.

"*Things like this make me sick, but in a case like this, I'll get away with it,*" he sang.

I laughed, but I also knew I couldn't imagine ever feeling this way about anyone else ever again.

"I love that song," I said.

"That's what I've always wanted. Can I kiss you?"

"You have to ask?"

He kissed me long and slow. If I believed in obnoxiously mushy shit, I'd say, "The earth moved."

When we pulled away he flashed me a smile. "I'm so happy," he said, beaming.

"So am I."

"This is larger than life." He stood, spreading his arms far apart.

"This is everything," I said.

Maybe both of us were a little overwhelmed by the intensity of the things we had said, maybe it was getting too heavy. I don't know, but Mark ran to one of the fountains, jumped onto the edge, and started dancing. He spun and twirled all around the fountains' wall. I was glad that the mood had eased up.

"Come up here with me," he called.

Within seconds I was on the fountain dancing with him. Usually, when I went out with someone, it was all about putting on airs, being whatever I thought would sell. But with Mark, I felt I could be me. I had spent so much time doing things for other people—acting like Heather's mother, acting like my ex Jason's girlfriend, acting like my mother's little girl. I'd forgotten that I liked to have fun, be silly and crazy and wild. I'd forgotten that I hated worrying about what other people thought of me.

I brushed against Mark and turned around. He was flailing his arms, trying to regain his balance. I reached my hand out to him, and he grabbed it, but not quickly enough. He went falling back, not letting go of my hand, pulling me in with him. I hit the icy water and immediately let go of his grip. It was freezing. My head emerged, and I found Mark inches away from me. We were both laughing. He pulled me to him in the cold water and wrapped his arms tightly around my waist, his teeth chattering. My teeth were chattering too as we kissed.

We walked home, our shoes sloshing with water, leaving a trail behind us.

Everyone—Malick, Tammy, Kurt, Brian, and Joe—was sitting in the den as if they had been waiting for me. I looked at Malick first and could immediately tell he was distraught. Finally, he stood and walked over to me, grabbed my hand, then looked somberly into my eyes. "I know everyone told you not to worry," he said.

A sick feeling came over me.

"Heather never came back," Malick continued, squeezing my hand tighter.

I was confused. She had just gone out to get something to eat, hadn't she? "What do you think happened to her?" I asked.

"I think the police came and took her early this morning."

"How would they have found her so soon?"

"Someone tipped them off, that's all I can think," Malick said, letting go of my hand.

All *I* could think was *Zacker*. He was such a fucking blister. I hated him, and I knew that he had squealed. I kicked myself for letting him see where we'd be staying. I should have had him drop us off on an entirely different block. Everyone's eyes were on me. It was nice that they were concerned about me; they barely even knew Heather and me. I was at a loss. If Heather was in police custody, I couldn't do a thing. I needed to get away from all the prying eyes.

"I'm going upstairs to dry off and change. I'll be back in a while when all this sinks in. Thanks for letting me know," I said.

I turned to beckon Mark with my eyes, and he followed me up the stairs. Once in my room I started taking off my wet clothes. Mark sat on the bed, watching. I felt no inhibitions with him. I stood in front of him naked, silently saying, *"This is who I am, love me."* I knew that he liked what he saw. But I knew if I had been out of shape, flabby, or just wrong, he still would have loved me. That's how it was.

"Do you want some dry clothes?" I asked.

"Sure, if you have something that'll fit me."

Naked, I walked across the room, then searched through the dresser drawer. I found the tie-dye T-shirt that I bought with Heather at the Dead show and an old pair of cut-off sweats I thought would fit Mark. I grabbed a tank top and some boxers for myself, then tossed the change of clothes next to Mark on the bed. I quickly got dressed, then sat on the other side of the bed. Mark was done watching me, now it was my turn to watch him.

He slowly pulled his wet turtleneck over his head, revealing a perfect six-pack. His arms were muscular, well-toned. He slid off his jeans, kind of stumbling but maintaining his cool. Every inch of him was smooth and cut; he looked like the ancient paintings of a god, bare and breathtaking. He was clearly turned on by me watching him. He stood motionless for several minutes, allowing me to take him all in. He was too perfect. I could never compare to someone as lovely as he was. In slow motion, he lazily put my clothes on his body. When he sat next to me, it took every fiber of my being to hold myself back from ravishing him.

"What are you thinking about?" he asked.

"About you." I bit my lower lip, trying to be sexy.

"Likewise. What about me?" he asked.

"That you're just too incredible for me."

"Nonsense. I could say the same about you."

"How do you know?" I asked.

"My heart aches for you."

"It's like electricity," I said, trying to match his tone, but the words didn't come out as smoothly.

"No, it's like blood. You're in my blood, pumping through my body. You make things beautiful. Even me."

"How did I do that?" I asked. An incarnation of Jim Morrison had walked into my life. I felt so flattered by the things he said, even though they made me a little embarrassed.

"I see through your eyes," he said.

"Is that why you dressed so slowly, because you want to see yourself through my eyes?" I asked. I was surely missing the point. Why couldn't we just have sex and forget about all the sap?

"Because I wanted that feeling to last forever."

"What feeling?"

"Butterflies."

"Are they gone?"

"They'll return," he said.

He grabbed his cigarettes and lit one for each of us, the way Heather and I used to do for each other. For a moment my stomach went tight, and I worried about where she was. What could I do to help her? I wracked my brain. Mark reached over me and lit the two candles at the head of the bed. He lay on his belly and motioned for me to lie next to him. I complied with a smile, staring into his eyes, watching the reflection of the candle flames flicker in his pupils.

"What do you want to know?" he asked.

I stared stupidly at him. "Everything," I said.

"Don't you know . . . you already do," he said.

"I want to know more . . ." I said. Or maybe I didn't. I didn't know what the hell we were talking about. He was too damn intense.

"It will come," he said.

I was starting to feel like he wasn't for real, like I'd walked into a movie. Everything had been perfectly written, only they'd forgotten to give me a copy of the script. I had to admit I loved it; the way he talked, the way the words sounded coming out of his mouth, all of it.

"It's dark now," I said, looking out the window at the half-moon staring back at me.

"It's late. Are you tired?" Mark asked.

"No, you?"

"No."

"Are you hungry?" I asked. I needed a diversion, a moment to get grounded.

"Not really, I just want to be here. Everything is so good, right now, with you."

"I don't understand why I feel this way. I mean, I've liked lots of guys but never . . ." What could I tell him? I'd only been treated like shit in the past.

"What is this?"

"This is extraordinary, it's kind of religious in a way," I said.

"In a way it is."

"Have you ever felt this way before?" I asked. I was dying to know if he talked to all the girls this way.

"Never," he said, firmly.

"Have you ever loved before?"

"No." Mark looked down at the blanket, his eyes running over the striped pattern of the fabric.

"Yourself?"

"What, loved myself?" he asked, drawing his eyes away from the blanket, then looking at me.

"Yes."

"Sometimes yes, mostly no." There was a sadness in his eyes.

I felt like I had said something wrong. My mother had always told me you couldn't really love someone until you loved yourself. I wasn't sure what to think of his answer.

"And now?" I asked, hopeful.

"Now, I think, yes." He paused for a moment looking down, then drew his eyes back to mine. "Do you know your eyes speak a language of their own?"

"I've been told." My mother always said she could tell if I was sick or lying by my eyes.

"It's marvelous," he said, gazing at me.

I felt a little uncomfortable under the weight of his eyes. "Thank you."

"Can I ask you a question?"

"I hope I give the right answer," I said.

"I'm almost positive you will."

"Okay."

He gave me a shy-little-boy look and his cheeks turned a touch crimson.

"What is it?" I asked, beginning to worry that something was wrong.

"Promise you won't laugh?"

"On my honor."

"Okay. If vanilla ice cream were a color, what color would it be?"

I wondered if he was serious. It seemed absurd. I thought about the question for about 1.1 seconds, because fortunately I'd pondered this question before. "Blue," I said.

He smiled as if he were relieved.

"What?" I asked. I felt a little annoyed.

"I've just always known I couldn't give my heart completely to someone who didn't answer blue."

"So what if I hadn't answered blue?"

"That didn't happen, did it?"

"But what if I'd said purple?" I asked. I wondered why he put so much weight on such a stupid question.

"I probably still would have loved you."

"Probably?"

"I'm glad you said blue. In a stupid way, it makes things right in my head."

I guess I was happy that he too could be foolish. Him worrying about ice cream made me feel a whole lot less stupid about never having the right thing to say. "Do you ask all the girls this question?" I asked.

"No, I've only asked one other girl. I loved her, but I didn't see stars, daisies, and fireworks when I kissed her."

"And when you kiss me?"

He kissed me. My eyes were open for a moment, and I saw the flame of the candle climb high. I didn't believe in spirits or shit like that, but the candle thing freaked me.

We talked like this into the early morning, never leaving the bed. We shared secrets, talked about our pasts, the present, and the future. Sometime during the early hours of the morning we fell asleep, intertwined, as close as two bodies could be. We didn't have sex. I would stir when I felt his arm slip around me, or his hot breath on my neck. I would close my hand around his, but then I'd fall right back to sleep.

CHAPTER 7

Mark's face came into focus, staring down at me.

"How long have you been awake?" I asked. His head blocked the sunlight from the window and cast a shadow across the bed. I thought about Heather with a pang of sadness.

"A little while," he said.

"Why didn't you wake me up?"

"I thought about it, but I was really enjoying watching you sleep. You purr like a kitten. It's adorable."

"I didn't really know that, but thanks," I said, feeling a little embarrassed.

"What do you want to do today?"

"Be with you."

"Kiss me good afternoon."

I kissed him gently and then pulled away. "Good afternoon."

Mark continued to look at me intensely, but it didn't make me uncomfortable. I wanted him to take all of me in. "Can I touch you?" he asked.

"Yes."

I felt comfortable, yet conscious. I was conscious of how different we were. I was the little schoolgirl, giddy with anticipation. He was the man, expert at touch and words and feelings. He brought his hands out from under the blankets. First he shut my eyes with his fingers, then he stroked my cheeks and my neck, sending shivers through my body.

"Can you take your tank top off?" he asked.

"Certainly," I said.

We sat cross-legged on the bed, shirtless, facing each other. His hand reached out for my neck again and his fingers slid down my throat and moved down to my chest, where he traced each of my breasts. My body tensed a little. I was silently hoping he wouldn't touch them for fear that he would be disappointed by their small size.

"Close your eyes again." he said.

"Okay."

"Lie down."

"Why?"

"Because I want to feel every inch of your body. I want to remember this forever."

His fingers lingered lightly on my breasts for a few more minutes, and my feelings of inadequacy subsided—I was terribly hot.

His fingers finally dropped below my chest as I lay on the bed. They slid over my ribs, outlining each one with his fingernails. He moved his fingers down my soft belly, over my jutting hipbones, then let them slide down onto my concave stomach. There, they circled my belly button several times, then slid to the band of my boxer shorts, then to the inside of the shorts. I was dying for him, wanting him so badly, but I kept my eyes completely shut, resisting touching him. My hips rose and fell involuntarily under his fingers.

I felt my boxers traveling down until they were no longer on me. His fingers were now on my thighs moving slowly up and down. His hands were near the place I ached for him to touch, but he wouldn't touch me there. His fingers moved below my knees and over my calves. They moved down my ankles until they reached the soles of my feet, and stroked them. Normally, this would have tickled me to death, but I was beyond that. Everything was completely erotic.

Now that he had touched practically every inch of my body, I was dying for him to be inside me. I lay still, expecting his lips to find mine. Instead, I felt his breath on my toes, hot and wet. He sucked each toe. I had never had anyone do this to me before, and I don't think I would have let anyone else do it. It was such a sensual feeling, I couldn't believe how insane it was making me feel. I was close to having an orgasm when he moved up to my calves.

He quickly moved his tongue up my leg until he was there, where I wanted him to be. I thought he was good at sucking toes but when he went down on me, I was in heaven. I'd never experienced anything like it before. When I was through, shaking underneath him, I asked, "Let me touch you."

"No, this is all for you. This is what I want. It pleases me more to see you sweating, see you shaking, see that glint in your eyes. This is what I've always wanted."

The whole experience was an awakening—parts of me that had been sleeping finally woke. I hadn't been satisfied in a long time, and I had never felt satisfaction mixed with love. My whole body was still quivering. When it was all over, my eyes filled with tears that rolled down my cheeks, landing on my breasts. Mark licked up every drop I shed, not the least bit concerned.

PART II

Alyssia

This Other World

CHAPTER 8

I feel like I need to go further back in time, to explain exactly what happened. How I got around to my first bi experience. It all started at the beginning of the last semester of my senior year, when I dropped out of high school. I was seventeen, and it was six months before I met Heather.

I had decided that school had nothing left to offer, so after a drunken splurge, I moved in with two guys I wasn't really friends with, then moved back home. It felt wrong to go back to my mother's house, even though I knew she was alone and had to be bored just watching television and whatnot. I had other places in mind for myself. I hated the suburbs of Chicago. We were only forty-five miles away from the "big city," but it took about two hours to get there with the constant traffic. So there I was at home, more miserable than ever. My mom and I were at each other's throats again.

I started dating this guy Jason who was friends with my previous boyfriend Matt. Jason was kind of dull, but he had a car, money, and his parents didn't mind if I stayed the night. I spent a lot of time hanging out with Jason, basically watching him skateboard. When he was at work, I would watch TV and keep an eye on his three little brothers. I didn't like Jason much, and I never had sex with him; it was just a ride and the cash I was interested in. Eventually, I moved in with him because of the building tensions with my mother. She was always pissed about how late I came home, and even more irate when I didn't show up at all. I thought I was too old to be told what to do.

After about two weeks of living at Jason's place, his mom started getting pissed. She told him I would have to find another place to crash by the end of the week. That was just lovely, because it was already Wednesday when she gave him this little message. He came to me with a somber look and explained how I would have to be moving on.

"Whatever, Jason, I don't really care. I just don't know where I can go," I told him.

"We'll worry about that later. Nick and his new girlfriend are coming over to watch some movies with us tonight," he said. I wondered why he was so lame.

"No doubt it will be *Hellraiser*," I stated, feeling a little irked at the notion of Nick and his "girlfriend" joining us tonight.

"No doubt."

I hated Nick. He was a totally weird guy. He lied all the time, about everything. It was so ridiculous, and everyone knew that he was lying. None of us had ever seen this so-called girlfriend, though we had been hearing about how wonderful she was for the past week.

"I'll make some food if you want me to, or are we just going to order some pizza?" he asked.

"Pizza sounds good."

"Fine with me, saves me the trouble of trying to cook." He picked up his skateboard and walked over to the door. "Could you make the boys some lunch, you know a sandwich or something? I'm gonna go skate for a while."

I shook my head and began getting the lunch meat and bread out of the refrigerator. I prepared lunch for them, then went into Jason's room to take a nap.

At about seven in the evening, Jason came into his bedroom and woke me. "Hey, Orleigh, Nick and his woman will be here soon."

"Okay, I'm up," I said, getting out of bed and stretching. Jason was watching me, and his gaze followed my shirt lifting up from my belly when I raised my arms above my head.

"It's too bad you never want to do anything," he said, staring more intensely at my midriff.

"What do you mean?" I asked, though I knew what he was talking about.

"You know, mess around."

I admired how cool he could be, how he could always find the best words to express his inner self. "Maybe later. We haven't been together for that long anyway." I knew if I really did care the right way, things would have happened by now. The truth was I just didn't give a damn.

"I know, but we sleep in the same bed. It gets frustrating sometimes. It's like you don't even want to touch me," he said, a sour look on his face.

I didn't want to touch him; I didn't even want to be with him. In fact, I was embarrassed that my situation had gotten so pathetic that I needed to live with him. I was actually thrilled at the thought of being kicked out of Jason's house—except for the fact that I didn't know where to go.

The doorbell rang, and I was relieved that I didn't have to explain to Jason how much I loathed him. It was easier to avoid talking about it altogether. I straightened my clothing, looked in the mirror, then went out to the den. I was astonished to see that Nick had brought a girl. She was not beautiful by any means. She had a shaved head, except for a few tufts of hot pink hair that stuck straight up. She was wearing a black miniskirt, although it was not very flattering due to her enormous legs. She had on black combat boots that hit just under her knees, and they were tied with rainbow-swirl shoelaces. Another stunning bit of style was her black leather jacket that was airbrushed with the names of various bands I'd never heard of.

Her name was Stormy. We gave each other the once-over and acknowledged each other's existence. She gave me the routine comment about how cool my own name was, and then it seemed we had nothing left to say to each other. Much to my chagrin, Nick piped in to the non-existent conversation.

"What are we doing tonight?" he asked.

"Orleigh and I thought we could order some pizza and watch whatever movies you brought," Jason said, and I wished he had left the movie part out. I couldn't bear the thought of sitting through *Hellraiser* movies all night.

"Sounds good," Nick said, tightly clutching his favorite horror films.

Jason took everyone's pizza requests, and in the process we discovered that Stormy was also a vegetarian. This made pizza ordering easier because usually everyone got mad at me for only wanting cheese. I tried to make small talk with Stormy, but she seemed less than enthused. I couldn't help but think that she was a total bitch. I already longed for the evening to be over.

"So, are we really going to watch movies all night?" Stormy asked.

"Yeah, honey, what did you think we were going to do?" Nick retorted, but I was already feeling a little hopeful, like, maybe Stormy had a better offer to throw on the table.

"I guess I thought we would be doing something fun," Stormy said.

"Well, there isn't much to do around here," Jason said.

I was in complete agreement with Stormy, and I wanted to find out if she had any better ideas. "What would you like to do, Stormy?" I asked expectantly.

"I don't really know. We could find something better to do in DeKalb if there isn't anything to do around here," she said.

"What's in DeKalb?" I asked.

"There's the Junction or the Morning After. The Morning After would be the best—good coffee and great music. Plus, there's usually something or someone interesting at either place." She slid her hand across her pink tufts of hair, waiting for our responses.

"I'm not feeling any dire urge to watch this movie, so I'm willing to go somewhere else. What about you, Jason?" I asked.

"I'll do whatever you want, baby." He smiled in my direction.

"Nick?" I asked, narrowing my eyes into paper-thin slits. I wanted to intimidate him.

"I suppose we could go somewhere else, it's just that I rented all these movies." He sadly looked down at the boxes still clutched in his hand. I kind of felt bad for him, but I was thrilled we weren't going to hang out at Jason's and watch movies.

Stormy smiled at Nick and grabbed his hand. "Hey, we can watch the movies later. Why don't we take your friends someplace cool? Is that all right with you?"

"Sure. We can watch the movies at your place, right?"

"Yeah, later," Stormy said.

Now that this was all settled, Jason decided to take off and get the pizza. I had to stay because the boys were home alone, at least until

Jason's parents returned from bowling. I could hear the electronic sounds of video games in the next room, and occasionally the boys yelled at each other about whose turn it was to play. I tried to tune them out, shifting my attention to the conversation Nick was having with Stormy. Nick was philosophizing about the character Pinhead from *Hellraiser*, how deep inside he was really a good guy, that he had been wronged by society, and now society was having to pay for its wrongs. This was about to make me puke; I mean, here's this figment of Clive Barker's imagination, and this guy Nick was trying to find deeper meaning in it. Fortunately, Stormy was captivated by Nick's speech, and I was able to gaze absently out the window, awaiting Jason's return. Eventually, Jason pulled into the driveway, and I announced, "Pizza's here!"

When Jason walked in the door, everyone got up and followed him into the kitchen. I pulled some paper plates out of the cupboard and got some cans of Coke from the fridge. I distributed them and Jason hollered out for us to dig in.

Except for the continual chatter from Nick about the highlights of Pinhead's traumatic life, we all sat around silently munching our pizza. Everyone was trying to eat, but Nick kept bringing up all these gory details that were making the pizza less and less appetizing. By the time we surrendered our desire to eat and gave up half the pizza to Nick, Jason's parents were pulling into the driveway.

"Perfect timing, now we can head to DeKalb," Jason said eagerly.

Stormy looked at Jason and me, exhaling a sigh of relief.

Nick sorrowfully stared at the empty pizza box. "I guess we can go now, there's no more pizza."

We all gathered what we wanted to bring to DeKalb and headed out to Jason's van. When he got into the van, Jason immediately turned the stereo up really loud, which enabled Stormy and Nick to make out the whole way and also provided Jason and me with a distraction from each other. It was a long ride, and by the time we pulled into town, I was thinking that this was probably a bad idea. Jason spun the knob on the stereo, lowering the volume.

"Where to, Stormy?" he asked, his long hair whipping me in the face when he turned.

"Oh, well, the Morning After is just to the right up a block. Park anywhere you can find a spot; it's pretty crammed on weekends."

Jason found a spot, and we all tumbled out of the van. Even though I wanted to get out of St. Charles, I was a little hesitant about where Stormy might be taking us.

Inside, something resembling a band was performing on a slightly raised platform in the center of the room. One guy was playing the bongos, and another a strange harplike instrument. There was a sign made from a tie-dyed sheet that read, "The Brad and Dean Experience." A wooden sign had been placed on a table next to the bongo drum player. It said, "LSD—Let's Save Dean," and there was a large bowl next to it filled with dollar bills and change.

We struggled through the crowd at the door and were almost instantly greeted by a waitress.

"Hey, can I get you guys anything to drink?" she asked in a high-pitched and slightly annoying voice.

"What kind of coffee do you have?" I asked.

She looked at me as if I were a complete idiot, yet in a sort of sweet, innocent way. "We have anything you want; any kind of coffee you like, we can make."

"Okay, I'll have hazelnut then."

She took everyone else's orders then cheerfully left us to listen to Brad and Dean play Dead cover songs. I initially thought Stormy might feel out of place here, but she seemed to fit in just fine. She waved to some hippies across the room, and I was surprised that she was friends with people like that, because she looked so hard-core punk.

The waitress returned carrying a large bowl. "Would you like some fruit soaked in vodka?" she asked.

We each helped ourselves to large chunks of vodka-saturated watermelon. I was starting to like this place. I was enjoying the fruit, the music, and waiting patiently for my coffee. Eventually, the waitress brought over four steamy cups and placed them in front of us. I looked around as I took a sip of piping-hot coffee. There were at least ten punk-rock people dressed like Stormy, some skinheads, then about half of the room were Deadheads, and the rest were preppies or wannabe somethings or other. It was extremely eclectic. And people's ages seemed to range from about thirteen to seventy. The music was so loud that talking was practically out of the question, so I sat and kicked back to Brad and Dean until they were finished playing.

The place started to clear out, and Stormy said, "Hey guys, we need to move to the back. That's where we always sit—it's the smoking section."

We followed her to a table where the air was cloudy with smoke. Through the haze, I saw that most of the people in this section wore black. Within a matter of minutes, the atmosphere of the place completely changed as the laid-back hippie crowd left with the band.

"Thank god all the tree huggers are gone," Stormy said. A new waitress came to our table, carrying coffee refills, which she sloppily set down.

"Can I get you guys anything else?" she asked with an attitude.

"No, coffee's just fine for now," Stormy replied, and I could sense immediately her familiarity with this whole routine.

"You have to order something more than coffee or you'll eventually get kicked out," the waitress said, looking directly at me.

I looked over at Stormy. She brushed the waitress off with a wave of her wrist, then giggled when the waitress turned to leave. I didn't understand what the deal was, and I certainly didn't mind ordering something else.

"Don't pay any attention to her threats. Kurt, the owner, doesn't like us sitting here all day only drinking coffee, but we *are* his moneymakers. We buy more here than anyone else," she said snootily. She leered at a guy standing behind the counter. "That's him."

I looked over at Kurt, a young guy, then into my coffee cup. I couldn't fucking figure out exactly who Stormy meant by "we." "Stormy, who is this 'we'?" I asked.

"Look around. See everyone wearing black and looking hard-core? Well, *we* are the best customers. We're here everyday, sometimes for lunch, dinner, sometimes breakfast, and sometimes just for coffee. So, as far as I'm concerned, Kurt can go fuck himself."

I was beginning to see that Stormy did have some kind of personality. Almost to prove this, it seemed, she gave a squeal and jumped out of her chair. We all watched, open-mouthed, as she not so gracefully ran over to some of her friends who had just walked in. It was kind of amusing—even her friends appeared a bit terror-stricken as she practically flung herself on top of each, hugging and kissing them incessantly. It was like watching a dog greet his master after a long day of being left alone. The whole event was a tad embarrassing, but fortunately we didn't look like we were with her. That is until she turned, pointed at us, then brought her punk-rock friends over to meet us. No one was overly excited about the introductions, and I got the feeling that these people didn't like Stormy that much. After her "friends" found their own table, noticeably far from ours, Stormy proceeded to tell us how tight she was with these guys.

I was considerably bored after about two hours of Stormy's constant babble about who all her friends were, what she did in her spare time, and how many ex-boyfriends she had. Nick watched her in a smitten daze. Go figure! I kept eyeing Jason, who sighed laboriously at the end of each tale Stormy spun. I could tell he was feeling ready to leave too, so I decided now was just as good a time as any to start my bitching.

"Jason," I said, "we really need to get going. Remember that I have to get up early tomorrow and start looking for a place to live." My tone was whiny and shrill, but I saw the relief in his eyes I had anticipated.

"You two have to leave this early?" Stormy asked, and I was surprised to hear sorrow in her otherwise bubbly voice. I gave Jason one of my do-or-die looks.

"Actually, Stormy, Orleigh really does have to start looking for a home, and I also have to watch the boys in the morning. It's not like we won't be able to do this again soon. It's been a lot more fun than staying at home," he said sweetly, trying to ditch her gently.

"Why are you looking for a place to live, Orleigh? Don't you live with Jason?" Stormy asked, pushing a pink strand of hair out of her eyes.

"Jason's mom doesn't like the impurity of our situation—you know, sleeping together without being married," I curtly explained.

But Stormy pried further: "So she kicked you out?"

"Not really, she just would rather me not live with Jason unless we're married." The idea of marrying Jason made me shudder inside.

"So where are you going to stay?"

"I don't know yet. I have to look around tomorrow and see what I can afford." It was true, but also a joke. I couldn't afford anything; I didn't even have a job.

"You could always come live with me," Stormy said, too enthusiastically. Her desire to help fascinated me. She barely knew me, and already she was inviting me into her home. I'd never met someone so desperate to make friends. For all she knew, I could have been a serial killer.

"That's really cool, Stormy, but let me think about it. You're kind of far away from where I live, you know?" I was ready to get out of there; Stormy was such a freaky chick.

"It would be free. Just call me if you end up not finding something."

"Thanks," I said.

As we headed out of the Morning After, Stormy gave another of her squeals. She had followed us, then clung to my arm, making us stop at a table.

"Hi, guys," she said. "I want you to meet some friends of mine."

I felt instantly like we were on display with signs on our foreheads that said *"Stormy's Friends: $5.00 an Hour."* All the people at the table stared blankly while Stormy introduced us.

"This is Orleigh, her boyfriend Jason, and my boyfriend Nick," she said with palpable pride.

A thin guy with wire-rimmed glasses barely averted his eyes. "Hey," he said.

"I'm Don," said a guy with a moustache, then he immediately stared down into his coffee cup.

A third spiky-haired punk rocker with striking blue eyes sat next to a girl. He took his time to smile at me. "I'm Sam," he said.

The girl sitting with them was dressed in black, but she didn't have that dirty, greasy punk look about her. She threw back her head to look at us as if she didn't give a shit, but then she smiled smugly and said, "My name is Alyssia. I'm bisexual."

Not knowing where this had come from, I looked at her and nodded. But I couldn't help thinking she was absolutely beautiful. Her lips were a deep, dark red, and her hair the same color. Her skin was pale, smooth, and lovely, like a saucer of cream. I stood there a while, maybe too long, astonished. She tilted her face, looking straight at me, and winked some of the most extraordinarily long lashes I'd ever laid eyes on. I was taken aback. Then Jason pulled me out of my stupor and dragged me to the door.

The whole time we drove to Stormy's house, I was lost in thoughts of Alyssia. She seemed larger than life. I don't know what it was about her that grabbed me the way it did, but whatever it was, I liked it. I liked it a lot.

The next morning Jason woke me up early to go look for a place to live.

"What, are you itching to get rid of me?" I asked.

"No, but my mom is," Jason said with a fragile smile. He kept peering around the room.

"You know I can't afford to move anywhere right now, which is why I'm staying here," I told him.

"You could always take Stormy up on her offer," he said, somewhat wimpishly.

"She's a little too strange for me." Stormy and I were so different, but I was starting to fear I might not have a choice.

"It's better than the streets, isn't it?" He laughed a little, then his shoulders slumped. I knew he didn't want me to leave.

"I just don't really like her." Pouting, I started playing with the blanket on the bed. I wanted to snap my fingers and be somewhere nice.

"You don't have to like her, honestly, babe; I'll come every night and hang out with you."

I have to admit I was a little moved by his kindness. "You would?"

"Promise." He sat next to me on the bed and put his arm around my shoulders. I wanted his arm off of me, but I let it stay there. My emotions for Jason kept swaying back and forth from hating him to liking him, and it was making my head hurt. I did need to get out of this house.

Out of pity, I rested my head on his shoulder. "You'll make sure I stay sane in the house of hell?"

He ran his palm over the top of my head. "I will," he said reassuringly.

I basically had no other choice but to go face the pain of Stormy's abode. How dreadful the thought of living with someone that (a) I didn't like and (b) I was afraid of.

"I mean really, Jason, she actually enjoyed listening to Nick ramble on about Pinhead last night. What's up with that?" I lifted my head off his shoulder, and his arm fell lifelessly off my shoulder.

"Maybe she likes Pinhead too," he replied. He opened his eyes wide and gasped.

"Maybe she's a freak." I snickered.

He squeezed my knee, then stood and stretched. "Maybe she is, but she'll have to do for now. All right?"

"Sure," I said, with every ounce of distress I could muster.

"You can call her later and give her the good news. Right now, I'm gonna go skate like I got the devil on my ass."

"See you," I said, but I didn't give a fuck.

He took off, board in hand.

The only thing I thought made the whole situation tolerable was that Alyssia lived in the same town as Stormy. I don't know why that made things any better for me, but it did.

"Jay has space at his place," Jason said, standing in the doorway to the living room, picking at a scab on his knee.

"Really?" I had been looking for better options than Stormy's all day, making calls, but had come up dry.

"Yeah, and it's just down the street at Walnut Manor," he said with a large grin.

"That's pretty cool. When did he say I could move in?"

"Today, but there's one thing you should know first." The smile vanished from his face as quickly as it had appeared.

"What's that?"

"Matt and Brandi live there too," he said, watching closely for my reaction.

Matt was my ex-boyfriend. He had driven me crazy. I was only fifteen when we'd gotten together. I would go to his house every day after school, and we would hang out until my mother got annoyed and came to pick me up. During our one-year relationship, Matt taught me everything I ever needed or wanted to know about sex. It was a totally experimental time in my life and doing things with Matt felt so adult and risky. At the time, I thought I loved him passionately. This went on until he became so heavily involved in drugs that I couldn't keep up with him. I finally had to leave him before it got too complicated, before I got too involved with things I couldn't handle. Nevertheless, we had remained close despite our differences. The thought of living with him and his girl-friend Brandi left a slightly bitter taste in my mouth. But at the same time anything seemed better than living with Stormy.

"That'll be all right, I guess," I said. "What choice do I have? Does anyone else live there that I should know about?"

"No," he replied.

"Then it'll be fine, and it will make your mother very happy." Resentment was just spitting out of me.

"That's not really the point," he said. "Even though she has no idea that nothing ever goes on between us."

I needed to begin packing my shit. He asked if I needed any help, but what I really needed was to get away from him for a while. I declined his offer and told him to go skateboard. That seemed to be the only thing that made him happy, because it certainly wasn't me.

Jason walked out the door, and I began to gather my meager belongings. It was good that I didn't have much stuff, because I imagined there wouldn't be much room for me. I kept thinking about how strange it would be to live with Matt. Even though it was over, and we had both moved on, there was still a strong bond between us. He *was* my first boyfriend. And I still thought he was sexy. I knew it would be rather sticky. We had occasionally carried on with our sexual relationship when we weren't seeing other people. But I was always careful not to get too involved. I knew that it would be difficult for us to be in the same place and not do anything.

I finished packing and went into the den to wait for Jason to help me move my things over to Jay's. I watched out the window as he skated back and forth down the street, then finally up to the mailbox to pick up the mail. He flipped his board up and caught it in mid-air; no matter how I despised the idea of us being a couple, he was a great skateboarder. He sauntered up the driveway, then into the house.

"You're done already?" he asked, placing his board in a corner of the living room.

"It's not like I had a ton of things to pack," I said.

He sat next to me and started looking though the mail. A rather large envelope from the American Heart Association had been delivered to his address by mistake.

"Look at this shit, like I'd really go collecting for the American Heart Association. How stupid." He tossed the envelope to the side of the couch.

"Let me see that," I said, snatching it up. I opened it and found badges and donation envelopes inside. It was put together so nicely. I slid it into my backpack. Jason helped me gather my things, then drove me over to Jay's apartment. As soon as Jason and I walked through the door, I noticed that the place was utterly squalid. No one but Jay was home, and he was sitting on a beat-up couch with cigarette butts all over it, smoking pot.

"Hey, roomie," he said, inhaling deeply. I set my bag down on the floor and looked around. I wasn't sure where I was going to sleep—it looked like a one-bedroom apartment. Jay absently followed my gaze, his long blond hair falling over his eyes. He was quietly humming along to the CSN tape on the stereo.

"Long time no see," I said, with less breathing difficulties than Jay seemed to be having.

"Hey, you can put your things basically anywhere, since you're going to sleep on that couch." He pointed at it. "This one's mine; Matt and Brandi share the upstairs. Enjoy," he said, and his finger stayed pointed in the direction of the couch for a long time after he spoke.

I knew right away that this was going to be a really fucked-up situation. Jay was obnoxious and always stoned. I'd never been good friends with him; well, actually, he wasn't my cup of tea.

The door swung open and Brandi and Matt entered, carrying lots of grocery bags. Brandi wore a tiny midriff and ripped-up blue jeans. On closer inspection, I noticed that her permed dirty-blond hair looked disheveled and greasy and her ruby-red lipstick emphasized her ruddy complexion—which I admit was catty of me. Matt turned his perfectly chiseled face in my direction, his cheeks dimpling with his smile. He was one of the most gorgeous guys I'd ever met. He had beautiful brown eyes with thick black lashes.

"Hey, chick, how are you?" he asked, setting bags down on the counter.

"Fine, Matt. Good to see you." I meant it.

"Same to you," he said.

"Hi, Brandi." I acknowledged her, trying to be as polite as possible.

"Hello, Orleigh," she replied in a cold, sinister voice. Then as she put things away in the cupboards, she kept glancing over at me, giving me the evil eye. "Orleigh, I don't know if you need any food, but we all buy our own."

"Orleigh won't be eating here. She'll still eat over at my house," Jason piped in. I'd almost forgotten he was there.

Thank god he had said something. Otherwise, I would have completely flipped on her. I didn't want her fucking food.

Jason came over and kissed me. "I'm leaving, babe. Got to take the boys to soccer practice. Why don't you get your things situated, then come over to my place in about an hour." He entwined himself around me, obviously trying to show ownership.

"What are we doing tonight?" I didn't care; I just didn't want him to leave.

"I don't know, but Nick said he was going to stop by for a little while."

"Really?" I asked, knowing that he was all nervous now, nervous that I wouldn't come over.

"*Sans* Stormy," he said, which I knew was an attempt to lure me.

After Jason left, I tried to find a home for my things. On my way to the torn-up and patched cream couch that was to be my bed, I noticed a few pot plants growing out of the carpet by the sliding glass door to the balcony. I stood next to them. They were about knee-high.

"Growing your own harvest here, guys?" I asked, laughing.

Matt looked over and smiled. "You know, it doesn't hurt to try. It would definitely save us money." He stared at the plants admiringly. "What are you doing today?" he asked.

"I'm going to put some things away and then try to find a job," I said, but in truth I was ready to forgo job hunting. I had already accomplished moving for the day.

Jay stood and walked to the bathroom.

"Sounds good," Matt said. "How much are you paying Jay for rent?"

"Jason's taking care of that. I don't really know." I felt somewhat stupid that I couldn't take care of myself.

"So, you've got the boy wrapped around your little finger, huh?" There was a twinkle in his eye. I think he loved it that I was taking advantage of Jason, and he certainly knew exactly what I was doing.

"I guess."

"How's the sex?"

"Nonexistent." My eyes shifted to the sliding glass doors that overlooked a Super 8 Motel.

"I can see why."

I was angry with him for implying mean things about Jason—that was *my* job. "Yeah, so can I," I said.

"So, are you lonely?"

"A little," I said. I was telling the truth. I had forgotten how easy it was to talk to Matt, and how nice it felt being near him. At this point in the conversation, Brandi came over and wrapped her arms around Matt.

"Not to worry, Orleigh, things always get better," he said.

I winked at Matt, and Brandi pulled him toward the stairs. "Let's go up," she said in a sexy voice.

"Why?" he asked, his eyes on me.

"You know why."

"Ah, good deal," he said slowly, taking her hand.

The two of them went upstairs, and I realized that the upstairs was completely open—within minutes you could hear the sounds of sex. Jay returned from the bathroom and reached over to turn on the stereo to drown out the noises, but Brandi's moaning was still audible over the sound of Hendrix's guitar. I felt frustrated that my life, especially my sex life, sucked so badly. Finally, I forced myself to go out and find a job.

Places for potential employment were limited around the apartment complex—a Pizza Hut, a gas station, a White Hen, and a Dunkin' Donuts. I decided that Dunkin' Donuts would probably be the best choice, so I headed in for a job application. Inside, two Indian people, a man and a woman, stood behind the counter.

"I'm interested in a job. May I have an application?" I asked, determined.

"Apple fritter?" the man asked in return.

"No. Application, for employment, for a job," I replied, a little annoyed.

"You want work?"

Finally we were getting somewhere. "Yes, I'd like to work."

"Here?"

"Yes, that is the case."

"Just in case?"

"Yes, I want to work here."

"Work morning?" he asked.

"Can I work mornings?"

"Work evening?" he asked, when I thought we were still dealing with the morning issue.

"At night?"

"You work both, right?"

I figured I would just agree with whatever he said.

"Fill out form," he said, then he handed me a coffee-stained application.

"Do you have a pen?"

"No pennies," he responded, and I was really getting pissed now. Like I was begging him for money or something?

"A pen?" I asked again, this time enunciating more clearly.

"Can't get in the register, do you want doughnut?"

I was tempted to just walk out. "No, a pen," I said rather smartly this time, then I made the gesture for writing, hoping this would clarify things.

"Oh, a pen," he said. I had finally made contact with the alien mind.

"Yes, a pen." I smiled.

He handed me a pen, and I began to fill out the application. When I had finished everything he handed me, I gave it all back to him.

"You know doughnuts?" he asked.

I wondered what the hell there was to know about doughnuts. "Sure, I eat them."

He reached behind the counter and pulled out a lovely shit-brown shirt with a pink collar. "Tomorrow at five," he said, as he laid the shirt on the counter in front of me.

"Five in the evening?"

"Five morning."

"Morning?" I asked, appalled.

"Yes, morning. Can you do?" He placed his hand on the shirt, as if he were about to take it away.

"I guess. That's early."

"Five in morning," he said, then lifted his hand off the shirt.

I grabbed it from him and walked out of the shop. This was really going to suck. Now I was going to have to get up so fucking early; I'd never been up at five a.m. in my life, well, unless I stayed up all night. I was pretty bummed out. I lit a smoke and began walking down the filthy back alley to the apartment. Big green dumpsters lined the alley, and it reeked of dirty diapers. The lids of the dumpsters weren't even shut because the garbage was piled so high. When I got back inside, it was apparent from the sounds of the bedsprings and grunting that Matt and Brandi were still going at it. This just made me physically ill, and I decided it would be best to head over to Jason's. I dropped my Dunkin' Donuts shirt on top of my other things in the corner of the den and left.

A car I'd never seen before was parked in front of Jason's house. Jason was skateboarding, and Nick and Alyssia—the bisexual girl from the Morning After—stood, chatting in the driveway. She looked me up and down, then smiled as I walked up.

"I remember you," she said, overtly flirtatious.

"I remember you as well," I said almost coyly, as if she were a guy.

She stared back at me with her intense green eyes. "Your name's Orleigh, right?"

"Yes, and yours is Alyssia." Her name had been seared into my memory.

"That's right. Nice to see you again," she said, slowly licking her lips.

"Nice to see you too." I was too shy to match her bluntness. I didn't know what else to say to her. I didn't understand why she was even here at Jason's.

"I was leaving Stormy's and trying to figure out how I was going to get back to my car," Nick piped in, "and that's when I bumped into Alyssia. Isn't she just the most beautiful woman you've ever seen?" His gaze lingered on Alyssia's breasts, then returned to me.

I felt embarrassed. Alyssia and Nick were looking straight at me, waiting for an answer. I wasn't sure what she was trying to achieve, so I quickly changed the topic. I pointed a finger at Nick, then moved it toward Alyssia. "So, are you two together?" I asked.

"I have a boyfriend," Alyssia said, creasing her brow as if the idea of Nick was slightly repulsive.

"How unfortunate for the rest of us," Nick remarked. I couldn't have agreed with him more.

I was starting to figure it all out: Nick wanted Alyssia, but she had a boyfriend and Nick kind of grossed her out. But then strangely enough, she gave Nick the same overtly sexual look she had given me. "Maybe not for long, Nick," she said. She was obviously toying with him.

"What are you implying, Alyssia?" he asked. His boyish charm amazed me.

"What are *you* inferring, Nick?" she shot back.

The two of them walked away, carrying on with their flirty banter, while Jason came up to stake his claim on me by cramming his tongue down my throat.

"Hey, stop it. What's up?" I jerked away from his prodding tongue and looked over at Alyssia and Nick. I was jealous Nick was getting all her attention.

"Nothing, I just missed you," Jason replied.

"It's only been about forty minutes," I said, easing backwards on my heels.

"That's way too long."

I ignored his attempt at sentimentality. "I went and got a job."

"A job, where?"

"Dunkin' Donuts."

"I'm sorry," he said, with tons of compassion.

"So am I. Now I have to work tomorrow at five in the goddamned morning. What's that? Who wants a fucking doughnut at five in the morning? Who in the fucking world is up at the motherfucking crack of dawn to eat doughnuts?" I looked back at Nick and Alyssia, who were chatting by the garage now; they seemed to be moving nearer and nearer. Alyssia was leaning against the garage door, and Nick had his arm stretched out, his palm against the garage door above Alyssia's shoulder. His face was entirely too close to hers, and I was worried they might kiss.

"Easy, girl. Look, if you try it and don't like it, just quit. It's not like a major career move or anything, so don't sweat it."

"Easy for you to say, you won't be up dealing with non–English speaking freaks before you can even focus, now will you?" I looked at Alyssia. How unfortunate; she was too beautiful to be devoting her attention to a jerk like Nick. Finally, Nick came over and interrupted us, only to tell us he was leaving. With him left the lovely Alyssia. I was sad to see her go in a strange sort of way. Not letting on, I focused my attention back on Jason.

We went inside and prepared a pasta dish that was Jason's only vegetarian specialty: diced eggplant, zucchini, and red sauce over fettuccini noodles. Very delicious meal. After the pasta was finished, the two of us sat down with some red wine and decided to watch *The Omen,* a movie that sent shivers up my spine. I only half-watched it, and the rest of the time I had my face buried in Jason's shoulder. For us it was a semi-romantic evening, and I didn't mind too much when he kissed me before I left his place and headed to my new crash pad.

There were, like, twenty people at Jay's, hanging out, smoking weed, and listening to music. Other than Jay and his girlfriend holding hands on the couch and Brandi, who sat on Matt's lap occasionally jabbing her tongue in his mouth, I didn't know any of the other people. The noise was only slightly annoying, since I had to be up so fucking early.

"How's it going, doll?" Matt asked in that smooth, sexy voice that had a way of easing all my tension. Brandi ran her fingers through Matt's curly hair and glared at me.

"Fine."

"Did you find a job?"

"Yeah," I answered, eyes downcast. I sat next to a girl lost in her long draping hair, smoking a bong that was being passed around. I figured I might as well try to start claiming my couch.

"Where?" he asked.

I felt myself blush. "Dunkin' Donuts," I said quickly.

"Sorry," he replied, which seemed to be everyone's reaction. I told him how early I had to work, and this made him laugh.

"Things will be winding down here soon. Would you like a beer?"

"Sure."

He rose, went to the kitchen nook, pulled a Miller Lite out of the fridge, then walked back and handed it to me.

"Thanks."

"Anytime."

He sat down, and Brandi hopped back in his lap, sitting sideways so she could watch both of us closely. He stared at me intensely, then we simultaneously turned our attention to Brandi, like lovers who'd been caught. She was looking extremely pissed.

"So now we get free doughnuts, right?" Matt asked, trying to ease the tension.

"I suppose, if you actually want them," I replied.

Matt gave his little half-laugh and eased Brandi off his lap to pick up his guitar. "What would you guys like to hear?" he asked the party.

A roar in the room went up, requesting Led Zeppelin. Jay turned off the stereo so Matt could play. After *Going to California* everyone began to leave, and I found myself alone in the room. Jay had left with his girlfriend and wouldn't be home for the rest of the night. I decided it was time to sleep but remembered that I didn't have an alarm clock. I was thinking about calling up to Matt to see if he could loan me one when I heard someone walking down the stairs. I was in the middle of undressing. I turned. Matt stood at the bottom of the stairs, an alarm clock in his hand.

"Hey, don't be shy, I've seen it all before," he said, approaching me cautiously.

"I know, but it's not the same anymore."

"Unfortunately."

My eyes shot up to the loft. "Quiet, your princess might hear you," I said.

"I brought this in case you needed it." He handed me the clock.

"Thanks, sweetie, I really appreciate it."

"You're welcome." He hesitated. "I better go back upstairs."

"Yeah, she might bust out a shotgun on your ass for loaning me this."

"She's just a little possessive and maybe a little jealous," he said with a wink.

"Why?" I asked mischievously.

"For good reason, I think."

"Really, you miss me or something?" I took a few steps toward him.

"Always," he said. He grabbed my hand and kissed my fingers, and I felt my body temp skyrocket. "Sweet dreams, darling."

I woke drenched in sweat. For a few moments I had no idea where I was. When my eyes came into focus I saw Matt, clad in boxers, sitting beside me.

"Bad dream?" he whispered.

I wiped the sweat from my forehead. "No, actually, kind of a good one."

"Then why are you all sweaty?"

"Like I said, it was *good.*"

He smiled. "Oh, that kind of good. Was it about me?"

"Don't flatter yourself."

"Who then, Jason?" he asked and chuckled.

"Wrong again."

"Who?"

I cast my eyes down to the shag carpet and quietly replied, "Alyssia," not knowing what his reaction would be.

"What? Who's Alyssia?" he inquired softly, though he looked alarmed.

"She's this girl I met last night in DeKalb, then I saw her again today. I don't know her well. She introduced herself, told me she was bisexual, and ever since she's been kind of checking me out."

He looked pleasantly surprised. "You think she wants you?"

"Maybe."

"Do you want her?" he asked, and the question threw me.

145

"Never really thought about it," I said.

"So you were dreaming about her?"

I gazed up at him shyly. "Yes."

"You know, you were moaning and making these really sexy noises."

"No, I wasn't," I said defensively, looking away.

"That's why I came down here."

"Really?"

"Yeah, I thought you were masturbating, thought you might need company," he said with his easy smile.

"Just dreaming."

"Tell me your dream." He leaned in so close I could feel the heat from his body.

"It was wild," I began. "I was out in a park, late at night, sitting on a bench wearing a long gown. Alyssia, this girl, walked out of the trees. She was wearing a leather outfit, tight and extremely sexy. She walked up to me and started making out with me, touching my breasts and caressing my neck. So I was getting really, really hot. Then she got down on her knees and crawled under my dress. I had no panties on, and she started finger-fucking me, but, like, I couldn't see her face or anything because she was under the dress. Then she started to go down on me. It was amazing. I'd never had anyone do it so good in my life. My whole body totally tensed up, and I was dying because she was teasing me by stopping, then starting again, bringing me to the point of orgasm, then just stopping for a second. It was making me insane, then I orgasmed like never before. That's when I woke up."

He grinned slyly. "Bummer you had to wake up at all."

"I know."

"Was she better than me?"

"It was a dream," I said.

"Was she?"

"In my dream, yes," I answered, and felt a little guilty.

"I bet in reality she's not."

"Don't know."

"You made me hot." He gave me those eyes, eyes I could never deny.

"It made me hot," I confessed.

"So, how bad do you miss me?" he asked.

"Lots. It's been a long time."

"I know, I miss you too."

"Then why Brandi?" I said, miffed.

"You wouldn't be my girlfriend again anyway," he said, looking down at his bare feet.

"You've blown too many of those precious brain cells. You know, I loved you for more than your body."

"So, why do you miss me then?" He looked up.

"The sex," I replied with a naughty little grin.

"We could fix that."

"We could?"

He climbed under the covers with me and began kissing me all over. Within two minutes my clothing was completely off. We groped at each other fervently. I loved the feel of his skin as I ran my fingers down his back. He began to stick his fingers inside me, getting me all worked up. He stopped and lowered his head further under the blanket, kissing my stomach. I knew he was going to go down on me, and it was made clearer when he lifted his head.

"I think I can make you feel better than your little dream," he said, then he slid his tongue down my belly.

"I know you can, after all, it was only a dream. You're real." I shut my eyes.

He must have remembered my description of the dream because he kept bringing me close, then stopping, then starting again. My body was shaking wildly, and I was trying desperately to keep my mouth closed. Just then I came. I let out a yelp as my legs began to shake underneath his body. I felt like I was in heaven, and he hadn't even entered me. Before the thought even passed, he appeared in front of my face and pushed himself into me with force and agility. He pressed his mouth down onto mine and his tongue probed in and out of my mouth. I could taste myself inside of his mouth, and this turned me on even more. The thought of Brandi upstairs flashed in my mind. I know this might sound cruel, but that also turned me on. I pushed my hips up to meet his and rotated them. This lasted for about fifteen minutes, then we both climaxed together. He held me for a while before he felt the need to return upstairs. I watched him stand and pull on his boxers.

"Don't go," I said, and held my hand out to him.

"I have to; she'll kill me if I'm not there when she wakes," he said, grabbing my hand.

"I know, but I want you here. I like the way you feel next to me."

"I like the way I feel inside you," he said, glaring back at me.

"Then don't go." I was almost begging.

"I have to."

"I'm happy you came down." I was saying anything to keep him a few more minutes.

"So am I, and I'm happy you shared your dream with me. You turn me on," he said, his fingers winding around mine.

"So do you."

"I think I'm going to enjoy this living arrangement," he said with a smile.

"So, I can count on frequent late-night visits?"

"Definitely."

"Well, I guess you can go then."

"Thanks, doll." He leaned over and kissed me, then he walked quietly up the stairs.

I rolled over and fell back asleep until the alarm blared in my ear at four forty-five, which wasn't much later. I heard someone laughing upstairs, and I looked up and saw Matt lean over the edge of the loft wall.

"Hey, baby, time to make doughnuts."

"I bet you've been waiting all night to say that," I said. I flipped him off.

He laughed, then disappeared behind the wall. I started to get ready for my slimy new job. I put the shit-brown shirt on over some jeans.

I was hating life as I walked out of the apartment that morning.

I quickly found out why I had to start at five in the morning. Matt wasn't kidding; it was time to make the doughnuts.

I tried to comprehend all the things this idiotic Indian guy was trying to tell me, but it turned out to be a total disaster. First, I *supposedly* mis-understood when he said only twelve cups of batter. I had heard him say twenty. This mistake, if you want to call it that, resulted in a major break-down in machinery. Of course, the breakdown caused this guy to yell incessantly at me, and I still couldn't make out what he was saying. The miscommunication caused several other mishaps, so by ten in the morn-ing I was completely distraught. Finally, I decided—after frosting dough-nuts with the wrong icing twice and getting yelled at again—I would quit. So I told the Indian freak what he could frost, and I walked out the door. It was a relief to be out of that hellhole and on my way back to the apartment.

When I walked in, I found Matt alone on the couch.

"You done making the doughnuts?"

"Permanently," I sighed.

"That doesn't sound good."

"It wasn't." I sat next to him. I leaned my head on his shoulder while I explained the tragedy of a morning I had had. He rubbed my neck a lit-tle as I told the story, which was nice.

"So you quit?"

"Precisely."

"Then why don't you take off that ugly brown shirt from the seventies and relax."

I got up off the couch, explaining that I had to get over to Jason's. I didn't have any idea how I was going to find another job, Dunkin' Donuts had been about the only place I could handle. I took off the work shirt and searched through my backpack to find a T-shirt. Nothing was clean. "Got any clean shirts I could borrow for today?"

"What would you do for it?"

"Come on—"

"No, you come over here and sit on my face," he said, and I thought, how crude!

"Romantic," I replied.

He grabbed me and pulled me onto his lap and started to unhook my bra.

"What are you doing? What if Brandi comes home?"

149

"She is home; she's still sleeping," he said with a devilish grin.

"Forget this!" I said, and got up off of his lap. I pulled on the first shirt I could find in my backpack, hurried to find some clean jeans, then slipped into my Birks. I didn't feel like being his toy for the afternoon. I had better things to do.

"Don't go after you just took all your clothes off in front of me."

I leered at him. "Look, not my fault, you're in my room."

"Stay," he said, and stared at me with those fucking eyes that slayed me. I was getting tired of those seductively sleepy eyes.

I glared up at the loft. "She's upstairs."

"She sleeps until about noon."

"What if today's different?"

"It won't be."

"Look, I need a place to stay for a little while, and I don't want to have serious problems my second day here."

"Then come over here and kiss me good-bye."

I walked over to him and gave him an innocent peck on the cheek. He grabbed my hand and pulled me down to his lap. His hand quickly went up my shirt and started fondling my breasts. By this time his tongue was making contact with my tonsils. I tried to pull away, which only made him grab me harder. Finally, I squirmed out of his hold, jumping up.

"Thanks for the love," I said.

"Anytime, doll."

"Look, you better watch it, or there are going to be problems around here."

"Yeah, and I'll meet you at the same time, same place as I did last night."

"Don't get too used to that," I said as I walked toward the door. Part of me wanted to jump back on his lap and fuck him right in front of Brandi, but I didn't want to get kicked out.

"Honey, I'm not just used to it, I expect it."

"How tactful you are."

"Do I have to be?" he asked, but he already knew the answer, already knew the comfort level.

"I guess not. Gotta go, bye." I scurried out the door to avoid any further conversation.

At Jason's house it was the same old, same old. I was instantly bored watching him do his usual skateboard routine. He had masterfully set up two enormous half pipes in his backyard and was now able to do more unbelievable tricks. This only caused me more depression because it meant he would be spending more time skating and less time taking me on errands and such. I sat inside and watched TV while he skated back and forth. After watching all the episodes I could possibly handle of a *Charlie's Angels* marathon, I decided it might be more entertaining back at the apartment. Easily giving up my comfortable spot on the couch, I walked out the door and headed back to Jay's, feeling a bit like a ping-pong ball.

Back at the pad the only one home was Brandi. I was wrong; this was not the better place to be. I had hoped I'd find anyone else but her. Hell, even she and someone else would have been tolerable. She gave me the evil eye when I walked over to the couch; if her eyes had been weapons, I surely would be dead.

"Where have you been?" she asked. She was opening and shutting cupboards in the kitchen, apparently looking for some of her precious food to eat.

"Jason's."

"I heard you quit your job already," she said smugly.

"So."

"I'm not working either; I just got fired." She grabbed a loaf of wheat bread from the cupboard and let it fall onto the countertop. Then she opened the refrigerator and pulled out a jar of strawberry jelly.

"Sorry," I said, and maybe I meant it.

"I wish someone would knock on my door and give me a million bucks." She had taken a knife out of the drawer and was spreading the jelly over the bread.

I leaned against the wall, dumbfounded by the fact that we'd actually said more than two words to each other and that she was being decent. It made me feel a little guilty for having fucked Matt.

"That would be nice," I said. I tried to think of jobs that worked like that. Pizza delivery jobs were the closest thing I could think of, but they required having your own car, and you had to knock on people's doors, and you didn't get to keep all the money people gave you, only the dollar tip. Then the American Heart Association envelope that Jason had received in the mail popped into my head. I wondered what would happen if I tried to collect money, wearing the cute little badge, then pocketed the cash.

"Brandi, it could be almost that easy," I said, as the wheels of my devious mind began to turn.

"How's that?" she asked, then took a large bite of bread and jelly.

"I have a package from the American Heart Association. It's to collect door-to-door. It even has name badges and little envelopes for donations," I said, rather excited.

"I don't get it."

I couldn't believe how dense she was—too much pot smoking, I thought. I wondered what Matt saw in her; she must be exceptional in bed.

"See, we could go collecting, and what we get, we keep. Instead of sending it in. Do you get it?" I asked, squinting my eyes at her.

"Yeah," she answered, her voice raising an octave. Houston, we've made contact, I thought.

"Want to do it?"

"Yeah," she said, but with a stoner's enthusiasm, then she was somewhere else again. She was clutching the half-eaten jelly sandwich in her hand, gazing dreamily at the pot plants growing near the sliding glass door. I wondered what people who got stoned actually thought about. They always seemed to be in another fucking zone.

"You want to go try it now?" I asked.

"Sure." She seemed to be getting it; she needed the money for her next quarter bag.

I got out the envelope, and we sorted all its contents. We made up fake names, which we wrote on the badges, then stuffed our pockets full of the little donation envelopes.

"Should we go around here, you think?" she asked me, as if I were some kind of expert.

"Sure, why not," I said. "We have to stay away from Jason's house though. I wouldn't want his mom to see us, or him for that matter."

We headed out of the apartment building with all our necessary Heart Association accoutrements and started walking in the opposite direction of Jason's house.

After two hours we were wiped and called it quits, so we headed back with our filled envelopes. When we got inside the apartment we discovered Jay was home. Brandi suggested we go upstairs to the bathroom in order to keep our new job a secret. I sat on the toilet and Brandi sat on the edge of the tub, while we both emptied our pockets of all the tiny donation envelopes. For a second, I felt guilt, like I had just robbed the collection plate at church. But then the feeling vanished. We had about thirty-some envelopes on the floor. We tore into them and began separating the cash into piles of ones, fives, tens, and twenties. We were both shocked by the amount we had actually accumulated after only two hours of door-to-door bullshit. Brandi looked at me with extreme pleasure as she grabbed all the money in her tight little fists and began counting it over again.

"Shit, Orleigh, we have about a hundred and ninety dollars here. In two fucking hours! Can you believe it?" We were bonding, and it felt strange.

"That much, huh?"

"That much," she said with a huge smile.

She divided the money and handed me ninety-three dollars. I was thrilled. If we could do this everyday we would have so much money, I thought.

"I'm gonna take off, Brandi. Got to go over to Jason's house to eat. Should we do it again tomorrow?"

"I'll be ready at eleven." I guess she was feeling greedy because Matt said she always got up at noon. She was clutching the money, staring at it dreamily, her greasy hair partly covering her gray eyes. I wondered if she ever showered.

"You're going to get out of bed early for this?"

"Hey, just imagine what we could do in three hours," she said, still staring at the money.

"Right. We could bring home three hundred seeing that we're averaging about a hundred an hour."

She finally peeled her eyes away from the bills and looked at me with a wicked smile. I noticed that her front teeth had begun to turn a little yellow, probably from all the pot. "Hey, don't tell Matt."

"Right back at you—don't tell Jason," I said, and the realization that we had a secret between us hit me full force. Were we becoming friends? I kind of felt like we were.

"Deal," she said with a smile.

"Deal."

I left the apartment after stuffing my money in the bag with my dirty clothes. I figured there was no place it could be safer. At Jason's I found him still skateboarding. It was flabbergasting how he could do this for hours. I made him come inside and talked him into taking me out for dinner and a movie. Anything was better than watching him go back and forth, back and forth.

CHAPTER 9

Brandi and I had milked the Kane County area dry in a week. We decided it was time to bury our little moneymaking scheme before someone caught on to us. I alone had a sock that contained five hundred and eighty-five dollars. We had hit a rut once we'd moved into the affluent neighborhoods; funny, they didn't give as freely as the middle-class areas.

I was growing tired of living in that apartment, having to listen to Matt and Brandi go at it every night. It was driving me crazy—especially now that Brandi and I were getting along better and Matt was still paying me late-night visits. The whole thing was plain uncomfortable and wrong.

I decided it was time for a change and that it wouldn't hurt to call Stormy and see if her offer still stood. I didn't really want to live with her, but I thought DeKalb might be a cool place to spend some time. She told me that she was still extending the invitation. I asked if it would be cool for me to move in that night, and she seemed completely fine with that. Jason helped me gather my stuff again, and I left my most recent roommates a lovely Dear John letter, then Jason kindly dropped forty dollars for rent on the table next to the letter, and we left.

Jason clutched the wheel of his van tightly in one hand and brought his other hand to his mouth, where he started fervently biting a hangnail. He had a look in his eye that was just not right.

"Is something . . ."

"No—" he cut me off tersely.

I waited for an explanation of his mood, but he was less than eager to share. I pulled a cigarette out of my pack; I almost always did this when life seemed to be getting too serious. I lit it and sat back further into the passenger seat. "What's wrong with you? You're acting as if you just got bad news or something."

"Or something," he snapped.

"Then what?" I asked, lacking the patience to play this game.

"I don't know."

"I see, then you're just wearing that face because you think you look good all twisted up in misery?"

"Yeah, that's exactly it."

"Come on, Jas, what's going on with you?" I asked fretfully.

He took a moment to collect his thoughts. "I'm just feeling blue."

"Why blue?"

"You," he said, and looked me dead in the eyes, then back at the road.

"What about me?" I asked, though I didn't really want to go there.

"You're leaving."

"Only to Stormy's."

"Yeah, but I'm not going to see you as often."

"You don't see me much anyway."

"Come on, I see you every day," he said, clutching the wheel even tighter.

"Yeah, between bouts of skating."

"What's that mean?" he asked defensively.

"It means you're always too busy skating to notice I'm around. I end up watching old reruns, and it's boring. I'm happy because it's a different place, with different people. Maybe I'll find some new friends. Sorry if you're sad, but we'll get to see each other still. You're overreacting. I don't know anyone but Stormy, so don't think I won't be calling you all the time. Plus, I won't be that far away."

I felt better after I'd let all that out, but Jason was still working his damn hangnail. I didn't know what else to say, but I honestly didn't care anyway; I just wanted the ride. I figured it would be rather pleasant if I never saw him again, but I couldn't very well tell him that.

"You know what, Orleigh? You're selfish. You take from me, but you never give, and you only care about yourself. What's that? What kind of a relationship do we have? It's not fair that you can get what you want all the time and I never get anything."

I thought maybe he could actually read my mind. I didn't know what to say. I knew he was completely right, but I wanted to tell him he had it all wrong. Yet, I knew that he wouldn't be convinced. I didn't want to confess outright that I used him.

"Look, Jas," I said quietly. "I know things haven't been going that great between us, but it's not only my fault. I don't just take, take, take from you; in fact, I'm always willing to do whatever you want. The sad truth is that you would rather be skating. How am I supposed to handle hanging out with your brothers and watching TV alone while you're out having fun? It's dull and mundane. Maybe space apart will make us appreciate the time we have together more. Don't you think? At the very least, it can't hurt us." That was the way to go, turn the whole thing around on him, make myself look like a victim and make him feel like an asshole. I was good at that. Now he could feel guilty, and I could go back to being void.

He was quiet for a while. "Maybe you're right, Orleigh. I guess it takes two. I have been concentrating on my skating a lot lately, especially after I built the half pipes. God, what a jerk I've been. Hopefully things can get better; they can't get any worse. I'm sorry I made you feel so lonely. I never meant to hurt you."

It had worked like a charm. "No problem, Jason, I'm sorry too. Maybe some space will help us out," I said, looking out the window. There was nothing but vast space all around me, space and the occasional barn. I started to worry that things might be just as miserable in DeKalb. DeKalb was a college town; Geneva, a rich little suburban shopping center. A college town had to be better.

"I'm sure it will," Jason said, and I was surprised at how easily he could be convinced.

"Where are we?" I asked.

"Stormy's."

"What?"

"Stormy lives here, in that one right there," Jason pointed to a small, dilapidated trailer.

I hadn't remembered it looking like this when we had dropped off Stormy and Nick. A trailer park was a far cry from what I had envisioned.

Maybe I'd hallucinated a nicer place when we'd been here before. I thought Stormy lived in a cool pad, with some cool people. How wrong could I have been?

"Wow, I didn't know I was about to become one of the elite trailer-trash folk," I said.

"Don't knock it, baby, it's home." He pulled his van into the gravel drive.

"Clearly only temporary."

"You going to come back to me soon?" he asked, too hopeful.

"Unless you want me to turn into a little hayseed, I think so."

"Do you want to stay here at all?" He slid the gear shift into park.

"I think I should, maybe for just a week. It'll be a little vacation in the trash can." I wanted to let him down easy.

"Okay, let's move you in then." He hopped out of the van as I silently and resentfully absorbed my surroundings before getting out.

We walked up to the screen door, which was slightly open (just enough for the bugs to get in). I peered inside before I knocked and noticed a pile of dirty dishes spreading over what I assumed were countertops and a table. I was horrified by the quantity of dishes; it looked as if an entire battalion lived in this tiny shack of a trailer. I looked at Jason and rolled my eyes. He smiled and rattled the screen. A little girl with a dirty face and a yellowed white dress came to the door. She didn't open it but simply stared at us.

"Hello," Jason said playfully.

"Is Stormy here?" I asked.

The little girl didn't speak.

"Misty, who's at the door?" a voice called out from somewhere inside.

"No one," the little girl said as she tugged at the hem of her dress. The little girl was actually going to play a little game: Ha ha, they're not really here. How cute. I decided to handle this one.

"Hello, is Stormy home?" I called to whoever was there.

"Come in," the voice replied.

We opened the door and walked around the little girl. I looked toward the direction the voice came from. No one was there. Instead of a person,

I saw a small cube with a couch, chair, and television. It looked like it was trying to be a den, but it wasn't big enough. Unfortunately, this confined space was also overloaded with clutter, laundry, and clothes that might have been dirty or clean, it was hard to tell. There were toys, especially dolls, strewn all over the place. It was frightening how much shit there was.

The voice called out again, coming from somewhere down a hallway. "Who's there? Misty, who is it?"

The little girl was apparently not going to talk.

"Misty, get in here!" the voice hollered now.

Misty picked up the hem of her dirty dress and ran down the hallway. Jason and I looked blankly at each other, not knowing what to do. The invisible person's voice was definitely not Stormy's, and I wondered if we were in the right place. I looked at Jason, who seemed to think this was all very amusing.

"Are you sure this is Stormy's place? It all seems very strange."

"Yeah, it's her place—" Before he could finish his sentence, the screen door swung open and in walked Stormy.

"Hey guys, been here long?" she asked.

"No, we were just trying to figure out where you were," Jason said, a hint of relief in his voice.

"Oh, over at the neighbor's house giving him a blow job," she said matter-of-factly.

"What, seriously?" Jason asked, his eyes wide.

"As a heart attack," she replied, her shoulders proudly arching back. "He's totally hot. Didn't have anything better to do for the last hour."

"You blew him for an hour?" Jason asked incredulously. I was getting very annoyed.

"Yeah, what about it, Jason? I'd do it for you for two hours." She smiled at him, like a snake at a rat.

"Really?" He shook his head in awe.

"If *she* didn't care." Stormy looked in my direction with this I'm-better-than-you attitude. Jason's eyes were popping out of his head as if he had just heard he'd won the lottery. I was getting sick to my stomach at just how lewd Stormy could be and how easily Jason could be sucked in.

"You know what? I don't give a damn what either of you do together," I said.

Jason came out of his fantasy world, smiled at me, and said, "I'm sure she was only kidding. Right, Stormy?"

"Sure, Jason." I saw her wink at him, but she didn't think I saw, because my eyes were cast down at the dirty white linoleum floor. Fuck, why did they get white if they couldn't keep it clean? I wanted Jason to leave. But what I really wanted to do was go back to the Morning After and find Alyssia. I didn't feel like staying here any longer. Jason mentioned he had a lot to do and that he had to go home, so I let him leave without kissing him good-bye.

"Sorry if I upset you," Stormy said, once Jason's van had pulled away.

"You didn't. It was just a little forward."

"Well, it's obvious *you* don't fuck him," she said, and this pissed me off even more.

"How so?"

"You two have no intimacy. You never kiss, never hold hands—nothing. So don't think the rest of the world can't see what's up between you. The relationship just reeks of convenience."

I was surprised at how perceptive she was. "Maybe you're right," I said, feeling slightly defeated.

"I'm right, no big deal. I just don't understand why you care."

"I thought it was kind of strange, I mean, *I'm* his girlfriend."

"Then act like it," she said.

"Go ahead and do whatever you'd like to him. I don't care anymore. I came here to get away from him. So, if you really want me to stay here, like you say you do, try and be a little nice, okay?" My voice sounded edgy. It was somewhat audacious of me to be scolding Stormy like a child. I barely knew her, and she was kind enough to let me stay with her. I inhaled then exhaled heavily.

"Sure, sorry. Hey, why don't I show you where you can put your things?"

She led me down the mysterious hallway that gave way to three bedrooms. We passed by what must have been the master bedroom (the door was closed and I thought this was probably where the disembodied voice

160

had come from), then a room with two little beds. On one of these beds was sprawled an overweight girl, reading a *YM* or *Seventeen* magazine. Misty cowered in the corner, rocking one of her many dolls to sleep. I assumed this was the children's room, which meant that the door at the end of the hall led to Stormy's. She opened this door to reveal a filthy bedroom with a large queen-size bed. She directed my attention to one of those little chair beds in the corner.

Pointing to the ugly, small, red thing, she said, "That's your bed."

For god's sake, I'm five-nine-and-a-half—what a nightmare it was going to be to cram my body into that dinky bed. I was saddened that I had made this choice. I had thought things couldn't possibly get worse. I dropped my bag to the floor and sat on my new so-called bed. Stormy looked at me as if I were an absolute bitch.

"Sorry, I just thought you lived alone, like, in your own apartment," I said. "I didn't realize your whole family lived here. It seems like an inconvenience—me staying here. Are you sure nobody minds?" I almost wished she would change her mind, that I would be forced into finding another place.

"My mom's cool with it, don't worry."

"Do you want to go out and do something?" I asked, hoping she'd say yes, and we could get the hell out of the depressing trailer for a while.

"I can't. I have school tomorrow." She pursed her lips.

"College?" I asked hesitantly.

"I'm still in high school."

"Seriously?" She must have been kidding.

"As a heart attack."

"I just thought . . ." I began, but I didn't want to go any further. I was going to be living with a high school kid. I felt like running out the door.

"A lot of people think I'm older. Sorry, I was thinking about maybe watching TV."

"I guess that would be cool," I lied.

We headed out to the miniature den, and Stormy turned on the television. Within moments the two girls came out of their room and sat directly in front of the box.

"Hey, you two, move, so that Orleigh and I can see," Stormy ordered the midgets, and their bodies inched on their behinds to the right and left.

"I want to watch cartoons," Misty whined.

"No cartoons on. We're going to watch what I want to watch," Stormy said with authority. She flicked the remote to MTV, and the two girls sat there mesmerized. Looking at the back of the adolescent girl's head, I deduced that she was getting homemade haircuts. Her hair was choppy and uneven. How could someone so young be so chunky? I wondered. Misty, the little one, must have weighed sixty pounds. When she turned to smile at me, I noticed that her front teeth were rotten. Shit, she had to be about five years old.

I didn't think this was how it was going to be. I thought we'd be hanging out downtown having fun. I didn't know the area, and I began worrying about how I'd get around. I felt like such an idiot for putting myself in this situation. What the hell I was thinking? Why was I so entranced by this Alyssia chick I hardly knew? So much so that I moved in with this trashy Stormy girl? I wanted to go back to Jason's house. Eventually, the children wandered off to bed. Stormy went to her room, and I decided to follow her and hit the red bed. Nothing to do but sleep.

"Come play with me," Misty called, waking me from a deep slumber. I opened my eyes. She was hopping around the edge of the red bed on one foot.

"Where's your mommy?" I asked, too tired to deal. I wanted at least another hour of sleep. When I felt depressed, I liked to sleep off as much of the day as I could.

"I don't know," she said, then hopped onto my chest. It didn't hurt at all. I wondered if anyone was feeding this kid.

"Is she here?" I tried to shove the kid's behind off of my breasts, but she had tangled her tiny fingers into my long hair, and when I tried to move her, she pulled. I shot a sidelong glance at the tiny left foot near my face and noticed that the sole was completely black.

"I don't know."

"Okay, let's go find her." I rolled her off me and stood. My body ached from head to toe. I hadn't slept on anything that uncomfortable in my life. It would have been better if I'd slept on the fucking floor, only there wasn't even a spot of floor to sleep on—it was covered with clothes, Wicca books, cassette tapes, candles, shoes, ashtrays, and Pepsi cans.

"I'm hungry."

"Okay, let's go get Mommy." I stumbled out of the room and started down the hallway, Misty at my side. I looked into the room Misty slept in, but it was empty.

"Summer's gone," the kid said, digging a finger deep into her nose.

"Yes it is. It's changed, kind of looks like fall."

"Summer's fall?" she asked, her finger still probing.

"No, it just looks like it's changing to fall," I replied, not really in the mood to discuss the seasons.

"She changed?"

"No, summer is fall now."

"Then why do we still call her Summer?" the child asked, scratching her scabby knee now.

"Who is *she?*" I asked.

"My sister."

"Oh, your sister is Summer, that's her name?"

"Summer's gone to school."

Now I got it; I supposed I should have introduced myself to everyone last night. I looked into the room where Misty was standing. There was a waterbed. It was empty. No mommy. Where the hell was she? Here was a little girl who could have been all alone, with no mother to care for her. I found this appalling. I was ready to call the child welfare society.

"Is Mommy at work?" she asked, her big child eyes beaming up at me.

"I don't know. Does your mommy work?"

"Yeah, I think."

"Where do you go when she works? Do you go to school?"

"No school. I stay here," she said, pointing at the floor.

"Does someone stay with you?" I asked, a little too hopefully.

"Sometimes."

"And what about today? Staying with you today?"

She pointed at me. "You."

"Oh, really." I laughed, but then became aware that nothing about this situation was remotely funny. I'd finally figured out what was going on

163

around here—Mom didn't need to come home because Orleigh the babysitter was here. Great. No wonder Stormy's mother didn't mind having people crash here—she got an instant babysitter out of the deal. This was bullshit. Like hell I was going to sit around and watch this little kid. I would have rather been living on the streets or back at the apartment, even at home with my mother.

I had to keep my mind occupied in this hellhole until I could find a way to escape. I was dying to get out of the trailer and back to the Morning After. For the remainder of the day, I played with the child. When Stormy and Summer returned, I immediately quit paying attention to her.

"Hey, is there any way I can get downtown from here, other than walking?" I asked.

"Yeah, why?" Stormy squinted.

I looked at Misty. "I mean, she's cute and all, it's just not my idea of fun."

Stormy informed me of a bus that stopped right across the street and went into town. Pleased that the dilemma appeared to be resolved, I found myself shifting into a better mood. Stormy decided to order pizza, and out of my appreciation for the bus tip, I paid for it.

"Stormy, where's your mom?" I asked, genuinely concerned.

"She works from four thirty in the evening until morning, then she usually comes home and sleeps. I think she got lucky last night, though, know what I mean?" Stormy winked.

"Got ya." A shiver ran through me. I couldn't believe that these kids' mother put her sexual satisfaction before the welfare of her children. They were the epitome of what I'd always thought of as trailer trash.

The pizza came, and we all sat down to eat; it was actually nice, kind of family-like. The television was tuned to MTV, and everyone watched quietly as they ate. After about four hours of TV-viewing pleasure, I got bored and sleepy, so I hit the little red bed.

CHAPTER 10

The next morning, I woke to the pitter-patter of little feet, followed by a thump on the bed, then small cold hands on my cheeks. I opened my eyes and saw that it was the little one again. I was thrilled to have my own personal, living alarm clock from hell.

"I'm hungry," she yelled, bouncing on the edge of the bed.

"Is your mommy here?" I asked, feeling a sense of déjà vu.

"Yes, she's sleeping," she told me as her little hand grabbed onto mine and pulled.

I wasn't ready to move yet, but I kind of felt sorry for this scrawny child. It was obvious that she wasn't well–cared for. She was still wearing that tired yellowed dress, and I gathered from its array of wrinkles that she'd slept in it. "What do you want for breakfast?" I asked.

"Cereal," she responded, bouncing with enthusiasm.

I brought Misty into the kitchen. The variety of cereal options was astounding: Cocoa Krispies, Count Chocula, Lucky Charms, Boo Berry, and Cap'n Crunch with Crunchberries. Unfortunately, all the bowls were crusted with the remains of various meals that had been consumed since the early eighties. It reminded me of a fucking archeological site. A disgusting smell of mold clung to the air, but I wasn't able to determine whether the smell came from the dirty dishes or the mountain of trash heaped in a corner. I looked for the bowl with the least amount of encrusted food so that I could give the pitiful little monster some cereal. I finally found one under a huge stack of dirty plates and bowls—a lime-green doggylike bowl that seemed to have contained cereal at one point, so I thought it was a primo choice. I cleaned it with hot water and the tiny drop of lemon dishwashing soap that remained in the plastic squeeze bottle. I put some Cocoa Krispies in it, then opened the refrigerator to find some milk. Luckily, there was a carton right in front of my face, though the stink that escaped from it almost made me puke. Misty looked over and plugged her nose. I flipped the top closed and tried to find a place for it in the already overflowing garbage. I put the bowl of dry cereal on the table in a tiny little space that wasn't covered with dishes and empty containers of Big Macs, Whoppers, Chicken McNuggets, and barbecue sauces.

"The milk's bad; you'll have to have your cereal plain," I said.

"I want milk," she said with a sigh.

"It's bad."

"So?"

"You can't drink it."

"Why?"

"It will make you sick."

"Oh." She picked up her bowl, walked into the den, turned on the television, and proceeded to eat her dry cereal with a spoon. Despite the circumstances, it was very cute. I went into the bathroom to take a shower before I headed out to the bus stop.

In the bathroom I immediately found that the filth was consistent with the rest of the trailer. The tiles in the shower were black with tiny specks of the original white showing through. Soap scum and shampoo drippings adorned the walls. Liquid Plumber may not have been an option for the shower drain, which was completely covered in hair. I decided I'd be cleaner by simply not taking a shower. I really needed to wash my hair—the grease had built up over the last few days—but given the conditions, I resolved it would be best to dress and head downtown. I didn't know anyone anyway, so it really didn't matter if my hair was slimy.

I got dressed then headed out the screen door just in time to see a bus pulling up to the corner. I ran across the street and jumped on. I shuffled through my pocket, but the driver nodded his head, signaling for me to walk on. This didn't make sense to me, until I saw the sign that said, "Students Ride Free." I guessed I looked like a student with my greasy hair and my backpack slung across my shoulder.

I sat back as the bus rolled away from Stormy's hell cave. I was thrilled to be free. After all, I'd come to DeKalb to see something different from St. Charles, and my idea of different was not a dirty little trailer home. The bus jerked back and forth down the main highway. We pulled up to a corner and two guys who looked vaguely familiar got on the bus. I stared at them, trying to place them. One had curly hair, cut pretty short; it looked like pubic hair. Even so, he was pretty cute. He had a long narrow nose and wore little wire-rimmed designer eyeglasses. If it weren't for his hair, I'd have thought he looked like John Lennon. He wore a snug-fitting black turtleneck, tight black jeans, and a bunch of thin black bracelets around his wrist. The other guy had piercing blue eyes and spiky raven-black hair. He reminded me of my ex Matthew because he exuded a similar kind of sensuality in his slow, graceful walk. I wanted to smile at him, but my hair looked so bad. They sat a few seats in front of me and began talking about a girl, raving about her. I couldn't make out her name, only that they seemed to think she was some sort of goddess. I wished I were her. The bus eventually pulled up to the front of the Morning After, and the two guys got off.

I stumbled off in my own very uncoordinated fashion, hoping that no one noticed how clumsy I was. I looked around the streets bustling with college students, some heading toward the campus that loomed in the distance. For a moment I fantasized about what it would be like to be a student at NIU, wondered if it was as cool as it appeared to be. The campus seemed overwhelming, huge. I could see myself getting lost on my way to classes, in the maze of sidewalks.

I opened the large wooden door to the Morning After. It was empty, save for the two guys I'd seen on the bus. It must have been prime time for classes. I sat in a corner booth from which I could watch the front door, as well as the two hot guys. I opened my backpack and pulled out my dog-eared copy of *Madame Bovary*. I was really starting to get into it. I identified with this Emma chick. She had the same trouble I did—she couldn't deal with the boring men in her life. And she was always looking to fill the tremendous void she felt.

I sat, quietly reading. Kurt, the owner, came over to my table.

"Hello, what can I get you?" he asked with a smile. He looked like an actor—blond, blue eyes, square jaw, and perfectly straight white teeth.

That whole thing. He was maybe a few years older than me. I always thought guys like him were cute, but they weren't my type. I needed a certain brooding darkness. I wanted the cowboy in the black hat instead of the white one. I wanted the villain in the Western movies.

"I'd like a cafe mocha with whipped cream," I said.

"Ah, a woman who knows her coffee." He gave me a friendly wink.

"Always," I flirted.

He walked away to fill my order. Even though I was burying my face in my book, I was aware that the two guys from the bus were ogling me. They were murmuring, but I couldn't make out what they were saying. I took a quick look at their table, and Blue Eyes held his coffee cup up to me. I quickly resumed reading my book.

The door to the Morning After opened and a very disheveled guy walked in. He looked skittish. His fingers moved rapidly at his sides while his eyes darted about the room. He spotted the two guys from the bus, then shuffled over to them. As he walked, he repeatedly touched the tip of each of his fingers on both hands to the tip of their thumbs. I swore I recognized all of them from somewhere, especially when the new guy sat down with them. He had a thin well-manicured moustache. I had seen this guy before. He didn't look like he would be friends with the other two. He wasn't as well put together, and he didn't wear the same characteristic black clothes. He had on a T-shirt and jeans with holes in the knees. The bus guys seemed eager to talk to him. I discretely watched them interact. They were acting more like women than men. When the skittish one had taken his seat, he placed his hands out on the table, tapping away, then he thumped his forehead down. The bus guys covered his hands with theirs, like comforting grandmothers. Blue Eyes put his arm around his shoulders, while the other embraced him too. All this behavior was very unfamiliar to me, but I liked it. I liked the fact that these three guys felt they could interact as intimately as they did, especially in public. I was impressed. They were looking in my direction again.

Then the door opened, and this time it was her—the bisexual Alyssia, dressed all in black.

She looked absolutely lovely. She had on a leather jacket, turtleneck, miniskirt, and knee-high suede boots. She took a drag from her cigarette and inhaled deeply as she paused for a moment, blinking, looking around the room. She made eye contact with one of the guys at the table and walked toward him, wearing a luscious glossy maroon smile. As she passed me, she exhaled a cloud of smoke that circled my head, making me feel insignificant. She hugged each guy before she sat at the table. Blue Eyes kissed her on the lips, which made me think they were a couple. But then she kissed the other two in a similar fashion. My friends always shook hands or hugged, never kissed on the lips. This was too much—realistically, she couldn't be with all three of them. After they finished fawning over each other, they began to talk. They spoke in such low voices, it was impossible for me to eavesdrop. I wanted to be a fly on their table. They looked in my direction again. Then Alyssia raised her voice:

"I know her. She's friends with Stormy."

"Really, Stormy? I wonder why," Blue Eyes asked.

"I don't know, but isn't she beautiful?" I could feel her eyes on me, but I pretended to read.

"Yeah, I was just saying that to Geoff before you got here," he said.

"I think she's just adorable," Alyssia purred, exhaling another thick cloud of smoke that floated over to my table.

"Why don't you go talk to her?" Four Eyes encouraged.

"She looks like she's really involved in her book."

It took all my energy to stay focused on the page. Kurt returned with my cafe mocha, which he placed on the table with a few napkins.

"I hope it's to your liking," he said.

"Looks wonderful," I told him, not looking at the coffee but at him. He reminded me of boys I had dated in high school. I was sure he'd been on his high school's football team.

"I added extra whipped cream," he said sweetly. He stood with a hand on his hip. I wasn't sure if he was waiting for me to try the drink, or if he just wanted to hang out with me.

"Thanks," I said, peering down into a mountain of whipped cream with chocolate sprinkles nestled into it. Feeling awkward, I stuck my finger in the whipped cream and scooped some into my mouth. Kurt smiled.

He walked away, and I tried to glance surreptitiously in the direction of Alyssia's table. They were all watching me. I looked back down at my book and the line, "Emma's heart beat faster when, her partner holding her with just his fingertips . . ." I read it over and over, then put my book down while I ate the whipped cream off the top of my coffee.

I sullenly sat spooning up mouthfuls of mocha, trying to ignore the now obvious glaring. If they wanted me to feel uncomfortable, they were doing a good job. I found myself glancing down at my cup, then up at the door, and down again. I turned my head in their direction—all eyes were on me, but I tried to pretend I didn't see them. I felt a blush creep into my cheeks. I knew they could see it. I wanted to get up and leave, but I didn't know where to go. I felt like an idiot. Then I was aware of a body standing next to me, not saying a word. I looked up. It was Alyssia.

"Hello, haven't we met before?" she asked, even though we both knew we had.

"Yes, here, I believe, then again at Jason's," I said, not mentioning I'd also met her in my dream. My cheeks burned.

"Right. You're Stormy's friend," she said, but it seemed like a question.

"If that's how you want to look at it."

She raised her eyebrows and gave me a quirky smile.

"I just live with her, really. That's the extent of the friendship."

"You live with her, since when?" she asked, wearing a puzzled expression on her pretty face.

"Very recently."

"You like it?"

"No."

"Care to join us?" She waved her hand at the other table, where the guys were staring right at us, involved in their own conversation.

"No, care to join me?" I asked, feeling a little feisty.

"Sure."

She motioned for the guys to come over. As they walked toward my table, it dawned on me that these were the guys I had met at the Morning After, the first night I had met Alyssia, but I had been primarily focused on her.

Alyssia and the guy with glasses sat across from me, Blue Eyes sat next to me, and the skittish one balanced himself on the backrest of the booth.

Blue Eyes grinned a wicked toothy grin. The kind of grin your first boyfriend gives you right before he takes you to bed and snatches up your virginity. "What's your name?" he asked, making me feel like I was the only person at the table.

"Orleigh," I said, almost shyly.

"Where you from?"

"Geneva."

"Switzerland?"

"No, Illinois," I said, laughing.

"Nice to meet you. I'm Sam."

He was flirting with me like crazy. He introduced the skittish one as Don and the curly-haired John-Lennon-look-alike as Geoffrey. I don't think they remembered meeting me, but they were all friendly. The whole time I could feel Alyssia's eyes burning into me. It was obnoxious how she stared. Then things got weirder. I felt a leg brush against my shin, but it wasn't a brush anymore; it kind of lingered and rubbed up and down. I couldn't tell who was doing it until I looked at Alyssia—her eyes were devouring me. It felt like she could see through my clothing, see everything. She winked at me, then asked if I needed to go to the bathroom.

"No, not really," I said, looking deeper into my cup. It was empty.

"Will you come with me?" she asked, standing.

"You can't go alone?"

"I can—I just don't want to," she said firmly, as if I were a bit dense.

"I see." I looked around at the guys, who all wore shocked expressions. What was the big deal? Lots of girls go to the bathroom with buddies, it's just a naturally feminine thing to do. I'd never seen such a reaction before—mouths agape, outright gawking—so I rose, turned my back to them, and followed Alyssia.

We entered the one-person bathroom. She gave me a look hard to describe—almost animal-like, very swift. She pressed herself against me, pushing me to the wall. I felt extremely uncomfortable, but my edginess didn't stop her. She ran her fingers up my sides and placed her lips against mine. I no longer felt uncomfortable. It all seemed very natural. Ferociously, her mouth tasted mine.

"You know you are beautiful," she said, as she slowly pulled away from me.

"No," I said.

"You are."

"Thank you." I tottered backwards on my heels.

"Am I making you nervous?" she asked.

"Not necessarily." I tried to play it cool.

"Do you like this?" She traced her fingers up and down my arm.

"I guess."

"You guess?"

"I do then," I said. I looked down at the floor.

"I thought so." She resumed kissing me deeply. She turned me around so I faced the wall. I felt her breath in my ear, then she lifted a scarf around my eyes and tied it tightly behind my head. I didn't say anything, this was all so bizarre to me. I had no idea what was going to happen next, but I didn't mind. I felt like a naughty little girl in trouble for something or other. Then I realized it wasn't trouble—it was bliss.

I was wearing a mini dress I'd purchased at a thrift store, one of my favorite buys, black with large yellow daisies. I had on thigh-high black stockings and a black T-shirt over the dress. I felt the bottom of my dress pull upward, then warm fingers grab my panties, inching them down to my knees, where they fell to my ankles and rested. I got a nervous queasy feeling as her hand found the place between my thighs. She kept touching me with her dexterous fingers. She knew every place to touch as well as the right way to touch me. I was hot, anxious, and sweating. She pulled me over to somewhere else in the bathroom, then her arms guided me to cold hard porcelain. Her hands helped mine find a grip. She placed a finger onto the small of my back, which I supposed was a silent order to bend down. She was still behind me, and her fingers went to play again on my softness, which was now dripping down my thighs.

"You are so wet," she told me in a sexy, husky voice.

I couldn't speak, partly because I was embarrassed, partly because I didn't know what to say.

"Let me help you then," she said in the same voice, and I could feel her body move down.

I felt something warm against my thigh, warm and wet—her tongue. It ran up and down the inside of my leg. It swept slowly back and forth. Finally, her tongue was there, where I wanted it to be. I had felt boys do this before, but it was not the same. Her tongue moved expertly, concentrating on just the right spot, just the right amount of time. She would bring me so close to the point of release, then stop. It was driving me crazy, but she was teasing me in a way I had never experienced, except oddly in that dream I'd had of her. After much teasing the release finally came. It was powerful. My body went limp and I quivered all over.

"You liked it, didn't you?" she asked. I felt her power over me intensify.

"Yes," I said, somewhat ashamed.

"I thought so. Never had it like that before?"

The air was so heavy it was choking me, cutting off my breath. "No, only dreamed about it."

"Stay there, just like that. I have a surprise for you." Her footsteps receded behind me. Click, clack, click.

I waited for her in the exact position she had left me in. My hands were gripping the bathroom sink, probably all white-knuckled. I could see light through the bottom of the scarf covering my eyes. My panties were still around my ankles, and I lifted my feet to kick them off. I heard the bathroom door open again, footsteps, which sounded like more than just Alyssia's.

Then I heard his voice: "Just look how sexy she is. What a beautiful tight little ass, and look at it just waiting for attention. Why don't we give her some attention, Alyssia?" It was blue-eyed Sam. "I think she deserves something for all the work she's been doing. Did you see her trying so hard not to look at us? She wanted to, and yet she restrained herself. She's in need of something special. And I may have just what she needs." He let out an evil laugh.

I was freaking out. What was he going to do, rape me? I heard a noise that sounded like air coming out of a pump. I contemplated pulling the scarf off, grabbing my things, then running like a scared child. Part of me thought that was the thing to do, just go, run, get away. But another part of me wanted to stay. Alyssia was magic, not because of what she had done to me, it was more than that. She was powerful, she was manipulative, she was a woman who got what she wanted. She barely knew me and already she had me under her spell. I was mesmerized by her.

"Have some of this," Sam said, and I felt something cold on my lips. I licked them and discovered it was whipped cream. He was squirting whipped cream onto his fingers, feeding it to me.

"Want more?" he asked.

"Yes," I said in a shaky voice that didn't belong to me.

"Then you better lick it off next time."

I didn't like his tone; it frightened me. But I did what he commanded, once, twice, three times. Then I felt the cold of the can between my legs followed by the spray of whipped cream, all over me.

"Are you hungry, Miss Alyssia?" he asked.

"No, I already ate her. Your turn," she answered flatly.

I was bent over and it began again. He licked the whipped cream off of me, sprayed more, and licked more. It was lovely and I orgasmed again. Nothing like the first time, though, nothing like her.

"Did you like it?" he asked.

I was too weak to answer, so I just moaned.

"I'll take that as a yes. Now, what should we do to the little girl, Miss Alyssia?"

"I don't know, maybe she would like more. Would you like more?"

I moaned again, still shaking. My legs felt like rubber underneath me, I was so hot. I had no idea what I wanted.

"I think she does want something, maybe she wants something from me?" Sam said.

"Maybe she does. After all, we've spent much time together. Maybe she's ready to move on to you. I need to go check on the boys anyway," Alyssia said, and I could hear her turn the door handle.

"No, you should stay," Sam demanded.

"I should?" I heard the doorknob release.

"Certainly, it's a two-person job."

I didn't want her to leave, I wanted her to stay. Maybe I wanted *him* to go. I heard motion; they were moving around in the tiny bathroom, rearranging the scene. I was still gripping the sink tightly, ass fully exposed.

"Come here," he said.

I heard his voice, heard the direction it was coming from. He was by the toilet, it sounded like he was sitting down. I didn't know where Alyssia was; she was silent as a mouse. A hand grabbed mine and pulled me.

"Sit down," he said, and I turned toward him.

"No, don't turn, just sit," he commanded.

I pivoted back to my starting position and sat down. I was on his lap. I could feel the hardness of him through his jeans.

"Comfortable?" he asked.

"Yes."

"Scoot up so I can get my pants undone."

I did what he said; his voice was soothing, sexy. I trusted him, for no reason. I heard his zipper going down. I felt sexy and erotic, despite how weird it all was.

"Now, lift your ass up about a.foot or two."

I complied without saying a word.

"You're not so hot anymore; are you scared?" he asked.

"Yes," I replied.

"Alyssia, help me get her ready again, I want her so hot she is screaming for it, begging me for what I have."

I felt someone's presence, directly in front of me. I could smell her. Her hands cupped my breasts, squeezed my nipples tightly, too tight. I flinched from the pain, and she let up a little. Someone's fingers were sliding in and out of me, but I didn't know whose. Things began to get confusing, all hands and fingers. Then Sam entered me, hard. I was not facing him, but someone was kissing me. I didn't know what to do. I came once, then again within moments. I could barely control my body's convulsions. I was finished, but he wasn't. His hands were still forcing my hips up and down. Then the strangest thing happened—someone bit into my neck.

The bite pulled me out of the trance I was in. I jumped off his lap and slid away from where I sensed the two of them were. My hand found the doorknob, and I turned it while I adjusted my skirt, then pulled the scarf from my eyes. The door opened and brought a triangle of light to the floor, which I followed out of the bathroom. I walked to the table where my belongings were, grabbed my backpack and *Madame Bovary*, then hurried out the door. I didn't look back at the Morning After, not once. As I hustled down the street, I ran right into Stormy.

"Hey, where are you off to?" she asked.

"Nowhere," I said, trying to regain my composure.

"Then why don't you come with me to the Morning After?"

"I don't really want to." I knew I couldn't go back in there now, especially with her.

"Are you okay? Your neck's all red." Looking puzzled, she tilted her head to study my neck.

"I'm fine. I'd just rather go somewhere else."

"How about the Junction?" she asked.

"Sounds good."

We walked quietly down the street in the direction of the Junction. I couldn't believe I had allowed myself to get involved in something so strange. Nothing made sense anymore. All I knew was it was her, it was all about her. I knew that I could love Alyssia; fall crazy in love with her. She was strong, sneaky, and downright sexy. However, the whole thing that had just ensued baffled me. She was stronger than any man I'd been with, not to mention better at sex. She made me sweat; I was sweating right now. What the fuck was my problem? She was way over my head, way more than I could handle. I didn't want to see her again, but I knew if I didn't I would die. This girl had gotten inside my head.

The smoking section at the Junction was crowded. Stormy led me to a table way in the back. I was thankful it was far from the maddening crowd. There was more animal hide in the Junction than in a slaughterhouse. I sat with my head in my hands, thinking of how fucked up everything had gotten. I didn't want to talk; I didn't even want to be there. I realized that I didn't have my underwear on anymore. I felt vulnerable. I hated the thought that my underwear was still at the Morning After, that they still had that part of me, like a prize.

We ordered coffee, and I tried to keep my head down so I didn't have to talk to Stormy. She continued to pry about what had happened to me, but there was no way I'd tell her. When I looked up to add cream to my coffee, I immediately saw that Alyssia, Sam, Don, and Geoffrey had entered the Junction and were walking straight toward our table. I stared intensely into my cup, so that they possibly wouldn't notice me. Unfortunately, when I looked up again, they were standing in front of me.

"Have a seat, there's plenty of room," Stormy told them, and my head started to reel.

Alyssia looked at me, smiled, and said, "Let's go to the bathroom, Orleigh."

"Let's not," I spat back, not looking up.

"I will," Stormy said excitedly. Thank god for Stormy. Maybe she and Stormy could get it on in there.

"No, actually I need to talk to Orleigh," Alyssia said, glaring at me.

"Sorry, but I'm not really in the mood to *talk*," I said.

"Come on," she coaxed. But then I didn't have a choice because she grabbed my hand and practically dragged me away.

"Look, I'm sorry that got out of hand," she said, blocking the door to the bathroom with her body.

"Whatever."

"No, I am. I like you. A lot." There was a softness in her tone that I hadn't heard before. Her lips parted in a sweet smile. It was strange to see her this way. She always appeared so icy.

"Good for you," I said.

"Hey, relax. I promise that won't happen again, but I didn't really see you freaking out about it while it was happening. In fact, you seemed pretty eager." Her countenance changed, she was being sterner, more like who I thought Alyssia was.

"Who cares now?" I said, but I could feel myself weakening.

"I do." She walked toward me and kissed me. She took her hands and ran them over my hair. Her kisses were so gentle, unlike before. She was making me feel comfortable again, making me relax. She pulled me into a stall and sat down on the toilet. I stood against the door, but she motioned for me to come sit on her lap.

"I want to talk to you." Her arms encircled my waist.

"About what?" I asked, feeling too easy.

"About us." She kissed me again, but this time her lips parted and her tongue lightly grazed my lips.

She was softening me with her delicate kisses. I knew there was lots to talk about, but I didn't want to talk.

"Actually, I was thinking you might have more fun staying at my place than Stormy's. How much fun can it be to live with her and her little sisters?"

"Not much," I said, somewhat thrown that she knew about Stormy's little sisters.

"Would you like to stay with me?"

"Do you have room?"

"Sure, I have a king-size bed. I think that's about all you would need."

I thought it was funny that the bed was the first thing she brought up. "A shower would be nice too."

"I can give you a shower." Her smile bedazzled me.

I wanted to stay at Alyssia's—the thought of sleeping with her and showering with her sounded fantastic compared to Stormy's. I could tell by the way Alyssia presented herself that she came from a clean environment. This made me incredibly jazzed. We were going to be in the same room together, sleeping enveloped in fresh linen.

"Then we should go pick your stuff up. I mean, unless you'd like a couple of days to think about it?"

"No, that sounds great. I just don't know how to tell Stormy." It was true, I felt kind of bad about it.

"I'll take care of that." She unlatched the bathroom door and started to head out, but before she opened the main door she laid another kiss on me, better than any she'd given me before. I wanted her. We walked out to the table where Stormy, Geoffrey, Don, and Sam sat. They were engrossed in some conversation, but when we walked up, all eyes were on me. I assumed that Sam had told everyone what had happened in the bathroom. I was going to be very pissed off if this was the case, but there wasn't enough time to find out.

Alyssia told Stormy that I was moving in with her, and Stormy asked no questions. I guess everyone was kind of intimidated by Alyssia. She grabbed my hand and led me out of the restaurant into the parking lot.

"Let's go pick up your things from Stormy's place and get back to my house. I'm dying to be alone with you," she said as she dragged me to her car.

We got in, and she sped out of the parking lot. She had her hand on my thigh, rubbing it up and down. I was getting extremely turned on, but I didn't know what to do, so I started thinking about what I would do if Alyssia were a guy. I would probably be giving her a blowjob by now, I thought. Obviously, that was not possible. I slid closer to her and rested my hand above her knee. I started kissing her neck as she concentrated on the road. I blew into her ear, then bit her earlobe. She was loving it, and her hips started to rise and fall as she drove onward. My hand was moving up and down her thigh now, and I wanted to get inside her. My fingers slowly crawled into her panties, and I touched her there. She was moaning like crazy, begging me to put my fingers inside her. I looked at her face, which was perspiring slightly, and I was so happy that I could make her sweat. She *was* a goddess. I told myself I had some of the same power she had as she drove, at least the power to make her moan.

We pulled up at Stormy's trailer.

"We'll be back at your house soon," I said, trying to get some control.

"I can't wait."

"Neither can I."

Reluctantly, we got out of the car and walked up the gravel driveway to Stormy's house. Inside, Alyssia walked right past the two little ones watching television without so much as a "Hello." But she could do that, walk undauntedly through a room. I loved her. I really loved her. I had never met anyone, male or female, who made me want to do things for them. I started to gather my belongings, and Alyssia helped me carry my mountain pack and some books. I felt so grateful. Within two minutes we were back in the car heading to her house. I was both nervous and excited at the thought of sleeping with her, but I was also afraid that I wouldn't know how to please her. I had never done anything with a girl before.

"What's on your mind?" she asked, sensing something from my quiet.

"Just eager to get to your place," I said.

"Well, I'm eager to have you. I mean, *really* have you."

"Yeah, me too."

"Really?" she asked, as if she didn't believe me.

"Yeah."

"Do you want me?"

"Yes," I said.

"What are you going to do with me?"

"I'll figure it out." I smiled broadly at her.

This flirty banter continued, along with some aggressive touching and petting, as we drove toward Alyssia's. I was so distracted by her presence, I was surprised when I saw that we were in a middle-class neighborhood. Alyssia pulled her car into the driveway of a quaint green house.

"Is this it?" I asked.

"This is it."

I grabbed my things from the backseat, and Alyssia grabbed some stuff as well. We headed up to the door, which was unlocked.

I followed her down a long hallway that ended with doors to the right and left. She opened the door on the left and dropped my belongings on the floor.

"This is my room."

"I like it." I took a few minutes to take it all in. It was a large room with a huge bed in the center. There were two dressers and a desk. Artwork covered the walls—lots of framed black-and-white photos of nude women. I stopped as I walked past one of the pictures, noticing it was Alyssia. In the photo she was standing with her arms crossed over her stomach, looking defiant and naughty. The picture showed her naked body from her head to mid-thigh. It turned me on so much, I felt my thighs tremble and a warmness gush out of me. I thought she had great taste, and a lot of guts to put a picture of herself like that on her wall.

"Why don't you put your personal stuff in the bathroom," she said, and pointed to a door that was painted hunter green. I opened it and discovered the coolest bathroom I'd ever seen. There was a large Jacuzzi that could have comfortably fit four. Tall glass doors encircled it.

Everything was black marble and chrome. I put my stuff under the sink in one of the cabinets, then placed my toothbrush on the little shelf under the mirror. I walked out of the bathroom and sat on the floor of Alyssia's bedroom. She'd already arranged my clothes in one of the dressers.

"What now?" she asked.

"Huh?"

"What do you want to do now?"

I could read the desire all over her face, but I needed to shower. I felt so grimy. "I would really like to get cleaned up."

"A bath or a shower?" she asked.

"I don't care, I just need to wash."

"Why don't you take a bath then? The tub's awesome."

"Anything I need to know?" I asked, not really sure how to work such a high-tech bathtub.

"Run the water, turn on the jet sprays. It's pretty simple stuff."

I walked into the bathroom and followed her directions. I quietly undressed, wondering why she hadn't offered to join me. Maybe she was just teasing me.

I eased myself into the bathwater and turned on the jets, relishing the pressure hitting my back. The tension of the afternoon's extravaganza evaporated. I was feeling so good, and the water was so hot it made me woozy. I kept thinking about how entirely strange all of this was; I mean, I never expected to have these kinds of feelings. I wondered if I was normal, if other women felt this way. None of the girls I knew in high school fooled around with other girls.

The door creaked open and Alyssia walked in nonchalantly. She was completely naked, her body utterly gorgeous. I gazed at her, drinking it all in: her stomach; her smooth hipbones jutting out; her breasts, full and round with slightly upturned rosy nipples; her legs, long and muscular. Everything about her was incredible.

After she cleaned me, she dried me off and walked me into her room. She guided me to her bed where it started all over again. She fervently attacked me as if it were the first time we had touched. I couldn't believe how many times I'd orgasmed in one day; I didn't ever think it possible.

I was totally crazy about her. I tasted every inch of her body, and she did the same to me. I seriously felt more strongly for her than I had for any man. We fell asleep naked, intertwined.

CHAPTER 11

Alyssia hollered that whoever it was could come in. I was shocked: We were both lying completely naked, and she was inviting someone into the room.

The door opened and Geoffrey walked in with a grin. "Hello ladies," he boomed.

Alyssia sat up, her breasts peeking out from the sheets, but she made no effort to conceal them. "Hi, Geoff, how are you?" she asked, completely at ease.

"Fine."

"Come over here and get in." She patted the spot between us. What was she thinking?

Geoff took off his shirt and climbed in. He kissed Alyssia on the lips. I watched their tongues combat. The phone rang, and they disengaged so that Alyssia could answer.

She mumbled lots of "yeahs" and "all rights" to the person on the other end, then hung up and smiled coyly. "Guess where we are going today?"

Geoff looked playfully at her. "Where, darling?"

"The zoo!" She smiled wide-eyed like a child.

"Sounds great. You in, Orleigh?" Geoff asked.

"I don't have anything else to do," I said, okay with the idea, although not sharing their enthusiasm.

"Good, then we should take a shower and get ready," Alyssia said.

Geoff smiled at Alyssia, while I sat there clueless. "Who should shower?" I asked, thinking that she was trying to get rid of Geoff.

"Who do you think? Let's go, guys." She climbed out of the bed.

We followed her as if she were a queen, as if whatever she said went, no questions asked.

Alyssia and I were already naked when Geoff began taking off his pants, and Alyssia turned on the shower. I looked at Geoff and saw that he already had a hard-on. Alyssia got in and waved for us to follow. Geoff and I piled in, then the seducing, kissing, and groping began. It was the hottest shower I'd ever taken. Hands and fingers were all over my body. Alyssia washed my hair as Geoff washed hers. I was tempted to head back to the bed, but Alyssia refused to get out until Geoff came, so we both gave him some extra attention. We got out, dried off, then went into her room to dress. I put on some jeans and a T-shirt over my underwear, but Alyssia gave me a dirty look.

"What's wrong?" I asked.

"I just wish you gave me better access; you know, jeans have to be unbuttoned and unzipped. That's too damn annoying." She licked her lips.

"What do you want me to wear?" I asked, even though I felt slightly uncomfortable with the idea of someone else dressing me.

"Can I pick something out?" she asked.

I looked at Geoff standing naked next to her, gawking at me.

"Yes," I said, surrendering against my better judgment.

She pulled out some navy blue drawstring pants and a white T-shirt with a v-neck. "I insist, no bra or underwear."

"Really, why?" I was not used to dressing so freely.

"Nothing but you inside my clothes, no added extras for me to worry about," she said, handing me the clothes.

We were finishing dressing when the doorbell rang.

"That's Rocky, the guy we're going to the zoo with," Alyssia said with an impish smile, motioning for us to follow her to the kitchen.

Geoff and Alyssia walked down the hallway, and I followed behind. I saw Geoff give Alyssia an annoyed look.

"Don't you mean he's one of your fuck-buddies?" Geoff asked, with obvious disdain in his voice, as we entered the kitchen.

"Whatever you want to call him: fuck-buddy, neighbor, I certainly don't care," Alyssia said defensively.

They passed angry comments back and forth, then stared each other down. I didn't like the tension in the kitchen and was relieved when Alyssia went to open the front door. Watching her walk away, I began to wonder how many *fuck-buddies* Alyssia truly had. She returned with a guy I assumed was Rocky and a girl.

"Hi, Lyssie, this is Abbie, my girlfriend," Rocky said, putting his arm around the plain-looking girl standing next to him.

"Hi, Abbie, these are my friends Orleigh and Geoffrey," Alyssia said, as she turned her eyes on us. Something was wrong, but I wasn't sure what. If Alyssia was upset about this Abbie girl, she had no reason to be, and Rocky looked like a huge jock, a fucking wrestler. He appeared to have been thrown against the mats too hard, too many times. He hadn't stopped smiling a slack-jawed jock smile since he'd walked in the door.

"Hi, guys," Abbie said with a toothy grin. She had the spirit of a sorority girl and the body of a plus-size model.

Geoff and I both made our introductions as we walked out to Rocky's bright red Jeep. Alyssia, Geoff, and I got in the backseat, then Rocky started the engine.

From the backseat, Alyssia made small talk with Rocky, and I noticed that Geoff's hand was inside her pants. She placed her hand on my upper thigh and began tracing it up and down. We were in public now, but that didn't stop her. Her hand had moved to the inside of the drawstring pants. Then her fingers were slowly gliding in and out of me. She covered my mouth with hers, before I could moan out loud. It was hotter than a freshly tarred roof in that car, and the black interior wasn't helping. I saw Abbie watching us in the reflection of the vanity mirror. She quickly looked away when our eyes met.

This went on the whole time we drove to the Brookfield zoo. Hands and mouths all over the place. Rocky and Abbie watched everything from their mirrors. Finally, we pulled into the parking lot. Everyone piled out and stretched, then we proceeded to the entrance.

We got a map of the zoo to plan our day's activities. The first order of business was the monkey house, then the bears, then the dolphin show. After we finished seeing all of these, time permitting, we would venture on to other points of interest. I felt like a little girl—I actually couldn't wait to see the monkeys. We hurried along through crowds of people to wait in the monkey-house line which was incredibly long. It looked like it would take quite a while.

Alyssia pulled me over to the railing surrounding one of the baboon pits. She pulled my body close to hers and pressed her lips to mine. This caused raised eyebrows. People began to whisper and point. I felt semi-uncomfortable, but also turned on by Alyssia's public display of affection. We made out, then joined the line again, moving a few feet forward, and resumed kissing. When we finally got into the monkey house, Alyssia was holding my hand as if we were a couple.

After looking at big apes, their cute babies, and exotic little monkeys, we were back outside. At the baboon pit, I placed my cigarettes on the ledge and looked down. Alyssia came up behind me and grabbed my chest, gently squeezing my nipples. I turned to face her, and her tongue instantly slid into my mouth. I backed up against the wall and slowly slid my ass on top of it. I circled my legs around Alyssia's waist and made out with her until Rocky interrupted us.

"Hey, your cigarettes dropped down there," Rocky said, leaning over the edge and looking into the pit.

"What?" I asked in a daze.

"Down there," he said, and pointed.

I looked down and saw the baboons fighting over my smokes. They were all grabbing at the pack and eating the cigarettes. It was both funny and upsetting—I was worried that they might get sick or freak out from eating the tobacco. Alyssia also looked concerned, and she grabbed me by the hand.

"We have to find a zookeeper," she said, pulling me along with her.

"Don't you think we'll get in trouble?"

"It was an accident."

"Yeah, but it's also cigarettes. How good can that be for them?"

"That's why we're looking for someone, Orleigh." She dragged me around long enough to find someone wearing a zoo uniform.

"Excuse me, sir, there's a bit of a problem," Alyssia said breezily.

"What, miss?" asked the zookeeper.

"Well, she dropped her cigarettes into the baboon pit." She looked directly at me.

Why did she have to do that? Whose side was she on?

"What?" he asked, slightly agitated.

"Well, it was an accident. Now the baboons are trying to eat them," she snapped.

The zookeeper gave us an extremely perturbed look, then ran to the baboon pit. We followed him back to where Geoff, Rocky, and Abbie were waiting.

Rocky was laughing as we approached. "What happened?" he asked.

"We just told the zoo guy," Alyssia said.

"So he didn't freak out on you two?" Rocky asked, concerned.

"Where is he anyway?" She craned her neck to look around.

We looked down into the pit and saw that the cigarette pack was no longer there. But a few of the baboons were still clutching cigarettes in their hands, smelling them, eating them. We decided as a group that it would be best to clear the vicinity, move on to the bears, when the zookeeper we had reported the incident to reappeared.

"I'm sorry, kids, but you all are going to have to leave the zoo." He stood, glaring at us, holding a long pole with a hook attached to one end. For a split second, I thought we were all in some slasher movie, and he was going to mutilate us with the hook.

Rocky looked at the guy incredulously. "Why, what's the problem?"

"It's the whole cigarette incident. That was extremely dangerous. We don't like things like that happening around here. Like I said, you'll have to leave."

"We paid money to park here and to see the animals. I don't think it's fair that we have to go. It was just an accident. Nobody meant the baboons any harm," Rocky said in our defense.

The zookeeper looked at Rocky and scowled. "Look, if the two lesbians didn't feel the need to make out on the edge of the baboon den, then this whole incident would never have happened. I tried to be nice to you all, but that didn't work. Now if you queers don't get out of here, I'll call the police."

Rocky flipped the guy off, Alyssia grabbed me and started kissing me fervently, then we all headed to the exit. I looked back while holding Alyssia's hand and saw that the guy and two others were following us, making sure we made our way out. We were not going to see the dolphin show. I felt a little sullen, even though we were all laughing hysterically on our way out of the zoo.

Alyssia and I joined Sam and Geoff in a booth and ordered coffees from Kurt. Alyssia held my hand under the table, and every once in a while leaned over to give me a kiss. Sam was smiling as well as staring at me, and eventually began giving me a lecture on the benefits of being a vampire.

"Look, Orleigh, it's not really a blood thing," he sermonized. "Vampires don't need the blood anymore—that was old-school vampires and movie garbage. Nowadays, it's all about the bite. It's not necessary to actually puncture the skin. What's important is the sexual anxiety of the bite. You know what I'm talking about? The man knows he's going to bite the woman, and he's overly anxious about the timing and the meaning of the bite—*that* makes it sexual. Plus, when the woman's actually bit, she's riveted by the feeling; its intensity and energy grab hold of her. It's not like it used to be, Orleigh, that's what I'm trying to explain to you; it's so much more than before."

"That just isn't something I've always dreamed about, Sam; granted, I can understand why some S & M chick would love being bitten, but it's not for me." I smiled a little.

"Have you ever been bitten?" he asked seriously.

"Just the one time you tried," I told him, not wanting to remember.

"But you didn't give it much of a chance; you just winced and left me hanging."

"I didn't like it!" I snapped. I wanted to drop this conversation.

But he continued: "Well, I want you to feel it, really feel it, my way."

"Maybe someday, Sam, just not now," I said, in a last attempt to shut him up.

"I told you before, the timing is everything."

Don, the skittish guy, walked into the Morning After and sat down at our booth. He didn't look very good—his skin was pasty and pale and his whole body shook.

"Do you feel it?" he asked our table, eyes wide with horror. He took the time to look at each one of us, but no one answered him. We stared blankly back.

"What, Don, what's to feel?" I asked.

"The electricity," he replied anxiously.

I sensed that he was waiting for something to happen. Probably waiting for aliens, I thought, and almost laughed out loud. "I don't know what you're talking about, Don," I said.

He held his hand out to me. "Touch my hand and tell me if you feel the electricity."

I grabbed onto his hand but didn't feel anything out of the ordinary. "No, I don't feel it, Don." I felt bad that I didn't.

"It's there, damn it! I'm full of this blue and green electricity. I feel sparks coming off the ends of my fingers. I know I shocked you just then, I felt it," he said, holding up his hands and waving them about.

He held a hand out to Alyssia, and she grabbed hold, then quickly pulled away as if it had genuinely hurt her. The others did the same when he offered his hand to them. They were either humoring him or they were all screwed up. They seemed in another world altogether. And things were not so normal in this world.

In keeping with this other world, they informed me that they all wanted to brush their teeth with a communal toothbrush, a small Jetsons toothbrush that Don carried in his pocket. Alyssia giggled as she helped me out of my seat. She kept saying that it was an initiation of some kind. So we all scurried into the bathroom and began to slop Muppet Baby toothpaste on the tiny toothbrush.

We took turns brushing each other's teeth then brushing our own, amidst lots of groping and touching. I didn't care anymore who touched me; we were all together in a weird kind of way. I mean, I loved them: Alyssia, Geoff, Sam. And I didn't even mind Don so much. I figured if Alyssia liked him, then he couldn't be that bad. There was an energy between us—not electricity, but energy.

Maybe we were all just a bunch of misunderstood freaks who had finally found others like ourselves.

Whatever it was, I felt at home with them. After brushing our teeth, we left the bathroom and returned to our table. Kurt came over and announced that there was a call for me.

"What? Who would call me here?"

"It's a guy," he said.

Sam raised his eyebrows. "Really?"

I felt a little edgy when I got up to go to the phone, which was in the kitchen. Everyone at the table was giving me the dirtiest looks. I felt like I was betraying them.

Kurt handed me the telephone, and I leaned against the kitchen wall.

"Hello," I whispered into the receiver.

"Hi, Orleigh," Jason replied.

Actually, I was a little pleased to hear his voice. "Hi, Jason, what's going on?" I asked, hearing almost too much excitement in my voice.

"I'm coming to see you in a little while."

"Tonight?"

"Yeah, my cousin Jeremy's in town, and I'd like you to meet each other."

"Oh, yeah?"

"I think you'd like him."

I hesitated a moment then asked, "Are you sure?"

"Yeah, I'm sure. Is that all right?"

"Yeah, there's a party later tonight at Geoff's, an after-hours thing," I said, then explained how Geoff lived above the Morning After. I gave Jason all the pertinent info.

"That sounds cool," he said. "Do you think the three of us can go out for dinner first?"

"I'll have to check," I said, whispering. Somehow I knew that they wouldn't like the idea of Jason being with me at all.

"Check? Check on what?"

"On what they're doing."

"Who's *they?*"

"Alyssia, Geoff, and Sam, you know," I said, but I knew he *really* didn't.

"Why do they matter?" he asked. "You're just staying at their place. Aren't you? That's what I heard from Stormy."

For a moment I questioned myself. Why did they really matter? I hadn't made plans with them. I was my own person, wasn't I? I could do what I wanted. "I'd like to check, you know, but don't worry about it, you can meet me here."

"At the Morning After?"

"Yes."

"Then dinner?" he persisted.

"Probably."

"You okay?"

"Yes," I lied. I didn't know if I was all right or not. I felt both a great desire to be with Alyssia and company, but also to be by myself. I had never functioned well in groups. In high school I'd never been cliquish, more of a loner. I was much better one on one.

"You sure?"

"Definitely," I said, trying to sound natural but failing.

"See you soon."

I hung up and walked back to the table. Everybody's eyes were on me. I sat down next to Alyssia, and she scooted away as if I had a disease or something. Sam stared at me, his forehead knotted.

"It looks like the circle has been broken," he finally said.

"What are you talking about?" I asked, somewhat annoyed.

"Who was on the phone?" Sam began to twist the straw he had been drinking from. He seemed indifferent, but I felt like I'd been caught doing something wrong by my father.

"Jason," I said, struggling a little to get his name out.

"Why?"

"He's coming here for dinner and maybe to go to the party." It came out like a question, and I silently kicked myself for cowering under his gaze.

"Who invited him?"

"Sam, he's my boyfriend," I pleaded.

Sam flung the straw into the air and looked at me skeptically. "Does he know what you're all about, Orleigh?"

I looked down at the table. "No," I said.

Alyssia decided to jump in and take control of the conversation. "Hey, cool it, Sam. She can have dinner with her boyfriend. It's not such a big deal."

"I think it is. Why do you even want to have dinner with him?" He still sounded chastising and paternal.

"Because he wants me to meet his cousin. Plus, I think I should try to end the relationship. Things have really changed, and I don't think we're right for each other anymore. Only it's become more obvious to me now." I felt defensive. I wanted Sam to leave me alone so I could figure shit out for myself. Maybe he was right, but I didn't like anyone telling me what I could or couldn't do. That was why I'd left my mother's house.

"See, Sam, she has her priorities in order. She needs to straighten her life out so that she can move forward," Alyssia said flippantly, but when she looked at me, her eyes were stern and unforgiving.

"I don't know why you have to see that guy," Sam said, and I caught a hint of dejection in his tone. He grabbed the straw again and began playing with it, but Alyssia put her hand over his fingers, and he stopped twirling it.

"That *guy* is currently my guy, and he deserves an explanation," I said forcefully. I was tired of Sam's bitching. It was no longer intimidating me.

"I don't think he's your guy," Sam said, not letting it go.

"Then who is?" I asked.

"Me." He looked coldly into my eyes.

My heart felt as if it had dropped into my stomach. I mean, I did like Sam, but I thought he was with Alyssia, and I thought I was with Alyssia too. I didn't know what to say. I didn't know who was with whom and I was beginning to feel confused and frustrated. "I didn't know we were supposed to be together. I thought you were with Alyssia," I said, as I nonchalantly darted my eyes around the room.

"I am, and you. Don't you see? Our group has no boundaries. You're mine. Not Jason's girlfriend, mine," Sam said, then slammed his hand down. The coffee mugs rattled on their saucers. "I don't want you seeing him any-more. End it all tonight and never talk about him again."

"Sam, you're just jealous because Orleigh has someone out of the group," Alyssia piped in.

"Maybe I am." I could see how tense he was.

"Well, relax, she'll take care of it." She squeezed his fingers and shot me a harsh look. I didn't know what the fuck she was angry about; this was my life, not theirs.

"I guess I have no choice but to relax and wait," he said, pulling his hand away.

They argued on about what I should and shouldn't do. It was starting to get on my nerves. Even though I had felt remarkably close to these people, we'd only recently met. Things were moving way too quickly. I was either going to run with them or run away from them. I wasn't sure. Alyssia and Sam were acting like my parents, for fuck's sake. Don looked over at me and smiled kindly as if he could read my thoughts.

"Orleigh, let's go for a walk," he whispered.

"Where do you want to go, Don?" I asked, a little startled.

"Just out, somewhere." He placed his hand on my shoulder and stood, waiting for me to join him. "Jason won't be here for at least a half an hour, right?"

"Right."

It didn't seem like Alyssia and Sam noticed Don and me leaving because they were so entrenched in their argument, but maybe it was because I was with one of their clan. Or maybe they just wanted to be alone. I thought it was cool of Don to have picked up on how tense I was. I was happy to be outside walking with him, even though I didn't get his electricity thing.

"How are you?" he asked quietly, his voice wispy and full of compassion. It occurred to me that he might be gay.

"I'm all right, I felt like I was getting the third degree."

"I could tell."

"Good call, thanks," I said, relaxing a little.

"I want to take you somewhere."

"Where?"

"To a special place." He smiled.

"Why?"

"Because you're not like them."

"What do you mean?"

"You're not like them. This fucked-up unit shit, you know. Like the tooth-brushing thing. I can tell you're not like that. You're better."

"I don't know about that," I said.

"I do."

I was afraid that he was trying to hit on me. He was tall and gangly, so jittery, and totally unkempt. He reminded me of a wooden puppet as he jangled along.

All I wanted was to get my life straightened out. Even though I'd told my mother I didn't want to go to college, deep down inside I kind of wanted to. I'd always thought of myself as a painter, but I wanted to learn more about art beyond having been good at painting and drawing in high school.

I felt alone, even though I was surrounded by these new friends. I didn't know who I was anymore.

"Here we are," Don said. He spread his arms out wide.

We were standing in the middle of a beautiful garden, bunches of multi-colored impatiens all around us. I stared at the two enormous weeping willows whose branches swept over hedges, thinking how I wanted to love Alyssia, but that it was getting all fucking twisted. It was all about control. Not that Alyssia didn't affect me, because she did, more than anyone ever had. But as far as "real" love was concerned, I didn't think I knew what that was. In order for me to ever love someone, I would first have to love myself, and I couldn't see that happening for a long time.

"You look really down," Don said.

"I know, I was just thinking," I replied quietly.

"What about?"

"How, well, how strange everything is," I said, not really sure how to explain my onslaught of emotions.

"Do you want to go back?"

"I probably should." I shrugged my shoulders and reluctantly began to leave.

"Yeah, Jason should be there soon."

"I know," I said, and I couldn't identify my own tone of voice.

"Do you love him?" he asked.

I took a moment before I could answer. The sky was nearly black, with long hazy white streaks where the moon's glow reflected off the clouds.

"I love the idea of him," I replied. "Real love hasn't happened to me. I fall hard, but it's seldom mutual. With Jason, he fell hard, and I took advantage of him." I felt sorry for myself.

"I'm sorry."

"You're really sweet, Don, even if I don't get your electricity thing."

"No one does, they all just pretend. I feel electric after my dad beats me. Does that make any sense? After he pounds on me, I feel sparks, shocks, all sorts of crazy shit."

I couldn't answer him. I didn't know anything about that, and suddenly I felt tremendous empathy for Don. We continued walking down the street, past an X-rated bookstore, where you could see all sorts of slimy guys hanging out inside through the display windows. They stood passively thumbing through porno mags. We turned down an alley between the bookstore and an old diner, and passed a green dumpster. The smell of garbage permeated the air.

Jason and an extremely handsome guy were sitting alone at a table. As I approached, I noted that Sam was sitting across the room from them. He was reading a *GQ* magazine, which he held upright, somewhat masking his face.

"Hey, baby," Jason said with his familiar smile, rising to greet me.

"Hello."

"How are you?"

"I'm all right," I said, trying to hide my current misery.

"Let me give you a hug and a kiss." He reached out and wrapped his long arms around me. It was actually a great hug. He kissed me on the cheek, which felt equally as good. Then he pulled away.

"Give me more," I said, surprising myself.

"You want another hug?"

"Yeah."

He reached around me again and pulled me close, and it was a great feeling. I knew it was only because I'd been feeling crappy (poor Jason!). But I felt happy. He introduced me to his cousin Jeremy, who was something else.

He had boyish good looks: rugged yet sweet. His blondish-brown hair was shoulder-length. He had big brown eyes and lips that made you want to kiss. After our embraces, Jason and I decided that the three of us should go to Pizza Hut. Alyssia and her crew looked very dissatisfied when I stopped by the table to say my farewells. Looking directly into Sam's distrustful eyes, I let him have it.

"I'm going out to dinner," I said harshly. "I'll be back in a while. We'll be back for the party."

"Have fun," he said, glaring back at me.

"I will. You have fun too," I said with a smile, not really caring. Fuck him, I thought.

"Bye, darling," Alyssia drawled charmingly, then blew me a little kiss. I looked at her for a moment. She was so wrapped up in this group thing. I wanted her, but I definitely wanted something more exclusive. Why did she have to devote herself to that many people? What was wrong with just the two of us? It didn't matter. I still had Jason, I deceitfully tried to convince myself. That's how it went—I always had someone to fall back on even if I wasn't in love with that person. But I was getting tired of my stupid little games. Alyssia and I stared each other down. For a moment I felt like the stronger one. She felt far away from me.

She quickly looked down, and I could see her vulnerability. I turned my back to her to join Jason and Jeremy.

"Those people were really weird, Orleigh," Jeremy said. I liked his voice.

"I know, but they are good people," I said.

"Yeah, I thought California had some strange ones, but those guys seemed *really* strange. That girl is something else, you know?"

"I know."

"She's really pretty, but I think she likes girls."

"Both," I told him.

"You mean guys and girls?"

"Yeah, AC/DC," Jason said and laughed.

"I don't know anyone like that," he said, looking at me and ignoring Jason.

"Now you do," I said, laughing to myself at my own little private joke. Jeremy seemed mesmerized by the way of life in DeKalb. Shit, we lived in the middle of fucking cornfields, we had to find ways to entertain ourselves.

"Look, Jeremy, those kinds of girls are freaks," Jason said. "Probably disease-ridden and what not. It would be better to stay away from someone like her." If only Jason knew.

"Actually, Jason," I said, "she's very nice, and she's very careful about who she sleeps with. It isn't that strange."

"I think it's strange." He looked at me askew as if he suspected me of something.

"I agree with Orleigh. I think it's pretty cool that she's that secure with her sexuality and daring enough to be different," Jeremy said.

"Whatever!"

Jeremy and I looked at each other and smiled.

We couldn't agree on toppings. Of course, I wanted cheese only, which predictably set off an argument about the finer points of meat. Jeremy helped alleviate the cheese-only problem by sharing with me. He was smiling bigger and brighter. All the normal and preppie guys I had dated in high school came back to mind as I stared at Jeremy. At least those kinds of guys were going to go somewhere. Sam, Don, and Geoff probably wouldn't. I could see Sam eventually working on a construction site, a barefoot, pregnant wife at home; Geoff I imagined employed at a "hip" record store for his remaining days; and I clearly foresaw Don's fatal end—institutionalized for drugs, alcohol, or some psychiatric disorder. On the other hand, I envisioned Jeremy as a stockbroker or lawyer or something like that.

As we walked back to the Morning After, we could already hear the laughter and screams of people and music blaring from blocks away. Jeremy was making lots of small talk about where he was going to school and what he wanted to major in. He was interesting, beyond the fact that he was completely sexy. He had been telling me how he had recently won an award for a screenplay he'd written at school. I was impressed. I couldn't imagine writing anything. I kept a diary every now and then, but I never kept it up. I did love to read though. Well, maybe Jeremy was bragging, but I was taken. We walked up the stairs to Sam and Geoff's place, where we were greeted at the door with green, blue, and red shots of liquor. Jason made his way across the apartment to some people he knew from high school, and Jeremy and I picked up bullshitting again.

"So, how much do you like my cousin?" he asked.

"We're not really together anymore, it's more like we're friends," I said, thinking that was probably the easiest way to describe my relationship with Jason, although I wasn't sure Jason would have agreed.

"You're not in love with him?"

"No, I'm not."

"Is he in love with you?"

"I think he's in love with the concept of me."

Jeremy looked confused. "What's that supposed to mean?"

"The idea of loving someone is much better than actually loving," I said, having made this realization about myself earlier.

"What?"

"Because that's just the way things are for me. I'm not right," I said, smiling shyly.

"Right? How do you mean?"

"In every way, I'm just freaky. Plus, I never know what I want. I drift, not really thinking about who I am or what I stand for. I'm all fucked up." The fact that Jeremy was almost a stranger made me feel compelled to confide. I needed to talk to someone who could be neutral. Let things out.

"Are we talking about relationships here?" he asked, genuinely curious it seemed.

"My life in general, in every aspect."

"Do you want to take a walk? Talk some more where it's quieter?"

"Where?"

"Anywhere."

We left the party and headed out to the neighborhood streets surrounding the campus of Northern Illinois University. It was a warm night, not too hot. I looked up at the indigo-blue sky and saw that the moon was full. It was wide and yellow. Jeremy reached for my hand. I let him hold it as we walked down the shadowy streets. He was quieter now; he knew he didn't have to try anymore. There was no reason to talk. He was like most guys (I hadn't fooled myself)—they talked the talk until they figured you wanted them bad enough. Then the only natural thing to do was fuck and later either pretend they didn't know you, or become madly infatuated with you. Usually with a guy like

Jeremy, I would have waited. I wouldn't have even thought about doing him, but I knew he was leaving soon. Plus I wanted him. It was more about a conquest than anything else. I needed to regain some control in my life. Alyssia and her swarm of devoted disciples had all the control. Under normal circumstances, I would have played the game with Jeremy, because I would have wanted him to call me. I could be coy and elusive when I wanted to be. But I didn't want anything from this guy other than his body, so what did it matter? That was how I felt when we walked into a two-story house that was under construction.

The house was quiet and filled with sawdust. It looked like it was going to be a *lovely* home for some perfect suburban family. Jeremy pushed me against a bare wall and began to kiss me. I was enjoying his mouth on mine, his hands all over my body. Everything moved with an intense speed. His hands were inside my skirt, then inside me. We went from standing to lying on the dusty floor within seconds. I felt drunk, stoned, and wired all at the same time. I opened my eyes to see his pants undone. He was touching himself. I found this extremely sexy and again became lost in the moment and closed my eyes—I felt incredibly naughty, the way I'd felt in the bathroom with Alyssia. That flashed in my mind. Then Jeremy was inside me, his moves smooth and easy. His hair fell around my shoulders and breasts as he kissed the parts of my skin that were exposed. He gave one quick, hard thrust that sent me into orgasm, and then apparently followed my lead.

After the heat of the encounter dissipated—as it does—he leaned down to kiss me. It was a soft kiss, minus the fervor of before. Beads of sweat dripped off strands of his hair onto my skin, cold sweat. I got up and dusted off my backside, which was covered with little wood particles. It was liberating to know that I was still attractive to the normal male, that not only freaks wanted me. We walked silently back to the party. We both knew that we would probably never see each other again, but I don't think either of us cared.

He looked at me before we headed up to the rooftop. With a slanted smile, he asked, "How do I look?"

"Like you just had sex."

"Really?" he asked. I'm sure Jason had told him how crazy he was about me, so he certainly didn't want him to find out.

"You look fine, don't worry about it," I said.

"Thanks."

"One more kiss before we part?" he asked, then like a modern-day Romeo he grabbed me tightly. At first I didn't resist, but I started panicking that someone might see us from the stairs—like Jason. I pulled away. He didn't say anything, so I headed up the stairs to the roof. The party was in full swing. Jason was playing bongo drums with some guys, and he didn't appear to have noticed that we were gone. Jeremy went over to hang out with him, and I found Alyssia, Geoff, Sam, and Don. It was obvious by Sam's expression that he was happy to have me back at his side. He handed me a drink, and I took a sip.

"Hi, love, back with the family?" he asked warmly.

"I guess," I replied. "What's this stuff?" I held up the drink and moved my tongue around in my mouth, trying to identify the taste.

"Vodka and grenadine; it's good. Drink up!" He smiled wryly. "Did you have fun out on your little walk with Prince Charming?" he asked, and I realized that his smile had been more menacing than friendly.

"Yeah," I said.

"Was he good?"

"What are you talking about?"

"You know."

I felt very uncomfortable and agitated. Who the fuck did this guy think he was? The way he was looking at me was scary. "No, I don't know what you're talking about."

"I followed you, and I saw the whole thing—it was beautiful." He narrowed his eyes.

"Fuck you, Sam," I spat, and turned my back to him.

"No, honey, I'm not the one you fucked," he said.

All of a sudden, I felt seriously ill. I couldn't get away from these people. They were way too consumed by my every move. It drove me crazy that he had followed me, though I wasn't surprised. Thankfully, Jason came over and saved me from murdering Sam.

"Hey, baby, I'm leaving."

"Let me walk you and your cousin down to the van," I said, encircling his waist with my arm.

"All right then."

The three of us headed down the stairs, and I considered leaving before things got worse. The only problem was that I couldn't quite leave Alyssia, she *had* gotten to me, as much as I was loathe to admit this.

As we stood by Jason's van, I knew that I wasn't going to go with him. I held onto him, clutching him as if he were the last piece of my sanity. I'd been unfair to him in every possible way. I'd been a terrible girlfriend, if I could even be called that. I needed him as a friend, but I knew that if he ever found out how shitty I'd been to him he would want nothing to do with me. I said my good-byes quickly, showing zero emotion toward Jeremy. Then they got into the van and left. The second Jason pulled away, I missed him, and I felt it was the last time I'd see him.

CHAPTER 12

I proceeded to get completely wasted. I didn't care what the end result would be; I wanted the freedom, the release. I stood on the roof, intoxicated and dizzy, thinking about what would happen if I jumped. I pictured my body heaving into the darkness, tumbling down, then hitting the pavement with a loud and final thump. But then, for a moment, my drunken haze cleared, and I realized that this wouldn't kill me, just maim me beyond recognition. I remembered hearing stories about drunks who'd survived car crashes because they were drunk and their bodies were so relaxed. Since being maimed was not quite the desired effect, I backed away from the ledge, then sought Alyssia.

Sam had apparently left for work, and it looked like Alyssia was on her way to visit him. She was fucked up, but not quite to the same degree I was.

"Look, Orleigh, we have to go see Sam. You really hurt him. As an *us* we can't really have that kind of tension. It's just not good for the whole of *us*," she said, her body wavering before me.

"What are you talking about?" This *us* shit didn't make any sense.

"Just that you need to make peace with Sam." She over-enunciated her words, placing her hands on her hips as if she were reprimanding a child.

"Who?" I asked.

"Sam. You've made him really upset, don't you get it?"

"No," I said, and her beautiful face started becoming mean-looking, ugly.

"You have to make things okay again or there'll be hell to pay."

"What kind of hell?" I laughed, thinking that I was already in some kind of hell.

"We'll have to let you go," she sputtered.

"Go where?" I asked, laughing harder.

"That's up to you. Do you want to make it better or not?"

"I don't even understand what I did." I felt dizzy. Her words dripped out of her mouth. I could see each word fall, each a different color and shape. I could see the words spelled out in different colors of the rainbow, some with big bubble letters and others as if they'd been typed out. My head was on fire and my eyes and ears burned.

"You went outside the group to find pleasure. How do you think that makes us feel? We're here to please you, and you're dissatisfied with us— you had to find other people. That's not the way we like things to go. Do you get it now?"

I was no longer thinking clearly. But somehow I managed to conclude that the only right thing to do was to make it up to Sam, even though I felt indifferent.

"Are you ready to go see him?" Alyssia snapped.

"Where?"

"At work."

"Now?" I wanted to sit down for a few minutes, get my bearings.

"Don't you think you should?" she asked, and a wave of guilt washed over me.

"Yes, I better," I said.

"That's our girl." She smiled and helped me stand upright. We were both swaying a bit.

Colored lights smashed against the windshield like tiny glow bugs splattering to their deaths. It was driving me crazy. My eyes were so fucked up. The light smeared out across the glass, and then I couldn't see where we were going anymore. I felt as if I were tripping balls, but I hadn't taken anything. I didn't usually feel this way when I was drunk. Alyssia's car slid and swerved like a slithering snake. The colors blinded me. Nothing was right inside my head.

By the time we pulled into Sam's work, I felt terribly nauseous. I didn't want to get out of the car. I knew it would be some kind of shock to my system to feel the pavement under my feet. I hurt; god, I ached. Bile made its way up my throat. I rolled down the window and stuck out my head, but I couldn't puke. Alyssia pulled me out of the car and onto the blacktop. The gas station was all bright lights and shiny metal. I was blinded.

"Let's go inside." She grabbed my hand and started to lead me to the double glass doors. My head spun the whole time she yanked me along. Once we got inside, I vaguely saw Sam sitting behind the counter, having a smoke. I felt like I was dying. I wanted to go home—*wherever that was.*

"Hey, beautiful," someone said, and it sounded like Sam, but everything was out of focus.

"Sam?" I asked, feeling lost in the bright light.

"Hey, girl, come here." I heard his voice, but couldn't quite make him out.

"No, I can't really see. Can you see me? I think I'm sick." I leaned against a wall.

"Maybe you need to cool off?"

"Yeah, I feel really hot," I whispered. Sweat was streaming down my face.

"Come with me then."

"Where?" I felt someone hold my hand, and I let myself be tugged along.

"We'll go into the cooler. It'll help your temperature chill out a little," Sam said. "Alyssia, watch the counter."

"Sure," she said. A form slid behind the counter and onto the tall chair there.

Sam dragged me into the cooler. I started to see better. Thousands of cartons of milk lined the shelves. It was creepy how much milk and cream was in there. Then again my eyes began to slip away, to somewhere else. I felt like I was in heaven for a minute—all whiteness, pure and pretty. Sam pulled me onto his lap. He was sitting on a milk crate. Things happened that I couldn't really put together. I remembered *The Wall*—the Pink Floyd movie—the flowers having sex. I felt a little bit of pain. My stomach twinged, and I puked out a mass of colorful vomit. It looked like someone had smashed Starbursts into the linoleum floor. Then I felt the pain again. I looked over at Sam who was getting ready to mop up the pretty colors I'd spewed. Then I can't remember anything else. I guess I just passed out.

Alyssia was shaking me. I couldn't see straight, but my body felt better.

"Hey, what time is it?" I asked, sitting up in bed.

"One," she said curtly.

"Morning or evening?" I asked, looking over at the clock.

"Afternoon," she replied.

"How did I get here?"

"Sam and I carried you to the car, then we put you in bed," she said, not changing her tone.

"What happened?"

"Some of the drinks at the party were spiked. But we have to go to the Morning After now. We're having a meeting to discuss *us.*"

"What happened last night?" I asked.

"You had sex with Sam."

"What? When?" I spat out, feeling betrayed and angry.

"In the cooler at the gas station. I watched you two—you were all over him."

"I don't remember." I didn't. I couldn't remember a thing except for the Pink Floyd flowers. I wondered if it were a lie.

"That's the drug."

"I didn't want to do that."

"Well, you did it."

"Why are you being so short with me?" I was getting sick of her attitude.

"Because we need to get going."

"Okay," I said. I got out of bed and put some clothes on. I didn't feel like taking a shower; I assumed this would make Alyssia even madder. I washed my face quickly and headed out the door with her. Nothing felt right—her mood was somber and serious. I felt as if I were being punished, as if I had done something terribly wrong *once again.* We pulled into the parking lot of the Morning After.

"Come on," she said, reaching over the seat for her bag.

Everyone was sitting at the table waiting for us. The whole scene made me uneasy. My brain hurt. I didn't want to be here, but I sat down like a good little girl, and Alyssia opened the conversation.

"Orleigh, we have something very important to ask you."

"Okay," I replied, but I already didn't want to be having any kind of serious conversation. I was so tired of them always discussing *important* things that were of no interest to me.

"I hope this doesn't upset you."

"Okay."

I felt sick again. I sensed that things were about to get ugly. I didn't want anyone to ask me anything right now. Everyone seemed to be doing their own thing, almost as if they didn't want to be there either.

"Well?" I asked, impatient with the silence.

"We did a little bit of talking last night while you were out, you know, getting fucked," Alyssia began. "We tried to figure out what would be the best way for us to unite. To be, well, you know, to be the *us* that we're trying to be."

I didn't like this whole "us" unity discussion—I was already feeling smothered. I scanned the table. Geoff was fidgeting with his hands, Don twirling a spoon over and over in his coffee cup, and Sam was staring out the window. No one but Alyssia seemed to care about any of this. "So," I said, nonchalantly, "What did you come up with?"

"Well, we figured that you're probably the purest person in our group, and therefore the one who is capable of carrying out the deed . . ."

"What deed? What are you trying to say?"

"We have appointed you to bring our child into the world. It would be the child of *us.*"

"What? How? I don't get what you are saying."

Alyssia gave me a look that scared the hell out of me—she was more than serious about whatever it was she was proposing.

"We want you to have sex with each of us, at the same time. Hopefully you'll get pregnant, and we can bring our beautiful baby into the world. That way we wouldn't know who the father was. It would be all ours. The child would be so special. It would exemplify everything we believe in," she said dreamily. She looked around at everyone at the table with a proud smile. They all looked blankly back at her.

I felt a major discomfort, accompanied by an urge to flee.

"What exactly is it you believe in, Alyssia?" I asked.

"Community, *us,*" she said, with an assured smile. It sounded like we were a corporate marketing conference or something. She seemed to be standing alone. I figured they'd been dragged here just like me, taken over by her power and charm. She was your quintessential cult leader.

"Not very original. Communes have been around for ever," I said. "And you guys honestly think this is a good idea? You think this is a healthy and normal way to bring a child into the world?" I looked around the table at the three pairs of averted eyes.

"Yes," Alyssia replied with absolute confidence, beaming, and her disciples all nodded their heads in agreement.

"And what the fuck happens to me and the kid when you all wake up out of this crazy fantasy? Huh? Who the fuck takes care of it then? I'll tell you who—*me!* I don't even know what to tell you people. I think you've all flipped. Fucking flipped! You guys need serious psychiatric help if you ask me. A group baby! It's just so fucking wrong, do you understand me? *WRONG!*" I yelled. I bolted up from the table and strode to the kitchen where I asked Kurt if I could use the phone.

I called Jason, gave him a briefing on what was going on, and asked him to come and get me immediately. I didn't know if he had heard about Jeremy and me yet, but he was willing to come and get me right away. I hung up and walked back to the dining area. They were all sitting silently at the table.

Sam looked at me with hatred in his eyes. "I knew you weren't strong enough for us."

"Good for you! You guys just reek of intelligence," I said, my arms folded across my chest.

"What are you going to do now?" Alyssia asked.

"None of your business." I grabbed my smokes off the table and gave my most hateful look to the whole table of freaks. I couldn't stand them looking at me. They literally made my skin crawl. I needed some fresh air. I knew if Jason came quickly enough I could head over to Alyssia's where the door was always unlocked, grab all my belongings, and be rid of them.

I walked out the door and sat down to have a smoke. I felt the poison go down my throat, through my lungs, and then back out my nose. It was purifying. No one could touch me, so I sat and waited for Jason's van to come and rescue me. I closed my eyes and concentrated on smoking.

PART III

Mark

Sometimes It Goes the Other Way

CHAPTER 13

I walked into our room at Tammy and Malick's place. A lot of the room-mates had moved out, so Mark and I could finally share one of the larger rooms. The Cure was playing softly on the CD player. There was an incredibly large piece of canvas covering the bed and the floor. Mark sat in the corner, his paint box opened. Various tubes of paint lay scattered on the canvas.

"Come here, honey," he said, patting the floor next to him, smiling eagerly.

I sat down, and he kissed me on the lips. His tongue quickly found mine and slipped something tiny onto it. I pulled away from him, horrified.

"What was that," I asked.

"Acid."

"Why?"

"Because I want us to do it together."

"Why?" I asked, sucking on the paper. It tasted like chemicals—I didn't like it at all, but for some reason I swallowed it.

"It's part of my Valentine's present to you."

My mind wandered back to Mark's birthday. I had slaved away for hours to prepare a special dinner for him. When he finally came home from class I could immediately tell that he was fucked up on something. He had been hanging out with Alyssia's new drug-dealer boyfriend Pat, working some drug deals with him, and I had a feeling he'd been sampling from whatever they were selling. When we sat down to eat, Mark admitted he'd taken acid. Then while we were eating, he grabbed hold of my throat and threw me down on the carpet. I tried to scream, but he had my throat totally closed off. I pulled my arm out from under his leg and smacked the shit out of him; he flew back, placing his hand on his reddened cheek. I completely flipped out on him, and he ended up telling me that he had hallucinated I was Alyssia, and he'd seen maggots coming out of my eyes.

"I know you've never tried this kind of shit," Mark said, "but you'll like it, I promise."

"Yeah, just like I liked being strangled, right?"

"Let's just get past that . . . please?" He grabbed my hands and began licking my fingers. He unbuttoned my shirt and pulled it off.

"What are you doing?"

"Just enjoy, baby, enjoy."

He unhooked my bra behind my back and slid it off. I had to admit that I liked what he was doing, despite the fact that I was pissed about the acid.

Things started to seem different fast—I was losing myself in the music, losing myself to Mark's touch. Within what seemed like seconds, we were standing completely naked before each other. I felt a little hazy about how the whole thing had transpired, but it was nice to just look at him, more beautiful than ever against the white canvas background. His skin was glazed with sweat, little droplets running down the sides of his face toward his chin. His lips appeared bigger and brighter than ever. I felt like I was seeing him for the first time.

My legs gave way like jelly, and I slid down onto the canvas-covered floor. Mark was unscrewing the tops off several paint tubes, which he began smearing on my body. In that moment I believed I loved paint more than anything—its texture, its smoothness and sliminess on my body. Paint covered my back now, and Mark was covering the front of me with it as well. I wanted some paint too, so I started touching his paint-covered hands, then touching him. The paint felt cool and so good to smear on his skin.

Frantically, we grabbed at more tubes and squeezed them into our palms, then onto each other. The many colors started to blend; paint everywhere at this point, handprints and footprints. Mark lay on top of me, kissing me fiercely. He had paint all over his lips, and I could taste it, but I loved its sharp metallic flavor. We rolled around on the canvas, leaving the prints of our painted bodies all around us. The room spun so fast I couldn't focus. I closed my eyes, and that's when he entered me with a force that almost made me faint.

The room was so warm and the paint so cold. Our bodies became sticky, and it was difficult to pull ourselves apart. Everything in the room grew blurry and distorted—colors flashed around me, my body changed positions every few seconds. I was on my knees, then my back, then on top of Mark, then on my side, then standing up, then sitting on his lap. I got dizzy every time he moved me. But when I orgasmed, I saw castles and horses and shit I'd never dreamed of before. I was in a bewitched garden where pixies were tossing their dust in my eyes.

I sat alone in the backseat. Pat drove, Mark beside him in the passenger seat. Pat kept glancing at me in the rearview mirror.

"Wicky isn't so bad," he said, his eyes darting from me to the road, then back to me again. "It just makes you really crazy. I cut it with weed so it's not that harsh."

He was aggressively trying to talk me into doing drugs. Pat had introduced Mark to drugs I'd never even heard of before, like wicky stick, which was supposed to be formaldehyde. The idea of smoking what people use to preserve dead bodies was really fucked up in my opinion. There was no way I would fuck with that kind of shit. I narrowed my eyes at his reflection in the rearview mirror.

We were on our way to St. Charles on a run to "off some shit," as Mark had put it. I didn't really want to go, and I knew Mark had asked me if I would come because he thought I would say no, but I wanted to see what he was up to with Pat. So I'd shocked him by saying I'd go. Pat kept persistently going at it, bringing up acid and a wide variety of other shit he dealt, trying to tempt me to try something.

Nothing sounded appealing, but then he mentioned coke. Mark had told me all about the last time he was out with Pat and tried it, how it was utterly wonderful and he thought it was a drug I would love.

"Okay, I'll give it a try. One time won't kill me," I reluctantly said. My eyes dropped to the rust-colored floor cover; I couldn't face them. They had finally broken me, and I felt shitty about it.

When I raised my head, Mark was dropping white powder onto a tiny mirror that Pat had handed him. He passed it back to me with a tiny piece of a straw.

"What do I do here?" I asked.

Pat laughed. "Haven't you seen people do it in the movies?"

"Yeah," I said. I remembered *Less Than Zero,* and the fear of what I was about to do crept into the pit of my belly.

"Well, like that. Put the straw on the line and inhale."

"In broad daylight?" I asked, worried that the other drivers would see me.

"We're cruising down the road, no one will see you. Do it quick," Pat said.

I held the straw up to the first little line and inhaled quickly, then I proceeded on to the remaining two lines. It tasted weird in the back of my throat, and my heart immediately began racing. I didn't feel that different, but when Pat dropped Mark and me off at the mall entrance, I was flying. I felt like I could run a mile without even getting remotely tired.

"How are you doing, baby?" Mark asked, as we headed toward the glass doors of the mall.

"Great, just a little out of it," I said. My hands were shaking out of control. I lifted my right one up to my face and watched it tremble. I held my breath as we walked into the mall. It was strange to come here with Mark, to the mall where I used to shoplift with Heather.

"You like the stuff?" Mark asked. "Pretty good, huh?" He grasped my trembling fingers.

"Yeah, I like it."

He winked at me. "Cool, we've found something you can get off on now."

"I'd rather get off on you." I smiled.

"Horny, are you?"

"Definitely!"

"Coke does that." He squeezed my fingers tightly.

"Then I like it even more."

"We're in your territory now, help me find the freaks."

It seemed a little risky to me to be selling shit in the mall, but what else could I do, I was too wired to think clearly about alternative locations. "Are you putting money into these drugs?" I had to ask.

"Just a little."

"Where you getting it from?"

"Don't worry about that; we eat, don't we?"

"Yeah, but I thought you were poor."

"Well, now I'm trying to get rich. Don't worry, all right?" He winked.

We sold a lot of the stuff we brought to the mall. Mostly acid and wicky sticks. None of the mall rats wanted the coke—it was too expensive. Then we headed back to DeKalb to the party our roommates were having. The whole ride home I was dying for more coke, but I didn't want to ask for it. I was afraid that Pat would get mad at me, and I was mortified by the fact that I had succumbed and gotten so quickly hooked. So I sat in the backseat quietly twiddling my thumbs.

When we hit the outskirts of DeKalb, Pat finally said, "Would you like a little boost for the party, Orleigh?"

"Sure," I replied casually. "Are you coming?" I was hoping he would, then the coke would still be around.

"No, I've got to get home to Alyssia. She gets pissed when I'm gone too long."

"Sounds like Alyssia," I replied snidely.

"Hey, be nice," Pat said.

"I am," I said, though I didn't feel very nice.

"Good."

Mark set up the mirror for me again. This time he laid out five thicker lines. I saw Pat glance at them. "Mark, what are you doing? That's too much, man."

"Hey, chill out, I'll pay for it."

"And you will." He shot Mark a sideways sneer.

"Fine, not like we didn't help you get rid of almost everything you had today," Mark snapped back.

"I guess you're right. Go ahead, give it to her," Pat reluctantly complied.

Mark passed the mirror back to me, and I did all five lines quickly. My head spun, but it felt so much better to be up again. I felt completely alive again.

Mark and I got out of the car and watched Pat drive away. He rolled down his window once he hit the street and hollered out, "Hey, I'll pick you up tomorrow. We have more business to tend to."

"No problem," Mark called back, then turned away from Pat and hugged me.

Music boomed from the house while Mark and I kissed. Someone screamed from the balcony. I looked up and saw Mark's ex Theresa.

"Do you two have to do that shit in front of me? It's so inconsiderate," she continued, bellowing down at us.

I shouted right back. "This is my fucking house, Theresa, and he's *my* fucking boyfriend. I pay the rent! Therefore, I can kiss him in my house, on this property, whenever I want. Get it?"

She turned her back to me and resumed talking with Sarah, Mark's sister. Mark and I walked into the front room of the house, the living room, where the party was already well under way. There were, like, two hundred people on the lower level of the house alone. Mark immediately headed upstairs to our room. I don't think he liked parties quite as much as I did. I wandered around and conversed with people, then I started to miss him and went to find him but got side-tracked by my roommate Kerrie who was standing in the doorway to her room.

"Hey, come in here, Orleigh," she said, grabbing my arm.

I entered the room, where it seemed she'd been waiting for me. I was reminded of the night I'd first met Mark; how I'd fallen in love with him in this room, Kerrie's room, when he sang "Pictures of You," leaning up against the wall. It had been exactly three months. She had painted the once-cream walls black, which made me instantly depressed.

"What's up, Kerrie?" I asked.

"You know, you really hurt Theresa's feelings," she said, looking at me with a tight frown that curved her entire plump mouth downward.

"Why, because I kissed my boyfriend in my driveway?"

"Well, you know it can hurt, don't you?"

I didn't give a shit if I hurt Theresa. I diverted my glance from her to take in all the bleakness of her dwelling space.

"Regardless, I pay rent here, she doesn't. Anyway, I didn't know she was out there watching us."

"I'm sorry, I thought you did it intentionally," Kerrie said, lighting a tall black candle. She walked slowly around her bed, then sat on the edge. I noticed there was a wooden Ouija board resting on top of her black silk comforter. The board gave me the chills for some reason.

"I'm not that mean," I said, but I knew I could be. I actually wished I had known Theresa was there, then maybe I would have fucked Mark on the lawn.

The door swung open and Joe busted into Kerrie's room like a warrior entering the battlefield, only in his silk pajamas. Didn't he know there was a party going on?

He sneered, his arms folded across his chest. "Hey, Orleigh, I saw Mark and Theresa hot and heavy in the hallway."

"Bullshit! You're always trying to start shit. You're always such a fucking instigator," I spat. I hated the way he always tried to fuck with me just cause I had turned him down.

"I'm not kidding!" he said with a sarcastic tone. He dropped his arms from his chest, glaring at me.

Theresa walked past Kerrie's door, then went out onto the balcony, which was visible through Kerrie's open window. She'd been coming from the direction of the bedroom Mark and I shared. I was pissed, seriously pissed. She moved directly into my line of vision, and I picked up Kerrie's favorite knife, which happened to be conveniently and strategically placed on the desk next to where I stood. It was probably there to open up letters or for kinky sex.

"Hey, Theresa!" I bellowed.

She turned and looked through the open window at me. She didn't see the knife in my hand.

"What do you want, Orleigh?"

I smiled at her, and I know it must have looked like a crazed fucking smile. Jack Nicholson in *The Shining*. I lifted the knife and threw it toward the window. Luckily I had perfect aim, and it went whizzing through the air, landing two inches from the top of Theresa's head in the window frame, making a loud thump.

"What the fuck? What did you do that for? What's your problem?" she yelled.

I ignored her, left Kerrie's room, and strode down the hall to my room.

"Hey, you," Mark said, as I walked in the door. He sat on the floor cleaning his brushes, listening to the Cure. He seemed rather pissed off.

"What's wrong?" I asked.

"Nothing. What's wrong with you?" he asked, obviously detecting how upset I was.

"I heard you were kissing Theresa." I walked to the window that looked out onto the back of the house. Malick's rusty orange Volkswagen bug was parked in the driveway. The half moon cast a glow on the rear window.

"What!" he asked.

"You heard me," I snapped back.

"Who told you that?"

"Joe."

"Figures. It's not true; I've barely seen her tonight."

I turned to look at him. He was methodically dipping each of his brushes in a bucket of mineral spirits. "Sure!" I said angrily.

He looked at me confused. "Why would you believe Joe? You do believe it, don't you?"

"Yeah, I do."

"Why?"

"Because it seems like something you'd do."

"When have I ever done anything like that before?"

"Never, but you also haven't ever been this fucked up before."

"What do you mean, fucked up?"

I couldn't believe that he didn't see what all the drugs were doing to him—wicky stick, acid, coke. They were starting to make him completely indifferent. He wanted to be alone all the time, and he seemed unaffected by things that were important to me. "I think you know exactly what I mean."

"I didn't touch her. I've just been sitting here cleaning my brushes."

"Likely story." I walked out of the room and back down the hall.

Theresa was standing in the doorway to the balcony. She was alone, and she glared at me as I approached.

"What the fuck is your problem, bitch?" I blurted.

"You could have killed me!"

"True, and *that* would have been so bad?" I said, my face inches away from hers. I felt insane. I wanted to bite her fucking nose off.

"You're such a fucking bitch." She tossed her blond hair over her shoulder and bit down on her lower lip.

"So?" I asked, leaning against the wall.

"So, you had no reason to do that." She was gnawing ferociously on her lip now. It was evident that she was angry, but nowhere near as angry as I was.

"And you have no reason to be here," I said.

"Yeah, I do, my friends live here," she snarled.

"What friends? No one here likes you." I knew I had hit below the belt, but it felt good. I watched her face contort into something that looked pained, and I felt satisfied—I had beaten the stupid bitch.

"Fuck you," she replied.

"No, fuck yourself. Why don't you just go the fuck away?"

"Why should I?"

"Because you have such a problem with Mark and me being together. It's just obnoxious. We live here, this is our home, and you expect us to tread lightly because you're all screwed in the head." I smiled triumphantly.

"You have no compassion for others."

"And you should leave."

"Well, I'm not leaving." She averted her eyes from my face.

"Really? I can make you leave."

"How, throw more knives at me?" She looked back at me and smiled, as if she'd said something extremely witty.

"I only wish." I pictured a circus side show, me throwing knives at Theresa, but missing the board behind her and hitting her vital organs.

"How, then?" she challenged.

"Easy."

"Really, then just try and make me leave. I won't leave, and every chance I get to fuck your relationship up, I will. I fucking hate you!"

Rage roiled inside me. I wanted her dead. I couldn't stand her attitude or her cry pity bullshit. She was so fucking . . . just so fucking unnecessary. My fingers clenched into a fist. She saw me resist. She watched me try to control my arm and backed up toward the stairs that led from the balcony to the driveway. I knew she was going to walk down them, knew she was afraid of me. That's when my fist flew up and cracked her right on the nose. She fell backwards, then rolled down the flight of creaky wooden stairs. I stood there, not doing anything to help her. I walked calmly into Kerrie's room and sat on her bed. I blew on my now-bloody knuckles to try to take away the sting. I could hear Theresa screaming for help, but I didn't budge. I just sat there until Mark came in.

"What's all the commotion about?"

"I knocked Theresa down the stairs," I said, not looking at him, but focusing on a droplet of blood that was trickling down my index finger.

"What? I told you nothing happened."

"That's not why."

"Why, then?" he asked, but I didn't answer. "Oh, fucking forget it. Is she all right?"

"Don't know, don't care," I said, still transfixed by the blood on my fingers, knuckles, hand. I couldn't tell whether it was mine or Theresa's.

"For god's sake, Orleigh." He stormed out of the room and headed out onto the balcony, then down the balcony stairs to Theresa. From Kerrie's open bedroom window I faintly heard their voices. Mark told Theresa he was going to call an ambulance, then he ran up the balcony stairs, across the balcony, and down the hallway past Kerrie's door toward our room. I still hadn't moved an inch. Mark's sister Sarah ran down the stairs, then Theresa was telling her everything that I'd said, somehow forgetting to include how she had provoked me—conveniently leaving out the part about fucking up our relationship. Mark ran past Kerrie's door again, then back outside. I listened to him explain to his sister that the ambulance was on its way, and that she better ride with Theresa. In a pathetically strained voice, Theresa begged Mark to ride with her.

"I don't think so. I need to stay here with Orleigh."

"Why would you want to stay with her? She's completely psycho. Mark, she threw a knife at me, then punched me in the face! I think she broke my nose. Come with me," she whined, then started sobbing loudly.

"I can't. I'm sorry."

Things were silent for a while, then Mark walked into Kerrie's room. "What happened?" he asked.

"Nothing," I replied shakily.

"Really?"

"Are you asking me my opinion?" I was so mad I couldn't look at him.

"Yes. Want to tell me what happened?"

"Not really." I wanted him to leave me alone.

"I think it was wrong of you to do that. You know, she's really sensitive about our break-up. I know you don't care, but she's been in therapy over it for a long time."

"That's my problem?" I half-yelled.

"It's not your problem, it's just something to think about."

"I don't give a shit. She told me she was going to try and break us up. To me, that sounds like a threat. That's why the bitch got the shit beat out of her."

"I didn't know," he said quietly. He was running his fingers through his shoulder-length hair and it almost looked like he was about to pull it out.

"Of course not, because you were too concerned about the little princess's fucking feelings. I didn't see you run to me and see how I was doing."

He crossed his arms and said, "You weren't sprawled out on the staircase bleeding."

"No, I wasn't. I'm just your girlfriend."

I got up and walked past him on my way out of Kerrie's room. I didn't want to talk anymore. I wanted to get the hell away from him, from this house. I didn't care anymore. I didn't care about anything. I went into our room, locked the door, then pulled out my mountain pack. I started to stuff it full with clothing, anything I thought I might need. I didn't know where I would go, but I knew I had to get away from Mark. I felt that tonight he had shown me where his loyalties were, fawning over Theresa the way he did. But ultimately I knew it wasn't about Theresa—she was but a minuscule part of what was wrong. *What was wrong?* We were falling apart. We didn't fit together anymore. Mark's head was crammed full of drugs all the time, and I could feel the end of the relationship creeping up on me. It was going to end with or without Theresa fucking it up. I didn't even know why I had hit her. After stuffing everything I could fit into my bag, I unlocked the door and stepped into the hallway, where Mark had been sitting on the floor right outside the door.

"Where are you going?" he asked.

"Away."

"Why?"

"Because I don't feel right about us anymore."

"Why?"

"Because tonight was too much for me to take."

"But I never touched her; I only wanted to make sure she was all right. Is that so bad?"

"Yeah, especially after the things she said to me." Maybe I was being unreasonable about the Theresa ordeal, fixating on it as an excuse. I just wasn't ready to completely accept the fact that maybe Mark and I weren't right for each other. And the Theresa thing filled me with resolve and energy to leave before things got worse.

"All I knew is what I saw," Mark said sadly.

"Yeah, and that gave you the right to defend her?"

"I wasn't defending her." He looked up at me with puppy-dog eyes.

"Really? *'She's in therapy, you need to be more careful with her feelings.'* What do you call that?" My hand clutched the strap of my pack so tightly that my fingernails dug painfully into my palm.

"Common courtesy."

"Whatever you say!" I said, starting to move past him.

"Don't leave," he said, grabbing hold of my pack.

I kept my back to him, trying to get to the staircase, but he was holding fast to my pack. "I have to."

"No, you don't," he said, not letting go.

I turned back to face him. "Yes, I do."

"Why?"

"Because I don't know how I feel anymore."

"Yeah, you do."

"No, I don't," I said, tugging at my pack.

"Can I play you something? Then if you want to leave you can."

We stared each other down. "Fine," I said reluctantly.

He pulled me back into our room, sat me on the bed, then put on a Cure CD. He fast-forwarded it to track eight, "A Night Like This." The song was about what would happen if this particular woman left her man, how he would go find her if it took him all night. As soon as it started playing, Mark began to cry.

I stood there debating silently with myself. I knew I loved Mark. I wanted to hold him and make him stop crying, but I also wanted to leave. I couldn't take the drugs. Shit, *I* was actually doing drugs. I'd been thinking about coke all night, wanting it so bad again—that rush, that intense energetic feeling. This wasn't supposed to happen to me. All of this weighed heavily down on me.

"Come here, please," Mark said, extending his hand.

"I can't," I said, staring at the neon-blue equalizer bars on the stereo as they bounced up and down to the music.

"Why?"

"Because then I'll stay," I replied quietly. I was ashamed of myself. I knew I'd given in.

"Then please come," he said, his hand still outstretched, waiting for me to grab it.

"Mark, I'm really unhappy."

"Maybe that's how you feel right now, but you know we'll work through this. Whatever is bugging you, we'll fix it. I promise."

I couldn't resist him. I was in love. No matter how I tried, I couldn't walk away, and I'm not sure I ever intended to. I grabbed his hand and sat down next to him, holding him while he cried.

I paced the floor, sweating because we were nearly out of coke. I felt panic-stricken. Out the window, Mark skated by. What the fuck were we doing here? We needed to get out of this town. Pat and Alyssia had both been arrested for selling cocaine; they had gotten caught with a couple of kilos on them. I hadn't known they'd been that seriously involved. Mark started to go to pieces after they were busted. He believed Pat would rat him out. I knew that Pat would never do something like that, but the stress had driven Mark to do more drugs than usual, and they were making him paranoid.

I was starting to worry about his sanity—he was so anxious about the Pat thing. I paced around, gnawing my fingernails, occasionally looking out the window. Mark skated back and forth in the driveway. Shit, I thought—he was starting to remind me of Jason.

Every time a car drove by he watched it pass, his neck craning to see if it turned or not. I wanted to call him upstairs, but I knew he wouldn't come. The vibe between us had dwindled to nonexistent. We barely had communicated since the night I'd threatened to walk out. I blamed Mark and all the drugs, but I wasn't much better. I had a stash of coke in the dresser drawer that I hadn't told him about. I had hidden it so I wouldn't have to share, or reveal the extent of my problem. I was equally pathetic, but no one else knew. Not able to resist any longer, I walked over to the dresser and rapaciously located the coke. I did a little bump, hoping it would help me focus.

As I snorted the milky white miracle substance, it hit me out of the blue: we had to leave. I didn't know where we would go, but then I remembered that Joe had recently told me that the Grateful Dead were on tour on the West Coast. I'd always wanted to go west. We could just pack up and head for the Dead, I thought. The only problem was money. We needed food, cigarettes, camping gear. We needed a car. I tapped on the window to catch Mark's attention and motioned for him to come upstairs.

The only thing that was really going to bum me out about leaving was the coke. And there was only a little bit left, about two eight balls, which was a lot, but not enough for a road trip. I didn't think it was going to last very long, especially if I told Mark I had it, in which case it wouldn't last a weekend. But despite how much I'd grown to love coke over merely a few weeks, I knew we needed to get away, get away from DeKalb and the drugs. I was half-tempted to take my stash to the toilet and flush it. But Mark was coming into the room, and soon I would need another bump.

CHAPTER 14

Cold. Too cold to sleep. I felt like I was breathing icicles. I tossed and turned, freezing my ass off. I could hear Led Zeppelin playing on our portable CD player, a soothing song called "Tangerine," but all I could think about was how cold I was. Mark and I had had sex, like, three times, to generate extra body heat, and now he was sound asleep. I snuggled closer. I wanted him on top of me.

Nighttime—no sun to warm things up. It was November. The temperature dropped as soon as it got dark in Estes Park, Colorado. I couldn't stand it anymore. I needed to get warm, so I nudged Mark awake.

"Hey, I was actually sleeping," he muttered. He turned around slowly to face me.

"I'm going to freeze to death."

"I'll miss you terribly," he said, pulling on one of my wayward strands of hair.

"No, you won't."

"Yes, I will."

"Whatever. Let's sleep in the car," I said anxiously, dying for the warmth of the heater.

"Anything you want."

"Can we turn the heat on?"

"I think we're going to have to."

"Is that a yes?"

"Yes, baby, we can turn the heat on."

He unzipped the tent and stopped in his tracks. His mouth dropped wide open. I thought someone was outside our tent. I had visions of *Friday the Thirteenth* movies, Jason, the psycho killer with the hockey mask, coming at us with an ax. It was the perfect scenario, a naked couple who'd just had sex, now innocently asleep in a tent, then the ax blade slicing the thin nylon to shreds.

"What's wrong, Mark?" I asked, frightened.

"Come here," he whispered.

I crawled to the opening of the tent and peered outside. In the darkness I made out five large forms, five four-legged forms with glowing yellowish eyes, huge antlers, standing completely still.

"It's cool, baby, don't worry. They won't do anything to us," Mark said.

I wanted to believe him, but he pulled his knife out of his backpack. I inched back into the tent and sat shivering, wondering what the hell he was going to do. He motioned for me to follow him, and we slipped quietly out of the tent, then moved slowly in the direction of the ancient VW Jetta Mark had acquired through a drug deal before we'd left. A branch crackled in the snow beneath his foot, and the elks were off, running from the sad wintry campsite.

"You can come to the car now," he said, looking back at me.

I ran across the luminous snowy path to the car, wrapped tightly in my bag, then crawled into the backseat with Mark.

"Hey, let's get warm." He smiled.

"How do you propose we do that, darling?" I asked, trying to sound sexy despite the chatter of my teeth.

Mark lay on top of me, and I soon felt him enter me, but my mind was not with him. I was way too focused on thinking about the remains of my stash, trying to figure out exactly how to ration what little was left. I wanted it to last until we got to California, and so far I'd been able to keep it all to myself. I would take one hit in the bathroom of every gas station we stopped at, when Mark went to pay for the gas. That was my rule. I was becoming a regular little cokehead, while I was diligently and lovingly trying to get Mark to give it all up. And he was doing such a great job. I was pathetic.

We woke in the back of the car, our bodies entangled. I couldn't breath. The night was gone and the day had brought a hellacious sun whose rays streamed through the car windows, toasting any exposed flesh. I was so hungry my stomach was grumbling loudly as I pulled a fresh shirt over my head.

"Looks like we have company," Mark said, his eyes lingering on my breasts as I tugged my shirt down.

An RV had apparently joined us in the lot at some point in the night. I shrugged it off. "I'm hungry," I said.

Mark got out of the car and set our Coleman stove up on the hood of the car. Then he began pilfering through one of our shopping bags of food. He pulled out a can of SpaghettiOs. What a yummy breakfast, I thought, as I stepped out of the car into the blazing sunlight and crisp mountain air.

"Where's the fucking can opener?" he asked.

"I don't know." I stretched my sore muscles, leaning back, then falling forward over my legs. The coke made me stiff.

"Could you at least look for it?" he snapped.

What the hell was his problem? He was being so fucking bitchy.

I looked through everything we had but couldn't seem to come up with the can opener. Mark was getting even more pissed off.

"Mark, honestly, there's no can opener. We could walk over to that RV. They must have a can opener," I said, hoping to calm him down.

"Fine," he snapped. "Go over there and see if they'll let you borrow it."

"Please come with me—we don't know who the hell lives in that thing. Could be a psycho killer for all I know."

"Fine, I'll go with you."

We headed over to the largely looming recreational vehicle parked at the corner of the rest stop, where Mark casually knocked on the door. We waited. Country music was playing inside, but there was no way to look in.

"Come on, baby, there's no one here. Let's just go back to the car," I said, because Mark was getting agitated again.

We began walking back to our shoddy auto but then heard the door to the RV creak open behind us. Both of us turned and saw a short, balding middle-aged man who had been apparently frolicking around in his underwear inside the RV.

"Can I help you kids?" he called.

"Actually, we were wondering if you had a can opener we could borrow?" I asked, smiling timidly. I felt a little embarrassed for him.

"Sure do, and a stove, a refrigerator, and many other things. What do you need opened?" He scratched his bald head, leering at me. He looked like a pedophile.

"A can of SpaghettiOs," Mark said.

"Why don't you bring them over here and cook 'em on my stove?" he said, leaning into the door frame. He smiled a wide, nicotine-stained, toothy smile.

"That'd be great," I said, despite the fact that I was a little afraid of him.

Mark looked over at me as if I were crazy, then we walked back to the car to get our can.

"Why did you say that?" he asked.

"Because it would be easier."

"I'd rather just eat with you."

"Can we just eat and then go back to the car?" I didn't really care what he thought, I wanted food, and quickly.

"Fine, Orleigh, whatever your little heart desires," he said, but his tone was mean and sarcastic.

"Little, huh?" I asked snidely.

"Okay, maybe not little, maybe just fucked up."

"Whatever!"

When we approached the RV, we both quieted down, not wanting to fight in front of this strange guy who was allowing us to prepare a meal in his home. We knocked again to let him know we'd returned. I figured he would have dressed by now; much to my surprise, he was still solely underwear-clad. "Come on in, kids, name's Sid, Uncle Sid if you like."

"Hello, Sid, I'm Orleigh, and this is my boyfriend, Mark," I said warily.

"The stove's over there, pots and pans under the sink, spoons in the drawer. Go to town!" He shuffled across the gray-flecked linoleum to sit down at the tiny rickety table that wobbled when he leaned his elbows on it.

Mark and I worked together to prepare the can of shit we'd brought over. This guy, Uncle Sid, was a total freak. I couldn't help thinking *serial killer, serial rapist, serial something or other.* He just looked insane—and the underwear, I couldn't get over the loose, droopy, briefs. I looked over at him sitting at the table, smoking a cigarette and drinking a beer.

"Where you two from?" he asked. His wet purplish lips smacked together, then he took another swig of beer.

"Illinois," I said.

"Running from the law, are ya?" He laughed nasally.

Mark decided to take over. "No, are you?"

"As a matter of fact, yes. My wife's after me on all sorts of alimony shit, so I packed up and left town." He scratched his balls in what I think was an attempt to be more manly.

"Nice move," Mark said, feigning a smile. "We're just following the Dead around, trying to make a buck here and there."

"Yeah, I done that when I was a youngster." He smiled, then shut his eyes for a moment. The smile grew larger, and I could tell he was recalling his lovely youth.

Mark was stirring the Os while I sat on the kitchenette counter and smoked, watching my hand tremble as I lifted it up each time I took a drag.

"Pretty girl you got there," Sid told Mark, his eyes resting dead center on my breasts.

"Thank you, but she really hates it when people talk about her like she isn't in the room," Mark said calmly.

Sid's eyes traveled from my breasts to my face, then back down again. "Uh, sorry. You're a pretty girl."

"Thanks," I replied coolly, averting my eyes.

"I need another beer. Anyone else want one?" Sid asked.

Mark and I nodded. A beer sounded great, especially since my remaining coke stash was nearly nonexistent. I needed something to take the edge off. Withdrawal was such a pleasurable experience. I was impressed by how cool Mark had been through his whole ordeal, but he obviously wasn't feeling things quite as severely as I was. Then again, he hadn't been partaking in coke this whole time as I had been. Sid walked to the fridge and pulled out three long necks. As he did this, the slit in his briefs, the one made for urinating convenience, separated, and his dick just "sort of" fell out. It was disgusting.

"Sorry," he said, adjusting himself with great show. "Seems I'm peeking out a little here. I *am* experiencing a little shrinkage from the shower I just took." He smiled weakly.

I couldn't believe he felt the need to make an excuse for his small penis. I hoped that dick-shrinkage wasn't something that happened to all men as they got older. I would hate to see Mark in thirty years with a toddler-sized dick.

Mark laughed under his breath. "Thanks for the beer, man. Got any bowls? We could go back to the car and get ours, but if you have some, we would certainly wash them when we're done."

"That would be great; I don't like to wash. If you look in the cupboard above your head you'll find a few bowls there."

Mark got two bowls, then poured a semi-equal amount of Os into each.

"Come hither, you two. Sit and enjoy your food," Sid beckoned.

We sat with him at the minuscule table, ravenously spooning up mouthfuls of Os. Sid watched until the last little bit of nasty orange sauce was consumed, then began chatting again.

"So where are you two going?" he asked.

Mark looked up from his empty bowl. "Not exactly sure right now, Sid. Somewhere a little warmer."

"Why don't you head over to Arizona? That's where I'm going."

"Where in Arizona?" Mark asked, running his finger across the bottom of the bowl, then licking the sauce off his fingertip.

"Well, there's this spot between Phoenix and Flagstaff called Camp Verde. It's a quiet, tucked-away place where you can camp. There's a couple of natural hot springs you can hang out in." His eyes shut, and he wasn't with us anymore. He must have had some fond memories of the hot springs because a smile spread across his face, revealing a few gaps between his yellowed teeth. Evidently, it wasn't only hair Sid had lost with age. His eyes snapped open, and he was back at the table in his run-down RV. He continued, "Really nice place. Really nice. Usually it's pretty mellow too; nobody there."

"When're you going?" Mark asked, and I detected interest in his voice, which caught me off guard. Like, he wanted to follow Sid?

"Not till tomorrow, but I could meet you there."

"Could you give us directions?" It seemed he had been taken in by Sid's description.

"Sure. It'll only take you a little while to get there, maybe six hours."

Sid rose to retrieve a pencil and paper. He was "peeking out" again. What a charmer. His blubbery belly jiggled as he shuffled back to the table. His chest was hairy. I'd never seen that much hair on a man. He sat and drew a map and some relatively easy-to-follow directions. Mark and I cleaned the dishes we had used, then left, promising to meet Sid at Camp Verde.

Camp Verde: I sat outside the tent at a picnic table, drawing tattoo stencils. Mark had acquired the tattoo gun before we left. He thought that since I was good at drawing and painting (he'd seen a few sketches and the painting in Joe's room) I should take up tattooing, so that I could do it at Dead shows while we were on the road and make some cash. I thought he was crazy, but I'd been practicing on the skin of oranges and tangerines. The guy who had given Mark the gun said it was similar to working on human skin. I was getting bored and frustrated with the fruit thing, but I had to wait to experiment on actual human skin till Mark was done beading a necklace he insisted on finishing.

I wondered if that Sid character would show up and thought how utterly pleasurable it would be to have his company. What I really wanted to do was relax in the hot springs with Mark, but instead I brought out the Coleman stove to boil the needles for Mark's tattoo.

We had been in Camp Verde for a couple of days. It was actually a pleasant place. A long, narrow *Dukes of Hazard* dirt road led down the canyon to the campground. Our car had barely made it through that road, and I couldn't imagine trying to get an RV down it. Our tent opened onto a narrow portion of the East Verde River within the Coconino National Forest. Across the water were enormous rust-colored cliffs. There were four small campgrounds, each with a picnic table, a fire pit, and a large tree stump to sit on while tending the fire.

Today we were going to make our first trip across the river to the hot springs. I was excited to see what hot springs looked like; I'd never been to one before. From my seat at the picnic table I watched Mark tie off his necklace.

"Ready to practice that tattoo?" he asked, looking over at me.

I thought he was fucking crazy, but I figured I'd give it a shot. I carefully removed the needle from the boiling water and inserted it into the gun. Mark took off his T-shirt, sweat glistening on his bare chest. He sat on the ground, and I sat on the stump. I had stenciled the outline, and I pressed the moistened paper to his skin. I dipped the needle into the ink, then lifted Mark's arm onto my lap. Hesitantly I began to follow the stencil of the Grateful Dead lightening bolt on the swell of his biceps. Mark seemed way too patient and calm while my hand shook over his soft skin. It seemed to take hours, and when I finished, it surprisingly looked good—not professional by any means, but not sloppy either.

Mark rubbed his fingers over the puffy skin and smiled. "I love it. Now we should truck over to the hot springs and celebrate." I put a dab of Neosporin on the tattoo, then placed a piece of gauze over it. After I taped the gauze on, Mark stood and shook out the tie-dyed blanket he had been sitting on. It made a cloud of dust around him, and he was still smiling at me through the haze.

I placed the tattoo gun in its black velvet bag, feeling proud. Maybe the guy wasn't kidding about practicing on fruit, no matter how ludicrous it had sounded.

"I'll get the CD player." He unzipped the tent and crawled inside, emerging moments later with the CD player and a fresh black tank top. I crawled into the tent and got a towel and some extra T-shirts, put on a pair of cutoffs and my bikini top. I pulled out my tiny baggie of coke and did what little was left, then licked the bag clean. I needed to celebrate. I felt so great about giving Mark the tattoo, especially at how happy he seemed with it. I was eager to get up to the hot springs and see what would transpire. I felt horny, and I wanted to be close to him again. I crawled out of the tent. Mark was about to get into the water. I wished we had some special shoes to walk across the river, but we didn't, so we were going to have to tough it out barefoot.

Mark carried the CD player on his shoulder and lunged right in. "Water's cold, baby," he said, turning slowly with a pained look. His nipples hardened under the black fabric of his tank top.

"It is? How cold?" I asked. I stood at the water's edge, looking across at the tree-laden cliffs. The other side of the river appeared majestic with its lush trees whose leaves shivered in the afternoon breeze. A rocky path snaked up the cliff.

"Really cold," Mark replied, bringing me back to the fucked-up task at hand.

He had already moved about ten feet forward, while I stood paralyzed at the edge, cringing, trying to force my feet to take the cold. I remembered being ten years old and full of dread, leaping into an ice-cold pool at six in the morning for swim-team practice. Then, I just gave up and headed in full force, holding my breath. A deep shiver ran through my body, but I kept moving, kept the blood circulating in my toes. We briskly walked across, holding our belongings over our heads, the water never rising above our waists. On the other side, the ground was craggy, covered with tiny pebbles and twigs. Mark looked up the side of the canyon, then down at my bare feet.

"Can you make it, baby?" he asked.

"I think so."

We stumbled up the side of the canyon. When we reached the top, there was a tiny wooden sign with crudely carved-out letters that read "HOT SPRINGS THAT WAY," with an arrow pointing toward a path. We followed it until we came upon a stone wall. The wall was about waist-high: rust-colored rocks from the canyon. We walked around it, and there, nestled in a nook, was a pool of greenish water, bubbles rising to the surface. Beyond the hot spring was a cave dug into the canyon; it looked like a crude train tunnel from an old Western movie. I peered inside its entrance and made out another pool of water surrounded by a smooth stone ledge.

"This is it, baby. Isn't it beautiful?" Mark had jumped onto the wall and was looking into the murky water from which steam rose. I walked around the hot spring and glanced again inside the cave. We had the option of bathing inside or outside. It was so desolate. The only sounds were of water bubbling, leaves rustling, and birds. I felt as sexy as one of Pan's nymphs surrounded by all this natural beauty.

"Take your clothes off." Mark had jumped down behind me. I turned to him, and the way he looked at me made me go limp all over.

"Should I leave my underwear on?" I asked.

"I don't think you should bother with that."

"What are you saying?" I asked coyly. I wanted the sex, I wanted to feel him inside me. I wanted to see him sweat and smell the sweat of our bodies coupling. Plus, I was beginning to come down from the coke, and sex was the best way to forget I was jonesing.

"I'm saying, get in the hot spring, and we'll see what happens."

Mark quickly peeled off his clothing, turned on a Zeppelin disc, then slipped ever so gracefully into the water. I undressed slowly, a little nervous that someone might come up the path and find us naked, especially slimy Sid. I slid into warm water. It felt so good.

"Come over here," Mark whispered.

"No," I teased.

"Come on," he insisted.

"I'm going to play hard to get," I said, inching backwards.

"Hard to get? Naked in steamy warm water?" He reached out.

I slid further away from him until I hit the slippery wall.

"Get your little butt over here," he said, his eyes glittery.

I doggie-paddled over to where he was. The water was deep, and I couldn't find anywhere to plant my feet. Once I was holding on to the ledge behind him, he started to touch me.

"Isn't this whole environment making you hot?" he asked.

"Yeah, it's really warm," I said, wiping beads of sweat from my forehead.

"That's not what I'm talking about." His fingers found my thigh in the cloudy water.

My tongue slid inside his mouth and we kissed. I felt like we were finally connecting again. He entered me awkwardly; it was obviously difficult to make love in a hot spring. The wall was slippery, and I

234

couldn't wedge my feet. But I slid up and down while he cupped my ass in his strong hands. My stash was completely gone, and now all I had was Mark. My hands steadily held his shoulders.

We trudged back across the river, our heads wrapped in towel turbans. I could see Sid's huge RV pulled into the campground. Mark took off his tank top and wrung it out, then placed it on the stump to dry. Then, too eagerly, it seemed to me, he headed over to Sid's RV, where he knocked on the door. I followed him full of apprehension.

We could hear Sid puttering around inside, then the screen door opened.

"Hey, kids, you should both know you don't need to knock." He stepped aside so we could come in.

"We thought you might be napping," Mark said. He walked up to the counter and leaned against it. I stood closer to the door, waiting for a chance to exit and get back to our tent. I wanted some more of what I had at the hot springs. Coming down made me want nothing but sex.

"No, I'm roaring to go," Sid said. A towel was draped over his shoulders, and he wore a pair of shorts. The brown hair on his chest was unruly, kinky, practically standing on end.

"Go where?" Mark asked. He looked at Sid, confused.

"On up to the hot springs," Sid said, with a little wiggle of his thick waist. He was clearly excited to be back at this memorable spot of his. I wondered if what had happened between Mark and me in the springs had actually happened to Sid at one time, probably a long time ago. The thought of this grossed me out.

"Actually, Orleigh and I just came from there," Mark said, shooting me a smile.

"I figured as much when I saw that your tent was empty," Sid said, scratching his chest.

"Yeah, we were just going to chill out." I backed up toward the door. I was trying to give Mark a hint, but he didn't seem to be picking it up.

"Why don't we make some dinner and drink some beer? Then we can head back to the springs," Sid said. He took the towel off his shoulders and set it on the bench by the kitchen table.

"Sounds good to me. Orleigh?" Mark asked.

"That'll work," I said, though I didn't mean it. I didn't feel like being a bitch when Mark and I were finally getting along. I certainly didn't want to go to the hot springs with Sid. He leered at me enough as it was when I was fully clothed. I didn't like the idea at all. Plus, who knew what kind of germs would slip off his body in that water, contaminating either Mark or me.

Sid made us up a heap of spaghetti that turned out to be quite tasty and better than SpaghettiOs. It was nice to have a cold beer too; Mark and I had been drinking the warm shit that had been sitting for about two weeks on the floor in the back of our car. After dinner Sid made small talk, explaining why he had taken so long to arrive. Apparently he had run out of cash and needed to sell some of his belongings to pay for gas. I found it pretty alarming that a guy over thirty could be so pathetic. He'd come across some Craftsman tools, which he sold at rest stops along the way, making a total of two hundred bucks. After he told his story, Sid was anxious to get to the hot springs.

It felt creepy taking my clothes off in front of Sid; he stripped down as if it were nothing, but I was not that comfortable in front of him. He jumped in the water, then started to coax us in after him. The whole situation seemed wrong. Mark undressed and slipped into the water.

"Come on, Orleigh," he called, his body undulating beneath the green water.

I reluctantly took off my clothes, but not quickly enough to avoid Sid's eyes or his sleazy comment: "So, you really are a natural blonde, Orleigh."

I didn't give him the honor of a response. Once I was in the water, I at least felt safer. I hung onto the stone wall near Mark. He was trying to touch me beneath the water, but I just couldn't get turned on with Sid there. What was he thinking? I certainly wasn't into having sex in front of old men. And I wasn't an exhibitionist under any circumstance. I edged away from Mark, noticing he was already distracted by something else. I followed his gaze to another cave entrance a little ways up the path. An extremely tall man in a long leather jacket was standing at its entrance. His hair was in complete disarray, and his beard fell to his chest. I thought, "hermit," as he walked down the path toward us. He was absolutely disgusting, unkempt, dirty. I was worried he might try to do something crazy.

"Hello, oh, you all, folks," the caveman sputtered with great difficulty. "So, hi. What are you? Ah . . . what's going on with y'all?"

Sid decided to field the question. "Paying a visit to old Camp Verde," he said, his fingers sliding shakily through the water as he attempted a doggie-paddle.

"Ah, my, uh . . . I guess you could if you want to, kind of call her, uh, my girlfriend, is . . . uh . . . making some stew, some really, ah, good vegetable stew, and we were . . . uh . . . wondering, since we, ah, made so much of it here, if you maybe would . . . uh . . . like to, uh, have some of this stew?" It was clear to me that the guy probably hadn't made it through kindergarten.

Sid looked at us, then back at the caveman. "Know what, buddy? We just ate a heaping helping of spaghetti, but if you'd boil up a pot of coffee, we'd love to join you."

"Sure, uh, we can, uh, do that for y'all," the caveman said.

"Come on and get dressed, kids," Sid said. He pulled himself out of the water and walked to his pile of clothing.

"These, ah, kids here, uh . . . they, uh . . . they're yours?" the caveman asked, perplexed.

"Not mine, but my brother's. They're on vacation with me right now," Sid said, reaching out his hand to help Mark out of the water.

I didn't like being associated with Sid in any way, shape, or form, but I figured he had his reasons for lying to the caveman. Maybe he was trying to protect himself, or us. The guy did seem a little scary, and I was less than interested in meeting his cavegirl, for fear they were going to chop us up and add us to their stew. But we all dressed and gathered our belongings, then walked into the cave, where a girl with stringy blond hair was leaning over a pot. No one had informed her that it was better to cook outdoors—less smoke. Regardless of their camping, or cave-living inadequacies, the stew smelled fabulous, and the girl had just started a kettle of coffee.

Sid was trying to work the cavegirl. She was a lot younger than the caveman, probably about my age. She was tall and thin, and she would have been pretty if she was clean and wearing something nice. Sid was helping her dish out the stew and paying her ample compliments on the good smells of her cooking. I was stunned to see him acting so considerate toward a woman. Surprisingly no obnoxious peeking-out-type comments were made the whole time we were there. It was touching.

After we drank our coffee, Mark and I took a walk with cavegirl.

"So, where are you from?" Mark asked. She had an accent that sounded Scandinavian.

"Neptune," the cavegirl replied. I turned to look at her, and she wasn't laughing or smiling, but completely serious.

"Excuse me?" Mark said, stopping short on the path that led back to the hot springs.

"The planet, Neptune," Cavegirl repeated, placing her hands on her hips.

"I see, and why are you here?" Mark asked, resuming walking.

"My father's a banker, and he sent me to earth to see what it's like," Cavegirl said, clutching a woven yarn pouch that hung around her neck and skipping between long strides. She seemed really happy.

"A banker on Neptune?" Mark asked, feigning surprise. I wasn't in the mood to attempt communication with the alien.

"Yes," she smiled. She had begun twirling around Mark, the little pouch around her neck swinging around and practically hitting me in the face. I didn't like her being in such close proximity to my boyfriend. I didn't want her body to come into contact with his—who knew what kind of creepy crawlies resided under her filthy rags.

"So, how are you getting by in America? I don't suppose we accept Neptune dollars here," Mark said smartly. He was moving from side to side to distance himself from the twirling freak.

She began to skip again, giving Mark some space. "My father changed them into American dollars. I've lots of money to get by," she stated proudly.

"Must be nice. Are you supporting the caveman too?" he asked.

She stopped walking, and we stopped next to her. She looked around the wooded path, somewhat puzzled. "No, I just cook for him. He gets checks for being poor."

"Ah, welfare, I see," Mark said. "So you just live here in the cave?"

She started to skip ahead again, lost in her own little alien world. I couldn't stand her. She was getting too close to my man, and she was so filthy. I kept giving Mark the eye, trying to tell him silently that it was time to go back to our tent, but he was engrossed in their little banter.

She suddenly stopped in the middle of the path and struck a pose—one leg bent at the knee in front of her and hands on her hips, which jutted out provocatively. "For now, I'm going to California. I want to be a movie star."

"I'm sure your chances are very good. I don't think we have anyone from Neptune in Hollywood yet." Mark chuckled.

"Thanks," she said.

We were getting pretty far along the path, a ways from the cave and the hot springs. The trees became denser, and it began to get dark. I wanted to go back to the campsite, and I was dreading having to cross the freezing cold river in the dark. Shadows loomed beneath the trees, and occasionally branches snapped and leaves rustled. I felt edgy. Only the light of the moon guided us, and it was barely visible through the tops of trees.

"I think we need to go back to our tent now," I finally said, tired of playing the evil-eye game with Mark.

Mark told the alien cavegirl to relay to Sid that we were heading back to the tent. Then he said something about how we'd probably see her and the caveman at the springs tomorrow. We walked away. I couldn't get over how fucking strange this chick was. Mark was so accepting of people, no matter how bizarre they were. He took people at face value, never judged them, and he always tried to help them if they were down and out. I hated people, couldn't stand it when I thought someone was stupid. Mark was this quiet shy guy, nice to everyone he met, and trusting. I guess we complemented each other.

"Didn't you think that girl was weird?" I asked.

"Yeah, but people think I'm weird too. No big deal."

"What was that Neptune shit about?" I asked, still frustrated from the whole encounter.

"She's just different. Maybe she has some problems; who really knows?" He grabbed my hand, and we scaled down the cliff.

My bare feet hurt. I kept stumbling over rocks. "I didn't like her," I said hastily.

"Of course you didn't, you don't like anyone," he said, letting my hand slip away from his.

"I like you; in fact, I love you," I whispered.

"You do?" He took my hand again and helped me over a particularly craggy spot on the path. We were approaching the edge of the water.

"Absolutely."

He put his arm around my waist to give me support. "Same here, baby," he said, kissing me on the cheek.

This time I waded into the water without hesitating. I wanted to get back to our tent and warm up, so I let Mark guide me across without a complaint. When we got back, we stripped off our wet clothes, then made love before we both dozed off.

"She said her father's a banker?" Sid asked, spooning Lucky Charms into his slimy mouth.

Mark and I sat across from him at the RV dinette table. "Yeah, that's what she told me," Mark said. He had been telling Sid everything that had happened when we left him with the caveman the night before.

"Interesting. I bet she has a lot of money," he said, then drank the remaining milk out of his plastic bowl, bringing it up to his lips. When he finished, he hurled the bowl into the nearby sink.

I was startled by the clank of the bowl. I looked at Sid. He was staring out the window, unaffected by the loud noise he'd caused.

"Doesn't look like she's heading back to Neptune for a while," Mark said, reaching in his pocket for his pack of cigarettes.

Sid turned away from the window and looked back at us. "Well, well, I have an idea," he said, smiling.

This conversation about Cavegirl's money seemed to be going in a bad direction. I could feel where it was headed.

"Are you thinking about taking her money, Sid?" Mark asked. Of course Sid wanted the money—he'd just sold off all his Craftsman tools, and I am sure he didn't know where his next dollar would come from. But now he did. I could see it in the gleam of his eye.

"Would that be a problem? Her father's a fucking banker. We could leave her enough money to get back to Neptune." He laughed.

240

"I don't know. I don't like to steal. I'm going for a walk. Are you coming, Orleigh?" Mark rose from the table and headed toward the door.

"No, I think I'll stay and make a cup of coffee and chill," I said, trying to sound casual. "I'll catch up with you." I didn't want him to know that my devious mind was already plotting plundering the alien's fortune.

Mark left the RV, and I knew he was contemplating how he felt about taking this girl's money. Personally, I had no qualms about it, and I wanted to know how Sid planned to go about it.

"What are you thinking we should do, Sid?" I asked, as soon as Mark was safely out of earshot.

"I was thinking about getting her to go naked in one of the hot springs. I'm thinking the one outside the cave. You and Mark could go in the other one inside of the cave, make it look like you're getting it on. Then one of you can get ahold of her clothes and check out the pockets. Easy as pie."

I kept thinking how truly pathetic Sid was. But what did I really care? I didn't have anything better to do, and I really didn't like the alien chick anyway.

"What if she won't go in the water?" I asked, intentionally trying to throw a chink in his plan.

"She will; she's crazy."

"When do you want to do it?" I asked, feeling a little excited.

"Tonight."

Mark didn't want to go through with it. He could sell drugs to people, but he couldn't take cash from a girl who thought she was from Neptune. I mean, I was a good person in some respects, but we needed the money. Well, if she truly had some. We had to move on to California via New Mexico in order to catch a couple of Dead shows. It was going to be virtually impossible unless we found a way to get some money. Unfortunately, we didn't have any Craftsman tools we could unload at rest stops across America.

We sat in the tiny hot-spring cave, while Sid and Cavegirl bathed in the outdoor one. It was the perfect setup. I crawled out of the water and crept quietly over to the entrance to the cave. I could see Cavegirl's clothing in a pile right in front of the entrance. It would be so simple to just reach out, grab something, and then start looking through it. In fact, I could see the little pouch she wore around her neck lying there. I had a gut feeling that that was where she kept her stash. I wanted to grab it, but I didn't want to upset Mark.

"Look, what if I take it, will it piss you off?" I asked.

He looked over at me. "I don't feel great about it, if that's what you're asking me."

"I'm asking if you would be pissed. I already know you don't approve."

"I won't be so pissed, and I'm not going to think any differently about you. I just don't really want to be involved."

"Okay. Then I'm going to get it," I said, feeling slightly more at ease. Mark wasn't going to judge me, and that was all I was worried about.

I crouched down on my hands and knees, sliding my arm out of the cave entrance. I felt around a little, then grabbed the string of the little pouch. I slowly slid it across the rocks. Once I had it in the tiny cave with Mark and me, I opened it. There was so much money inside it. I quickly thumbed through it. There had to be over a thousand dollars in hundreds and smaller bills. I couldn't believe this crazy chick was walking around with this much money around her neck. She really was from Neptune. I took everything save for a hundred dollars in small bills, which I wrapped around a small stone to make the pouch somewhat heavier. I briskly began dressing. "Let's go back to the tent."

"How much?" Mark asked.

"Enough," I said, slipping my T-shirt over my head.

"How much?" he asked again, not moving from the water.

"A lot." I slid my shorts on.

"Did you leave her anything?" he asked.

"Yeah, enough to take a bus, make a phone call, eat a meal."

"How much?" he asked.

I was getting annoyed. "Around a thousand," I said, through clenched teeth.

"What?" he asked, finally getting out of the water.

242

"Around a thousand dollars." I was trying to be quiet so that Sid and Cavegirl wouldn't overhear.

"That much?"

"Yeah," I replied.

We started to walk back to the tent. Sid was trying to get it on with the cavegirl when we waved to them and continued down the path. I figured he'd fuck her with her consent or without, then come back to our tent to try and get some of the money. Mark and I crawled into the tent and lay on the sleeping bags.

"Let me see."

I pulled the bills out of my bra and handed them to Mark.

"Holy shit! That's a lot of money. I don't think I've ever had that much money at one time."

"I know. I haven't either," I said proudly. "How much should we give Sid?" But in truth I didn't think he deserved shit. He was getting sex from the girl, after all, which was all he really needed.

"One hundred is all," Mark said.

I smiled inside—we were both feeling the same way. "Oh, okay, Mister Generous. Why don't we just get the fuck out of here? Sid's going to be banging Cavegirl for a while. This is probably the first time he's had sex this century."

"Then let's go," Mark said. I was surprised he agreed with me. Usually he was too damn honest. What was the deal? Was I finally rubbing off on him? I wondered, only a tad troubled.

We scrambled to pack up our camping gear. We were fortunate we didn't have much to pack because we were basically living out of the car. I threw everything into the trunk as Mark started the engine. Within moments we were back to feeling like Bo and Luke Duke as we headed up the wild dirt road.

I wasn't sure how long I'd been asleep when I was torn from an awesome dream by the shaking of the car. In my dreamy haze I peered over at Mark, who looked pissed off.

"What's wrong?" I asked.

"The car is freaking out."

"Why don't we pull over?"

"Fine."

At the side of the road Mark got out to inspect the car. He walked behind the car, and I could see his face contorting in the rearview mirror. He gave the car a hard kick. This was obviously something pretty bad. The plan was to catch up with the Dead in Flagstaff. The show wasn't starting till the following night, so we had decided to check out the Grand Canyon on our way. We were excited to see the Grand Canyon, which had been one of the goals of our road trip.

Mark came back around and opened the door. "We have a flat tire," he said.

"Do we have a spare?"

"No."

"What are we going to do?" I asked, tapping my Birkenstock-clad foot on the dashboard.

"I suppose we wait. A cop has to drive by eventually," Mark said, climbing back into the driver's seat.

"A cop?" I asked. What the fuck! All we needed was an encounter with a cop.

"Yeah, who else is going to help us?"

"I don't know, shouldn't we try and walk somewhere?"

"Do you see anything around here?" He waved his hand back and forth like a magician. Nothing but desert flatlands, with large red rocks looming in the distance.

We sat in the car for around two hours, endlessly waiting. I smoked about two packs of cigarettes and drank four Pepsis. Eventually, Mark's wish came true—a sheriff drove past us and squealed to a stop.

"He's getting out of the car," I said, watching the sheriff's every move in the rearview mirror. Mark didn't move—maybe he was a little afraid too.

"He's coming, Mark."

"Good, that's what we wanted," he snapped.

Smiling, the chubby sheriff strode lethargically to our open window, a cigar butt stuck between his teeth. "Howdy, kids. See you got yourselves a flat."

How observant. Maybe he had figured out that we were ex-druggies and thieves as well.

"Yeah, and we're not from around here, so we don't know where to get it fixed," Mark replied nonchalantly. He didn't appear anxious at all.

"Why don't you let me take you over to the mechanic's. He's a personal friend of mine, and I'm pretty sure he can help you out."

I climbed into the backseat of the police car, and Mark got in the passenger seat. I didn't like anything that had to do with cops, but at least the fat fuck was kind enough to give us a ride. After about forty minutes of driving in complete silence, we pulled into the police station. Mark looked back at me completely distressed.

"Excuse me, sir, but aren't we going to the mechanic's?" he asked. My first thought was that Cavegirl had already managed to call the cops.

"We sure are, son, he's located right behind the station. I'll walk you back there if you'd like."

Mark breathed a sigh of relief, and so did I.

"No, sir. Thank you. I think we can find it all right on our own," Mark said, getting out of the passenger seat.

We headed behind the station, where we found a dusty mechanic sitting on a lawn chair, smoking and drinking from a bottle of Jack Daniel's. He looked like he used to ride in a Hell's Angels motorcycle gang but had contracted AIDS somewhere along the way.

"Yeah?" he said, looking up at us from the lawn chair, a pile of engine parts cluttered around his feet.

"We have a flat tire down the road," Mark said.

"What do you want me to do about it?" the mechanic asked, digging a finger deep into his nose.

"The sheriff told us you'd be willing to lend us a hand. We don't have a spare." Mark looked around. A crooked red sign that read "Jethro's Garage" hung over the garage entrance. An old yellow rusted-out Chevy truck sat disassembled in the middle of the garage, and tires were stacked up all around on the cement floor.

"Fine, I'll take care of ya, but it will cost you," the mechanic said. He growled deep in his throat as he rose from his lawn chair. He shamelessly scratched his balls, then adjusted the waist of his baggy pants.

"We have some money," I replied.

"You can count on losing about fifty dollars," he said, taking a long swig from the bottle of JD. "Especially if I have to drive you both back to your car." He smashed his liquor bottle, throwing it against the ground, giving a triumphant guttural laugh as it shattered.

The idea of this guy driving Mark and me anywhere was scary, but Mark didn't seem a bit concerned. He continued talking to the guy, and they picked out a tire for our piece of shit. Male bonding at its finest. I was starting to think we wouldn't be able to see the Grand Canyon. I was ready to go somewhere where we could eat and crash for the night.

We crawled into the bed of the mechanic's truck, and he drove us back to our car. He was kind enough to help us get the tire on. When he was through, he took our fifty dollars, scratched his exposed butt crack, then drove away.

"Ya want anything else?" our mouthy little waitress said, snapping her gum while she rudely slammed our check on the table.

"No, thanks," Mark replied.

"Suit yourselves." She turned on her heels and, shaking her saucy thirty-something ass, walked away.

After we finished our okay meal, we headed out to the car, discussing how tired we were. We decided to park in the truck stop and sleep. Behind the restaurant we found two parking lots. One was jammed with trucks, engines running. The other had only a single truck in it, so it seemed it would be best to park there—definitely quieter. We drove into it, then went to sleep.

It was a bright and sunny Arizona morning, and for some reason I woke feeling more in love. Mark straightened his shaggy hair in the rearview mirror, and I couldn't take my eyes off of him.

"Breakfast, baby?" I asked through a yawn.

"Evil-truck-stop restaurant?"

"Lovely, maybe Flo will be there."

We spent a few minutes trying to make ourselves at least presentable. I started the car, but it wouldn't move. I stepped on the gas pedal and nothing happened. Mark looked at me, then out the window.

"I'll go check it out. Hopefully it's not another tire." He stepped out of the car, and I watched him trudge around it. He looked like he was moving in slow motion, then he started slipping and sliding. "Fuck!" he yelled.

"What the hell's going on?" I asked, rolling down the window.

"Mud, it's all mud. No wonder there was only one semi in the lot, it would take a semi to get the fuck out of here!" I could tell by his tone that he'd reached the ultimate point of frustration. He walked behind the car and started to push as I pressed on the gas. Nothing happened; we didn't budge.

Mark circled the car, sinking deeper and deeper in the mud. Then he just lost it, kicking the car with his heavy boots. He climbed on top of the hood and jumped up and down, bouncing and swearing. I sat in the driver's seat listening to him above me. I wondered if he was going to completely lose it and trash the whole thing. Then I didn't hear him anymore. I eased the upper part of my body out of the open window, planting my ass on the bottom of the window frame. Mark was sitting there on the hood, his head in his hands, crying.

I felt like I was going to cry too, but I held back my tears.

"It's not worth all the effort," Mark said sniffling. "What are we doing? Life was better before. We had an escape; I had an escape. I could always get away from whatever was bringing me down. Now I have nothing but a piece-of-shit car and money problems."

"You have me," I said, trying to comfort him.

"I love you."

"Let's get this car on the road," I said, grabbing his wet hand.

He pulled his hand away from me and wiped more tears from his eyes. "Baby, we can't."

I looked around the parking lot and saw some large pieces of plywood, so I pulled myself onto the roof, then slid my body down the side of the car. I trudged through the mud, then dragged a piece of plywood over to the car and placed it under the back tire. Once I had four pieces, I shoved them so as far under the tires as they would go. I got back in the car and started it.

"Mark, honey, could you get off the roof and push again?" I called up at him.

He slid off the roof, shaking his head, then went behind the car to push. With one push, the tires broke free, and the car moved forward. I was so thrilled to get the hell out of that parking lot, I didn't want to stop completely, so I just slowed down enough for Mark to climb in.

CHAPTER 15

Mark had painted a sign that read Jewelry & Tattoos. Almost instantly after setting up on our tie-dyed blanket, two guys came over asking questions about tattoos. Mark let them look through my book, and they both picked a tattoo.

"Can you do the dancing bear?" asked the shorter one with long dirty hair.

I didn't want to tell them that I'd only tattooed fruit and Mark. I couldn't look the guy in the eye, but I mumbled that I could. He sat down on a corner of the blanket, away from the jewelry, and I started up the battery-operated tattoo gun, then stared at the guy's puny upper arm. I was afraid I was going to screw this up, even maim the guy.

"Hey, girl, you want to get stoned before you do this? You look a little nervous," he said as I prepared the stencil.

"No, but thanks for the offer." I wet the stencil with alcohol then centered it on his arm, pressing down lightly. When I peeled the paper off, I noted that the stencil had come out perfectly. Too bad I couldn't pretend that the stencil was the actual tattoo. I was afraid to tattoo a total stranger. Who knew what he would do if I fucked up.

"Well, I'm gonna smoke some shit before you start. Is that okay?" he asked, pulling a little red glass bowl out of his shirt pocket.

"That's cool," I said, anxiously biting my lower lip. I looked around for Mark, feeling protective of him, hoping he didn't see the weed. What was I thinking? We were at the parking lot of a Dead show—if he wanted weed he could easily get it.

When my victim finished smoking, he adjusted his arm for me. I dipped the needle into the ink. I was terrified as I pressed it into his skin. I could feel it bury deeply, but I wasn't sure if it was deep enough for the ink to take, so I pushed harder.

"Ouch," the guy gasped, jerking back his arm.

"Uh, sorry, but it's going to hurt a little." I smiled reassuringly. I don't know if I was trying to convince him or myself that I could do this.

His tall friend came over to see what I was doing. "How's it going, man?"

"A little painful, dude," the guy said, and I dipped the needle into the ink again, then blotted the little bubbles of ink on his skin.

"I've got something that'll ease your pain," the friend said. He reached into his pocket and pulled out a tiny brown glass bottle. I knew immediately what was inside it; I'd seen that kind of bottle before. The guy unscrewed the cap, revealing a tiny spoon. He dipped it into the bottle, pulling it out to reveal a minuscule mound of cocaine. He held it under his friend's nose. He inhaled deeply, then shook his head.

"You want some?" the friend asked me. God, I wanted some. My hands began to shake. I looked over at Mark peddling his jewelry.

I shook my head. "No thanks, man. It'll break my concentration." I stuck the needle back into his skin.

It took about half an hour to finish the tattoo. When I finally wiped it clean, it looked really good. I was relieved that I had done a decent job. The guy examined it and let me know that he was pleased. I was lucky it was his first tattoo, or he would have seen how utterly inexperienced I was. And the gun was shoddy and the ink cheap.

Mark sat on our blanket surrounded by a group of people, playing the bongo drums. They all looked stoned, and I wondered if Mark had done anything. I'd been so good about the coke. But he gave me a reassuring look as I walked up to him. He had evidently sensed my concern. I knelt down ·beside him and touched his hand.

"Hey, girl," he whispered. "I made us quite a bit of money."

"Good, baby. What did you sell?" I asked, looking around, worried that someone might overhear us discussing money. But the Deadheads hanging out on our blanket didn't seem aware of us.

"Lots of necklaces." He smiled, showing me his necklace holder, which was practically empty.

"Cool," I said. I was relieved. I'd made a hundred and twenty-five dollars off the stoner guys, and they'd thought my crappy tattoos were actually good.

"Want to try and get into the show?" Mark asked.

"No, this is fine. I like sitting out here with you. I see you made some new friends." I looked around at the four drummers. Their eyes were closed as they obliviously beat on their pigskins. A boy with long black dreads led the circle. A girl pounded a drum while shaking a tambourine in her other hand.

"Actually, they are attracting a lot of attention to my jewelry."

My hand and my back ached from giving tattoos. I decided to take a walk to ease some of my tension. As I moved through the crowd, I was approached by a hippie chick, carrying oranges in her skirt. I felt kind of sorry for her.

"How much for two?" I asked.

"Twenty dollars," she replied, staring back at me deadpan. I didn't know how to respond. I considered walking away, but then I thought how these people sometimes desperately needed the gas money. Mark and I had enough money to make it far ourselves, and we could honestly spare a twenty for someone in need.

"Sure, I'll take two," I said. I paid the girl and brought the oranges to Mark. The drummers had vanished as bizarrely as they had appeared. They'd gone spreading their bongo love elsewhere. We sat on the blanket, eating our fruit. It tasted so good to eat something juicy and fresh. But ten seconds after I finished the orange, I began to feel nauseous. Then I found myself on my hands and knees, leaning off the blanket, heaving and throwing up orange-tinted vomit. I looked over at Mark, vomit clinging to the dirty strands of hair that fell in my face. He was leaning against our car, clutching his stomach. He bent over, mouth agape, and a flood of vomit projectiled from his rosy lips. My head fell uncontrollably forward, and I continued puking and retching until there was nothing left in my stomach. I stood, wiped the tears from my eyes, and stumbled over to Mark, who was now dry heaving. He was gagging and spitting, drool spilling from the corners of his mouth, dribbling down his chin. Fucking oranges, I thought.

Mark lifted his head, wiped his drool with his shirtsleeve, then

251

glared harshly at me. "Orleigh, where did you get those fucking oranges!"

"From some girl," I answered, barely able to stand. I felt horrible. I put my arm around his waist, but he moved away from me.

"Where? What girl?" he asked, craning his neck and scanning the crowd through teary eyes.

"Over there." I pointed in the direction where I last saw the girl, and Mark stumbled off in that direction.

The crowd became translucent, fluttering in and out of focus, like butterfly wings. I watched, mesmerized. A child in overalls was spinning around in front of me, a daisy clutched in her hand. I wanted to touch these people, see if my hand would go right through them. I felt like it would. The beat of the drummers pounded in the distance, a loud pulse in my head. I became deaf to all other noise. I saw Mark in the distance walking back toward me. He looked like an angel. He was floating just a few inches above the ground, his body swaying with the rhythm in my head.

He was standing in front of me. "It's peyote," he said. His voice sounded like a tape recorder playing at slow speed. I felt like we were underwater.

"What?" I asked, wanting to see his mouth form the words again.

"Sit back and relax; this is going to be a long ride," he said, slipping down onto the blanket.

What went on the rest of that night I don't think I will ever fully remember. The beat of the drummers was calming, the colors vivid. Mark was angelic. I had a vision in which we were together forever. It began with a big stone house. We had children, two beautiful boys. Mark pulled into the driveway in a convertible. He got out of the car, wearing an expensive-looking suit and a tie, holding a briefcase. The boys ran to him gleefully, calling out, *"Daddy, you're home!"* Then the vision turned on me, became a black-and-white movie, a gray haze distorting the picture. I was alone, sitting at Mark's grave, singing "Pictures of You" to his body beneath the earth. Then I saw myself at a river, where a man with a ferry was waiting to take me to the other side. I paid him with the coin clenched in my fist. I was in a church, on the other side, and Mark was there, cold and blue. I kissed his mouth and there was blood in it.

Everything turned crimson. I tasted the blood as I touched Mark's ice-cold skin. I wanted to be with him, but I wasn't real. I wanted to love him, but I couldn't get inside him anymore. I kissed him, stuck my tongue in his mouth, desperately trying to be with him again.

I awoke on the blanket in the parking lot, surrounded by the cars of crashed-out Deadheads. I felt as dazed as I had the night before—I wanted to stop tripping.

"Mark," I moaned as I rolled over. He was propped up on an elbow, his face pasty white, his countenance pained.

He looked directly at me, but I could tell he didn't see me. His eyes were glassy, distant. I crawled over to him, held his face in my palm, then snapped my fingers in front of his eyes. He didn't flinch, didn't even blink.

"Mark, Mark," I whispered. I stared at his face for what seemed like forever. A tear rolled out of his eye, then another. He looked at me, but he wouldn't speak. Then his eyes became vivid, clear and focused, and he smiled at me as if nothing were wrong.

"Mark, are you all right?"

He still didn't seem to hear me. My thoughts were so twisted up in my head. I worried that the drugs had made him brain-dead or that he didn't want to be with me anymore. I kept staring into his face, wanting a reaction, but his dulled expression remained unchanged. I placed my head in his lap, sobbing quietly. He didn't attempt to comfort me. I needed to be close to his body, feel him.

I sobbed myself to sleep, my head nestled in his lap. I'm not sure how much time went by, but I woke to him trying to get his legs out from under me. My eyes snapped open, and I sat up.

"How you doing, darling," he asked, smiling, playing with my hair.

"Fine. How are you?"

"Great."

He was acting as if nothing had gone wrong. "Do you remember anything?" I asked.

"Not really, just eating the oranges and getting sick. But I'm fine now," he said, reaching his hand out and pulling me off the ground.

The first place we went when we arrived in California was Newport Beach. Baker, Heather's old boy toy, had a brother named John who lived there, and I wanted to drop by and say hello. I thought that Mark and I could maybe crash at his place for a day or two before the Los Angeles Dead show. I remembered when I first met John at Baker's—he was an extremely attractive guy. He said he was a hair model in L.A. He did have gorgeous hair. He had told us all about his beachfront condo. And there was this beautiful woman who took care of him. I was so excited to see his place, and I hoped his sugar mama wouldn't mind us staying.

Mark and I found ourselves in front of a run-down apartment building. It was the correct address, but there was no beach in sight. We walked to the front door and knocked. After a long wait, the door opened, revealing an old man in a 7-Eleven work shirt.

"Can I help you?" he asked, looking shocked that he had company.

"Is John here?" I asked, puzzled. I was convinced we had the wrong place.

"He's sleeping," the old man said to my surprise, then pulled a hanky from his shirt pocket and blew his nose.

"I'm a friend from Illinois. Just wanted to see him while I was in the area." I smiled sweetly.

The 7-Eleven guy stepped away from the door. I wasn't sure if that meant he was done with us, or if he was going to get John. Mark gave me a weird look, and I shrugged my shoulders. We stood there for about two minutes, then John appeared at the door.

"Hey good-looking, what are you doing here?" he asked, standing in the doorway, lewdly licking his lips.

"Came here to see you again," I said. I was flirting, but mainly because I wanted to find us a place to crash.

John walked out onto the tiny front porch and gave me a hug and a more-than-friendly kiss. I pulled away and introduced him to Mark.

"So, you have a boyfriend now?" John asked, eyeballing Mark.

"Yes," I said, looking at Mark, smiling warmly.

"That just sucks, Poolside," he said, slapping me gently on the ass.

"Sorry," I replied.

I couldn't believe he called me "Poolside." That nickname brought back the horrible memory of the one and only time John and I had been together. We were all skinny-dipping at a pool in a friend of mine's neighborhood. And somehow John and I got to doing it by the side of the pool on a lounge chair in front of everyone. It was totally crazy, and I never got over it. Not that I didn't get over him—it was the idea of what I did with him I couldn't get over. It felt amazing and thrilling in the moment, but in retrospect I was mortified.

"Where you staying during your visit in Newport?" John asked. He sat down on a porch step and lit a cigarette.

"We're not sure," I said, fishing out my own cigarettes from my shoulder bag. I lit one for Mark, handed it to him, then lit one for me.

"Why don't we get some lunch at this bar down the street?" John said, rising from the porch step, inhaling his cigarette deeply. "You know, you're welcome to stay with me if it's all right with Ernie."

"Ernie?" I asked.

"The guy who answered the door. I'm sort of staying with him right now, for lack of a better place. Unfortunately, my love life has kind of taken a spill, and I'm stuck with very little cash. You know me, though, I make ends meet." He squashed his cigarette butt under his ratty tennis shoe.

What a loser, I thought. "That would be great if we could crash for a night." I looked over at Mark, who was silently smoking. He gave me a disapproving look.

"Let me check with Ernie; hang out here for a minute," John said, walking back inside. Soon I could hear a muffled conversation. Mark looked at me, then down at the ground.

"What's wrong?" I asked, though I knew he was upset about John's forwardness and my flirtatiousness.

"I don't like that guy. I think I'd rather sleep in the car."

"In the car?" For god's sake, wasn't he tired of living in the car? Wouldn't a bed, for at least one night, be nice? I stared back at him, but he wouldn't look me in the eye. He knew that something had gone on between John and me; John certainly hadn't tried to conceal it.

"You two had something. Don't try and lie about it," he said, his anger clearly detectable.

"First of all, I wouldn't even think about lying to you," I said defensively, placing my hands on my hips. "Secondly, it was nothing. It was a one-night stand that meant absolutely nothing to me. The only thing we have going on is friendship. I like John as a friend, nothing more."

John returned from inside the apartment, and I abruptly shut up. "Hey, guys, you can stay if you'd like. But only two nights."

"Sounds good to us," I said, shooting Mark a look to keep him quiet.

Relieved that I didn't have to sleep in the car again, I felt more than willing to give John a ride to a few places, but then we spent the whole day running errands for him. I'm not sure if he was selling drugs, but it did appear that way. After several hours of dropping him off places, picking him up, then driving him to yet another location, we wound up at the bar where we were supposed to have lunch hours before. It was a shady little hole in the wall, and we ate our grilled cheese sandwiches quickly.

When we were done we returned to John's lovely "condo." It was so small: a kitchen, a bathroom, and a minuscule bedroom. In the bedroom there was a bunk bed and a couch, and it was made apparent that Mark and I would be sleeping on the couch. Ernie and John both got in their bunks, John on top and Ernie on the bottom. The whole living-arrangement thing was bizarre. It was only eight o'clock, and they were getting ready to go to bed. Ernie shouted out, "Who has the remote?"

I looked down at a tiny table by the couch and saw the television remote. "It's right here, Ernie," I said.

"Then turn on the television and have a seat. That's where you'll be sleeping anyway." He snickered.

Mark and I sat on the couch, and I handed the remote to Ernie. John threw us a blanket, and we crawled under it. I really didn't care if we went to bed or not. It was so strange to see John living like this, especially after all the tales he'd spun at Baker's. He'd made it seem like he had such a glamorous life, filled with money, women, and parties. But here he was living with a seventy-or-so-year-old guy in a piece-of-shit apartment.

When Mark and I returned from breakfast at Jack in the Box, John was sitting on his tiny front porch, looking very unhappy.

"What's up, John?" I asked.

He frowned. "You guys can't come back inside."

"Why?" I asked, utterly confused. Had we done something wrong?

"You didn't fold up your blanket," he said, looking at me. He seemed distraught. "You just left it on the couch."

"We ran to get a bite to eat. Not like I was going to leave it like that all day or anything," I said defensively. I did feel a little guilty until I realized how ridiculous this was. I was relatively conscious of being a good guest. This was just a blanket though; I didn't see the problem.

"It's not me, Orleigh, it's Ernie. He's the one who has the problem. I'm sorry, guys, you can't stay here anymore." He dropped his head between his knees, focusing on his shoes. He was embarrassed. Maybe he was upset that I'd caught him in such a huge lie. Maybe it was that he was living with someone who could be his grandfather. Mark and I stood there awkwardly in silence.

I had nothing left to say to John. It wasn't like Mark and I really cared about staying there.

"Sorry about the blanket, dude," Mark said. But I could tell he was being completely insincere.

We walked away, and once we got in the car, we busted out laughing.

"Now you young folk should know better. Leaving a blanket unfolded on the couch! What, were you born in a barn?" he mumbled, imitating Ernie's old-man voice. I couldn't stop laughing.

"What was it with that John guy? What kind of relationship did you two have?" Mark asked, turning serious.

"It wasn't a big deal."

"He acted really weird around me."

"He acts weird around everyone," I said. There was no way I could explain to Mark what had happened between me and John. If I told him all the sordid details, he would have assumed I was a slut. Well, maybe I had been, but the poolside incident with John had been one of the biggest mistakes in my life. The thought of sex with John made me shudder.

We drove to Palm Springs. We had some extra money and thought it would be nice to get a hotel room and live it up. We found a hotel that cost eighty dollars a night. It looked fabulous. We sauntered into the relatively posh lobby, where we were completely out of our element. Neither of us had showered in days, and we weren't exactly dressed to kill—we both wore filthy jeans and tie-dyes imbued with the stench of the road. Regardless of our freakiness, we were able to get a room when we placed our wad of cash on the hotel clerk's counter. After the bellhop led us to our room, we slammed the door in his face without giving him a tip. The room was elegant and clean.

"I'm going to get washed up. Want to join me?" I asked Mark, winking seductively. I caught a look of myself in the mirror, noticing that my hair was clumpy and greasy, my eyes blood red from lack of sleep, my lips cracked and chapped from the sun. I looked horrible.

"Can I watch instead?" Mark asked.

"You want to watch me take a shower?" I asked incredulously.

"Yeah," he answered with a mischievous grin.

"Why?"

"Because I think it's sexy."

"Why don't you just get in the shower with me—isn't that sexy?" I asked. I wanted to get clean and fuck in the shower.

"I'd rather watch from the outside; it feels better that way."

Maybe he was just being polite because I smelled awful. That was understandable; I had been catching unpleasant whiffs of *him* lately. "Whatever," I said as I walked toward the bathroom.

Mark followed me, and I started the shower. The hotel had kindly placed several bottles of shampoo, conditioner, and bath gel inside the shower. The expensive stuff too. I slowly undressed, then walked into the delicious hot stream of water. I could feel the dirt slide off my body. I glanced at Mark who sat on the floor. He was smiling.

I began to wash my extremely greasy hair. To shampoo was a gift from the gods. I couldn't handle how great it felt to be cleaning myself. I finished washing my hair twice, then I grabbed a washcloth and some shower gel. Once I began to soap my body up, I noticed Mark was masturbating, still sitting on the floor. Seeing this made me even hornier.

When I got out of the shower, Mark was obviously through assisting himself, so he got in. I dried off and went into our room. I opened the curtains and the sunlight poured in, blinding me. The carpet around the window was illuminated by the rays of sun. I stood in the square of light and felt the heat soak into my naked flesh. The view was unbelievably bright. All the little shops looked so upper-class. Ladies in designer outfits and large sunglasses strolled down the street, carrying armloads of shopping bags. The fronds of palm trees swayed in the breeze.

Mark came out of the shower and started groping me all over as I moved away from the window and lay on the bed. I was thrilled by the feel of clean sheets and the idea of being in a room instead of the backseat of the car. And Mark had the greatest tongue. I waited until it found the place where it was most desired, then I closed my eyes as my body began to slowly tense.

There were so many reasons why I loved Mark.

The sun was still shining when we left for dinner. It spilled through the leaves of the palm trees that lined the hotel's drive. We ambled down a sidewalk, also bordered by palm trees. I'd only seen these trees in movies, but they were everywhere here. I felt like we were in paradise: palm and banana trees, climbing bougainvillea, the warm sun, and the wide open sky. You could see the Santa Rosa Mountains off in the distance, their peaks capped with snow.

At a quaint little Italian restaurant, we were seated at a corner table, a comfortable distance from the other customers. I ordered pasta; Mark, a pizza. It would have been nice to drink some wine, but the waiter carded us, and we had to drink Pepsi instead. Regardless, it was the most fabulous meal either of us had eaten in weeks.

Hotels, fine dining, shopping. We went from the lush life to being down-and-out once again. I dug my hands deep into my overall pocket and pulled out a fifty-dollar bill. That was all we had left even though we were sitting outdoors on the patio of a coffeehouse in downtown Huntington Beach drinking expensive mochas. I placed the bill on the table between Mark and me, and he gave me a knowing smile. Then I saw that two guys were approaching us.

"Hey, I got a question for you." The gruff voice came from a sardonic-looking guy. His eyes were a flat black and peered out from beneath strands of dyed-black hair. He fidgeted back and forth on his black Converse high-top sneakers. The other guy stood with both hands in the pockets of his ripped-up black jeans. He had reddish-blond unruly hair that stuck out from a baseball cap, and a long beard that had a tiny braid down the center. He stood quietly, staring at Mark, at me, then at our table. I glanced at the bill on the table, wondering if I should pocket it again.

Mark studied the two guys, looking baffled. "Go ahead, shoot," he said.

"You know where we can get some good drugs around here?" the guy in the Converse sneakers asked. The other one leered at me from under the rim of his baseball cap.

"What are you looking for specifically?" Mark asked, then took a long sip of his mocha.

"I don't know, like acid or ecstasy. Either or," he said. His friend continued leering in silence.

"I can probably hook you up with some acid," Mark said, not looking directly at the Converse guy, but focusing his attention on me, silencing me with his eyes.

I didn't know what Mark was thinking because there was no way he could get find acid around here. What a complete freak, I thought. He was only going to get these guys completely pissed off. I didn't say anything though; I just sat there and watched them interact. The Converse guy continued bouncing on the balls of his feet as he talked with Mark. Mark arranged for them to meet us back here in two hours. When they walked away, I glared at Mark.

"What were you thinking?" I said.

"This is a chance for us to make money, baby." He calmly downed the rest of his drink.

"Yeah, but how are you going to produce the goods, Mark?"

"I'll figure that out in a few minutes," he said, focusing his attention on the etched glass tabletop.

"When? We only have two hours."

"Look, I have an idea, but I know you won't think it'll work."

"Lay it on me," I said bitterly, already fearing what his mind had conjured up.

"I was thinking I could buy some heavy art paper and perforate it. Then I could, like, color it or stamp it, and it would look like a sheet of acid. We could sell them a sheet or two or three at maybe a hundred dollars apiece. What do you think?"

I cast my eyes to the ground. How could it hurt? I thought. I mean, we were planning on leaving that day, so these guys would never see us again. Plus, they were about as brain-dead as a roach on the Raid highway. "I think it should work just fine," I said.

We walked a few blocks from the coffeehouse and found a stationary store where we purchased three sheets of art paper, a smiley stamp, a blue ink pad, and a brown envelope that could hold all three sheets. Each sheet of paper was large enough to make one hundred tabs of fake acid. The whole thing seemed like it would work like a charm. When we were done making our purchases, we walked back to the coffee shop and found an outdoor table behind a large tree in the corner. Mark laid out the art supplies, and we were discreet enough that no one could tell what we were doing.

He took the safety pin that was holding his jacket sleeve together and began to perforate the paper into tiny little squares, which took forever. When he was done making a sheet, I took the stamp and inkpad and placed a tiny smiley face in the middle of each square. I was worried that the guys would return before Mark finished all the sheets, but they ended up being late.

We had completed three sheets, placed them into the brown envelope, and were drinking yet another cup of expensive coffee when the guys pulled into the parking lot of the coffeehouse. They casually walked over to our table.

"Hey, what's going on?" Converse said, throwing his shoulders back, attempting to look tough. His friend leered at me again, and his tongue darted up like a lizard's catching a fly.

"Nothing," Mark replied. He tapped a corner of the envelope on the glass tabletop.

Converse greedily eyed the envelope. "So, were you able to help us out?"

"Yeah, I think so," Mark said easily. I felt utterly uncomfortable. I kept looking up at the green-and-white-striped umbrella that shaded our table from the glaring sun. I didn't want to be a part of any of this, and I was beginning to think Mark and I had made a terrible mistake.

Converse smiled, continuing to stare at the tapping envelope. "What do you have?"

"Acid," Mark said, smiling triumphantly. I could not share in his enthusiasm, but I admired his audacity. I was mostly trying to avoid the gaze of the greasy lizard guy.

Lizard peeled his tiny eyes off of my face and settled them on Mark's. "How much?" he asked.

"Three sheets of one hundred."

Lizard cracked a sinister smile. "What do you want for them?"

Mark scratched his scalp, staring at Lizard. "A hundred for each sheet," he said, smiling.

"Sounds good. We have to take them to this guy though," Converse said.

My attention snapped from the gum-crusted brick patio to Converse's scruffy face. Nothing about this felt right to me. "What?" I asked, staring this guy straight in the eye.

He paid no attention to me. Instead, he continued looking at Mark in silence, then said, "Yeah, she can ride along with us. It'll only take a few minutes."

"I can ride with you guys," Mark said. He stood. The two guys towered over him, and Mark was six-feet tall.

Lizard Guy shook his head. "No, only her," he said blankly.

I looked at Mark with complete despair. I didn't want to go anywhere with these guys. I didn't know them, and I didn't trust them either. Mark pulled me aside, away from the table and out of their earshot.

"Honey, if you go we stand to make three hundred dollars," he said, though I could hear the uncertainty in his voice.

"If I go, I stand to get raped or murdered!" I replied a little too loudly, and the two guys looked over.

"That's ridiculous. We need the money, just go," he whispered. I could see he was feeling empathetic, but he was pretending not to.

"But I'm scared!" I persisted. I was flabbergasted. He was asking me to take a ride with this freak-show crew. What was he thinking? He was supposed to love and protect me, not pimp me for three hundred bucks.

"If you don't want to go, I understand," he said, changing his tactics.

I wasn't going to fall for his selfish niceties. "Why won't they let *you* go?" I asked, dumbfounded by his stupidity.

"I don't know. Why don't you just ride along with them, and if anything happens, jump out of the car."

I stared at him aghast, but nothing changed in his countenance. "That sounds *really* reasonable!" I spat at him, tired of dealing with this bullshit.

"Please go."

"Fine, I'll go, but if I don't come back I hope it was worth it to you," I said, bubbling with frustration and anger.

"You'll come back," he said reassuringly.

We walked back to the table where the guys were waiting. Mark told them I would ride with them. I took the envelope from Mark's hand and cautiously walked to the car, following the two guys. I looked back at Mark, who was sitting at the glass table, his face buried in his palms.

The Converse guy opened the front door for me, and I sat down in the passenger seat. My heart beat out of control as Lizard Guy slid into the backseat directly behind me. I felt like I was suffocating in the heat of the car. Sweat drizzled down the sides of my body from my armpits.

They drove away from the coffee shop, and I wondered if it would be the last time I saw Mark. For a moment, I almost didn't care. He was making me do this for a measly three hundred dollars. I would never have done something like this to him. On the dashboard, a picture was nestled in the corner by the speedometer. It was of a crucifix with an upside-down Jesus, his eyes glaring red, his tongue forked and hanging out the side of his mouth. Goose bumps rose on my arms. Now perspiration was sliding down my forehead toward my chin. I watched out the window as we made several turns on different streets. I desperately tried to remember each street name—Palm Canyon Drive, Sunrise Way, Ramon Road. We pulled into an alley behind a bar.

"Is this where your friend is?" I asked nervously.

"Sure," Converse said, as he pulled the emergency brake.

Then I felt something cold and sharp touch the nape of my neck. This was it—I knew I was going to die.

"We have a knife at your neck; you better give us the shit," Lizard hissed behind me, his hot breath grazing my neck, sending icicles down my spine.

I handed over the envelope without so much as a peep. I shut my eyes to try to keep my tears back. I knew they were going to do something horrible to me. I could see Lizard Guy flicking his tongue in and out of my mouth as his friend held me down, arms pinned above my head. There was no way I could jump out of the car with the point of the knife resting on my jugular. I watched Converse open the envelope and run his fingers across the three bunk sheets. I was afraid they were going to test the acid, and I would have to wait until they discovered it was fake. Then they would kill me for sure.

"Now get your ass out of the car," Converse shouted. The knifepoint eased away from my neck, and Lizard Guy laughed sinisterly.

"What? I don't even know where I am!" I cried, instantly realizing just how stupid I was. They were letting me go.

"Get out," Converse commanded.

I didn't feel like arguing with guys who had put a knife to my neck, so I opened the car door and got out quickly. I started walking, trying to remember the direction we had come from. Panicking, I turned down streets that I didn't remember at all, wishing I knew where the fuck I was. I wandered aimlessly, hoping I'd come across Mark.

I found him about an hour later. He stood in the middle of a side street, looking around like a lost dog. I stopped and watched him search for me. He didn't know I was there. He looked so sad and scared. For a moment, I thought about walking away, making him suffer some more, but I was so relieved I'd found him. I hollered out, and he came running.

"I guess I don't have to tell you that it went badly," I whimpered. He threw his arms around me, squeezing me so tightly I could hardly breathe.

"I don't care about it anymore. I didn't think I was ever going to see you again." He nestled his head deep into the nook of my neck. I felt wetness.

I stroked his hair. "I'm here."

"What did they do to you?"

"They held a knife to my neck and made me give them the sheets."

He pulled his head away from me and peered into my eyes. "Did you?"

"Of course, they were fake. Then they told me to get out of the car, and they drove away."

"Did they hurt you?"

"No, just scared me. Why did you let that happen? Why didn't you go?"

"I thought about it as soon as you drove away, thought about how stupid I was to let you go. I'm so sorry." His eyes were brimming with tears. "I'm so fucking sorry and so happy that you're here with me now. I thought something awful had happened."

"Something awful did happen."

"Yeah, but you're back now!" he said, and ran a hand over his cheek.

In San Francisco it felt like Mark and I were two of the many homeless. There were, like, two hundred thousand residing in Golden Gate Park alone. We woke in our car somewhere downtown, near some condolike apartments. We counted our dollars and cents before hitting the road. The show the night before, our last Dead show, had rocked. We'd made quite a bit of cash. We totaled it up to around five hundred, most of which came from the tattoos I had given, which were improving, I must say.

"Want to leave now or get something to eat?" Mark asked.

"Can we *afford* food?" I asked, somewhat spitefully, because we'd had a fight about buying food the previous day.

"I think we can," he said, slightly huffy.

Luckily, we made it to McDonald's during breakfast and were able to get some Egg McMuffins sans meat. It was an even worse scene than I thought it would be. People were eating food out of the garbage can.

We were both anxious to get back to DeKalb, not like it was any better a place than anywhere we'd been, but at least there we knew what sucked. In DeKalb no one really fucked with us because we were friends with Alyssia's boyfriend Pat, and apparently he had lots of "connections."

We headed back to the car and jointly decided that Mark would be the first to drive on the long trek home. He sat in the driver's seat and turned the key in the ignition, but the engine didn't turn over. He tried again and again, but it still didn't work. At this point both of us were extremely upset. The tension was building between Mark and me, and I had no idea why. Well, maybe it was because we were running out of money, or maybe we'd just been on the road together too long. But, also, after that knife at my throat, I'd become rather short-tempered. I was having trouble trusting Mark.

Mark got out of the car and opened the hatch. I knew that something bad like this had to happen. Just as we were about to finally get out of there, the car decided to play possum. Sometimes I felt we were cursed. Mark returned rather grimly to the driver's side.

"Fuck," he stammered, looking as if he were about to cry.

I sighed heavily. "Let me guess—there are no jumper cables?"

"Correct. Chalk one up to your overwhelming brilliance," he replied snidely.

"Hey now, there's no reason to get gritchy with me," I said in my defense.

He grabbed my hand through the open window and caressed it. "Sorry. We need to find some way to start this piece of shit."

"Why don't you just knock on someone's door and see if they have jumper cables?"

"You're coming with me if I do."

I yawned, stretching my arms above my head. I was getting tired of arguing, tired of traveling. "No, I'm not." I sighed.

"I think you are; remember your firsthand experience with a knife not too long ago?"

I found it fascinating that *he* wouldn't risk going anywhere by himself. I got out of the car and slammed the door behind me.

"Fine, let's go!" I practically yelled.

We trudged up the stairs to the condo we had parked in front of. The first one we saw, therefore the best choice. Mark pounded loudly on the door, and we waited. The door opened, revealing a tiny man in a tacky Hawaiian shirt.

"Hello," he said in an overly feminine voice. It sounded more like a question than a greeting. Well, it was really like he was saying, *I don't know who the fuck you are or what you want, so go away.* He seemed to be posing. His hands rested on his hips, which protruded forward. He ran his hand through his long thinning blond hair and stared at me.

I decided I should do the talking. "Hi, we're looking for some jumper cables," I said, making my own statement sound like a question. "See, our car is parked outside, and it won't start."

He smiled a little at me. "I can't help you, but when my husband gets home he can probably jump-start your car. He handles all those *messy* car problems. I don't know anything about that kind of stuff." He giggled, then peered around us at our car.

"Great, what time will he be back?" I asked, somewhat annoyed by Fruitloop's dramatics.

"In about an hour; he went to get our car washed. You can come in and wait if you'd like to?" He stepped back to show us in.

I wasn't in the mood, but I did notice that the foyer was tastefully decorated with what looked like expensive art.

"I think we're going to hang out at the car. It's a beautiful day, and I could use the sun right now," I said, taking in his fake orange tan, knowing he'd understand.

We walked back down the stairs to wait for the husband. Mark started laughing when we hit the bottom of the stairs.

"That guy was whacked out. Married?"

"They're gay, Mark," I said, brushing him off.

"Obviously. You know they can't really be married though." He sat down on the curb next to the car.

"I guess they just consider themselves married. It's no big deal." I sat down next to him.

He was looking over his shoulder at the apartment door. "Right, but the Bible doesn't condone same-sex marriages."

I couldn't believe he was throwing Christian-ideology shit at me. "When did you give a shit about what the big book said?" I suddenly felt like I didn't know him.

"It's just common knowledge, that's all I'm saying."

I looked away from him to the car, then back to the apartment door. "I can tell you this much, that gay couple is loaded." I was so frustrated by our situation. Nothing was going right, and I didn't even feel like I liked Mark anymore, let alone loved him. Especially after that homophobic statement.

"What does that matter?" he asked.

"It doesn't really. I was just thinking that you might want to head up there with your skateboard and bash the fag's head in. Then we could take all their valuables and get the hell out of here!" I said, surprising myself. Maybe I'd been pushed too far.

He looked me in the eye, shaking his head. "Right, sounds like fun."

"I'm serious."

He seemed astonished. "No you're not."

"I think we should."

He stood up and leaned against the car. I could tell he was feeling uncomfortable. "I could never do something like that."

"You could spend hours perforating bunk sheets of acid, but you couldn't hit someone with your skateboard?" I asked, though I knew the two were far from related.

"No! Plus, we don't need the money all that bad."

"Fine!" I sat on the curb. I wasn't sure if I'd been serious about the head-bashing thing. I had never hurt anyone like that. I figured I was testing Mark, seeing how far he would go. Sometimes I did things like that for absolutely no reason.

Mark came and sat down beside me, but I continued to stare at the pavement, waiting for him to say something.

"Car won't start?" a voice behind us asked.

Startled, we both turned and saw a rather hefty, good-looking guy standing there.

"No, it won't. We're waiting for someone to give us a jump," Mark said softly.

The guy smiled broadly. "That would be me," he said.

He strode to the front of our car and lifted the hood, then inspected the engine as if he knew exactly what he was doing. After he had studied the innards of our car, he walked over to a Jeep Wrangler and pulled some jumper cables out from the back, which he hooked up to our battery.

"I don't know if the jump's going to get this car working or not. This is a pretty old machine, and it looks pretty bad under that hood. But let me bring my car around and see if we can get this baby running."

He walked to his Jeep, started it up, then pulled it up next to our car. Mark and I looked around aimlessly. The guy put the other end of the cables onto his battery and hollered for Mark to try to start our car. Nothing happened. The guy checked the cable connections and told Mark to try it again, but again nothing happened.

"Looks like it's more than just a dead battery, guys. Sorry. Don't know much about these ancient cars. I can get you a phone book if you'd like to call for a tow."

Mark looked as if he were about to cry. "We'll take a phone book," he said.

The guy walked upstairs to retrieve it while Mark and I silently waited by the curb.

"How fucking great! Now we have to flush more money down the toilet!" Mark finally said, slamming his fist onto the hood of the car.

"Why don't we just ditch it? We could sell it for parts or something, take a bus home."

Mark didn't say anything, he just stood there with his clenched fist resting on the hood.

"At this point I don't really care. We can call one of those numbers in the phone book where they take your car and give you a little bit of money for it," I said, trying again.

He sighed wearily. "Not a bad idea."

When the guy came back with the phone book, we frantically looked for a number of a tow service that bought cars. After we found one, Mark ran up to the apartment and called the place. I waited with the husky guy for Mark to return. In some dark place in the back of my mind, I could see Mark bashing the weak little man upstairs in the head. I could picture us getting the other guy somehow, snatching up all their valuables, then taking them home with us on a Greyhound bus. We'd have a fresh start in DeKalb and lots of money. But mostly I was relieved that this madness was soon going to end.

The tow truck came and hauled our junker away. We were left on the street corner with all our belongings. We had no way to get to a bus station, no transportation, and too much fucking shit.

"We need to get to a Greyhound station," I said, hearing the edginess in my voice.

"You want to bus it?" he asked.

"Isn't that what we agreed? What other way do you suggest?"

"I don't know. Fine with me, I supppose." He wiped the back of his hand across his sweaty forehead.

A little girl popped out of a peach-colored condo, bouncing a pink rubber ball on the orange brick driveway. A shudder went up my spine. I hated everything about this place. Everything was peach, orange, some beautiful earthy color. I felt like I was going to puke.

"Let's get going," I said, full of resentment.

"You want to carry all this stuff?"

"How else are we going to get it on a bus?" I picked up my shit and started walking. A bunch of convertible cars lined the street. I wished I could jump in, steal one, and drive off into the sunset. End of story.

"Cab?" Mark called behind me.

"Fine. Find a pay phone and call a cab then," I said, turning to him.

Mark left, and I waited on the street corner. People were looking at me as if I were crazy as they walked by. I just scowled at them and watched the cars zoom by. Everything seemed so fucked up. I was drifting away from Mark.

I felt that I'd changed him somehow. I was getting bitchier. What if he didn't come back? I could almost understand if he left me right then. We hadn't touched in days. He had to be as miserable as I was. But when it came down to it, I didn't want him to leave me. I sat next to our pile of stuff and rested my head in my hands. A stray tear spilled out of my eye, and I lifted my finger to brush it away. Then I saw Mark walking back.

CHAPTER 16

Mark's father drank too much and his mother stood by watching. A typical night went like this: Over dinner, Mark's father laughed about a porn star's name—Orgazma—so hard that he fell out of his chair and hit his head. Moments later he rose, blamed Mark's sister for his spill, and chased her around the house with a spatula, slapping her on the ass.

Mark and I had been living with his parents for about a month. It certainly wasn't an outtake of *Little House on the Prairie*. It was more like *Little House of Nightmares*. I couldn't stand the thought of leaving Mark there alone, but I felt like I was going to have a nervous breakdown, until I received a certain phone call.

"It's Heather," the voice on the other end said, and I felt my heart jump.

A series of questions rushed out of me: "Heather, where the fuck are you? How did you get this number? How are you?" I was so excited to hear from her.

"I'm in Indiana with my aunt. I got your number from Baker. The cops came and got me that morning, early, and they brought me home. My choices were pretty grim, so I decided to stay with my aunt . . ." She rambled on.

I told her about my road trip with Mark and how pathetic it got.

"So, when are you coming?" she asked.

"Where?"

"Portage, Indiana."

"Where the hell's that?" I asked, laughing, but inside my heart fluttered a bit at the prospect of getting away and seeing Heather.

"Exactly! It's actually a lovely suburb of Gary, Indiana," she said. I could hear the smile in her voice.

"I didn't know Gary had suburbs."

"Well, it does, and let me tell you, it sucks ass."

I laughed. It was probably the first time I'd laughed in weeks, and it felt good. "You're doing a wonderful job of selling me on this coming-to-visit idea."

"So, you coming or what?" she asked impatiently.

"All right, call and get ticket information for the next train there. I'll come ASAP." I was already eager to get packing.

"What's the earliest you can come?" she asked.

I felt so excited to leave I sputtered out, "Today."

"All right, I'm on it," she said, and hung up the phone.

I sat on the edge of Mark's bed, watching him sleep. I'd been waiting for about two hours to hear back from Heather. I kept wondering if it had been a dream, if I'd never really heard from her at all. I needed to get away from this house, but I didn't know if leaving Mark right then was the best idea because we were falling apart.

My feelings for Heather had been over a long time ago, but I missed her friendship. I missed our walks through the field after summer school.

The phone in Mark's room rang, and I was afraid it would wake him. I ran to the dresser across the room and grabbed it.

"Hello," I whispered.

"It's me," Heather said.

"Hi," I said, relieved.

"How soon can you get to the train station?"

"What time do I need to get there?"

"You could take the two thirty or the four o'clock train. Whichever one you want."

I looked at the clock on the dresser. It was one. There was no way I could get things together in less than an hour. "I'll be on the four o'clock," I said.

She explained to me what I should do and told me to get off at a stop called Portage.

"I'm on my way," I said, hanging up and looking around Mark's room at all the things I needed to pack. I wasn't planning on taking much, because I figured that I'd only be there a little while. But then I grabbed my mountain pack and started stuffing everything I could fit inside it. Mark began stirring in the bed, and I wasn't really sure if I was ready to discuss my departure with him. He peaked his head out of the covers and looked at me, then the mountain pack on the floor.

"What's going on, Orleigh?" he asked sleepily.

"I'm leaving." I stuck a folded T-shirt in my mountain pack.

His face contorted. "You're leaving me?" he asked.

"Not you, just town for a while," I said, but I didn't know if I believed myself. Maybe I was leaving him.

He sat up. "What are you doing?" I could tell he was getting angry.

"Going to Indiana to see Heather."

"When did you talk to her?" he asked now, more curious than angry.

"This morning. She called. She got your number from Baker."

"So you're going to visit or stay?"

"Visit."

I continued packing things, watching him watch me out of the corner of my eye. I felt uncomfortable in the silence. I wanted him to talk to me. I folded another shirt, holding my breath.

He sighed deeply and swung his legs over the edge of the bed. "How long?" he asked quietly.

"I don't know, maybe a couple of weeks."

"I don't want you to go," he said.

I looked at my mountain pack, then caught his soft gaze. I could see the pain in his face. I wanted to touch him.

"Come with me, then," I said, surprising myself.

His gaze fell from my face to the floor. "I can't, not right now."

Something inside me broke. All of a sudden I desperately wanted him to be with me. "Why?" I asked.

"We have no money. How can you even afford to go to Indiana?" He banged his fist on his knee, glaring at me.

"It's not that expensive," I said defensively.

"Well, maybe I can head out there in a few days." He looked so tired. It wasn't just a physical thing. I could see it in his eyes, and the way his shoulders were always hunched lately.

I wanted to fix things. For the first time I really felt like it could be over between us. "I wish you'd just come with me now."

"I can't."

"There's something you're not telling me."

"No, there isn't," he said simply.

"This just isn't like you. You never want to do anything without me; now you're just letting me go like it's no big deal."

"What else am I supposed to do? You're going to go even if I want you to stay. I mean, it's totally obvious you're just itching to get out of here." He leaned back against the headboard of the bed and ran his hands through his tousled hair. He looked up at me, sighing heavily. "You packed your bags while I was sleeping. It's like you were planning on sneaking the fuck out! Do whatever it is you feel the need to do. I'll still love you no matter what, but I'm not going to Indiana right now." He threw back his shoulders defiantly.

"Sorry," I said, placing a pair of shoes into my mountain pack.

He watched me closely. "About what?" he asked.

"I just can't do things the way you think they should be done."

"How's that?" I could hear a twinge of anger in his voice again.

"Your way," I said slowly.

His head fell dramatically into the palms of his hands. "It's not about that."

"It's all about that," I said. I closed my mountain pack and placed it on the bed in front of him.

He looked at the pack, then up at me. He seemed tired and desperate. He reached out his hand to me. "I think you're being a bitch because you don't want to leave me," he said, smiling.

I stood with my hands on my hips, not wanting to take his hand. "And I think you're lying to me about why you can't come with me," I snapped.

He dropped his hand to his lap. "Fine," he said wearily.

"Fine." I picked up my mountain pack and walked out of his room. I didn't care if I ever saw him again. I knew he was completely full of shit, and, right then, I just didn't care anymore. Nothing seemed right between us.

I opened the front door of his house, and sunshine poured into the foyer. I turned to take a last look around. Maybe it was to see if he was coming after me. But then maybe it wasn't. He hadn't followed me down the stairs. He was probably still sitting in bed. I walked out the door and closed it behind me. It wasn't a long walk to the train station.

I was an hour early and the train hadn't arrived at the station yet. I sat outside near the track, chain-smoking and fretting over Mark. I felt so bad about our fight, but I didn't know what to do. I had to get out of his house; his dad was driving *me* to drink. I thought about Mark all the time, wanted to be with him all the time, and I loved it when we fucked, but something had changed. We no longer held each other afterwards but sat silently smoking cigarettes. Maybe I had made a mistake dragging him on the road with me. I felt hands on my shoulders and turned around. Mark was standing there.

"I love you," he said.

Relieved, I turned to face him. "I love you too."

"Don't leave me," he said softly.

"I have to get out of your house for a while." I sighed. "It's not personal. Please come with me."

"I have a big deal to make at the end of the week. I stand to make a large sum of cash. I just can't go."

I knew there was something he hadn't been telling me. "What big deal?" I asked, pissed off.

"Something Pat worked out for me." He paced a little, then kicked the iron railroad track.

"Isn't Pat in prison?"

Mark picked up a stone and threw it. It bounced off the tracks and landed on the wooden piece between the ties. "Yeah, this is something he set up from inside, and I have to follow through with it."

I looked at my watch, then peered down the tracks. The train was nowhere to be seen. "Great! What's the deal?" I asked, but I had a feeling I already knew.

He couldn't look me in the eyes. Instead he focused on another stone that he was tossing up and down in his hand. "Coke," he sighed.

"How much?"

"Lots." He smiled broadly.

"How much is it worth?" I stared ahead at the midwestern sunset. The sky had turned a beautiful purple-pink, large popcorn clouds exploding all across the horizon.

"About two grand's worth."

"How much would *you* get?" I asked, watching him avoid my gaze.

"About a grand." He laughed a little.

I felt pissed, but I had no energy left to fight. A grand was really not that much to risk getting caught. "Do it then, and when you're done, get your ass to Indiana." I shaded my eyes and looked down the railroad tracks. There was still no train.

He smiled sheepishly, but I still found him incredibly sexy. "I will," he said, sounding sure of himself.

I tried to hide my concern, but I don't think I did it very well. "I feel better you told me. I'm not particularly happy about it." I was silent for a moment, waiting for his reaction, but he said nothing. "I mean, don't you think it's just a little bit stupid to get involved with Pat again? Look where he is now."

"He wants to get some money to Alyssia—she's not doing very well."

I felt my stomach tighten. A mixture of anger and passion swelled inside of me. Alyssia still had some power over me—just the sound of her name caused me to feel uneasy and a little queasy. "So half the money is for *her?*" I asked.

"Yeah," he said nervously.

"Why doesn't *she* do it then?"

"There are eyes all over that girl; every move she makes is monitored. The cops have been on her ever since they got Pat. I'm the only one he worked with that they don't know about."

I could hear the train approaching, and I didn't feel like spending our last seconds arguing. "Just don't get caught," I said, smiling.

The train was pulling into the station, and Mark's eyes began to tear. I knew he was hurting as bad as I was, and now I was terribly concerned for him. I hated that he was going to get involved in stupid drug-deal shit again. Plus, I knew that much coke was a felony, and I didn't want him to wind up in the cell next to Pat's.

He grabbed hold of my hand and tugged me close. "Don't go, baby."

I kissed him on the cheek. "Don't stay," I said, then I picked up my mountain pack and slung it over my shoulder.

"This is a stupid argument. It's obvious we've both made our choices."

"Yeah," I said, squeezing his hand.

He squeezed my hand tighter. "Call me tonight."

"You know I will."

His hand reached toward my face, and his fingers grazed my cheek. "I'll miss you." I felt as if I were about to cry. "I miss you already," I said, looking over my shoulder at the train door.

We hugged each other tightly. The train was looking like it was about to leave any second, but Mark's hug felt so right, his strong arms so comforting. His heart beat against mine, his hot breath in my ear. I loved him so much I felt like I could explode. I wanted to shrink into something tiny and crawl inside of him, live there forever. I didn't care if the train left me standing there clutched in his embrace.

"Baby, you better get on that train," he said, his eyes lighting up for a second, then he shut them and kissed me good-bye. I pulled away from him and ran into the train just as the doors slid closed.

The train pulled into the lovely Portage station—it was terrifying. I really had no fucking idea where I was, but I knew this was definitely Hicksville, and I wasn't sure whether you would call the station an actual train station. It was more like a shack with a ticket agent and a couple of benches. I didn't like the looks of it at all, but then I looked up and saw Heather leaning against a white Chevy Bronco. I felt awkward for a moment, the way I had when Mark mentioned Alyssia's name. But I didn't feel queasy. It's not that I was still interested in Heather; it was just that the past had happened, and it wasn't easy to overlook it. She looked different. Her hair was back to its natural color, longer and in a ponytail again. She was dressed in a Grateful Dead tie-dye and blue jeans. Her face had grown slimmer, along with the rest of her body. She looked so good, natural, not all dolled up in Tammy's disguise. I sauntered over, feeling my smile widen as I approached her. For a moment I felt like kissing her on the lips because I wanted our greeting to be intimate, but I thought she might take it the wrong way, so I kissed her on the cheek.

"Hey, good-looking, what's cooking?" I said.

She adjusted her hair, then threw her arms around me. "I'm glad you're here."

She stepped back from me and gazed at my face. I stared back, then glanced around the station. Everything was so desolate. "I'm glad I'm here too. So what do we do in this dive town?" I asked, wondering how in the hell she spent her time here.

"First, we get you checked into the hotel." She unlocked the passenger side of her car. "Where's Mark?"

"He's coming. Later," I said hastily. "And what's this about a hotel? I don't have a lot of cash."

She smiled reassuringly. "Taken care of. I got your ass, that is until we get you some money."

"How do you plan on doing that?" I threw my mountain pack in the backseat.

"We'll just have to steal a bunch of shit and return it. It still works for me like a charm."

"Sounds good, I guess." I had thought my klepto days were over. "Where's the hotel?"

She rolled her eyes. "Well, it's not something to write home about, but it'll work for now. My aunt can't really know you're here or else she'll tell my mother, and that would be cause to drag my ass away again." She climbed into the driver's seat, and I followed her lead, sliding into the passenger seat.

"Cool, don't worry about it," I said, slamming the door.

She started the engine, and it rattled ferociously as we pulled out of the crude parking lot.

Little shacks posing for houses flanked the street of the station. A sense of dread came over me. What the hell was I going to do here? There was nothing around but shacks. I supposed we could lift some lawn gnomes if we got really bored. Heather drove rather frantically down some twisted and dark little streets. The houses all started looking the same. Heather and I were from middle class suburbs, and I couldn't help feeling like we were in the slums. The houses looked like the gardening sheds behind our parent's homes. Finally, Heather pulled up to what looked like a no-tell motel from hell with a sign that read, "We have ooms!" Apparently they had rooms but were out of bulbs for the neon letter "r." I was a little worried about how damn scary the place looked. It reminded me of *Psycho,* and I half expected to see Norman Bates behind the desk. But once we were inside the room, it wasn't so bad. The place had a kind of tasteless, circa late-seventies flair about it; I figured if I wanted to disco this would be the place to do it. We sat on the bed and I lit two smokes, just like old times.

I passed the lit cigarette to Heather, and she smiled warmly at me. "You happy to be here?"

"Overly," I said, in an exaggerated way.

"How are things going with Mark?"

I hesitated a bit. "Good, I guess."

"Why didn't he come with you?"

I nervously twirled the cigarette between my thumb and index finger. "Big drug deal he's doing. He's going to make a small fortune off it or something," I said, sighing.

"Are you mad at him?" She kicked her shoes off and lay back on the bed.

"Not mad, just disillusioned. I thought we had it all together for a while. I pulled his ass out of DeKalb and got him off all the drugs. For what? He just got back to town and started exactly where he'd left off." I tapped the ash into the ashtray and smiled weakly.

Her lips parted and her eyes searched mine. "Is he doing the drugs or just dealing?"

"It looks like just dealing but how am I to know? You know he is, like, the most awesome person I've ever met in my life, but then he goes and fucks it all up." I lay down on my stomach next to Heather and rested my chin on my fist.

"That's how they are, isn't it?"

I focused my attention on the orange and yellow diamonds on the wallpaper; they matched the bright orange bedspread so well. "If it weren't for his little problem not being able to say no, our relationship would be perfect."

She nudged me on the butt with her toe. "Your relationship is perfect.

I know he loves you, Orleigh. I could tell that the first night at that party. You rocked his world." I was happy she wasn't angry about that night anymore. She'd grown up a little. She seemed much more relaxed, and what she had said made me feel all weak inside, but it wasn't enough to comfort me.

"It's different now," I said. I wanted a drink.

Heather finished her cigarette, yawned and stretched, then told me she would come back tomorrow. She had to get back to her aunt's. We hugged each other good-bye. She pushed a strand of hair out of my eye in a motherly way. I watched her get into the Bronco, then I sat on the bed alone thinking about her. I had missed her so much. Despite all the things that had happened between us in the past, she was still my best friend.

I dreamed about Mark. He was tied to a tree on an island. Several pigmies surrounded him, holding long sharp spears. They began chanting as they honed in on him. I was watching the whole thing from a hill in the distance. I wanted to run to him, to save him, but my legs wouldn't move no matter how hard I tried. All I could see were the little men creeping closer to him.

I woke to knocking at the motel door. I stretched my arms high above my head, thinking about my phone conversation with Mark the night before. He told me the deal would be wrapped up by Friday, then he would come to Indiana. Feeling like the living dead, I slid out of bed and went to open the door of my lavish living quarters. Heather stood there, an evil grin on her face.

"What's the look for? Did you bring me here to kill me?" I asked, stepping back a few feet to let her in.

"Yeah, because you stole Mark away from me, and then let the cops get me in DeKalb. It's time for revenge." She sneered as she slid past me across the carpet and glided on over to the bed.

I laughed a little uncomfortably. "Look, I take no blame for those crimes."

"You shouldn't. I still love you. Now it's time to go borrow some shit from a few stores."

"Where we going?" I asked, curious about what Portage, Indiana, had to offer, other than the squatter shacks we'd driven past on our way here.

"The mall," she said with a smile.

"They have those out here in the sticks?"

"Yeah, we have a mall. Make sure you dress properly."

For a moment I thought she meant there was a dress code for the hicks, then I realized she wanted me to wear baggy clothes for shoplifting. I emptied out the clothes from my pack onto the bed and looked for the best thieving gear. I had a pair of baggy jeans and a roomy sweatshirt. I figured I could probably get enough shit under my clothing to pay for the room for the next month. Luckily, I had also packed my favorite stealing jacket with umpteen pockets. I dressed quickly, and we headed out to the mall.

There were about twenty stores—not what I really considered a mall. We separated to make ourselves less conspicuous, then went to work. I concentrated on baby clothes, since they were expensive and no one ever questioned a "mother" returning baby stuff. I walked to a rack filled with tiny outfits. I checked the price of a little jumper. Forty bucks. I slid it off the hanger and into the large inside pocket of my jacket. A young girl stood behind the checkout counter, talking on the telephone. It was all too easy. I continued slipping the clothing into my pockets, then the girl hung up. She headed toward where I was standing, sliding the little hangers across the rack, trying to appear interested.

"Can I help you find something?" she asked shyly.

"No, I don't think so." I smiled and turned to walk away. I hated when salespeople approached when my pockets were filled. It always felt *a little* uncomfortable. But the salesgirl was way too caught up in other things—I looked back over my shoulder, and she'd already resumed chatting on the phone.

Heather and I had planned to meet back at the car within a half an hour. It'd been about thirty-five minutes so I figured I was done. I waltzed out of the mall—no big deal. No one even gave me a second look. This was always puzzling to me. Maybe I just had an honest face.

I arrived at the car, but Heather wasn't there yet. It was actually not a very good idea to separate for these shoplifting sprees, but better if one person did it, and the other surveyed the area. But this time we needed to separate, due to our urgent need for lots of cash, therefore extra items to return. Heather was the best I knew. After all, I had trained her in the art, and she had been an excellent pupil. I watched the mall entrance; the hillbillies in sweatshirts that said "I'm with stupid" or "My grandson went to Arizona and this is all he bought me." It was enough to make me vomit. Kids went running and screaming to crappy rusted-out pickup trucks, with bumpers held on by bungee cords. Impatiently, I watched the entrance for Heather. Fifteen minutes had passed since our scheduled meeting time, and my heart began to thump hard and fast. I thought about going back into the mall, but then I saw her walking out, her head held high—the sign of a successful kill.

I smiled with relief as she approached the car. "Hey, girl, how'd it go?"

"Fabulous. You?" Her eyes were laughing with delight, which made her look absolutely beautiful.

"Equally fabulous."

She padded her clothing and got into the car; she looked pregnant. A couple walked to a pickup parked next to Heather's car. Their bumper sticker said, "I never kill what I won't eat." What a lovely sentiment, I thought.

I looked at Heather. "I went for the baby clothes this time. You?"

"Stuff, good stuff. Got two pairs of Calvin Klein jeans."

"Let's get the fuck out of here."

We began unloading as Heather drove, throwing our booty into a pile in the backseat. At the motel we would change into good clothes to do the returning. It was such a fine system.

"I don't really want to take back these Calvin Klein jeans," Heather said, once we were back in the motel room. The jeans lay beside her on the bed, and she was running her finger affectionately across the waistband's leather label.

"Slave to the label?" I asked, as she continued fingering it as if it were Braille.

She lifted her finger from the familiar Calvin Klein letters, then rested her hands in her lap. "What's that supposed to mean?"

"It's just that you never seemed to care about those things before. I remember when three-dollar secondhand jeans were good enough for you," I said.

"Well, I don't really care much. I'd never buy jeans this expensive for myself, you know? I mean, I always get the three-dollar kind, and it would be a nice change to have some new ones."

I stood up to switch shirts. "Change into the label. Do whatever you want! I don't care."

Heather smiled at me mischievously as I pulled my clean shirt over my head. "There's a pair in your size too," she said, seductively patting the pile of clothes on the bed.

"So!" I said spitefully.

I sat down next to her. She smiled. "So, do you want them?"

I was shocked that she would even think I'd be interested in jeans that were more than ten dollars. "No," I said, with a nasty tone in my voice.

"Why not? They're free," she taunted.

"I just don't care about that kind of shit, plus I've got plenty of three-dollar thrift pairs."

"Fine," she said snottily.

I watched Heather change her clothes as I smoked a few cigs, sitting crosslegged on the bed. None of the old sexual excitement brewed inside me. She even took extra time putting her shirt on, flaunting her bare breasts in my face, while she searched through my clothing for something to wear. I wondered if she was doing it on purpose to test me. She hadn't changed that that much—same old tease. I leaned back and closed my eyes, ignoring her. It was important that we waited a while before returning to the mall, because after five o'clock the sales-people usually rotated. The daytime shift left and the evening shift came in. Our system was foolproof only if executed properly. I had to admit I *was* a little twisted up inside about the jeans. I mean, I don't know if I really wanted them or not; but I guess I *kind of* did. But I knew I had to preserve my I-don't-give-a-fuck-about-what's-socially-desired image. I did think I would be damn sexy in those jeans. I could even wear them when we went to pick up Mark. I knew he would appreciate a pair of jeans that actually fit me, instead of the baggy ones I wore. But that wouldn't really be me. I needed the three-dollar jeans, needed to remain cool.

Heather had a stash in her car of all sorts of different shopping bags from the stores at the mall, and she had brought them inside the motel room. (It was a good thing Heather's aunt was a shopping fiend and saved all her damn bags.) That way we could return our stolen goods in the proper bags. She had covered all the bases just as I'd trained her.

She grabbed a shopping bag from the department store and started stuffing the baby clothes in it. "I'll be the mother with the new baby; I look older even though you are," she said.

I opened the County Seat shopping bag and slid both pairs of Calvin Klein jeans into it. "And I'll be the slave-to-the-label teenager with the Calvin Klein jeans," I said, gently grazing the leather label Heather was so fond of.

We walked back into the mall, carrying the appropriate bags for the stores we had ripped off. This time we planned to meet at the car in forty-five minutes—the returning of goods often took longer than the actual pilfering because of the various forms to fill out for each return.

Once I had successfully returned all of Heather's goods, including reluctantly handing over the CK jeans, I headed back to the car. I never liked to be in any mall for a long period of time, especially after I'd done so much dirty work. When I got into the car I emptied out my pockets and counted my dinero—about two hundred dollars. I knew Heather would come back with even more because I'd stolen her so much expensive shit. Eventually she came out sporting a large empty bag.

"How'd it go?" I asked, as she slid into the driver's seat.

She gave me her easy smile. "Really well, not one problem. You?" she asked. She turned the key in the ignition and started the car.

"I did great, about two hundred dollars," I said proudly.

She looked over her shoulder to pull out of the parking spot. "We can count mine at the motel. Let's get out of here," she said, stepping hard on the gas petal.

Once out of the lot, we headed to the motel. We paid the front desk guy for six days with part of our money. I wouldn't be going anywhere for a while.

I slipped into a pair of dirty rotten jeans and walked out of the bathroom. I wished I hadn't been so stubborn about those Calvin Kleins; Mark's train was due at ten thirty, and I was so anxious to see him. Luckily, Heather and I beat the train, which was a good thing. I knew that if we'd been late picking Mark up, he would have panicked.

The night before Heather had stolen a bottle of Jack Daniel's from her aunt and uncle, and we had drunk ourselves silly. It was so bad that we'd started giving each other tattoos with the needle and few bottles of Indian ink that I had found at the bottom of my mountain pack. It'd been a long night and my pounder headache made it all seem so stupid.

I went to get a cup of coffee in the coffee shop across from the train station, to dissipate some of the fog in my head. My eyes were so heavy I could've fallen asleep right there at the counter. I felt a little better when the boiling-hot liquid finally passed my lips and went scaldingly down my throat. All I wanted was to feel alive again. I watched the train arrive through the coffee shop window. I ran out, Styrofoam cup in hand. Heather was looking around as people got off the train, but Mark was nowhere to be seen. My head reeled. Maybe he had been arrested, I thought. Maybe he'd gotten back with Theresa. Then I saw a guy jumping out of the last car, off the step and onto the pavement. He dropped his bag and turned, looking directly at me.

"Hello, girl," he shouted.

A rush of relief washed over me. "Hey, Mark," I shouted back.

I hurried to him and immediately wrapped my arms around him. His kiss sent shivers through me.

"I thought you might have gotten busted," I said, leaning back and looking into his soft eyes.

He laughed and squeezed my butt. "Never say die."

"Okay. I'm happy you're here." I grabbed his hand and pulled him toward Heather who stood on the platform with her arms crossed, a smile forming on her lips.

Mark smiled brightly. "Oh, my god, I didn't even see you standing there. How are you, doll?" He threw his arms around her neck.

When we'd finished embracing, we all jumped into Heather's car and headed to the shoddy little motel.

Something about being in a sleazy motel room was turning me on, and I loved the way Mark's wet skin felt, loved the way he tasted, all soapy and clean. I rested my hands against the grimy shower wall and let him enter me from behind. As he fucked me, I took in the lime deposits and dirty grout. And there, in the filthiness of that bathroom, I fell in love all over again.

When we were through dodging cockroaches and doing the cucaracha in the shower, I lay on the bed, watching Mark put on his snug black clothes. He looked at me with those crazy dark eyes that always said more than I think he intended. He looked relieved. Relieved to be with me and, I believed, relieved that he hadn't gotten busted.

He sat on the bed and ran a hand up my naked thigh. "I've really missed you, girl."

"I've missed you."

His eyes sparkled and my thighs began to tremble slightly from his touch.

"I love you," he said shyly.

"Not as much as I love you."

"It was so hard being away from you. Tell me you're coming home with me," he said, as he squeezed the flesh of my inner thigh.

I was getting turned on again, but I felt reluctant to simply agree. "Only if we can get our own place."

"That could be arranged."

"Would you go back to school?" I asked insistently.

"I don't know. Would you?"

The thought of returning to school made me cringe. I decided it'd be best not to comment.

I could see him grow frustrated with my silence, then his expression changed and he asked, "Can we always be together?" He smiled as his hand continued traveling up and down my leg.

"I think we can," I answered.

He gave me a shove, pushing me away from him, and I fell off the bed. "What do you mean, think?"

I pulled myself up off the floor and sat back down next to him. "I think we can, but I realize that you're too good for me."

"What do you mean?"

I sighed and grabbed his hand on my thigh and held it. "You're just too good for this evil planet."

He squeezed my hand tightly and kissed me on the cheek. "I think I belong right here with you."

I let his hand fall back onto my thigh. "I don't deserve your love."

"And what kind of love is that?" he asked.

I smiled. "Great love."

"And what is it you think you deserve?"

"Something horrible, something that's completely wrong. I mean, when it's all you've ever had, it's all you expect. With you it's something more. You know what I'm talking about."

The door to the no-tell motel room was rattling. I wrapped a dingy yellow-white towel around my naked body and opened the door. Heather stood there, smiling, a large bottle of vodka and a quart of OJ in her hand.

She looked over my towel-clad body and stepped around me into the room. I gathered up some clothes and went into the bathroom to dress. When I came out, Heather and I jumped onto the bed, leaning back against the pillows. Mark took the cellophane wrappers off the plastic glasses from the bathroom and placed them on the television table. He prepared the drinks, brought them over to us, then conveniently weaseled a space between Heather and me on the bed. I took a sip of my screwdriver. As soon as Heather and I had downed our drinks, Mark rose and made more. Within an hour we were all pretty drunk.

"I think I'm going to finish my tattoo," I said, laughing. I felt dizzy from the last cigarette I'd smoked.

"Do you have your gun with you?" Mark asked.

"No, I left it at your house, but Heather and I were fucking around with a needle and some India ink," I said, stumbling off the bed, searching for the ink and needle. I found them on top of the TV.

This was going to be fun. Finishing our tattoos half-cocked on screw-drivers suddenly seemed like the most brilliant idea.

Mark lay on the bed with a fresh drink, watching me dip the needle in the ink. Heather and I were trying to design matching tattoos on the inside of our ankles—big roses with "Dead" above them and "Head" underneath. It was a beautiful tattoo, but neither one of us had pressed deep enough the night before for the ink to take to the skin.

This time, I stabbed the needle into my ankle and screamed; the vodka wasn't enough of a painkiller. Heather wanted to get in on the action. She crouched down beside me, cigarette in one hand, drink in the other. She set down her drink, picked up the needle, dipped it into the ink, then pressed it into the skin of her ankle. "Fuck!" she yelled.

"It won't take, Heather," Mark said.

"Then you do it for me," Heather stammered.

She went to sit next to Mark on the bed. Mark drove the needle deep into her pale ankle, gripping her high-arched foot.

"I'm going to pass out," she squealed. "That hu-u-urts!" She pulled her leg away and lay back on the pillow, sweat streaming down her temples.

"Do mine," I said to Mark, tipping a screwdriver onto the carpet. I walked over to where he was sitting and brought my leg up onto the bed, resting my foot in his crotch.

"Ouch!" I yelped. He pressed the needle into my skin. I pulled my leg away. "I don't want to do this anymore."

I kissed Mark deeply and then turned to take a swig of my drink. "I have to pee," I said, falling off the bed and stumbling to the bathroom.

In the bathroom I studied my reflection in the mirror. My hair fell down in front of my face, with nothing but my pink lips peering through. I thought I looked sexy, in a hazy, rock-star way. I sat on the toilet. Pee gushed out of me in a long hard stream. My toes curled in drunken delight. I wiped, flushed, and walked back in the room. Mark was studying the tattoo dots on Heather's ankle, rubbing his fingers over them. I climbed onto his lap and stuck my tongue in his mouth. His hand slid inside my shirt, then caressed my back. I took his hand and placed it on Heather's lap. I opened my eyes and saw it run up Heather's thigh. He stopped kissing me, then kissed Heather on the lips. I felt a twinge of jealousy, and my stomach tightened, but then Heather stopped kissing him and began kissing me.

Mark got up while Heather and I were making out and made us more screwdrivers. Then he was taking Heather's shirt off and trickling drops of screwdriver onto her breasts and licking them off.

"Now you," he said to me. He drizzled more of his drink onto her breasts, and I licked them. Hands and fingers were everywhere, groping and plunging. I was so lost in the sensations that I wasn't troubled anymore by Mark and Heather touching. Her tongue was probing my lips. As we kissed, I noticed that Mark's hands were between her thighs, slipping in and out of her. Then I felt like I wanted to puke. I got off the bed and rushed to the bathroom. I knelt down in front of the pubic hair–laden toilet bowl and hurled out a stream of orangish liquid mixed with the grilled cheese sandwich I'd eaten earlier. When I returned to the bedroom Heather was pulling her pants back on. I guess she thought my puking was her cue to leave. She said she was worried about not being able to drive home. Mark looked at her, dejected, telling her she didn't have to leave yet. But actually, I wanted her to go. I didn't want things to get overly complicated between us, as they were before. Heather put her bra back on, and Mark watched her the whole time. She was doing her now-familiar tease routine. I walked her to the door and said good-bye, after she promised to return in the morning.

I took off the rest of my clothes and slid between the sheets next to Mark. The thought of him with his fingers inside Heather was making me unusually horny, now that Heather was gone. Funny how things work.

"Make love to me, Mark."

"Anytime," he said. He touched me gently.

"Harder," I said.

He looked a little baffled. "Touch you harder?" he asked.

"Yeah."

"What do you want me to do?"

"Do the usual but different," I said sternly. "You, but wilder."

He rolled onto his side and began scratching my stomach with his fingernails.

"Harder," I grunted.

"What?" he asked, stopping.

"Tie me up," I said. I was thinking of the wild times I had had with Sam and Alyssia. I wanted to feel the same heat again, but with Mark.

"With what?" he asked. His chest was dripping with beads of sweat.

I put my wrists together above my head. "I don't give a damn, just do it. Now!"

He grabbed a T-shirt and ripped it into two long strands. He took the pieces and tied my wrists tightly.

"Now tell me what you want," he asked, his erection in my face.

"Anything you want," I said. "You're in control."

He flipped me onto my stomach, then scratched my back and spanked me like a child. I pleaded for him to do it harder and harder, and each time he complied. Then he finally thrust himself in me. I felt like he was pounding into my intestines. We were fucking, and it was sleazy and trashy in the scary little motel room, and I loved every minute of it. I felt sexier than ever. When it was over I thought of walking out, leaving him there alone, as if I were a stranger who had just walked into his life. But instead we curled up next to each other and fell asleep.

Morning came and I instantly felt strange. It wasn't the claw marks on my back or the red handprints on my ass, but a funny pinching feeling on the right side of my belly. And, for some reason, without prior experience, I knew I was pregnant. I called Heather and told her to get over to the motel.

As soon as Mark woke, I said, "I think I'm pregnant."

He shook his head, bewildered. "How do you know?"

"I know."

"Don't you think we need to confirm that?"

I smiled as big as the Cheshire cat. "Yeah, I'm just telling you what I think."

He wrapped his arms around my shoulders. "Sounds wonderful. I hope you are."

"You do?" I asked, surprised.

"Too many babies are brought into this world for the wrong reasons. It would be nice to have one for all the right reasons."

"Don't you think we're too young?" I asked. Mark was eighteen, a year younger than me.

"If we're old enough to make love, then we're old enough to deal with the consequences." He kissed me on the cheek.

I walked over to the bathroom door and leaned against the wall. "I suppose you're right, but wouldn't you be just a little bit afraid?"

He smiled a beaming smile, and he seemed so confident just then. The light poured in through the cracks of the motel curtains, casting a glow around him. He appeared luminous, angelic. He tilted his head, casting a shadow across the bedspread, his hair falling to one side. I wanted to be sitting in the sunlight with him, but I stood against the wood-paneled wall and watched him from the darkness.

He lifted his head and grinned. "Everything we do is beautiful," he said.

Two weeks later my period did not come on time, and Heather drove Mark to a drugstore to buy a pregnancy test. He returned with seven different kinds. I took all of them at different times throughout the day, and all of them came out positive. I was right. I was completely unprepared to deal with the situation, but Mark seemed happier than ever. He insisted that we go back to DeKalb and tell his parents; he wanted us to get our own apartment. I loved him for believing in us, loved him for all his crazy faith. I watched in astonishment as he packed our things to head home. I had no idea how I could ever tell my mom. I was shocked that he was dying to tell his parents everything. I wanted to run away and hide.

PART IV

Willow

Tracing Footprints

CHAPTER 17

Today, when I finally rose from bed, I felt different. A darkness engulfed me, and I couldn't shake it. I kept going over my last doctor visit, how he had informed me that if I didn't find ways to relax, the baby could be born prematurely. That conversation had done nothing but cause me more anxiety.

I was distracted by a sudden desperation for food—more than likely it was the child within me screaming for sustenance. I opened all the cupboards, only to find them empty except for a package of saltine crackers and a packet of instant oatmeal. My stomach turned fucking somersaults. It wasn't unusual for us not to have food. Ever since we moved into our little dive of an apartment—which was semiclose to Malick and Tammy's old John Street place—we had lived rather pathetically.

I slammed the cabinet door shut, and my mind began sorting out the argument I would have with Mark when he returned from work. I would hurl at him that I was pregnant and hungry, that I couldn't walk all the way across town to get food, and that even if I could, he didn't leave me money to do so. I could hear him defending himself, but I would retaliate by reminding him how much money he made at his new job and how much he scored in the underhanded drug deals he made for Pat. I had the whole fight planned out, every detail. In the meantime, I would await his return, hunger pains and all.

Things had changed so much between Mark and me now that we were expecting a child. We were children ourselves. We could do it, but I wasn't sure if I liked the way we would have to live. Mark's parents were actually being nice, helping out a little, but I knew we would have to go on welfare and Medicaid. I thought about things like this all the time, but Mark never did. He was optimistic, excited. Maybe he was living in a dream world or maybe I was being overly pessimistic. I still hadn't told my mother, and I wasn't sure if I'd ever be able to. I did love Mark's enthusiasm, I just wished I wasn't so terrified to be a mother.

Someone knocked on the door. I was expecting Mark, so I slowly shuffled to the foyer, my bloated belly sticking out in front of me. Why he didn't use his key was beyond me.

I opened the door and saw Mark's friend Lee carrying a to-go bag from Tom & Jerry's. He handed it to me without saying a word. I couldn't believe how nice he was being—he barely knew me. I thanked him and immediately sat on the couch, inhaling the greasy fries.

"I feel like I'm supporting you and this baby," Lee said gruffly, sitting next to me.

"Come on. I didn't ask you to bring me food," I said, feeling ashamed.

He put his arm around my shoulder. "I couldn't let you starve."

I felt deeply indebted to Lee. "Sorry, I've just been really hungry lately," I said, continuing to gulp down the delicious greasy food. I lost all will power to eat slowly.

Lee flipped through the television channels as I ate. Now and then I would look over at him to admire his tough exterior—all leather and hardware. Combat boots, tightly laced. Black motorcycle jacket (he wore it no matter the weather). Spiked, dyed-black hair.

He must have realized I was staring at him, because he turned and looked at me as if it were the first time he'd ever seen me. "I can't even tell you're pregnant," he said nonchalantly, watching me munch on two French fries at one time.

"That's because I was only a hundred and five pounds when I got pregnant," I said, through a mouth full of half-chewed fries.

"You're not really showing."

I stuffed another fry in my mouth. "I am when you look at my bare stomach."

His eyes focused on my belly. "Let me see it."

I swallowed my food then lifted my shirt, exposing a slightly rounded, super taut belly. It had horrible, deep purple, snakelike stretch marks on it. They ran all across my stomach, like a road map of my own personal hell.

Lee looked at it, horrified. "I didn't know it looked like *that.*"

I laughed and stuffed another fry in my mouth. "What were you expecting?" I asked.

"I don't know. It looks painful."

I pulled my shirt back down. "Not really, it's more painful to look at."

He patted my knee. "No, it's beautiful; you're beautiful."

Taken aback, I looked into his deep blue eyes and saw a compassion that I hadn't seen there before. We both gazed into each other's eyes for a while, not speaking. Then he leaned into me and kissed me. For a moment I was taken in by his soft lips, pressing against mine, but then I pulled away, my eyes darting to the floor. Why was I feeling so fucking vulnerable lately?

Lee looked frightened. "I'm sorry; I shouldn't have done that."

I reached for another handful of fries. "No, really, it's all right. You just surprised me, that's all."

"You're not mad at me?"

I swallowed the food. "No, I'm not mad. I just don't understand where it came from."

He sighed laboriously. "It's always been there, what can I say? You know you're just so damn cute and sweet."

I laughed under my breath. He knew nothing about me. "I don't know about that," I said. "Compared to Mark I'm not." I wanted Mark to get home, I missed him, and I wasn't even angry anymore. I couldn't believe what I'd just done.

"Wrong!" Lee said.

"What do you mean *wrong?*"

"Mark's different, that's for sure, but he's not better than you."

I stared at him, perplexed, waiting for him to continue.

"There's something dark about him, and when it comes out, it's a terrible thing," he muttered.

My throat tightened, and it was difficult to breathe. "I've never seen it," I said, but I wasn't so sure.

"You wouldn't. He loves you too much to let you."

Our botched bogus drug deal flashed in my mind. "Oh sure, and you've seen it?" I asked.

"Mark and I have always had a special relationship."

There was no way Lee could know Mark the way I did, but I wondered what kind of predicaments Lee had gotten into with Mark back when he knew him in high school. "I don't understand," I said, fishing for more.

"You're not supposed to," he said.

Our conversation was quickly interrupted. The door opened and Mark walked in with an armful of grocery bags. "I brought you some food, honey," he said, obviously proud he'd remembered the grocery list that had been sitting on the baby-shit-yellow Formica counter for the past five days.

Too little, too late, I thought. "Thanks, hon, but Lee just brought me some," I said, my frustration evident in my tone.

"That's fine, but can you take some of this food and make Lee and me some dinner or lunch? Whichever."

"Can you stay, Lee?" I asked quietly, having trouble looking in his eyes after what had happened, especially now that Mark was home. God, it was just an innocent kiss. What was wrong with me?

Lee smiled lightheartedly. "I can always eat," he said.

The door opened again and Albert, Mark's other sidekick of late, swaggered in. I pondered how nice it was that he didn't feel the need to knock. And Albert made my skin crawl. He was only a kid, but there was already something noticeably wicked about him. He constantly looked at the floor, even while he spoke to people, obviously unable to look them in the eye. He was shifty. His droopy body language could be seen as a lack of confidence, but I knew he was a snake lying in wait, ready to strike. He had latched onto Mark, and Mark, for reasons I couldn't fathom, tolerated him.

"Hello, Albert," Mark said indifferently. He seemed distracted, as if he were far away from this room, these people, and me.

"Hi," Albert replied to the floor. He took his usual seat next to Lee on the couch.

Mark and I unloaded the groceries, then I began preparing dinner. Everyone was in good spirits now, even Mark's mood had changed. But I was preoccupied by the sense of danger I had felt swarming in on me since I awoke. I could barely breathe. What if the baby did come early? I thought I had a little over a month to get ready. Could I ever be ready? Was I prepared to be a mother at all? I grated a piece of mozzarella, then placed the slim pieces of cheese on top of a premade pizza. Questions swam through my head, but the answers were obviously swimming in a different pool.

I slid the pizza pan into the oven, feeling strange about what Lee had said about Mark not being who I thought he was. Maybe he wasn't all that I thought he was. I knew he had moments when he could be a little selfish, but he was always looking out for me, I believed. As I was pondering over all of this, Mark came in the kitchen and wrapped his arms around my belly. My body relaxed. I had been craving his touch lately.

I did the dishes while the boys watched the guests on the Jerry Springer show scream and holler. The scent of lemon dish soap wafted up to my nostrils and made me nauseous. I walked the five feet from the kitchen and opened the bathroom door. I slid down onto the gray bathroom mat in front of the toilet. I sat there for what seemed like forever, waiting to puke, then Mark opened the door and sat next to me on the floor.

"You okay?" he asked.

"It passed," I said, staring into the stained toilet bowl.

He looked into my eyes. "You know, you are the best thing that's ever happened to me. I love you so much. And I'm so excited about the baby. Scared, but excited. I want to be the best father and the best man for you," he whispered.

"Thank you," I said. I felt like I was going to cry.

"You want to get up?"

"Yeah."

He reached for my hands and helped me rise, then wrapped his arms tightly around me.

I encircled his waist with my arms and squeezed back. My tears gushed out, but the oven timer was buzzing in the kitchen. I let go and wiped my eyes.

We all sat down, and everybody began making small talk about the weather and whatever. Something was off. It wasn't so much that we had company, because we usually did, but it was the way everyone was acting—soft-spoken and overly conscious of their manners. After dinner we turned the television on and everyone vegged out.

"Mark, I really want a chocolate shake. I'm having a craving, baby," I said, still perturbed by the unusual atmosphere and what Lee had said about Mark.

Mark placed his hand on my leg and squeezed it reassuringly. "I'll go get you one." He grabbed his skateboard, smiled hugely at me, and walked out the door. I wanted to ask Lee about what he had been saying earlier, but not in front of Albert. Albert never came over unless his visit somehow involved an ulterior motive, namely drugs. This time he was hanging out and eating dinner. Something was up. I sat, staring at Albert and Lee, who were talking about nothing, nothing that seemed like it might be something, or that would give away a surreptitious plan.

"Shit, that's funny," Albert said. He picked up the remote and changed the channel.

Lee looked quietly at the TV, tapping his foot nervously, beating time.

The door opened and Mark walked in, holding a Styrofoam cup in his hand. He handed it to me, smiled, then glanced mischievously at the other two. I wasn't stupid—I could tell something was up, but they certainly weren't going to discuss it in front of me.

Mark suddenly boomed, "Orleigh, I have a surprise for you."

I didn't respond, just stared at him vacantly.

"We're going to Chicago," he said.

Maybe it was the flicker in his eyes, maybe the coy smile pushing up his lips—whatever it was, he knew how to charm me. I was instantly pulled back to the night we met, to how I felt he would never hurt a soul. I remembered his blue-black hair tumbling over his eyes as he leaned into me.

"Why?" I asked, smiling back.

He sat down next to me and swung an arm over my shoulder. "I was thinking we could go to your house and visit your family, even your friends if you want. Then we could hop on the train and visit Carl," he said. He widened his eyes at me inquiringly.

I stared at him in a daze; he didn't know my friend Carl that well. Carl called our place every once in a while to catch up with me, but in reality we hadn't been close since high school. I'd only seen him once since graduation, and that had been months ago. I wondered if Mark was trying to set up some sort of drug deal with him.

"Sounds good, honey. When do you want to leave?" I murmured, despite myself.

"Now would be good, if you're ready. Geoffrey is going to give us a ride to Geneva." Mark lifted the blinds and peered outside. "In fact, he's outside right now."

I turned to face him, shocked. I hadn't seen Geoffrey since the day I'd screamed at him, Alyssia, and that whole crowd, then stormed out of the Morning After. I was extremely reluctant to go anywhere with Geoffrey.

"When did you arrange that?" I asked angrily.

"Today," he said, aloof. "So, you ready?"

I felt my face flush as I thought about seeing Geoffrey again. This was going to be so uncomfortable. Everything Mark did—even when he tried to be nice—had been making me nervous lately. I looked around the room for my purse and saw it on a chair. "Let me get some things together, that is if we're going to spend the night," I said, completely flustered.

Mark watched me with an air of curiosity. "You don't need anything, baby."

"But if we're sleeping there, I'll need my things."

"No, you don't." He slid the strap of my purse onto my shoulder.

I felt extremely tired and gave in. I slid my shoes onto my swollen feet and let my head loll onto Mark's shoulder. It didn't make sense that he had asked Geoffrey to give us a ride to Geneva; he knew how I felt about the Alyssia crowd.

Mark looked over at Albert and Lee. "You two ready?" My mouth gaped open in astonishment. Why was he inviting them?

Albert picked up his knapsack. "Yeah, I'm ready."

Lee looked at the floor, scuffing the tip of his combat boot into the carpet. "Mark, uh, I'm not going to go with you after all."

Mark and Lee stared each other down. What the hell was going on here? I really was beginning to think there was a drug deal in the works. Maybe Lee and Albert were contributing money, hoping to make some quick cash. But whatever was going on, I didn't want to be part of it. Honestly, I couldn't have cared less if Lee joined us or not. I was getting twisted up inside, angry and stressed. I needed to relax. My belly grumbled.

Mark broke off the stare down with a look of disgust. "You're not going? What the fuck do you mean, *you're not going?*"

Lee leaned against the door, and the safety pins on his leather jacket tinkled. "I don't really feel like heading out to Geneva. I don't want to get involved in this fiasco."

Lee's reaction confirmed to me even more what this trip was about. "Mark, they don't have to come," I said uncomfortably. "I think they'd be bored anyway."

"Shut up, Orleigh," Mark shot at me, then sneered. "Lee you *are* coming."

"No, I'm not, dude." Lee walked past me whispering, *"Be careful"* into my ear. Then he walked out the door.

The twist in Mark's lip betrayed that he was seriously pissed. Something was definitely not right. But what I couldn't figure out was why Lee was so concerned about me. Outside, Geoffrey began honking the horn. Mark came up behind me and shoved me out the door. Everything was rushed. I didn't want to go. This trip obviously had little to do with me visiting my family and friends.

"Let's go, guys!" Mark said with exaggerated cheer and enthusiasm.

Albert and I followed Mark out to Geoff's car. As I approached, I stared at Geoffrey, and he stared back at me. Memories came rushing back. He smiled awkwardly at me as we said hello. I saw him glance at my belly, and I wondered what he thought in that fleeting moment. I wondered if he, like me, was remembering that long ago discussion about the *Us* baby, and if he now saw how crazy and ridiculous it had all been.

"It's Mark's," I said, patting my stomach.

"That's what I thought," he replied, smiling kindly.

I got into the car, and we headed out to Geneva. As we drove, Geoff occupied most of the conversation, talking about everything that had happened while Mark and I had been on the road.

He told us how Sam had a nervous breakdown and moved to California. Don was in a mental hospital, which was no big surprise. He had stopped hanging out with that group. We had moved on, and all of that now seemed long ago. The current news was more important. He gave us the scoop on how Pat had gotten busted for dealing coke. The police had nabbed some of Pat's clients while they'd been snorting lines in a restaurant bathroom. After grilling them for a few hours, they had given the cops Pat's name. According to Geoffrey, those two guys had not been seen in DeKalb since they'd gotten out of jail, which led him to believe they might have been killed by gang members. He rambled on.

"Now I'm working in telemarketing, making excellent money." He combed his hand through his curly hair. He hadn't changed much physically, but he appeared more grown-up.

I leaned back into the bucket seat and watched the cornfields roll by, spying an occasional red barn, bales of hay, the silos in the distance. As I peered out the window, I kept wondering what Lee had meant when he said to be careful. I feared that all this anxiety would cause my water to break and my eight-month-old fetus to spill out of me right there in the car.

On Route Sixty-four we pulled up to a stoplight in St. Charles, the town right next to Geneva, where I had grown up. St. Charles might have been called a town but was actually a McDonald's, a Pizza Hut, a couple of gas stations, and a few buildings smack in the middle of a cornfield.

Mark began barking out orders. "Hey, let's stop here, guys. Actually, Geoff, you could drop us off right here. I know you need to get going."

I recognized one of the handful of buildings. An old high-school friend named Tracey lived there with her boyfriend. Last I heard they hadn't moved. Geoffrey pulled into a gas station, per Mark's orders. It was a Clark station that was notorious for never letting anyone use the bathroom, and I had to pee. One thing pregnancy offered was an eager bladder, always about to explode. I thought my friend Tracey wouldn't mind me using her bathroom, if only I could get Mark to let me stop by there.

"Mark," I piped up from the backseat. "My friends live in that building. Can we go and see them? I really need to pee."

"Sure, baby," he replied, all nice.

For a split second I thought things had returned to normal. I believed that we were here to visit my friends and family. I wanted to think that this wasn't about a drug deal, that Mark sincerely meant for this time to be mine. Then I looked over at Albert's reptilian grin and knew that I was merely deceiving myself—the plan, whatever it was, had nothing to do with me.

We got out of Geoffrey's car and said good-bye. Walking toward the apartment building my bladder ached, and the pain doubled as we made our way up the stairs. I hadn't seen Tracey or her boyfriend Reggie in a long time, and I felt a little guilty and awkward bringing my posse with me. But the thought of a bathroom propelled me upward. I knocked on the door, and soon Tracey answered, cheerfully surprised.

"Just thought I'd drop by and say hi for a few minutes while I'm passing through town," I explained. "Oh, and this is my boyfriend Mark and his friend Albert."

"Come in, sit down." She smiled, but I could tell she was a little uncomfortable about me popping in so unexpectedly.

"Can I use the bathroom, Trace?" I asked, ready to quickly make the dash.

"Down the hall, second door on your left," she said.

I set my purse on her plush velvet couch and headed to the bathroom while Mark and Albert sat down. I shut the door behind me, grateful to be alone, if only for a moment. I sat on the toilet, looking down at the huge lump that had grown in my belly. I felt repulsed. I hadn't told Mark what the doctor had said. Maybe if I had, we wouldn't be here right now with me getting all stressed out. I flushed the toilet and stood. A pain jetted up my spine. I washed my hands, watching my reflection in the medicine cabinet mirror twist in agony. When the pain subsided, my face returned to normal, and I was surprised at the youthful image looking back at me. My face hadn't changed much. Maybe it was a little fuller, but I still looked pretty. My pale-blue eyes were clear and bright, my lips rosy, and my cheeks glowed in a way I'd never noticed before. It didn't seem possible that I could look so good and feel so shitty. I felt old, tired. When I opened the bathroom door, Mark and Albert were no longer on the couch.

"Where'd they go, Trace?" I asked with a sense of panic.

"They said they were hungry, so I sent them over to that ice cream place you and I worked at when we were in high school. Mark said to tell you that he took a couple dollars from your purse."

I was amazed that there were a few dollars in my purse.

"Oh, and we're supposed to meet them in the parking lot in ten minutes. I offered you guys a ride to the train station. Why are you guys going to Chicago?" She looked quizzically at my face, then my stomach. I imagined she thought our impending trip had something to do with the baby.

"We're going to see Carl. Remember Carl?"

"Yeah, you two used to be best friends." She smiled.

"That was a long time ago." I sighed. I had thought we were going to my mom's house in Geneva first.

"I'm sorry, Tracey, we don't need to be in that big a hurry, there're lots of trains to Chicago."

"Don't worry about it; it's just nice to see you. Everything going okay?" she asked, her eyes meandering over my pregnant belly.

"I think, I mean, well, being pregnant kind of sucks. And Mark's acting so weird lately. I feel kind of lost. He's brought me here to see my family, and now we're leaving for Chicago. My mom's house is in Geneva. It's only five minutes away. We just got here. I don't get men."

Tracey laughed. "Join the club, sister. It's always confusing." She smiled softly at me, and for a moment I felt comforted.

"I think it's time to meet your man." She stood. "Need anything before you take off? It's a long train ride."

"No, but thanks for letting me use your bathroom." I rose slowly, lacking the energy that Tracey's thin and healthy body possessed. I followed her as she bounded down the stairs. We opened the huge metal door to the parking lot, which was filled with old cars and rust buckets, then walked to the VW bug that Tracey had owned since high school. I leaned against it.

"Do you remember that time we made vodka slushies outside the amphitheater in the park?" I asked, wishing I were there again instead of waiting for Mark in a suburban apartment-complex parking lot, pregnant.

"Yeah, Orleigh, I remember everything." She laughed a little, then looked at her watch. "Do you think we should go pick them up?"

I looked out across the parking lot and saw Mark and Albert running over a small grass incline at the end of the lot. "No, it looks like they're coming," I said.

As they ran, Mark's eyes locked into mine. He looked worried, probably thought I was pissed off about waiting for him. I didn't really mind. It was nice to talk to Tracey.

"Let's go, we're gonna miss the train," Mark said, winded.

Tracey got behind the wheel, and the rest of us piled in. I sat in the front seat with Tracey. She slowly pulled out of the parking lot, and we were off again, set further into a whirlwind of motion that didn't seem to stop. I glanced in the rearview mirror and noticed that Mark and Albert were changing their shirts as Tracey sped toward the train station.

"Are you two cold?" Tracey asked.

"Uh, yeah, and it's even colder in the city," Mark replied, his voice muffled by the long-sleeve Dead T-shirt he was pulling over his head.

I wasn't cold, but I thought maybe it was just my hormones fucking with my body temperature. I was constantly feeling overheated these days.

"Can you drive a little faster?" Mark asked.

I looked over my shoulder and shot him an evil look. Why was he being so fucking rude? He didn't even know Tracey.

"I guess," Tracey said, then she accelerated a bit.

We were entering Geneva. We passed the movie theater where I used to hang out in my early teens. There was a cement wall in front of it where all the burnouts would stand, smoking cigarettes. When the movie let out, they would hit on us. No one was hanging out there now. Things had changed.

I heard the drone of a police siren. Turning around, I saw that the police car was tailing us. The bright blue and red lights flashed over the rear window. I was pretty pissed that Tracey was going to get a speeding ticket on our account.

When I turned around a second time, there were five cop cars, all flashing their lights.

Tracey pulled into the train station parking lot. A sick feeling crept into my belly.

The cops surrounded Tracey's car, and one came over and ordered us to get out. I stood next to Mark, watching the cops hone in on the car. Two cops were opening the back passenger side door and peering inside.

We were told that they were taking us to the police station. I looked at Mark, then back at the cop who was now rifling through Albert's knapsack, which he had retrieved from the backseat. A cop approached Mark and me, grabbed my arm, and walked me over to his squad car. Mark was looking at me, and he had tears in his eyes, but I was too stunned to care. The cop pulled out his Smith and Wesson handcuffs. He yanked at my wrist, then snapped a cuff around it. I was overwhelmed by the scent of his uniform. He smelled of pipe tobacco, like my grandfather, and for a moment I felt oddly comforted. Mark and Albert were also being handcuffed. Mark was bitching about the cuffs being too tight. I'd lost sight of Tracey, but her car was still there, so I assumed she was probably in one of the squad cars. My pipe-smelling cop helped me get into his car, placing his hand on my head so I would duck and not bump it.

It's amazing how little attention you give to things like your hands until you can't use them anymore, I thought.

I sat in the back of the cop car, and it all came to me in a flash. I remembered a night after our road trip when Mark and I sat in his room, drinking Hawaiian Punch spiked with Everclear. I told him about the ice cream parlor where Tracey and I had worked while we were in high school, and how she now lived across the street from it. I told him about the large sums of money the owner stashed in the freezer. We desperately needed money then, and I had jokingly suggested we could rob the place. It seemed so long ago, and in the interim things had changed. Mark got a job and worked for Pat on the side, making extra cash. And it wasn't anything I'd really go through with, it was just a moment of drunken craziness.

They took us in through the back of the station, where the first order of business was to gather all our stories. Then they started questioning those stories. I sat across from my own personal officer. The fluorescent bulbs above me buzzed loudly. I felt dizzy, like I might faint. The cop's ice-blue eyes glared at me while I coughed nervously.

"What do you know about what happened this evening?" he asked. He licked his finger and turned a page of his yellow legal pad.

"Nothing," I said shakily, looking at the floor.

"I think you must know something," he said, staring intently at me.

"Can I smoke?" I pulled a cigarette out of Mark's pack, which was still in my purse.

"Sure you can." He set an ashtray on the desk. "Is there anything else I can get you?"

I lit my cigarette, the first one I'd had in a really long time, and looked around his office. There was a pop machine in the corner. I was thirsty, so I said, "I'd like a Pepsi. Not Coke, Pepsi."

The officer rose and got me a Pepsi from the machine. When he returned, he placed it in front of me, and my interrogation resumed.

"So, why don't you tell me what you know?" His beady eyes shifted from me to the legal pad. He licked the tip of his pen, which I thought was completely bizarre. He obviously thought I had something of importance to tell him.

"I already did. Nothing, really! I'm sure Mark and Albert will tell you the same thing. As far as I knew, we were coming here to visit my friends and family. Of course, that was just another empty promise. We were going to go to Chicago afterwards to meet a friend of mine. So we were on our way to the train station, and we got pulled over. Now we're here. Maybe you can tell *me* what happened?" That was the best answer I could give him. My head was reeling. I was so scared I could barely sit still. My legs were crossed, and my foot swung uncontrollably up and down. I was having trouble smoking; my throat kept tightening. I wanted to see Mark and ask *him* what had happened.

"So you were just in the area, visiting friends and family? Tracey was one of these friends?" he asked with a sly smile.

"Yeah, well the guy who gave us a ride here needed to go somewhere else, so Mark suggested that we get dropped off at the apartment building. I knew Tracey lived there, and I thought it wouldn't be a bad idea to drop by and visit a little." I didn't want to say too much. I wasn't sure if what I was saying would help or hurt Mark's situation. The cop stared at me, apparently trying to intimidate me. It wasn't working.

"So visiting Tracey was not part of the original plan?" he asked, as if he were on something, or merely high on the power of being a cop. His smile sickened me.

"There was no plan; we were just hanging out," I said.

"Then what happened?" With every question he gave me this strange look, as if he were a spider and I the fly twisted in his web.

"We were at Tracey's. I was in the bathroom when Mark and Al got hungry and took off to a restaurant. Tracey and I went down to the car to meet them, then we headed to the train station. We never quite made it onto the train, and I'm assuming you know the rest of the story," I said snidely. I didn't know what the fuck he wanted from me—I certainly wasn't going to tell him about the night Mark and I had plotted a robbery in a drunken haze. I tried turning the tables around on him again: "Why don't you tell me what this is all about?"

He snickered. I looked at his stern face, wondering if it was his line of work that had made him so hard. His face looked blockish, all rough sharp angles instead of soft curves. Whenever he asked me a question, he furrowed his brow, causing a large crease to form between his eyes. I felt like I was sitting across from a growling bulldog. And I really didn't like the good-cop/bad-cop game he was playing. First, it was all *"You can smoke, let me get you a Pepsi,"* and now it was *"Let me be a real ball buster because I don't believe you."*

"Have you ever watched *CHiPs?*" I asked.

He looked up from his notepad. "Yeah," he said, surprised.

"Well, anything you get from me is inadmissible unless you read me my rights," I said, feeling proud that I'd remembered that bit of information. Who says television doesn't teach us anything?

He was shocked, like I'd caught him in a major fuck-up. "Cute, very cute." He took a few moments to snottily read me the Miranda Rights. "Would you like to add anything to your story?" he asked, once he had finished.

"Look, I told you what I know, and I'm sure Mark and Albert will confirm my lack of knowledge. Perhaps you can let me know what they did?" I was dying to know exactly what had gone down. My gut told me that Mark had carried out the plan from our drunken conversation. He had done it, and he hadn't wanted me to know. I wished he would have told me, then we wouldn't have wound up here. I would have never let him go through with it.

"Your boyfriend and his buddy robbed that restaurant at gunpoint," the cop said, watching me closely for a reaction.

I stared at the officer in complete disbelief. Mark was a pacifist. I couldn't even picture him holding a gun. I had thought he would have just bullied the owner and tied him up. The cop must have read my incredulous look.

"It wasn't a real gun they used, it was a pellet gun," he said. "But they can seem real when they're being held to someone's head. They walked out with a little less than two thousand dollars. Was it really worth it?" He made this last question sound as if I'd really want to answer it. The hard angles of his face softened. I think he really did believe that I hadn't known what Mark was up to.

"I doubt it," I blurted, an extreme sadness building up in my chest. It was all over now. Mark was going to do time for this. My heart ached, and I wanted to run to him and comfort him. "Can I see Mark?" I asked.

"Absolutely not," he said gruffly, the bad cop returning. "I imagine you two won't be seeing each other for quite some time." There was a tinge of sympathy in his voice now. "Do you know why he did it?"

"I do. He did it for me. He did it for our baby." It was the truth, and it simply came out. I wished it had been about drugs, anything else, then at least I could resent him or be angry with him. I felt horribly guilty.

"Pretty big risk to take when you have a baby on the way," he said, and I couldn't tell if he was trying to be nice or not. "Did you ask Mark to do this?"

Baffled, I said, "No." It was all I was going to say from this point on. My heart hurt, my brain hurt, everything hurt. There was a knock on the door, and he got up to answer it.

"Wait right here, will you?" he asked, as if I could go anywhere else. It was a little difficult to escape from a police station. I nodded my head up and down, then cradled it in my hands.

I was left in the room alone for an exceptionally long time—about two hours. I couldn't believe my parents paid these assholes' salaries. What would have happened if I had to pee? For god's sake, I was pregnant and no one had even checked in on me. I gathered they were trying to put together all of our stories to make some sense out of the robbery. Finally, the officer returned to the room and sat down across from me.

He spoke in a heavy tone, looking more like the bulldog again, clearly agitated. "You forgot to tell me that you used to work at that restaurant. That you knew where the money was. You forgot to mention that you and Mark talked about robbing this place before." He continued spitting out accusations. It was as if he had discovered a gold mine, but I didn't care.

I was surprised that Mark had told him about that night. He must have freaked out because he was scared. Cops could be pretty intimidating. I knew he hadn't meant it. "That was a long time ago," I blurted, with a little hostility.

"Well, the fact that you two talked about all this means you did know something. You know what we call you, Orleigh? We call you an accomplice." He spoke triumphantly, but I still didn't give a shit.

"We're going to take you to another room now. We have to book you. That means we have to take some mug shots and get your fingerprints." He stood up and motioned for me to follow. Thank god he'd finally read me my rights. I followed him. His butt cheeks clenched tightly as he walked. I observed his thinning hair from behind. I felt sick to my stomach.

When we got to the back room, I saw Mark handcuffed to a bench. We stared at each other. He looked guiltily at me, but I wasn't angry with him. It wasn't his fault he had told. I smiled at him, as my bulldog cop pointed to a spot on the bench. "Sit down right there and be quiet."

I sat next to Mark, and he turned to me, his eyes downcast. "I'm sorry," he whispered. "I love you."

"I love you too. Don't worry. Whatever happens, I'll be here." I gave him the best words I could muster. I did love him, and I could never stop loving him. This was all just a big mistake, a giant fuck-up.

The officer in charge of Mark came to take him away. He seemed really nice compared to the cretin I had got stuck with. He undid the cuff that was around the metal part of the bench and snapped the now empty side onto Mark's left wrist. I didn't want them to separate us.

"Hey, kid, you best say good-bye to her," Mark's officer said softly. "It might be a while before you see each other again. I'll step aside for a minute here."

The officer moved out of earshot, and Mark clumsily got down on his knees in front of me. His hands were cuffed together so he couldn't wipe the tears from his eyes. "I never meant for you to get involved in this shit. I'll try to see to it that they let you go. I tried to explain that you had nothing to do with any of this. They refuse to listen to me, baby. I love you. I love our little baby too. Love you both so much."

Mark was sobbing now, his words coming out all muffled. "And I wasn't the one who told." His voice sounded pained. "I told Albert, and I think Albert told the cops."

I wiped the tears from his face, and he took his cuffed hands and cupped them to my stomach; then he gave me gentle kisses as he slowly stood up—on my belly, my face, my hair. When he pulled his head away, there were wet marks all over my shirt.

"I love you too, Mark. Love you forever. Things will work out all right for us; they always do," I said, even though I found the words hard to believe.

"Okay, let's go, kid," Mark's officer said, laying his hand on Mark's shoulder.

I mouthed the words *I love you* as he walked away. He gave me a wink and a weak smile.

CHAPTER 18

Olivia,

My love, I miss you terribly. It has been awful here, separated from you. I want so badly to be with you. I only wish I could break out and find my way to you. It wouldn't be too difficult; I sense your presence everywhere around me. Sometimes I even think I smell you.

How is our beautiful baby girl? I got the ultrasound picture you sent. Even through the blur of fluid, I can see she is stunning. She is perfect, just like you.

I dream you are with me at night. I feel you underneath me. I smell you, I taste you in my mouth. Then I wake and cry. The nights are hardest. Remember how we used to sleep spooned? Your body fit perfectly against mine. I miss you so bad it hurts.

Some terrible things have happened since I last wrote. The guys here beat me up badly. They think I am a fag because I cry about you. What do they know? I doubt they have ever had anything like our love in their lives. They held down my arm and put their cigarettes out on the tattoo that you gave me when you were practicing in Arizona. I think it will be okay when it heals but for now it is as ugly as my bruised face.

My parents and sister are coming to see me this Saturday. This will be the first time I've seen them in a long time.

Please write to me soon. Tell me all about the baby. Tell me if you are fat now. You know you wear pregnancy well. You're so beautiful. Dream of me, like I dream of you. I love you forever.

Beetlejuice

Beetlejuice,

Darling, my heart aches to be with you. My mom comes every Saturday, but she won't get me out of here. I can't stand being away from you. That is the hardest part of all.

The baby is well, as well as can be expected here. I'm still smoking on occasion; I don't know what else to do. All day I fantasize about us being together. I keep dreaming of you, me, and our beautiful daughter high in the Colorado mountains. I see us lost in our own little world, the three of us. That would be all I need to be happy, my love.

I'm devastated about what they did to you. I hope everything will be better. I have to go to court on Tuesday, so hopefully you'll be there, and I can at least see you. I miss you as much as you miss me, if not more. I picture you so clearly. Your hair falling over your eyes when you're about to kiss me. Write soon, please. I dream of you every night. You are always in my thoughts.

Olivia

Dearest Olivia,

I will also be in court on Tuesday. I think my parents are going to bail me out. I have begged them to get you out as well, but the bond is so high, they can only afford to get me out.

Don't worry though, I will come and visit you immediately. I'm dying to see you, see your belly. I wish I could lay my hands on your stomach and feel our child kicking, moving. It's a father's deepest desire, to touch the baby through the skin of the one he loves.

Please be strong for the baby and me. I will talk to you on the phone every day. I promise that things will be good. They always are with us, aren't they? I love you. I love you too, baby. What are we going to name her? I have some ideas to share with you. I'll save them for our first visit. I'm dreaming of making love to you right now. I love you forever.

Beetlejuice

Beetlejuice,

You think you are going to get out? That's wonderful. I'm so envious. But I think things are harder for you than they are on my side. People are pretty nice to me here; I think because I'm pregnant.

I can't wait to see you tomorrow. I know you will be as beautiful as always. I saw the doctor today. Baby is wonderfully healthy. You are right—she is stunning. She moves all the time. Sometimes, I see a foot or a hand pressing on the skin of my belly. So tiny. Little hands and feet. I already love her more than words can express. She is ours, everything that we are, welded together into one beautiful baby. Could anything be more perfect?

I am tired now, tired all the time. Hopefully, I can fall asleep and dream of you as always. Don't forget me when you leave here. Please don't forget me. I love you so much. You are always in my thoughts.

Olivia

I slept through the night into the morning. There wasn't much more to do in jail—either watch TV or sleep. I was trying to make myself look as good as possible. It was going to be the first time I would see Mark in two weeks. I was ashamed he had to see me in the orange jumpsuit I was required to wear.

They wanted me to testify against him. I would rather slit my throat than send him away to prison. Being sent away to boot camp for four months was better than being a narc. Everyone thought I was stupid—my mother, my lawyer, everyone—all because an innocent pregnant girl would rather see her love free in four months than be responsible for sending him to prison for at least five years. I hoped if this stupid boot camp thing went through we would be there at the same time. I couldn't bear not seeing him for another four months.

The loudspeaker crackled loudly as it turned on for an announcement.

"Ladies, anyone due in court today, please line up at the door," the monotone voice said from somewhere outside the bars.

They called steel bars a "door." How fucking homey! I lined up behind three other women also going to court.

"You got your smokes?" Marie, a Mexican prostitute who was arrested every other week, asked me.

"No." I shrugged my shoulders.

"I got extra for you and your bambino." She smiled a toothless smile at me. Her clients must have loved her services.

I gave Officer Tate my name as I walked out so she could verify it on the list of women expected in court that day. So many formalities. There were only six women in the jail—how could the officers not know our names by now?

I proceeded down the hall until a fat male guard bearing handcuffs met me. I was used to the routine. I held up my wrists to be cuffed, no questions asked. I stood with the three criminals against the red brick wall. The ladies laughed, talked to each other, and flirted with the male guard. I was silent. The whole situation made me ill.

Officer Tate walked up to us, smiling broadly. "Okay, ladies, follow me to the van." The zillions of pieces of hardware on her body clinked together as she led us toward the gate where we would be searched before we got in the van.

We reached the holding pen, which was actually a garage. It consisted of two ramps: one for men and one for women, separated by a waist-high red wall. We walked down the ramp, then stood in front of a metal gate. It was similar to the lines at amusement parks, except when this gate opened it led to a high-security van instead of a roller coaster. My eyes scanned the line of men waiting to be led to the ramp. He was there. I could see him searching for me through the crowd. As soon as our eyes met, we smiled. He mouthed the words *"I love you,"* and I did the same. Then Officer Tate walked the men down the ramp to the van that transported them to the courthouse. I kind of felt sorry for her; some of the guys were making comments about her ass, but I guess that was one of the perks of her job.

When we got to the courthouse, we were brought to a holding cell in the basement. It resembled the hard-core prison cells in movies. It had a thick steel door with a tiny window in it. In the corner stood a lone toilet with no toilet paper. It smelled atrocious. The gray walls were graffitied with pencil; inmates were never allowed pens or markers. I held my breath and slumped against the dingy wall, waiting for my name to be called.

Eventually I was ushered into a plush room adjacent to the courtroom, where Officer Tate instructed me to wait in silence for my case to be called. I looked around the room and saw Mark sitting alone, but Officer Tate directed me to a chair that was on the opposite side of the room. I sat down and our eyes locked. Stunned, I watched Mark stand and start striding toward me. A male guard halted him with his arm.

"Where you going, son?" he asked, surprised by Mark's boldness.

Mark lifted his cuffed hands and pointed at me. "To her."

The guard laughed under his breath. "I can't let you go over there. Sorry."

"Sir, she is my life," he said, his shoulders hunching. "She has our baby inside her. I need to talk to her for just one minute. She has been all alone for weeks. Please, let me go to her."

"One minute," the guard said, obviously touched by Mark's plea.

"That's all I ask. It's all I need."

My vision became blurred and watery as he walked across the room. He sat down beside me. "Hello, baby," he said, as his eyes lit up the way they used to.

"Hello, love."

He looked down at my big round belly. "How's she doing?"

"A little kicky at times," I whispered. "Probably misses her daddy resting his head on her."

He smiled, and with his cuffed hands touched my belly. I felt weak all over. I had missed his touch more than anything.

"So you're getting out today?" I asked. I felt excited for him but still terribly sad.

"Yes, and I can't wait to come visit you."

"Neither can I. How can I call you?"

"Call me at home tomorrow, around ten." He smiled warmly.

"In the morning?"

He seemed thrilled about us being able to communicate by phone instead of writing. "Yeah, the parents will be at work," he said.

"Are you worried about today?"

"Court?" he asked.

"Yes."

"I guess I am, a little. You know you should have testified against me. You could have stayed home and raised our daughter." He sighed. "I know you were looking out for me and all, but I feel horrible that I got you involved."

I could barely get my words out. "I couldn't testify," I stammered finally.

"I know, and because of that you are saving my life, but I've ruined yours."

"It's a small sacrifice for you," I said, even though I feared it might be a huge mistake.

His eyes lit up again. "I love you."

"I know. I miss you," I said, but my mind was filled with thoughts of the baby.

Our names were called, and we went into the hallway. Mark kissed me ever so lightly as we passed through the door, and the guard didn't say anything or try to stop him. He probably felt sorry for us. I figured our situation looked pretty dismal.

My lawyer was waiting for me in the hallway. He basically outlined the next six months of my life: I would deliver the baby, then after two weeks' rest I would go to boot camp. All this for saying *guilty*. It seemed so unfair. I wasn't even in the fucking restaurant when Mark robbed it. I just had to protect him. My choices were grim: plead guilty and do boot camp or testify against Mark and be free. When I originally agreed, it seemed like a fair trade—six months of my life for what could be five or more years of his. But then I thought about our daughter, and I wasn't sure it was the best decision.

I looked at Mark, who was standing across the hall. He winked at me, and in that hasty moment I told the lawyer I would take the plea bargain. I would go away. It would even be an easy way to shed the pregnancy pounds. The lawyer made one more feeble attempt to get me to testify against Mark, but it was fruitless—I could never hurt him like that.

It was time for me to appear before the judge. I was so scared I had to pee. I was called before Mark, and when I glanced back at him, he gave me a reassuring smile. I walked through the door into the courtroom. I sat on a bench and waited for them to call my name. I saw my mother—she was crying. I wanted to tell her that everything would work out for the best, but I wasn't so sure myself.

I approached the bench in my orange uniform and handcuffs. It was brief. The State demanded four months of my life in just a few minutes. I mean, I knew it was going to happen, but I didn't know how bad I would feel. When the judge gave me my sentence, fresh tears swelled in my eyes. I was so afraid of what was going to happen to my baby, to Mark, to me while I was at this fucking boot camp. All I could envision was barbed wire, big gates, and soldiers barking out orders: a concentration camp.

I was ushered back into the hallway where I would soon be returned to the holding cell. I passed Mark. He was also crying. It was all so confusing. We left the room, and I sat down on a bench in the hallway next to Officer Tate. We had to wait until four more prisoners, who had just gone through the same process I had, joined us before we returned to the basement cell. Then I would have to wait until all of the prisoners were done getting their sentences.

Mark walked back into the hallway, a guard following close at his heels. He sat right next to me, not even asking for permission this time, and the guard shrugged his shoulders at Officer Tate.

"What happened to you?" I asked sullenly.

"Same thing as you."

"Can you get out today?" I asked. I almost hoped he couldn't. I felt angry that he was getting out and I was going to have to stay in jail.

"Yes," he said, smiling a little.

I didn't return his smile. I looked down at my stomach, then back him. "Then what?"

"When you're done with boot camp, I have to go," he said, trying to hold my hand.

I was taken aback. "We don't go at the same time?" I asked.

He shook his head back and forth. "No, they won't let us."

I clasped his hand in mine and patted my stomach. "What about the baby?"

"I'll have to take care of her until you're done." He smiled again.

I resented his smile. I pushed his hand off my belly. "This whole thing is so fucked up. I feel horrible. I can't stand it anymore," I said bitterly.

He reached toward me, and we clasped hands for a second, then

Officer Tate grabbed my elbow to help me up. It was time for us to go back to the holding cell. He kissed me before he got in line. This time it didn't make me feel any better.

I hated being locked up. It was cold and surreal. There was a large room with shit-brown carpeting, four large metal tables in the center, and four seats bolted to the floor. A window opened onto a lovely view: a cement wall where a few rays of light seeped in for an instant around eight in the morning. Most of the inmates spent their time on the wrap-around brown couches that faced the TV. The guards controlled the channels, but no one objected. Behind the couches loomed a huge yellow steel gate that kept us inside and the guards at a comfortable distance. The gate also sealed us off from the doctor's quarters, the room where inmates met with their lawyers, and most importantly, the visiting rooms. We were only allowed out of the cell for emergencies, visits, or court dates. Then there were our bedrooms, hidden behind twelve steel doors, a window in each. We were not allowed in the bedrooms until "lights out," which was around ten p.m.

Inside the "day room," as the jailers called it, there was not much to do. I sat alone on the floor by the window. I'd been contemplating it for days, and I finally arrived at Willow. I couldn't wait to tell Mark. It made perfect sense: sturdy and strong and sad. It was a name that would represent the first year of her life—half the time spent without a mother and the other half without a father.

My name spit out of the intercom. Mark was right on time. I walked into the visitors' room, sat behind the plate glass, and waited. The door opened, and he walked in. As soon as we saw each other the tears started pouring out of our eyes. We were both so fucking cheesy. He picked up the phone and signaled for me to do the same. It took every ounce of energy to lift the receiver.

"Hello, darling," he uttered quietly.

"Hello."

"How are you?"

I heaved a sigh into the phone. "Good, I guess. Better now that you're here."

"I miss you," he said, his hand sliding over the plate glass.

"Likewise," I said.

He smiled because I had used the word he always used with me. His eyes were twinkling, and he laughed.

"Aren't you happy that we no longer have to be Beetlejuice and Olivia?"

"Yeah, except I liked it. So, is it nice to be out?"

"It's better, but it would be nicer if you were with me," he said sorrowfully.

I felt guilty for resenting his freedom. "Well, that's just *not* going to happen." My tone was edgy. I glimpsed at my belly, then back at Mark. It wasn't his fault that I couldn't get bailed out.

He looked forlorn. "What's wrong with your mother?"

I laughed a hideously contemptuous laugh. "She doesn't think it's safe to let me out. I might go crazy and start killing people. You know how I can get."

He smiled at me and placed his hand against the glass. I put mine up there too, but the act was so cliché that we both dropped them immediately.

"Have you thought about a name yet?" he asked, trying to turn the conversation to a more cheerful topic.

I told him about the name Willow, which I'd been dying to tell him, and why I had chosen it. His eyes turned glittery.

"I love it," he said. "She will definitely be Willow."

"So you approve? You said you had some ideas?"

He looked at me with pride. It was the first time I'd felt even a modicum of happiness in this rotten place.

"None that compare to yours," he said sweetly. "Stand up and let me see our little girl."

I felt reluctant to stand. He was wearing street clothes, and I was stuck in my nasty orange uniform. I didn't even look good in orange. It made my face and hair look washed out. He motioned with his hand for me to get up. I stood so that my belly was visible. It hadn't grown that much in the past few days, but I was due to pop any minute. I felt enormous, like a fucking orange balloon.

He laughed heartily. "You're huge."

I sat down quickly, feeling embarrassed and ashamed of my body. "Thank you," I said, sneering.

"Huge and pretty," he said warmly. "I wish I could wrap my arms around that big belly."

I blushed and started to feel a little better. "You're silly."

"No, I'm in love," he said.

The female guard Alma walked in to let him know that we were out of time. She waited at the door for me to wrap up my visit, but I didn't want it to end.

Mark looked at me, smiling. "Call me tomorrow."

"I'll call you every day," I said. "You have no idea how much it means to me to talk to you in person."

A guard appeared on his side of the glass and tapped him on the shoulder.

"Bye, Olivia," he said, and hung up the receiver.

"Bye, Beetlejuice," I said to his back.

As I watched him walk away, my whole body collapsed in the chair.

He came to visit me once a week, and each time the desire to tell him what I had been considering became more difficult. Today was the day I had to make my final decision—whether or not to sign the adoption papers. It was getting near my delivery date, and I had made arrangements for the baby. I hadn't told him that I was seriously considering giving our child up, that I had met with a couple who wanted to adopt her. I wanted to talk to him about it, but I knew it would break him. He'd been working at Arby's in order to buy things for the baby. I don't know how he thought he could support her with that kind of an income. I just couldn't tell him that I didn't think it was going to work out the way he planned.

I needed to tell him, but I couldn't find the courage. The people who wanted to adopt her were due at the jail in half an hour, and as the time approached, I struggled with wanting to call him. Maria, the toothless Mexican prostitute, was on the telephone jabbering away in Spanish. I wanted to make the call before these people arrived, but Maria wouldn't get off the fucking phone. She ignored me. I waited, glaring at her, absently glancing at the TV now and then. I was tempted to go up to her and disconnect her call, but Maria was not to be fucked with. She had once bashed a girl in the head with the phone receiver for mouthing off to her.

The guard came and announced that my prospective adoptive parents' lawyer was here to see me. I wasn't going to do anything without talking to Mark. The huge yellow bars slid open. I walked out of the cell, feeling momentarily free, and then into the little office set aside for lawyer visits. The lawyer was there with the couple. Their faces beamed when I walked into the room. A slew of papers for me to sign had been spread out on the table. A sharp pain stabbed my back. It got worse when I sat down.

"How are you?" the lawyer asked, shuffling more paperwork.

I stared at his bloated face, his bright red nose, the flared nostrils. I wondered if he was a drunk. He was Irish, which I had gathered from his business card, Danny McClure or something like that. He took off his suit jacket, revealing the yellow stained pits of his white shirt. The shining clean faces of the couple caught my eye, and the pain in my stomach worsened.

"I'm actually feeling a little sick," I mumbled.

The lawyer's face contorted into some kind of a concerned look. I gathered that it must have been painful for him to feign sympathy. Like he gave a damn about a stupid convict's feelings. All he cared about was the money these people were paying him to get my baby.

He shuffled the papers again. "We should probably get started so that you can lie down soon."

Fuck you, fuck you, fuck you, ran through my brain. You money-hungry devil, what do you know about pain? I thought, but, "I guess so," slipped out of my mouth instead.

"I've prepared all the paperwork for you to sign," the lawyer said while the couple watched me eagerly.

My eyes concentrated on the faux wood table. "I haven't talked to my boyfriend yet. I would like to discuss this with him first," I said to the table.

"You could still sign the paperwork, and if you have a change of heart we could figure that out later," the lawyer said, too enthusiastically.

I knew he was trying to dupe me: *Just sign the papers and everything will be all right.* That's what the police had told me when I got myself involved in this crazy fiasco. The pain in my back was killing me. I didn't know what I should do. I desperately needed to lie down.

"I'm in a lot of pain," I said through clenched teeth. "In fact, I think I need the doctor."

The woman looked at me with alarm in her eyes. "Is it the baby?" she asked.

I began breathing heavily. "I don't know," I gasped. "It hurts."

The lawyer ran out of the little room and got the guard, who came down the hall to check on me. I was sprawled out on two chairs that the couple had kindly arranged.

It was Officer Tate, and she looked worried. "Are you all right?"

"I think I need a doctor," I cried. The pain kept intensifying.

"I'll call him right away. Should I call an ambulance?" Officer Tate asked.

"I think so."

She ran out of the room into her office to make the calls. I could hear her freaking out on the phone. It was difficult to believe she was being so nice. Officer Tate came back and led me to a cot in her office, so I could lie down until the ambulance arrived. She asked me if I needed anything.

"I need to make a phone call."

"Can I make it for you?" she asked.

I breathed heavily and grabbed hold of the flimsy cot mattress. "No, I need to make this call."

She asked me for the phone number, then dialed it for me.

"Do you know what hospital they are taking me to?" I asked, as my eyes began to water.

"Delnor, it's always Delnor."

"Thank you."

The phone was ringing in my ear. It rang three times, four times, and then I heard his voice.

"Hello," he said.

"Mark, I need you to get to Delnor hospital. It's happening," I said, trying to control my breathing.

"It's time. Oh Jesus, it's time. Fuck! Honey, how are you doing?" he asked tenderly.

I had no patience for his niceties. "Don't talk to me, just hurry up and get there," I spat out.

"I'm on my way. Don't worry. I'll be there as fast as I can. Chris will take me on his motorcycle. I love you, baby, I love you so much."

"I love you too. *Hurry!*"

I heard the phone crash to the floor, then Mark's frantic footsteps, and "Fuck, fuck, fuck," being muttered.

I waited in pain until the paramedics came with the stretcher to wheel me to the ambulance. I'd never been in one before, and the interior surprised me—it was kind of womblike, safe, so many machines that could save my life if I needed to be saved. All I could think of was getting the baby out. I wanted the pain to end. The ambulance felt as if it were going a million miles an hour, jostling the stretcher back and forth, my body aching with every jolt. Two men were poking and prodding my body, looking between my legs, talking about centimeters of dilation and other things I didn't comprehend.

We arrived at the hospital, and they rushed me to the maternity ward and wheeled me into a birthing room. Once I was in the room, the pain had become immeasurably worse. The doctor ran in and began his diagnosis.

"She's four centimeters dilated. It won't be long now." He snapped some rubber gloves onto his hands.

I noticed that I didn't have the orange jumpsuit on anymore and couldn't remember when it had come off. The pain was all I could think about. Mark finally arrived and rushed to the side of the bed. He grabbed my hand and kissed my sweaty forehead.

"Drugs, I need drugs," I wailed, reminding myself of that Lisa girl from the Dead concert yelling, "Dose me!"

"Doctor, can she have some drugs?" Mark asked. He winced as I squeezed his hand.

The doctor shook his head. "It's too late, this baby is coming fast. I have to break her water," he said.

I felt a sharp prick between my legs, and then it was as if the Hoover Dam broke, flooding the hospital floor. I was panting like a dog. "What should I do?" I asked between gasps of breath.

The doctor looked at Mark. "Breathe with her, like you did in Lamaze classes."

"We never made it to Lamaze classes," I heard Mark say.

"Then follow my lead." The doctor made these funny breathing noises, while Mark watched, then tried to mimic them with me. It didn't work. I gripped his hand tighter and screamed. It hurt so fucking bad.

"Push," the doctor said calmly.

"I am!" I cried out, my stomach muscles tightening.

"Harder!" The doctor said, raising his voice so he could be heard over my wailing.

Tears were streaming down my cheeks. "I can't!" I screamed.

"You have to," the doctor replied forcefully.

I felt my bowels move. I was worried. "I feel like I'm taking a shit," I said nervously.

The doctor nodded his head. "You're supposed to feel that way. Now push!" he commanded.

I tried pushing. Clutching Mark's hand in my sweaty palm, I let out another scream. I wanted her out of my body. She hadn't really bothered me for nine months, barely any morning sickness, nothing. Now she was *killing* me.

Eventually the doctor smiled. "I see the head; the head is out. Push again," and I pushed like this for about half an hour.

Mark dropped my hand and ran to look at our baby's head.

"Push, baby. It's coming. I can see it," he said, smiling proudly.

I screamed at the top of my lungs and pushed with all my might.

"Baby, she's out. I see her. She's beautiful. She is so beautiful," he yelled, and he did seem awestruck. He was touching her bloody head.

I couldn't believe the whole thing was over. It took about forty-five minutes. It was incredible. The doctor was stitching me up, but it didn't hurt very much. After that, nothing hurt.

A nurse came in and started massaging my stomach. I had no idea what was going on. A few seconds later a tiny baby was placed on my belly. She was wearing a little pink hat, wrapped in a pink blanket. She was absolutely gorgeous. She had my eyes. Big, baby-blue eyes. She had

Mark's cute nose and his big full lips. She was the most beautiful thing I'd ever seen.

Mark came over and sat on the bed next to us.

"Oh, Willow, you're such a beauty," he said, taking her tiny hand in his.

He pressed his lips to mine, and I could feel his body trembling. A nurse came in to check on Willow and me, and said she would be back shortly to take Willow for a while. After the nurse left, I just touched her tiny hands, her tiny face. She smelled so good.

Mark went to get water and didn't come back for a while, and when he walked back through the door he was wearing a somber look.

"What's wrong, honey?" I asked.

His shoulders slumped, and he wouldn't look me in the eye. "There're some people out there that say they are adopting Willow. Can you tell me what that's all about?"

"I was thinking about it. I mean, I am thinking about it." I fell silent. I was speechless.

He sat next to me and took the baby from my arms. "She's *ours,*" he said.

"I know, but so many things are going to happen to us now. So many bad things. I want her to have the best life. Can we give her what she deserves?"

He kissed Willow's forehead. "I hadn't given it much thought. I imagined everything would work out. I just thought everything had to work out for us."

It pained me to watch him with her. He was so tender. "Does it seem like it is?" I asked.

He looked at Willow tucked in the crook of his arm. He bent his head and kissed her face several times, then tears began rolling down his cheeks.

"Tonight it does," he said, adjusting her pink blanket.

"What about next week when you have to buy her diapers, food, clothing, and everything else? What then, Mark?"

"I'll make it work," he said.

"I know you'd do your best, baby. What I'm asking you is, is your best good enough for her?"

The nurse interrupted us to take Willow to be examined. Mark reluctantly released her as if he would never see her again. When the nurse left the room, he turned his attention back to me.

"I don't know if my best will be good enough," he said. "The selfish side of me says that I deserve at least a chance. The unselfish side says Willow deserves at least a chance. I don't know what to do." He collapsed on the bed by my side.

"I think we need to give her a chance," I said, feeling awful.

"I don't want to let her go."

"Neither do I, but I think we both know it's right. We're both going to be all fucked up this year and maybe for a long time after that. Is it right to take her down with us?"

"No, but it hurts," he said, sniffling.

"I know." I took his clammy hand in mine.

"If none of this ever happened, if we both weren't going to boot camp, what would've been?"

"You know it would have been different then."

He climbed into the bed with me and snuggled up. We were both crying. I didn't know how to comfort him, and I didn't think he knew what to do either. I felt his moist tears on my neck, felt his lips kiss my neck. I was in agony, but I didn't know what else to do. After some time he fell asleep. I heard the guard stationed outside my hospital room door walk in and check on me. When she realized I wasn't going anywhere, and neither was Mark, she went back to her post. I lay there remembering how we got to where we were. How, no matter how much we loved each other, we had fucked things up. I wanted to go back to DeKalb, back to NIU, and start everything anew.

CHAPTER 19

I hung up the phone and went to the cabinet to take my mother's spare set of keys. She was out shopping with friends, and I needed her car to get to DeKalb. I opened the garage and got in the driver's side. I started the car and with that my tears started to flow freely. After one hundred and twenty days of separation, we only had three days to connect before Mark left for boot camp. It was over for me. Now Mark was about to go to his own personal hell. I didn't want him to have to go to that awful place. I wished I could do it all over again, so he wouldn't have to go. Everything was always so hard for him.

I saw him looking out the window as I pulled into the driveway. He wasn't wearing a shirt, and his face looked anxious and happy from behind the glass, framed by the white curtains. I got out of the car, the door to his house flung open, and he was running out to take me into his arms. It was exactly like those dorky closing scenes in movies.

"I love you, girl," he said with a smile.

"I love you too." He had no idea.

"Tell me everything about this place I'm going to." I could see ten thousand questions in his eyes.

"I will, but first tell me everything about you, everything I've missed." I wanted to know what he'd been thinking, what had been going on in his life. Since the day we were arrested we hadn't been able to talk freely to each other.

We stood on his blacktop driveway, a slight breeze blowing through the leaves of the large white oak tree that loomed in his front yard. Little droplets of sweat dripped down between his nipples.

"What do you want to know, baby? I've been biding my time away, waiting to be ripped away from my life and my love again." There was pain in his eyes as he spoke and a hazy grayness that had never been there before. Maybe it was the darkness Lee had told me about. He seemed different, but maybe I was the one who had changed.

"Are you ever going to tell me about that night? About why you did it? Was it for the money?" I had so many questions.

"I did it for you, for our baby, and for me. I did it because I thought that was what you wanted me to do," he stammered. He looked sheepish as he nervously ran his fingers through his hair.

My body tensed. I never wanted it to be about me. I had given him some information in a fleeting moment of desperation. What was I thinking anyway? I was always pushing him to see just how much he'd do for me. I'd never wanted any of this to happen.

"Don't ever do anything crazy for me again," I said uncomfortably.

"It's all about love, baby. Love *makes* you do crazy things." This time he smiled. I couldn't tell if it was genuine, but it was a smile.

"You seem sad," I said.

"That's just how it is, baby. Too much."

I wanted him to touch me the way he used to, but when he did his fingers felt cold.

"What's going to happen to us? I mean, are we over?" I asked.

"I love you, Orleigh. I always will. I have to give my body to the state for one hundred and twenty days. Who knows how things will be when I get back? I don't want to leave you. I want things to be like they were before, but they will never be that way again."

"Are you breaking up with me?" I was in a panic. My eyes flitted from him, to the tree, to my mother's car. I looked into his dark eyes, feeling completely inadequate. I always thought I knew what he was talking about, but now I realized he was more than I could ever fully understand.

"Not breaking up, just, well, I don't know what to tell you. I love you, baby, so much. . . . I feel really weak. Love me, I guess, just never stop loving me." He looked down at the blacktop driveway, then back into my eyes. I still felt panic-stricken, despite his reassurance.

"Does that mean we are together, or aren't we together?" I asked.

"Orleigh, don't you understand? Words don't matter. I love you; how come that can't be enough? Can't you walk away with that, and just, just feel good?"

I was still confused. "I just was wondering what it all means, Mark. I mean, I don't know if I'm your girlfriend or not." I nervously wound strands of my hair around my index finger. I hadn't done that since I was five.

"Orleigh, I'm trying to tell you that it's all insignificant. All irrelevant. I love you, why isn't that enough?" His smile was awkward and rigid.

I stared at him coldly, my mind overrun with thoughts of him and another girl. "Have you found someone else? Is that what you're trying to tell me?" Tears began sliding down my chin.

"No, there is no one else. There is only you, there has always been only you. You are the one I love, the only one I have ever loved, the only one I will ever love. It has always, and will always be you. Whatever else you are trying to get from me doesn't matter. We are all that matters, the way we are and the way we have been. That's what matters, baby. You've always been the only one." He wiped my chin.

"So we are together?" I asked expectantly.

"Yeah, baby, we are together, and we will always be together. Our hearts will always be attached."

"Make love to me then," I said, my feelings of despair leaving me.

"Come upstairs."

I followed him up the stairs, thankful that we had finally worked this whole mess out. We still loved each other, and we were still together. I lay on his bed and waited for him to touch me. His hands reached out slowly, in a labored way. He touched my face and let his fingers rest upon my cheek. He didn't undress me, so I started to pull off my shirt.

"Slow down. Please, let me do this my way," he said, with a touch of desperation in his voice.

I stopped and let him continue to touch my face. Tears rolled down his cheeks and dropped onto my body. He began to undress me. I could tell he was trying to look deep inside me, but the tears in his eyes were clouding his vision. I wanted to feel him inside me. My clothing was almost all on the floor, and he undressed himself, weeping the whole time. I wanted him to stop crying, he was scaring me. It wasn't like he was never going to see me again. It was one hundred and twenty days.

He lay on top of me and entered me gently. It was slow and easy all the way. Cold tears dropped onto my hot skin. I couldn't seem to pull him out of the daze he was in. I didn't make any noise, and I don't think he knew when I orgasmed. He lay, wrapping himself around me. I held him while he sobbed like a child for over an hour, then I dressed to leave. I knew he needed something, but I felt at a loss.

"Do you want me to stay with you?" I asked, hopeful.

"No, it's time for you to leave," he said somberly.

"Will I see you again before you leave for boot camp?" I asked, my panic returning.

"No, I actually have to leave tomorrow. My parents are driving me there, and they want us to stay in a hotel the night before they take me away forever." He sounded so pessimistic, so unlike himself.

"Well, that's nice of your parents. Will you call me when you get back?"

"I will always let you know when I'm back."

We kissed good-bye, once, twice, then he just held me tightly. His sobbing began all over again, and I wanted to help him, wanted to make it all better. He finally let his hold of me loosen, and he stepped back to look me over. The way he looked at me then, I will never forget. A part of him drifting from him to me.

I didn't want to go, but my legs willed me up and away from him.

Later that night, the phone rang at two in the morning. My mother never answered the phone that late, and neither did I anymore. It rang five times, then stopped. I lay in bed and started drifting back to sleep. Just as I was falling into my coma world my mother knocked lightly on my bedroom door.

She walked in with curlers in her hair and cold cream on her face. "Honey, the telephone is for you," she said quietly.

"Who is it?" I was hoping she wasn't mad at me for getting a call this late.

"It's Sarah."

"Mark's sister?" I asked, feeling foggy.

"Yes, dear."

332

There was a tone in her voice that I couldn't place, one I hadn't heard before. I wasn't sure if she was ticked or upset or fine about the phone call. All I knew was she was acting weird. I picked up my phone and waited for her to walk out and hang up hers, hear the click.

"Hey, Sarah, what's going on?"

"I don't exactly know how to tell you this, Orleigh." She sounded like she had a cold. I was instantly afraid that Mark might have run away, that the idea of boot camp was too much for him.

"Orleigh, Mark freaked out tonight," she said, and her voice wavered.

"What happened? Is he okay?" I blurted, hearing my voice crack.

"When he didn't come home tonight we all started getting worried. We searched everywhere for him, but after several hours my dad gave up and called the cops to report him missing. They told us that we would have to wait twenty-four hours before we could fill out a missing person's report, but they said they would try to keep an eye out for him. About an hour later . . ." She was breaking up. She could barely get her words out. I wanted to know what the fuck had happened to Mark. She sniffed a little, then resumed talking softly. "Some kids on campus found him at the fountains. He'd taken a knife from the kitchen, Orleigh. He stabbed himself in the heart. Orleigh, Mark's dead."

I couldn't say a thing. I didn't know what to say. I couldn't speak.

"Orleigh, I think he'd been considering this for a long time. He left some letters behind. He left a bunch of things for you. I'll get everything he wanted you to have. I'll give it all to you at the funeral. My parents haven't made any arrangements yet, but I'll let you know when the wake and funeral will be."

Sarah continued to sob on the other end of the line. I let the phone fall onto my bed. I had no words for her. I had nothing. My mother came into my room and compassionately got off the phone with Sarah. She put her arms around me and held me while I cried. The tears did not stop for weeks, and my mother was always there to comfort me.

Mark was cremated three days later, and I was there to receive his ashes. His parents tried to put them in this gold urn, something I knew he would have been repulsed by. I made him a plain clay urn. His parents weren't overly thrilled when I showed up with an alternative to the nasty gaudy thing, but I'd started making it the day after he died. I needed to do it for him. His parents would just have to deal. I'd gone back to my high school and worked for two days in the art room on something that was more appropriate for Mark. I was lucky that I had such a wonderful relationship with my old high school art teacher. She was extremely supportive and helpful. When I was through, it was absolutely beautiful, and I placed several things inside of it. There was the ultrasound picture of Willow that he'd always held onto, some hairs from his favorite sable paintbrush, a picture of us, one of his necklaces, and a cut-up Cure CD. I waited with his parents while they burned his body, then the man returned with my urn full of everything that I knew Mark loved. Now Mark was also in that urn.

I took the ashes and the large box Mark had left behind for me. It was obvious that he had thought about this. He had left specific instructions for his parents. He had also written a will. It was all very sad. I had no idea he was ever this unhappy.

I didn't know what to do with his ashes. I needed to think about it all, needed to clear my head. I couldn't handle everything crashing down on me.

One week later I was sitting on top of Mark's grave in a lush green cemetery with sprawling oak trees. A wrought iron fence surrounded the grounds. The sky was a pale blue, and the sun harsh and bright. I still had the majority of the ashes in the steel urn, but Mark's parents wanted a little bit of him in a resting place they could visit. I complied.

The drive to his grave had been long and extremely upsetting. I had the box of stuff he left me, but I was beginning to think I wouldn't be able to open it.

I sat there staring at the box, at the red roses I'd carried with me to lay on his grave, at the CD player I'd brought along so I could play the Cure to him.

I had to open the box. Maybe it would help, maybe it would hurt, but either way it had to be done. I slowly pulled the lid off and peered inside it, tears blurring all the contents. It was filled with so many things, I didn't know where to begin. The first thing I pulled out was a large brown envelope. Inside there were several hundred-dollar bills rolled up in a rubber band. I didn't know exactly how many, and I really didn't care either. This told me nothing. Next I opened an equally fat brown envelope. Inside was a journal. I opened it and thumbed through the pages, each covered with his handwriting. I had never known he kept a journal. I put it to the side, figuring I would read it later. There was yet another envelope, but this one was white and my name was written across it in black ink. This one scared me. Everything was about to get personal, and I was afraid of what I might find out. I finally gained some courage and broke the seal on the envelope. Inside there were several sheets of paper containing Mark's thoughts—his suicide note to me. I didn't want to read it, but I had so many unanswered questions. I lay back against his headstone, lit a cigarette, and turned on the CD player. As the Cure began to softly whine, I started to read.

Orleigh,

If you are reading this letter then you know that I found the strength to do what I had to do. Don't think that this is your fault. This is definitely not your fault. I love you, I always will. I promise I am watching you reading this right now and I am loving you. I will always be watching and loving you from wherever I am. Never forget this. Next, and equally important, please don't go doing this to yourself. We don't need any sappy Romeo-and-Juliet thing going on here. Shakespeare would turn over in his grave. I did this for me and I did it for us. Please don't get any crazy ideas.

That stated, I want you to know that I completely understand how you are feeling. I am inside of you, living through your pain, just as you have always been there through mine. I know also that you have a million questions. I will try to give you answers to the ones that I can, the others will be answered with time.

First, I have been thinking about this for a while. After we gave Willow up, everything changed for me. I was never angry with you about the decision, but I always felt like I was slighted in some way. I wanted the opportunity to love her and raise her to be a beautiful young woman. This was my dream, and it was shattered when they took her. Maybe it was all wrong and we never would have succeeded, but I never got the chance. I hurt so deeply after that day in the hospital, and I have never been able to get over it. That is when I knew that I wasn't going to be here much longer. That is when I began to get things ready for my death.

Second, was obviously the crime. What happened was such a horrible mistake. I never wanted you to go down for me, but I let you anyway. I was scared and childish. And that is just another thing never to forgive myself for. I could never express to you how it broke my heart to see you in trouble, and how much I appreciated everything you were willing to do for me.

Third, I have dealt with the pain of living for too long. All the sad and horrendous things around me every day, well, they're too much for me. It sounds weak, but this world is much too cruel for someone like me. I am weak and too sensitive. The way I see it is that I never chose to be here, therefore, I can choose when I am ready to leave. It all makes sense to me.

This is brief and maybe you want more details, but for that you will have to read my journal. Orleigh, things are really strange within me. I feel terrible for the things I have done. I feel like I have sinned and sinned. I will never know what brought me to this, if it was all the hurt I felt at the hand of my father or the drugs I did, or if it was that I couldn't find my own niche in this harsh world. You are different, and I have always envied you for that. You are strong and self-assured. You may call that a facade, but I have always seen your strength come through, again and again. Everything bogs me down, and I can't help being wrapped up in all my hurt. I can't escape it, no matter how hard I try. All my old antics are failing, and I am left with a bitter heart and a numbness that won't go away. I don't feel real anymore.

The crimes and terrible things I have done are too much. I started down the wrong path, then I lost myself. The bad grew greater, and I became numb. And I was afraid that you and I were catalysts for one another. We were two people with so much love, but together we took all the goodness and destroyed it. I am not bunking our relationship. I think if we had been a little more mature, and a little less consumed by the evils of the world, we would have been one hundred percent perfect together.

This whole fiasco of evilness had to have an end and this is the only way I knew how to end it. So it was a mix of evil and pain that caused my demise. All I want from you, now that you are free from me, is to turn it *around. Make things different for yourself. I left you as much money as I could put together. I want you to take the money and get Willow back. It's still early enough for the adoption to be reversed. I want you to take the most precious part of our love and let her learn what we were all about. Teach her how to be a good girl; teach her all about her daddy. This I want more than anything in the world. You will need her to be complete. Things will never be easy for you in this life, especially now that you've lost me. I am not being conceited here; I just know how I would feel under the same circumstances.*

Orleigh, please get Willow back, and please never stop loving me. I am with you always. I will never not love you. I love you now as I write what hurts more than ever to write. I am doing this for me, for you, and for us. I love you more than anything, and I think that makes it easier to leave you. I know that I will live in your heart eternally; I will live through Willow, no matter where she is. These are things I know and understand.

I have left you some of the few belongings from my life. All the contents of this box are all the things you must keep. I have also left you my paintings. You know what needs to be done with those. I trust you completely to do the right thing. You have my ashes, and wherever you are right now, reading this letter, what remains of my body is with you. I asked my parents in my will to give them to you. I know you can't think about things clearly now, but eventually you will discover where they should go.

Again, baby, I know this letter isn't enough. I know that you need more. Read my journal when you are ready. Take time to heal. I wouldn't recommend jumping into another relationship, like you so often do. This time, let the hurt lessen before you start something new. I'm not there anymore, but I want you to be happy. These things take time. If you get Willow back, make sure you find her a strong and stable daddy, but also make sure she knows who I was and how much I love her.

My heart is killing me and soon I will kill my heart. I can't even cry anymore. My eyes have dried up from the millions upon millions of tears I have shed. Never forget, baby, that you are my love and you mean more to me than anything. I love you, girl, I love you, Olivia, I love you, Orleigh, I love everything about you, and I always will. You are now going to be my heart. I don't need this cold black thing beating inside my chest,

I only need you. Go on, my love, be strong. Always remember who you are and what you stand for. I love you forever. Good-bye for now, baby.

Mark

Stunned and feeling a pain like none I'd ever felt, I lay there and shut my eyes. I'd never known these things he felt, and now that I did, I loved him even more. My heart was broken, my spirit and my hope gone. I felt so terribly alone. How he could leave me, I'll never know.

I looked inside the box and found his stack of Cure CDs tied with a red ribbon, his paintbrushes, and two necklaces. One necklace was long; it was obviously for me. The other was very tiny and it didn't take much to figure out who that was for. It was so hard to grasp that this box was all that remained of my love. This box held everything that meant something to him. In fact, this box was Mark; it was all I had left of him. I turned off the music and placed everything back inside it, my tears spilling endlessly. With the urn, CD player, and my box of memories, I stumbled to my car.

EPILOGUE

I am on a plane to Arizona. Willow is being fussy—I don't think she likes to fly. I have been trying to explain to her that we are going to put Daddy in his place of rest. She is way too young to understand me—she can't even speak yet—but I like saying the words anyhow. The airplane is crowded, and our seats are cramped. A balding businessman sits next to us, sipping Bloody Marys, and occasionally making goo-goo faces at Willow. Exhausted, I clutch her to my chest and try to sleep through the flight.

The landing is unbearable. Willow wails at the top of her lungs as the plane lunges downward, levels off, then lunges again. The businessman seated next to us is no longer making cute faces. After the plane makes its bumpy landing, I scoop Willow into my arms, gather my things, and disembark.

I rented a car to take us to Camp Verde, and the Avis man at the rental stand hands me the keys to a dark blue Honda Accord. A baby seat is already in the backseat of the car, and I feel nothing but relief as we head out of the airport.

Everything is in red-orange tones. The sun blazes on the horizon. As we approach the entrance to Camp Verde, I feel an overwhelming nostalgia. It's almost like Mark's here with me, and we're on the road again. God, how I miss those times.

We're not going to camp; Willow's too young to rough it. I plan to hang out at the hot springs all day, then spend the night at a hotel in Flagstaff. This isn't supposed to be a long visit; in fact, it is going to be a short but harrowing one. I have carried this urn with me everywhere lately, and it is time I stop holding on to it.

Willow and I spent one afternoon at the fountains on campus, leaving

339

a little bit of Daddy there forever. His absolute two favorite places in the world were those fountains and the hot springs of Camp Verde. He loved nature and everything beautiful. He loved the places we had shared. I want a part of him to always be at these two places.

We hit the *Dukes of Hazard* road, and I am a little concerned about Willow making it down the hill without bouncing out of the car seat. I stop and climb over the seat to make sure she is as secure as possible. She grabs a fistful of my hair and tugs hard. I untangle her little fingers, and feeling confident that she won't bounce out of the seat, I head down the long and winding path to the hot springs. When we finally reach the bottom, both of us a little shaken, I see that the campground is eerily vacant. We park at the campsite where Mark and I once loved, fought, and dreamed. I lift Willow out of her seat. I have a little child-carrying backpack that I purchased specifically for the trip across the river. After she is all hooked in and my shoes are off, I slip her onto my back and pick up the other things I have brought with me to take across the water.

The water is icy cold, and I wish I remembered how craggy the bottom is; I would have brought along some water shoes. But instead I stumble along barefoot, trying to balance the things in my hands and keep Willow above water. The water gets to be about waist high, and I rear up on my toes to keep Willow from getting wet. She tugs at my hair and shrieks with excitement. The scenery is as gorgeous as it had been the last time I was here—verdant foliage grows out of the clay-red land.

I'm not used to having someone so tiny with me all the time. It was all kinds of messy at first, but the adoptive parents turned out to be very compassionate when they heard the whole story. After I let them read Mark's letter, there was no way any person with a heart could let his dying wish go ungranted. Even though I felt unprepared for motherhood, I've loved every minute being with Willow. When I look at her I am reminded of Mark, which is great at times and devastating at others. But I know it is right, and I love her.

By the time we reach the top of the canyon and then the hot springs, I'm feeling really blue. I unhook the straps of the baby carrier and pull it off. I set Willow down on a little blanket on the ground, then sit next to her. She is smiling her daddy's smile, obviously thrilled by the adventure we're having.

"Honey, I have to figure out where to spread your daddy's ashes. Do you have any ideas?"

She cocks her head at me. I watch as she manages to stuff all her chubby little fingers into her mouth, then kick her legs in the air.

It occurs to me what we should do. I stand and take off all my clothes. I undress Willow, diaper and all. Her pinkish baby skin glows. When we are both completely naked, I pick her up, cradle her in my arms, and slowly slip into the soothing warm water. With Willow in one arm, buoyant in the water, I reach out for the urn. I open the lid and empty the ashes into the water with Willow and me. I know that would be the way Mark would want it. He is floating in the water with the two people that he loved most in the world.

We sit there for hours and watch the sun sink behind the canyons. I glance up at the cave entrance, but the caveman is nowhere in sight. I feel Mark all around Willow and me. I can feel him here with us, not just his ashes, but something more.

I keep thinking about whether I'll be a good enough mother for Willow, but then I remind myself that Mark thought I was good enough, and it is what he wanted. I love him so much for believing in me. Whenever I doubt myself, I remember his faith in me.

I look forward to the day when I can explain to Willow how wonderful her daddy was, and how every time I look at her I see him in her face. I want her to know everything. I hold her tightly as my tears trickle into the ashy water. She looks into my eyes and giggles and coos.

Also from Akashic Books

Adios Muchachos by Daniel Chavarría
245 pages, paperback
ISBN: 1-888451-16-5
Price: $13.95

"Daniel Chavarría has long been recognized as one of Latin America's finest writers. Now he again proves why with *Adios Muchachos*, a comic mystery peopled by a delightfully mad band of miscreants, all of them led by a woman you will not soon forget: Alicia, the loveliest bicycle whore in all Havana."
—Edgar Award-winning author William Heffernan

The Big Mango by Norman Kelley
270 pages, trade paperback
ISBN: 1-888451-10-8
Price: $14.95

She's Back! Nina Halligan, Private Investigator.

"Want a scathing social and political satire? Look no further than Kelley's second effort featuring 'bad girl' African-American PI and part-time intellectual Nina Halligan—it's X-rated, but a romp of a read . . . Nina's acid takes on recognizable public figures and institutions both amuse and offend . . . Kelley spares no one, blacks and whites alike, and this provocative novel is sure to attract attention . . . " —*Publisher's Weekly*

Michael by Henry Flesh (1999 Lambda Literary Award Winner) with illustrations by John H. Greer
120 pages, trade paperback
ISBN: 1-888451-12-2
Price: $12.95

"Henry's the king. He writes with incessant crispness. Sex is reluctantly juicy, life is reluctant and winning-even when his characters lose. What's it all about, Henry? I think you know."
—Eileen Myles, author of *Cool For You*

Kamikaze Lust by Lauren Sanders
287 pages, trade paperback
ISBN: 1-888451-08-4
Price: $14.95

"Like an official conducting an all-out strip search, first-time novelist Lauren Sanders plucks and probes her characters' minds and bodies to reveal their hidden lusts, and when all is said and done, nary a body cavity is spared." —*Time Out New York*

Once There Was a Village by Yuri Kapralov
163 pages, trade paperback
ISBN: 1-888451-05-X
Price: $12.00

"If there were a God, then *Once There Was a Village*, Yuri Kapralov's chronicle of life as an exiled Russian artist on the Lower East Side, would have gone to Broadway instead of *Rent*. Only the staging of this book, set amid the riots of the late '60s and the crime-infested turmoil of the early '70s, might look like a cross between *Les Miserables* and *No Exit*." —*Village Voice*

Manhattan Loverboy by Arthur Nersesian (author of *The Fuck-Up*)
203 pages, paperback
ISBN: 1-888451-09-2
Price: $13.95

"Nersesian's newest novel is a paranoid fantasy and fantastic comedy in the service of social realism, using methods of L. Frank Baum's *Wizard of Oz* or Kafka's *The Trial* to update the picaresque urban chronicles of Augie March, with a far darker edge . . ."
—*Downtown Magazine*

Heart of the Old Country by Tim McLoughlin
224 pages, paperback
ISBN: 1-888451-15-7
Price: $14.95

"Tim McLoughlin writes about South Brooklyn with a fidelity to people and place reminiscent of James T. Farrell's *Studs Lonigan* and George Orwell's *Down and Out in Paris and London*. Among the achievements of his swiftly paced narrative is a cast of authentic and frequently complex characters whose voices reflect dreams and love as well as desperation to survive. No voice in this symphony of a novel is more impressive than that of Mr. McLoughlin's, a young writer with a rare gift for realism and empathy." —Sidney Offit, author of *Memoir of the Bookie's Son*

These books are available at local bookstores. They can also be purchased with a credit card online through www.akashicbooks.com. To order by mail, or to order out-of-print titles, send a check or money order to:

Akashic Books
PO Box 1456
New York, NY 10009
www.akashicbooks.com
Akashic7@aol.com

(Prices include shipping. Outside the U.S., add $3 to each book ordered.)